ANTON BRUCKNER–
A DOCUMENTARY BIOGRAPHY

ANTON BRUCKNER–
A DOCUMENTARY BIOGRAPHY
Volume 2

Trial, Tribulation and Triumph in Vienna

Crawford Howie

Studies in the History and Interpretation of Music
Volume 83b

The Edwin Mellen Press
Lewiston•Queenston•Lampeter

Library of Congress Cataloging-in-Publication Data

Howie, Crawford, 1942-
   Anton Bruckner : a documentary biography: trial, tribulation and triumph in Vienna /
   Crawford Howie.
      p. cm. -- [Studies in the history and interpretation of music ; v. 83b]
   Includes bibliographical references (p.) and index.
   ISBN 0-7734-7302-5
   1. Bruckner, Anton, 1824-1896. 2. Composers--Austria--Biography. I. Title.

ML410.B88 H69 2002
780'.92--dc21
[B]
                                                                           2001042755

This is volume 83b in the continuing series
Studies in the History and Interpretation Music
Volume 83b ISBN 0-7734-7302-5
SHIM Series ISBN 0-88946-426-X

A CIP catalog record for this book is available from the British Library.

       The Edwin Mellen Press   The Edwin Mellen Press
            Box 450   Box 67
       Lewiston, New York   Queenston, Ontario
       USA 14092-0450   CANADA L0S 1L0

                       The Edwin Mellen Press, Ltd.
                       Lampeter, Ceredigion, Wales
                       UNITED KINGDOM SA48 8LT

                    Printed in the United States of America

Volume 2: Table of Contents

CHAPTER 5

Bruckner in Vienna: The Second Ten Years (1878-1887)

Bruckner's financial position took a turn for the better at the beginning of 1878 when, at Hellmesberger's recommendation, he was appointed a salaried member of the *Hofkapelle* with an annual income of 800 florins. In his official letter to the Lord Chamberlain, Hellmesberger also made it clear that it would no longer be necessary for Bruckner to continue in the posts of assistant librarian and singing teacher of the choirboys for which he had received an annual honorarium of 300 florins 'no doubt graciously granted to him in view of his poor financial circumstances'. Furthermore, Bruckner was by no means 'impoverished' and 'in need of financial aid'. His salary at the Conservatory amounted to more than 1200 florins. Hellmesberger's recommendation was accepted and Bruckner was officially informed of his new appointment on 24 January.[1]

Hellmesberger's reservations about Bruckner's alleged financial straits were not without foundation. The cost of living in Vienna c. 1880 would have enabled Bruckner to live well within his income. According to Orel:

---

1 For Hellmesberger's letter to the Lord Chamberlain, dated Vienna 3 January, 1878, the official acceptance of Hellmesberger's proposal (19 January, 1878) and the letter to Bruckner, see *ABDS* 1, 90-95.

The material struggle for existence which Bruckner allegedly had to endure in Vienna really belongs to the realm of fantasy. The mere fact that he left 10,000 florins in cash alone puts a large question mark over Bruckner's 'poverty', because this sum was the product of savings which Bruckner had been able to make from his regular income.[2]

Bruckner's main concern, however, was that he should have enough 'quality time' to compose and that he should not have to rely on money from private teaching to supplement his salaries from the Conservatory and the *Hofkapelle*. He obviously had in mind a particular level of financial security which would afford him the time and space to follow the creative Muse. His 'Stundenplan' in the *Neuer Krakauer Schreibkalender* for 1877 shows that his teaching commitments were two hours at the University (Monday, 17.00 - 19.00), 16 hours at the Conservatory (Tuesday, 9.00 - 14.00 and 17.00 - 19.00; Thursday, 9.00 - 14.00 and 17.00 - 19.00; Saturday, 17.00 - 19.00) and 13 hours' private teaching (Wednesday, 9.30 - 10.30, 11.00 - 13.00, 17.00 - 19.00, 19.30 - 21.30; Friday, 10.00 - 13.00; Saturday, 9.00 - 12.00), 31 hours in total. His teaching commitments for 1878 included the same hours at the University and Conservatory and ten hours' private teaching (Wednesday, 10.00 - 11.00, 16.00 - 19.00; Thursday, 15.00 - 17.00; Friday, 17.00 - 19.00, 19.30 - 21.30), 28 hours in total.[3] In later years Bruckner re-scheduled his teaching commitments by cramming them into two or three days each week, thereby leaving himself complete uninterrupted days for composition. Bruckner also had regular commitments at the *Hofkapelle* and had to ensure that his duties would be covered by another organist during his annual vacation which he normally took from the middle of August to the middle of September. In order to avoid having to pay a deputy to fulfil their duties the *Hofkapelle* organists came to a reciprocal arrangement among

---

2 Alfred Orel, 'Bruckner und Wien', in *Hans Albrecht in memoriam* (Cassel, 1962), 228.

3 The diaries are located in the *ÖNB*, shelf no. Mus. Hs. 3182.

themselves during the holiday period. In 1878 and 1879, for instance, Bruckner substituted for Rudolf Bibl from mid-July to mid-August and Bibl no doubt returned the favour when Bruckner was away from mid-August to mid-September.[4] Bruckner and Pius Richter also substituted for each other several times between 1878 and 1890, not only in vacations but also during 'normal' periods of duty.[5] In 1878 Bruckner spent part of his summer vacation at St. Florian giving harmony lessons to the new organist, Josef Gruber.

Bruckner was a past master, however, at making maximum use of the free time that was available to him to pursue his compositional activities. During the course of the year he wrote two secular choral pieces, *Abendzauber* WAB 57 and *Zur Vermählungsfeier* WAB 54, and a sacred choral piece, *Tota pulchra es* WAB 46, completed his Symphony no. 5, carried out revision work on his Symphony no. 4, including the composition of a new Scherzo, and commenced work on his String Quintet in F, WAB 12.

The composition of *Abendzauber*, the words of which were again provided by Dr. Heinrich Wallmann (Heinrich von der Mattig), was completed on 13 January and the work was dedicated to his friend Carl Almeroth in Steyr. It is written for male voices, tenor/baritone soloist, three distant yodelling voices and four horns. The male voices are required to hum throughout until the last section where there is a proper text underlay. According to Franz Bayer, another of Bruckner's friends from Steyr, the three yodelling parts were intended for female voices and were modelled on the Rhinemaidens' music.[6]

---

4 See *ABDS* 1, 99f.

5 See nine letters from Bruckner to Pius Richter in the *ÖNB* - ÖNB-H 126/58-1-9.

6 The autograph score of the work is in the library of the Vienna *Männergesangverein* which gave it its first known public performance on 18 March 1911. In the first edition of the work (U.E. 2914, Vienna, 1911), Viktor Keldorfer, the editor, sought to make the earlier choral parts more secure by providing a text underlay derived from the words of the solo part. As Bruckner did not provide any

Bruckner's landlord, Dr. Anton Oelzelt von Newin, was married in November and Bruckner wrote an unaccompanied male-voice chorus, *Zwei Herzen haben sich gefunden* (*Zur Vermählungsfeier*) for the occasion. Although the original intention was to have the work performed at Klosterneuburg, Auer suggests that it was too difficult for the Klosterneuburg Male Voice Society and that the wedding did not take place at Klosterneuburg Abbey in any case as Oelzelt von Newin was a Protestant.[7]

On 5 June Franz Josef Rudigier celebrated the 25th anniversary of his office as bishop of the Linz diocese. To commemorate the occasion, Bruckner, at the instigation of Johann Burgstaller, the director of music at Linz Cathedral, wrote one of his most effective short sacred pieces, the Marian antiphon *Tota pulchra es* WAB 46. It was composed on 30 March and first performed at a special benediction service held in the Votive Chapel on the evening of 4 June. Rudigier, its dedicatee, received a signed copy of the work on 30 May.[8]

---

specific syllabic underlay for the yodelling parts, Keldorfer also added what he considered to be 'yodelling syllables corresponding to the typical way of singing in the Austrian alpine districts'. For a general discussion of Bruckner's male-voice works, including *Abendzauber*, see Andrea Harrandt, op.cit. in *BSL 1987* (Linz, 1989), 93-103.

7 See *G-A* IV/1, 520-21 for further information; but the date of composition is given wrongly here as 11 November 1878. The autograph, dated 27 November 1878, is in the *Gesellschaft der Musikfreunde* library. The piece was published for the first time, ed. J. Kluger, in the *Jahrbuch des Stiftes Klosterneuburg* III (1910), 133. It was published again 11 years later, together with *Ave regina coelorum* WAB 8, by Universal Edition (U.E. 4980), edited and with a foreword by Josef V. Wöss, in the series *Kirchenmusikalische Publikationen der Schola Austriaca*.

8 See *HSABB* I, 178 for the text of Bruckner's congratulatory covering letter to Bishop Rudigier; the original is in the *Bischöfliches Archiv*, Linz. Burgstaller conducted *Tota pulchra es* as well as the first performance of a *Te Deum* by Karl Waldeck and a *Litanei* by Johann Habert. Rudigier's signed copy is now in the library of the new Cathedral. The original autograph in the *ÖNB* (Mus.Hs. 37.286) was used as the engraver's copy for the first edition of the work, printed by Emil Wetzler (Julius Engelmann) as no. 1 of *2 Kirchenchöre* (Vienna, 1887). There is a modern edition in *ABSW*

At the beginning of the year, after a long process of refining and improving, Bruckner put the finishing touches to his Symphony no. 5 in B flat major WAB 105. The first draft had occupied him from 14 February 1875 until 16 May 1876. Other dates in the autograph indicate that he refined the Finale first, completing it on 18 May 1877.[9] He then worked on the first movement and completed it on 9 August before leaving for St. Florian. Finally, he turned his attention to the Adagio and worked on it until 4 January 1878.[10] Liszt was in Vienna during the month of April and played through Bruckner's symphony, making favourable comments to Hohenlohe-Schillingsfürst, the Lord Chamberlain. In a letter to Wagner on 20 May, in which he was typically effusive in his praise of Wagner's 'immortal masterworks', Bruckner described Liszt's gesture as 'certainly my last comfort in Vienna'.[11] At the

---

XXI/1, 107-12. For further information, see *G-A* IV/1, 493-96, *ABSW* XXI/1, viii and *ABSW* XXI/2, 98-101.

9 The autograph is located in the *ÖNB*, Mus.Hs. 19.477.

10 In his application for the post of assistant director of music at the *Hofkapelle* on 31 October 1877, Bruckner mentioned his compositional activities and stated that his 'Fifth Symphony would soon be finished'; see Chapter 4, page 335 and note 269. An entry in the *Neuer Krakauer Schreibkalender* for 1 January 1878 reads 'Sinfonie Nr. 5 im 4. und 5. Bogen Zeichen Br.', indicating that Bruckner had inserted changes in the time-signature in the fourth and fifth sheets of the Adagio. There is a facsimile of bars 95-97 of the movement, fol. 45' of Mus.Hs. 19.477, in *ABSW V Revisionsbericht* (1985), 59. There is also a later insertion made in the first movement below bars 477f. - 'NB 1.2. Trompete neu' - in October 1878. Nowak describes this as the 'last date which can be ascertained of Bruckner's involvement with the Fifth' in *ABSW V Revisionsbericht*, 67, footnote 1.

11 See *HSABB*, 177 for the text of this letter; the original can be found in the *Nationalarchiv der Richard Wagner-Stiftung* (IIIA 14-4). See also Peter Raabe, *Liszts Leben* I (Stuttgart/Berlin, 1931; Tutzing: Schneider, 2/1968), 311, and Egon Voss, 'Wagner und Bruckner' in Christoph-Hellmut Mahling, ed., *Anton Bruckner. Studien zu Werk und Wirkung* (Tutzing: Schneider, 1988), 230; and *G-A* IV/1, 481f. concerning a possible reply to this letter which has been lost. For Liszt's visit to

turn of the year 1878/79 Liszt was in Rome where he was also generous in his praise of Bruckner. Once again Bruckner was grateful for his recognition.[12] The symphony was dedicated to Karl von Stremayr and presented to him on his name-day (4 November) in a copy score with a title-page beautifully prepared by J.M. Kaiser.[13] Bruckner never heard an orchestral performance of this work of epic proportions with its majestic display of contrapuntal skill in the final movement. In Nowak's words, it 'reveals the utmost technical mastery of form, structure and instrumentation. For all who have ever set foot on the mighty edifice of its polyphony, its melodic wealth and its chorale, it remains an unforgettable experience.'[14]

In his letter to Tappert in October 1877 Bruckner had already announced his

---

Vienna in 1878 see Ernst Burger, *Franz Liszt. Eine Lebenschronik in Bildern und Dokumenten* (Munich, 1986), 272.

12 Bruckner referred to this when writing to Tappert in Berlin. See *HSABB* I, 181 for this letter, dated Vienna, 9 December 1878; the original is in private ownership.

13 This copy is in the *ÖNB*, Mus.Hs. 6064. Bruckner wrote to Kaiser on 13 October 1878, thanking him for his 'newest great masterwork' and enclosing payment of 40 florins. See *ABSW V* Revisionsbericht, 67 and *HSABB* I, 181 for this letter; the original is in the *ÖNB*.

14 From Nowak's foreword to *ABSW V*, transl. Richard Rickett. For informative articles about the structure of the work, see Armin Knab, 'Die thematischen Zusammenhänge in Bruckners 5. Sinfonie' in Heinz Wegener, ed., *Knab: Denken und Tun. Gesammelte Aufsätze über Musik* (Berlin: Merseburger, 1959), 18-36; Leopold Nowak, 'Anton Bruckners Formwille dargestellt am Finale seiner V. Symphonie' in *Miscellánea en homenaje a Mons. Higinio Anglés* (Barcelona, 1961), 609ff., repr. in *Über Anton Bruckner*, 43-46; Gunnar Cohrs, 'Der musikalische Architekt: zur Bedeutung der Zahlen in Bruckners 5. und 9. Sinfonie' in *Neue Zeitschrift für Musik* cli (July-August 1990), 19-26; idem, 'Zahlenphänomene in Bruckners Symphonik. Neues zu den Strukturen der Fünften und Neunten Symphonie' in *BJ 1989/90* (Vienna, 1992), 35-75; William Carragan, 'Structural Aspects of the Revision of Bruckner's Symphonic Finales' in *BSL* 1996 (Linz, 1998), 182f.; Robert S. Hatten, 'The Expressive Role of Disjunction. A Semiotic Approach to Form and Meaning in the Fourth and Fifth Symphonies' in *Perspectives on Anton Bruckner* (Aldershot: Ashgate,, 2001), in preparation.

intention of 'thoroughly revising' his Fourth Symphony. No sooner had he completed the Fifth than he began revising the first movement of the Fourth on 18 January. Work on this movement and on the second movement occupied him until the end of July. From the beginning of August until the end of September he pruned the Finale from 616 bars to 477 mainly through significant cuts in the development section and in the coda of the movement. The latter is, to all intents and purposes, a new composition. In the preface to his edition of the 1878 Finale, Nowak aptly uses the term 'creative revision' in his description of Bruckner's revision work.[15]

Bruckner's inscription 'Volksfest' in the copy of the movement in the *ÖNB* suggests that the main purpose of the revision of the Finale was not only to shorten it but to give it a lighter character. As well as revising the first, second and fourth movements, Bruckner wrote a completely new Scherzo in November. He provided details of this mixture of revision and new composition together with information concerning work on other symphonies in two letters to Tappert in October and December. In the first letter he also reminded Tappert that Bilse had still not returned the score and parts of the original version of the Fourth:

> ... I have now produced a new and shorter version of the 4th ('Romantic') Symphony (1st, 2nd, 4th movements) which should be effective. All that remains to be written is the new Scherzo which portrays the hunt, while the Trio is a dance tune which is played to the hunters during their meal.
>
> A large part of Symphony no. 2 in C minor has also been revised. Herbeck was very pleased with this work.
>
> I have made some changes too in the Symphony no. 3 in D minor (dedicated to Rich. Wagner) - a work which has been maligned so much, could not be rehearsed properly and appeared on the

---

15 See Leopold Nowak, 'Finale von 1878', *ABSW* IV/2 (Vienna, 1981); originally published by Haas in the appendix to vol. 4 of the first Complete Edition (1936). The first sheet of the autograph score is in Kremsmünster library and the remaining sheets are in the *Stadt- und Landesbibliothek*, Vienna. There is a copy (Mus. Hs. 3177, vol. 3) in the *ÖNB*.

programme at a time when the audience is accustomed to leave.[16]

Could I recommend to you for performance my 2nd Symphony in C minor which is probably the work that will be most easily understood by the public. No. 3 in D minor is also ready for performance. Professor Schelle looked through the score of this symphony, said that I had been treated most unjustly, had the most flattering things to say about its originality and contrapuntal invention and asked me to recommend it to you and request that it be performed in Berlin as soon as possible. (I do not dare offer anything for performance in Vienna until it has been played abroad.)

(Willner [sic], court music director in Dresden, has also invited me to send him a score, as has Rubinstein, director in Moscow.) But all that is of secondary importance.

It is only in Berlin that I have the good fortune to know such a celebrated and excellent critic as Professor Tappert in whom I can truly confide and from whom I most earnestly request favour and goodwill, albeit from some distance away. Otherwise I have no-one else here below!!!

In St. Florian - an abbey with a very large organ - where your famous reviews have recently been the talking-point, everyone was delighted to learn that I had the good fortune to know you etc.)

Concerning the choice of symphony [to be performed], I have no real preference, except that the 2nd should take precedence over the 3rd.

Once again, may I make a fervent request for your assistance! Bilse, the music director, has still not returned the music of the impractical old version of the 4th Symphony. Would you be so good as to remind him of this, dear Professor, if you have the opportunity.

If Herr Bilse is no longer inclined [to perform one of my symphonies], perhaps someone else can be found. The director of the Court Opera also knows me.[17] I can guarantee that either of the symphonies can and will give pleasure, provided that they are rehearsed carefully. I trust, nevertheless, that Music Director Bilse has not written me off completely. Please be so good as to convey my respects to him. In any case I should like to send him the score [of

---

16 The symphony was in the second half of the traditional Sunday morning concert when the attention of many members of the audience would be turning towards lunch!

17 This is a reference to Karl Eckert (1820-1879) who was opera director in Vienna from 1853 to 1860 and took up an appointment as director of the Royal Opera in Berlin in 1869.

one of these symphonies] so that he can peruse it.
Once again please don't be too annoyed with me for pestering you
so much. You know the situation in Vienna well enough and what it
means to be neglected.
Herr Rättig wants to have the piano scores of the symphonies which
I have mentioned so that he can publish them...
P.S. My address now is 1ˢᵗ district, Hessgasse no. 7.[18]

In his second letter, written two months later, Bruckner somewhat apologetically
renewed his request for Tappert's assistance and informed him *inter alia* that he had
completed his revision of the Fourth Symphony and had begun work on a String
Quintet:

Please forgive me for daring (no doubt somewhat presumptuously)
to repeat once again the request I made two months ago. The scores
and parts of the C minor and D minor symphonies are still reserved
for Berlin in spite of requests from Rubinstein in Moscow and others
to send them something. I find it impossible to believe that you would
abandon me although I have been pestering you continually. Perhaps
I will still be able to find an opportunity of expressing and confirming
my gratitude. Bilse, the court music director, has obviously not had
the time to write or to have the old material returned.
In the meantime, the 4ᵗʰ (Romantic) Symphony has been completely
finished but the parts have not yet been written out. I hope to give
you particular pleasure with this work. At present I am writing a
String Quintet in F major which Hellmesberger who, as you know, is
very enthusiastic about my works, has repeatedly urged me to
compose. I learned recently that Liszt had made complimentary
remarks about my 5ᵗʰ Symphony and other current works of mine not
only to Hohenlohe but also to people in Rome.
Please don't leave me in the lurch - I await a favourable response

---

18 See *HSABB* I, 179f. for this letter dated Vienna, 9 October 1878; the original is in private
possession, but the *Musikwissenschaftlicher Verlag*, Vienna possesses a photocopy. For Willner read
Wüllner. See page 458, footnote 246 for further information about Franz Wüllner (1832-1902).

with anxiety...[19]

No further correspondence between Bruckner and Tappert has survived. The two men met on several occasions thereafter at Bayreuth. Although Tappert no doubt made every effort to arouse interest in Bruckner in Berlin in the late 1870s, the first performance of a Bruckner work in the German capital did not take place until January 1887 when Karl Klindworth conducted a performance of the Symphony no. 7.

As well as pursuing his teaching activities and his vocation as a composer, Bruckner did not entirely neglect social pleasures. A friendship with a young lady called Julie Joachim was typical of many of his short-lived 'affairs of the heart'. In this particular instance, Miss Joachim wrote to Bruckner on 9 January 1879 and made it clear that she did not wish to take the brief friendship any further. At the same time she was bold enough to ask him for some free concert tickets![20] Bruckner's *Hochschulkalender* for 1879 also contains references to other activities. At the end of a carnival ball on 15 February he danced with a Baroness Scala and at the end of another ball three days later he danced with Fräulein Waldheim, noting her address in brackets - 'Pharmacist, Himmelpfortgasse'. The entry for March 15 - 'Orgel-Concert, Improvisation in Akademischen' - refers to his participation as an organ soloist in a concert given by the *Akademischer Gesangverein* in the large *Musikverein* hall. Bruckner played for half an hour and ended his recital with an improvised four-part fugue. On 11 May he also played the organ at a benefit concert for the pension fund of *Concordia*, a society for journalists and writers. The concert was advertised in the *Wiener Zeitung* on 7 May and there was a short but favourable review in the

---

19 See *HSABB* I, 181 for this letter, dated Vienna, 9 December 1878; also see footnote 12

20 See *G-A* IV/1, 569 for details of this letter.

same paper on 12 May.[21]

There are also some references to Bruckner's state of health in the 1879 diary. Bad migraine headaches are recorded on 21 and 22 October and again in December. The early onset of winter must have surprised him - the first snowfall during the evening of 16 October is duly noted. As usual the names, and in some cases, the addresses, of his private pupils are written down. Among the names for 1879 are Hans Rott, Rudolf Krzyzanowski and 'Dietrich', probably Rudolf Dittrich who had organ lessons in Bruckner's flat as well as studying at the Conservatory from 1878 to 1882.[22]

Although Bruckner had little sympathy with the ideals of the Caecilian Catholic church music reform movement, he responded to an invitation from Ignaz Traumihler, choir director at St. Florian and a keen supporter of the movement, to write a motet for the feast of St. Augustine on 28 August by composing *Os justi* WAB 30 for four-eight part choir *a cappella*. A week after completing the motet he sent it, with an accompanying letter, to its dedicatee and went out of his way to stress the deliberately archaic style of the piece:

> I convey my heartiest congratulations to you on your name day with all speed before you go to Linz. May God bless you, keep you in the best of health and preserve your customary mental alertness for years to come. May He also grant you the same zeal and undiminished energy in your artistic and religious activities!
> Many thanks for remembering my own name day in such a friendly way.

---

21 See *HSABB* I, 182 for an official letter of thanks to Bruckner from Edgar von Spiegel, a member of the committee and Zacharias K. Lecher, the president of *Concordia*. It is dated Vienna, 13 May 1879; the original is in St. Florian.

22 Dittrich (1861-1919) spent seven years in Japan (1888-1894) as the artistic director of the Imperial Music Academy in Tokyo. He was appointed court organist in Vienna in 1901 and succeeded Vockner as Professor of Organ at the Conservatory (1906-1909).

If I am not mistaken, you wanted me to write an 'Os justi'. I take
the liberty of sending it to you and have been so bold as to dedicate
it to you (that is, if you accept).
Is this the complete text? I would be delighted if you liked it.
There are no sharps or flats, no seventh chords, no 6/4 chords and no
chordal combinations using four and five different notes
simultaneously. I propose to have it sung in the *Hofkapelle* at the
end of October when my D minor Mass is being performed.[23] My
Quintet is finished. Hellmesberger, the court music director, is quite
beside himself with joy and intends to perform it. He is completely
changed and makes a huge fuss of me. My holidays begin on 17
August. If Herr Bibl returns a few days earlier, however, I can come
to St. Florian immediately. My thanks also for the invitation - I hope
to find you in excellent spirits. My respects to the abbot and to the
dean...[24]

According to Franz Wiesner, who was a choirboy at St. Florian at the time,
Traumihler was not completely satisfied with the piece after the first rehearsal and
asked Bruckner to make some changes, particularly in the middle section.[25] Bruckner
complied with Traumihler's request and, on 28 July, added the organ-accompanied
versicle 'Inveni David' which follows the closing 'Alleluia' of the gradual. In
response to Bruckner's query 'Is this the complete text' in his letter to Traumihler,
the latter no doubt reminded him that the 'Inveni David' verse was used both at the
feast of Silvester on 31 December and the feast of Augustine on 28 August as well
as pointing out that there were some differences between the *Os justi* text which
Bruckner set and the appropriate text for the feast day of St. Augustine.[26]

---

23 It was sung as the gradual on 9 November 1879. The 1861 *Ave Maria* was the offertory
hymn.

24 See *HSABB* I, 182f. for this letter, dated Vienna, 25 July 1879; the original is in St. Florian.

25 See *G-A* II/1, 269.

26 The autographs of the first and second versions are located in the *ÖNB*, Mus. Hs. 3158 and Mus.
Hs. 37.284 respectively. There is a facsimile of the autograph of the first version between pages 568
and 569 in *G-A* IV/1. The autograph of the concluding 'Inveni David' is also in the *ÖNB*, Mus. Hs.

During his summer vacation at St. Florian Bruckner was asked to play the organ for some high-ranking officers in the army. Wishing to use a military theme as the basis for improvisation but not knowing any, he asked one of the priests, Matthias Lehner, for his advice. It is possible that this theme inspired the main theme of Symphony no. 6 which Bruckner began shortly after his return to Vienna. Mahler's use of military signals in some of his works provides an interesting comparison here.

Bruckner's major compositional activity in the first half of the year was the String Quintet in F WAB 112 which was begun towards the end of 1878 and, according to dates in the autograph, completed with the Scherzo on 12 July 1879.[27] Hellmesberger, who commissioned the work, evidently found the Scherzo too difficult and Bruckner wrote an alternative third movement - an *Intermezzo* WAB 113 - which he completed on 21 December.[28] No alternative Trio was written. In the first edition of the work, however, the original Scherzo was reinstated, and the Intermezzo was not published until after Bruckner's death.[29] In the original autograph, the copy used for engraving and the parts used by the Hellmesberger Quartet, the slow movement is placed second. But a more satisfactory order of movements in which the slow movement is placed third was eventually adopted both in the engraver's copy and the parts, almost certainly with Bruckner's approval. Bruckner made some alterations and additions in the engraver's copy but did not copy these into the

---

6069. Traumihler's dedication copy is located in St. Florian, Bruckner-Archiv no. 19/12. The work was first published by Theodor Rättig as no. 3 of *Vier Graduale* (Vienna, 1886). For a modern edition, see *ABSW* XXI/1, 113-17. For further information, see *G-A* IV/1, 563-68, *ABSW* XXI/1, 188, *ABSW* XXI/2, 102-17 and Leopold Nowak, 'Die Motette "Os justi" und ihre Handschriften' in *Mitteilungsblatt der IBG* 22 (Vienna, 1983), 5-8; repr. in idem, *Über Anton Bruckner*, 246-49.

27 The autograph is in the *ÖNB*, Mus. Hs. 19.482. See also Bruckner's letters to Tappert and Traumihler (footnotes 19 and 24) in which he mentions work on the Quintet.

28 The autograph of the *Intermezzo* is also in the *ÖNB*, Mus. Hs. 6080.

29 First edition of the Quintet with the original Scherzo - Vienna: Gutmann, 1884 (A.J.G. 500). First edition of Intermezzo - Vienna: U.E., 1913 (U.E. 2922).

autograph. After the first printing, however, he made some alterations in the autograph, particularly at the end of the Finale.[30]

Hellmesberger and his quartet did not perform the work until January 1885. In the meantime, one of Bruckner's most dedicated pupils, Joseph Schalk, arranged a private performance in the Bösendorfer hall in November 1881. On this occasion, a quintet of young enthusiasts played the first three movements only. The first performance of the complete Quintet was given by the Winkler Quartet, with Franz Schalk playing the first viola part, at another musical evening arranged by the Wagner Society in the Bösendorfer hall on 7 May 1883. Joseph Schalk also arranged the work for piano duet. It took some time for the Quintet to become established in the chamber music repertory. Perhaps the fact that it shares several compositional features with the symphonies, for instance the 'massive' octave-unison gestures and rich textures, militated against this. But it cannot be denied that there are many passages in which Bruckner displays a lively awareness of the chamber medium and creates a more intimate sound world.

---

30 For further details, see G-A IV/1, 535-63 and Leopold Nowak, foreword to ABSW XIII/2 (Vienna: Musikwissenschaftlicher Verlag, 1963). Nowak has also provided an informative article about the structure of the first movement in his 'Form und Rhythmus im ersten Satz des Streichquintetts von Anton Bruckner' in Horst Heussner, ed., Festschrift für Hans Engel zum siebzigsten Geburtstag (Cassel, 1964), 260-73; repr. in Über Anton Bruckner, 60-70. A perceptive comparison of Bruckner's Quintet and Brahms's Quintet in F op. 88 (1882) for the same grouping of two violins, two violas and cello has been made by Wilhelm Seidel, 'Das Streichquintett in F-Dur im Oeuvre von Anton Bruckner und Johannes Brahms' in BSL 1983 (Linz, 1985), 183-89. There is a comprehensive survey of the documentation of the Quintet (including references in letters and concert reviews) in Gerold W. Gruber, 'Anton Bruckner, Streichquintett in F-Dur (WAB 112)', BJ 1994/95/96 (Linz, 1997), 99-133. In a recent article, 'Late-Nineteenth-Century Chamber Music and the Cult of the Classical Adagio', in 19th-Century Music 23/1 (Summer 1999), 33-61, Margaret Notley discusses the slow movement in the context of other chamber-music slow movements of the period, particularly those of Brahms.

In the latter part of 1879 Bruckner also carried out some revision work on his Symphony no.2 and began writing the third Finale of his Symphony no. 4. One of his favourite pupils, Felix Mottl, joined forces with Hans Paumgartner to play the second and third movements of the Third Symphony in Mahler's arrangement at a *Wagner Society* concert in the Bösendorfer hall in Vienna on November 12. The critic for *Die Presse* reported that there was 'no more reliable indicator of the worth of a musical work than the effect it has when heard more often, and this work made a thrilling and electrifying impression'.[31] Mottl and Paumgartner also played an arrangement of the Andante and Scherzo movements of the Fourth Symphony at a *Wagner Society* concert in Vienna on 4 February 1880 and a piano arrangement of the first movement of the symphony later in the year just before Mottl left Vienna to take up the position of musical director of the court theatre in Karlsruhe.[32] On the same day as the first of these concerts, an article entitled 'Anton Bruckner. Porträt eines Wiener Musikers' and signed 'C.B.', obviously someone who knew Bruckner well, appeared in the *Deutsche Zeitung*. It touched on various aspects of his

---

31 From a report which appeared in *Die Presse*, 19 November 1879. There was a review of the same concert in the *Neue Wiener Zeitschrift für Musik* 1/6 (20 November 1879). Also see Andrea Harrandt, *Die Bruckner Klavieraufführungen im Wiener Akademischen Wagner-Verein*, *BJ 1994/95/96* (Linz, 1997), 223-34 for an account of the two-piano performances of movements from Bruckner's symphonies in meetings of the Vienna *Academic Wagner Society*. There is an English translation of this article in *Perspectives on Anton Bruckner* (Ashgate: Aldershot, 2001), in preparation.

32 This second concert was on 7 October 1880. Theodor wrote an enthusiastic review of the first concert in the *Neue Wiener Zeitschrift für Musik* 14 (10 February), 110. Mottl (1856-1911) remained at Karlsruhe until 1903 when he moved to Munich to become musical director at the opera house and the *Akademie der Tonkunst*. He conducted at Bayreuth for the first time in 1886. For further information, see Oskar Kaul, 'Felix Mottl' in *MGG* 9 (1961), col. 670, and David Charlton, 'Felix Mottl' in *The New Grove* 12, 650f. Hans Paumgartner (1844-1896) worked as a lawyer until 1880 but then embarked on a musical career. He was a repetiteur at the Vienna Opera and music critic for the *Wiener Zeitung*. In 1882 he married the famous opera singer, Rosa Papier.

personality - his appearance which would lead one to suspect that he was either 'a younger relative of our present archbishop or a monastery cellarer travelling incognito' but certainly not 'one of the most richly endowed sons of St. Cecilia', his large appetite, his shyness which the writer attributed partly to the fact that he had spent many of his formative years 'in the seclusion of a monastery' and which came to light, for instance, when Bruckner was rehearsing his Third Symphony - and on his relationship with Wagner who had apparently promised to perform this particular work.[33] Recognition was slow in coming but at least there were signs now that his work was being taken more seriously. Franz Liszt wrote to him at the end of March, saying that he had 'read the score of the D minor symphony with interest' and 'would not hesitate to recommend it enthusiastically to conductors of my acquaintance'.[34]

During 1880 there were two performances of the D minor Mass, with *Locus iste* as gradual and *Os justi* as offertory hymn, in the *Hofkapelle*.[35] Oddo Loidol, a young

---

33 Article in the *Deutsche Zeitung*, 4 February 1880. See Manfred Wagner, 'Bruckner in Wien' in *ABDS* 2 (Graz, 1980), 41-44. Franz Scheder, *ABCText*, 350 suggests that C.B. could be the initials for Cursch-Bühren, a Leipzig lawyer and music journalist who also wrote for the *Leipziger Tageblatt*.

34 From Liszt's letter to Bruckner, dated Vienna, 30 March 1880. See *HSABB* I, 183; the original is in St. Florian. On 20 August Liszt wrote to Ludwig Bösendorfer (probably from Weimar), enclosing copies of the score and four-hand piano arrangement of Bruckner's Third Symphony, and asking him to return them to Bruckner and to reassure him that he had recommended the symphony to several conductors. See *HSABB* I, 185; the original is in the *Gesellschaft der Musikfreunde* library.

35 On Sunday 6 June and Sunday 24 October.

priest from Kremsmünster who was studying in Vienna at the time and attended Bruckner's lectures at the University, recalled that Hellmesberger was greatly impressed with the Mass. This is corroborated by the following testimonial which Hellmesberger supplied at Bruckner's request:

> The great Mass (in D) written by Professor Anton Bruckner, the imperial court organist, can be described as a true masterwork. It is an inspired composition and a superb musical realisation of the text, and has never failed to make a great impression on all connoisseurs of music when it has been performed in the court chapel.[36]

Before the second performance in the *Hofkapelle* Bruckner wrote to Loidol, congratulating him on being received into holy orders in Kremsmünster and requesting that he ask the music director of the abbey to return the score of the Mass:

> Be so good as to forward it to me yourself. This Mass is being performed more often now and is beginning to become unusually popular.[37]

As in the previous year Bruckner's duties at the *Hofkapelle* kept him in Vienna until the middle of August. He stayed at St. Florian from 13 to 20 August. On 22 and 23 August he saw the Passion Play at Oberammergau. He then travelled to Switzerland, visiting Zurich and playing the organ in Zurich cathedral on 28 August. His itinerary took him next to Geneva (29 August), Chamonix (30 August - 4 September; including a trip to La Fléchère), back to Geneva where he played the organ in the cathedral (5 September), Lausanne (6 September), Freiburg where he

---

36 This testimonial is dated Vienna, 16 July 1880. See *G-A* IV/1, 603. There is a copy (but not the original) in the *ÖNB*.

37 See *HSABB* I, 187-88 for this letter, dated Vienna, 17 October 1880; the original is in Kremsmünster abbey.

played in the cathedral after a concert given by Eduard Vogt, the resident organist (7 September), Bern where he made a great impression on Dr. Jakob Mendel, the cathedral organist (8 September) and Lucerne (8-10 September). He returned to Linz by way of Munich and Salzburg on 11 September and spent the few remaining days of his vacation at St. Florian. In his diary he noted down some details of his journey, including the names of several young ladies who had attracted him. In Oberammergau he made the acquaintance of a 17-year-old girl called Maria Bartl who was one of the 'daughters of Jerusalem' in the Passion Play. On his return to Vienna he wrote to Maria several times. According to information given to Göllerich by Henry Wright, these letters contained information about 'many of his musical works, his successes, ideas and projects'. Unfortunately, they have been lost, 'some of them as a result of fire damage, the rest destroyed by their recipient after her marriage'. Maria's husband, Josef Albrecht, who read all the letters before they were destroyed, confirmed that Bruckner was passionately in love![38] Four of Maria's letters to Bruckner have survived, however. On 9 September 1880 she sent a photograph of herself with an accompanying postcard which included the following note from her mother, Lina Bartl, who apparently wanted something more permanent to result from the relationship:

> It would be very fine... to have the good fortune to see my daughter at the side of such a worthy man. Youth and shyness on their own make life gloomy. Now, however [she will] have much better prospects as she is convinced that she is loved by such a man. A girl who has only attended the village school and lacks experience until she reaches maturity is not disposed to abandon herself and her love to the big wide world...[39]

.

---

38 See *G-A* IV/1, 611 for further information.

39 See *HSABB* I, 186 for the texts of both letters; the originals are in St. Florian.

In a letter written two months later, on 7 November 1880, Maria thanked Bruckner for sending her his photograph and regretted that he had been ill. She was glad that his trip had been so successful and hoped to visit him in Vienna with her mother. One suspects that it was the mother who prompted some of the following words:

> It gives me increasing pleasure and honour to be acquainted with, indeed to be admired by, such an important person, and the more I read your esteemed words, the more I am amazed. I reflect thoughtfully on the work with which the bride-to-be is occupied today as she has always been. I always have your dear picture very close to me...[40]

The relationship came to a sudden end the following year. On 5 May 1881, Maria thanked Bruckner for the gift of a prayer-book and for sending her a page from a newspaper which included an article about him. Although she would be happy for him to visit her in Oberammergau, she and her mother would prefer to come to Vienna.[41] The final letter which has survived is dated 10 June 1881. It contains the information that the rehearsals for the play 'Philippe Welser', in which Maria had an important part, would begin soon.[42] This was perhaps an indication that she would not be able to visit Vienna as originally planned. While it would appear that Bruckner was genuinely very fond of Maria, he must have realised that marriage was out of the question. If he himself often felt out of place socially in the Austrian capital, what would an 1 8-year-old girl from a village in Germany have felt? And life

---

40 See *HSABB* I, 188 for the complete text of this letter; the original is in St. Florian. The illness referred to was a foot complaint which had confined Bruckner to bed for a few days at the end of September.

41 See *HSABB* I, 191-92 for the text of this letter; the original is in St. Florian.

42 See *G-A* IV/1, 613 and Leopold Nowak, *Anton Bruckner. Musik und Leben* (Linz, 1973), 195 for information about this letter.

with a 56-year-old man, now firmly set in his ways, would not have been a bed of roses!

Before embarking on his vacation trip, Bruckner learned that the Vienna *Männergesangverein* required a new assistant conductor. He wrote to Eduard Kremser, the chief conductor, offering his services:

> I have learned that the assistant choirmaster of the Vienna Male Voice Society is to be appointed in October. You are probably not aware that I was director of the *Frohsinn* choir in Linz at one time. When I conducted the choir in a performance of Kücken's 'Wachet auf' at a special festival in Nuremberg in 1862 I received the highest praise from Herbeck among others. Although I have never sought to push myself at any time in my life, I am making this approach to you now as I know that you are well disposed towards me and an important supporter of my music. Should there be a possibility of obtaining the position of second choirmaster, I ask you sincerely to give serious consideration to this request and application for the post. If there is no possibility, please treat this letter with confidentiality so that it does not become public knowledge needlessly. In a few days I am going to Upper Austria, St. Florian and then Switzerland...[43]

Bruckner was unsuccessful in his rather unorthodox application for the post. To his dismay, what he had hoped would remain private became public. His request for discretion was not heeded. In October he wrote again to Kremser, asking if at least he could be allowed to rehearse *Germanenzug* with the choir as a guest conductor:

> Since the beginning of the school year I have been suffering from a foot complaint and have had to spend a week in bed already. I heard on several occasions that, unfortunately, I have no hope at all of obtaining the position in your Society - you are the best judge of

---

43 See *HSABB* I, 184-85 for the full text of this letter, dated Vienna, 9 August 1880; the original is in private possession. Eduard Kremser (1838-1914) succeeded Johann Herbeck as choirmaster of the Vienna *Männergesangverein* in 1869 and was director of the *Gesellschaft* concerts from 1878 to 1880.

that. If Herbeck was alive he would say what kind of choir director I am; (it is well known in Linz and in the *Akademischer Gesangverein*, with which I rehearsed *Germanenzug* four years ago, how thoroughly I prepare a piece.)

I have already let it be known what Herbeck said to me about this a few weeks before his death and on many other occasions.

In order to salvage some honour, I beg you to agree to this request that I be allowed to rehearse my *Germanenzug* just on one occasion. It would never enter my head (as I said in my previous letter) to push myself, and I do not begrudge anyone the position. But as my name has been mentioned in the papers and I have to put up with a lot of vexation, I would like at least, with your influential help, to regain some self-respect by being allowed to rehearse my *Germanenzug* once. I wish to reiterate my original request that my name be never mentioned on any future occasion if there is absolutely no hope for me.

You know very well that I have little success in Vienna. As God wills! Depending on and trusting in you...[44]

Nothing came of Bruckner's request. Kremser and his male voice choir were among the composer's staunchest advocates throughout the 1880s and 1890s, however.

In 1880 Bruckner began to receive a regular income for his Harmony and Counterpoint lectures at the University. First of all he was given a special payment of 800 florins by the Ministry of Education on 30 June as a remuneration for the 1879-80 lectures.[45] Five months later, on 28 November, he was informed by Dr. Conrad Eybesfeld, Minister of Education and Culture, that his formal request on 13 November for a fixed annual salary had been approved and that he would receive henceforth 800 florins per annum, to be paid in two six-monthly instalments. This

---

44 See *HSABB* I, 187 for this letter, dated Vienna, 2 October 1880; the original is in the *ÖNB*.

45 This was in response to a request formally made by Bruckner on 23 June. The original of the letter from the Ministry of Culture and Education is in the *ÖNB*.

was confirmed by the board of the Faculty of Philosophy on 16 December.[46]

Bruckner's diary entries for the year contain more frequent references to migraine headaches. He attended several balls in the Carnival season (February/March) and, as usual, noted down the names of ladies with whom he had danced. There are the names of private pupils and, under January, Gustav Mahler's address: '4. Bez. Floragasse N 7 Florabad 4. Stiege 3. Stock'.[47] In June there is a reference to the performance of his D minor Mass in the *Hofkapelle*: '6. Juni (2. Aufführung meiner Messe in D in kk. Hofkapelle unter meiner Direction.) Grad. Locus iste. Offert. Os justi'. In August, the entry '8000 Meilen von den ersten Menschen' is almost certainly a reference to the Austrian expedition to the North Pole which was of great interest to Bruckner.

Bruckner's compositional activities during the year included further work on Symphony no. 6 and a third Finale for Symphony no. 4. Dates in the autograph of Symphony no. 6 indicate that Bruckner began work on the first movement on 24 September 1879, was still working on it on 9 June 1880 and completed it on 27 September while 'lying in bed with a foot complaint'; the second movement was also completed in sketch form two months later - at the University on 22 November - and composition of the Scherzo / Trio was finished in mid-December.[48] The revised Finale of Symphony no. 4 was begun on 19 November 1879 and completed on 5 June 1880. The first three movements of the symphony were performed at the end of 1880 / beginning of 1881 at two rehearsal evenings of the Conservatory student orchestra, the first conducted by Hellmesberger, the second by Bruckner himself. Josef

---

46 See *G-A* IV/1, 619 and Manfred Wagner, *Bruckner* (Mainz, 1983), 142f.

47 On 27 April, Bruckner wrote to Mahler, saying that he had something important to discuss with him and Krzyzanowski and asking them to meet him at the Conservatory in the early evening or later at the *Zum roten Igel* inn. The original is not available, but there is a copy in the *Internationale Gustav Mahler Gesellschaft, Sammlung Ernst Rosé*.

48 The autograph of Symphony no. 6 is in the *ÖNB*, Mus. Hs. 19.478

Venantius von Wöss was present at both rehearsals and related that Hellmesberger, who led the viola section in the second rehearsal, played the viola theme in the Andante movement so beautifully that Bruckner embraced him afterwards.[49]

A comparison between the first (1874) and second (1878-80) versions of Symphony no. 4 reveals several changes in details of scoring and a more rigorous handling of structure in the latter. Reduction in length goes hand in hand with a much more concise presentation of material. While the Finale is longer than the '1878' version, it is still 75 bars shorter than the original Finale. The most striking addition is the quotation of the main theme of the Scherzo at the beginning which establishes an obvious connection with the previous movement.

1881 began well for Bruckner. On 2 February his D minor Mass was sung once again in the Hofkapelle, with the 1861 Ave Maria and Locus iste as the gradual and offertory motets respectively. A few days before this, on 27 January, Bruckner was elected an honorary member of the Akademischer Wagner-Verein,[50] and this society arranged a private performance of the Fourth Symphony by the Vienna Philharmonic conducted by Richter on 20 February in a concert which began with Beethoven's King Stephen overture and also included Beethoven's Piano Concerto no. 4, in which Hans von Bülow was the soloist, and von Bülow's own symphonic poem, Des Sängers Fluch.[51] While von Bülow was well known to the Viennese concertgoers

---

49 See G-A IV/1, 631. Wöss (1863-1943) later worked for Universal Edition and was responsible for editing several of Bruckner's compositions..

50 This is the date given in G-A IV/1, 630 and Manfred Wagner, Bruckner, 144; but 22 January 1885 is probably a more reliable date. See Hellmut Kowar, 'Vereine für die Neudeutschen in Wien' in BSL 1984 (Linz, 1986), 83 and 89; Andrea Harrandt, 'Bruckner und das Erlebnis Wagner' in Mitteilungsblatt der IBG 38 (1992), 12.

51 In a letter to an unnamed person (possibly a reviewer for the Neue Wiener Tagblatt), however, Richter made it clear that his 'fellow musicians' in the Philharmonic had not rejected the Fourth (implied in a report in the paper on 13 February). There had simply been a difference of opinion

as a fine pianist and his interpretation of Beethoven's concerto was admired, his symphonic poem made little impression. Bruckner's symphony, on the other hand, elicited an enthusiastic response from the audience. The critical response was mixed, ranging from Eduard Kremser's warm appreciation of Bruckner's compositional skill in *Vaterland* to Max Kalbeck's scathing review in the *Wiener Allgemeine Zeitung*. Kremser's review must have been particularly gratifying to read, and Bruckner was no doubt reassured that lack of success in his application for an assistant choirmaster's post the previous year was not the result of any animosity on Kremser's part. Bruckner was so delighted with the review that he mentioned it, as well as another review in the *Vorstadt-Zeitung* which had been sent to him, when writing to Father Ernst Klinger in Taufkirchen on 11 March.[52]

In his review, which is not specifically about the Fourth Symphony, Kremser makes a distinction between Bruckner the unremarkable, unassuming person and Bruckner the outstanding organist and composer:

---

between those who argued that it would be better to perform only part of the symphony and those who considered that it should be played in its entirety The text of this letter, which is in the *Wiener Philharmoniker Archiv, ÖNB*, can be found in Imogen Fellinger, 'Brahms' und Bruckners Verhältnis zu ihren Interpreten', *BSL 1983* (Linz, 1985), 86, Otto Biba, 'Eine Miszelle zur Uraufführung von Bruckners 4. Symphonie', *Mitteilungsblatt der IBG* 26 (1985), 27 and *HSABB* I, 189. The paper printed a correction of the original report on 15 February. It was five years later, on the occasion of a rehearsal of Bruckner's Fourth in the summer of 1886, that von Bülow allegedly described Bruckner as 'half genius, half imbecile'. See Hans-Joachim Hinrichsen, 'Halb Genie, halb Trottel' in *Mitteilungsblatt der IBG* 55 (December 2000), 21-24.

52 See *HSABB* I, 191; location of original unknown. First printed in *ABB*, 154. See also *HSABB* I, 190 for a letter to Josef Thiard-Laforest (1841-1897), conductor of the *Linz Musikverein* at the time, in which he asks him to make sure that his friends in Linz are informed of the success of the performance of the symphony and recommends certain reviews. The letter is dated Vienna, 2 March 1881; location of original unknown; first published in the *Preßburger Zeitung*, 18 March 1897.

... There is nothing outwardly brilliant about Bruckner, nothing charismatic, hardly anything winsome; on the contrary, he is not only an unassuming but also a very humble person. He is an outstanding organist - one of the best there is - but attaches very little importance to this fact. With all his modesty and humility, however, he is filled with a great self-assurance. It has been related to me that, on being asked why he did not give any organ concerts, his reply was 'my fingers will be buried, but what they write will not be buried!' That is a profound remark, but not unjustified. And while it presupposes rather strongly that there will be a future response, there is no doubt that Bruckner has the right to give greater prominence to his activities in the area of composition than many other more famous people.

Bruckner is the Schubert of our time. There is such a flow of invention in his works and one idea follows another in such a way as to cause one truly to marvel at their abundance; one ought not to be in the least surprised, however, that he has not yet found the most suitable setting for such a great number of precious stones. The excellent organist, a product of the old contrapuntal school, would not find it difficult to move just as easily within the conventional forms and express himself just as precisely in them as many other composers for whom technical mastery of these very forms is the be all and end all. Bruckner is simply struggling for a new form, but as yet the struggler by no means gives the impression of being victorious. The one who strives never produces the pleasant picture of something finished and complete. He always appears to be in a state of continual development, and the bold pioneer is regarded all too frequently as a mere student in the eyes of the faint-hearted who have no understanding of the excellence of such a process. This is why many treat him as a mere imitator of Wagner. There is little truth in this, and it is perhaps even less true of him than it is of the composer who believes that he is completely free and independent of Richard Wagner's direction. What is important when it is a question of the independence of an artist? Pride of place is probably given to the originality of ideas. Now I would like to get to know any contemporary composer who possesses more inventive directness or originality of ideas than Anton Bruckner! I hope that such a composer will be born soon. Today at least he is not yet moving among us, preaching his wisdom in the streets.

Bruckner is a Wagnerian but just in the same way as Wagner is a Beethovenian or Beethoven a Mozartian, and certainly not in any other sense. He works with themes and motives of his own invention and, at the same time, avails himself of all those developments in the areas of modulation, motivic combination and thematic organization as well as instrumentation which have been promoted in music of our time. Is one, therefore, a mere imitator because one makes use of what has been handed down and inherited from earlier? It is only a question of how this happens, whether one employs the material which has been handed down in an original manner. And Bruckner has assuredly done the latter more than any other contemporary composer; he sings his own song, he plays on his own instrument. He has something of his own to impart to the world, and it is only to be wished that he would have more frequent opportunities of doing so than has been the case up to now. If only Herbeck was alive! But Bruckner can wait. There are already a few who are able to appreciate him, and what he writes will not be buried with him.[53]

Contrast the above with Kalbeck's review. Kalbeck began by describing the symphony as 'the work of a child with the powers of a giant'. He continued:

... A young Hercules who strangles two snakes in his cradle would perhaps compose music in a similar fashion. Unfortunately, however, this boisterous child is a professional musician of mature years who is universally admired as an experienced theoretician and excellent organist. Indeed, if the innocent old man was still an inexperienced youth who, in his natural naivety and touching ignorance of human affairs, was blindly following the impulse of his impetuous will and was making music come what may, unconcerned about God and the world, we would add our voices to the enthusiastic cries of his admirers and rejoice, 'Behold, a new Beethoven. Blessed is he who comes in the name of the Lord!' There is no doubt about Bruckner's musical talent; he demonstrates it brilliantly in many places in the symphony. But he does not organize or control this precious possession in the correct manner. He thinks it is inexhaustible and throws it out of the window with both hands; consequently he starves afterwards. He also lacks the ability to judge size and measure distance; he reaches for the sun in order to kindle the little fire in his hearth and hurls a spear at a mosquito.

---

53 From the review in *Vaterland*, 3 March 1881; see *G-A* IV/1, 637-40 for text.

The four movements of his work are a veritable symphony-tetralogy and each on its own is sufficient to kill off an unprepared orchestra. The disorder of a study, in which everything is in a muddle and only the head of the house can just about feel his way, governs the musical physiognomy of the work. It is precisely those ideas that are the most feeble and ordinary which are spun out endlessly and repeated *ad nauseam*, while those that are truly original and worthwhile are shunted on one side without any attention being paid to them. A Richard Wagner in reverse who does not know the limit of his capabilities and searches for them most eagerly in those places where they are least likely to be found! Bruckner over-values his inventive powers one moment and his creative ability the next. He likes to make good his weaknesses not with strengths but with new weaknesses. If he were to understand, like Wagner, how to make virtues out of his deficiencies, he would perhaps be a great symphonist and it would not be necessary for us today to describe his work as a failure for the most part. Bruckner either pays no attention to or is unaware of the important rule which applies just as much to artists as to diplomats - to remain silent at the right time. He has so much to say to us and would rather say it all at the one time. As this is out of the question in spite of timpani, trombones, horns and trumpets, he goes as far afield as possible, makes continual digressions, repeats himself countless times, gets entangled in muddled contradictions and just cannot stop. These characteristics are combined with an aura of mystical profundity which Bruckner has in common with many gifted people. It is noticeable that there is nothing false or pretentious about this, and that he has even at times provided a visionary glimpse into the heavenly heights and oceanic depths of music. And this gives his music an undeniable power over the public who will always prefer the most extravagant and intricate work of the visionary to the clear, comprehensible work of the many normal artists. We do not need to affirm that such a phenomenon is also of far greater interest to us than a dozen dull Kapellmeisters but, at the same time, we must not forget that one's interest in the pathological and personal outstrips one's interest in the aesthetic and technical.

It would be very tempting to discuss details of the work, insofar as it offers us abundance of material for critical comment and detailed study. As we must beware of making the same mistake as Bruckner and of not knowing when to stop, we will content ourselves with a few observations and add the following details - that the symphony gives the impression of being a music drama without text, that the first movement is by far the most substantial and significant, and that the overall structure as regards instrumentation, atmosphere and mood, as well as individual phrases and details, is clearly reminiscent of Wagner. 'Lohengrin', 'Dutchman', 'Valkyrie' and 'Twilight of the Gods' have all been actively involved although there is no recognizable thematic influence. The Philharmonic under Hans Richter really worked wonders in playing the symphony which lasted a whole hour and kept everyone in suspense. They were largely responsible for the extraordinary success enjoyed by the composer who was applauded several times after each movement.[54]

Writing in the *Neue freie Presse*, Hanslick mentioned the successful performance of the symphony very briefly in the edition of the paper for 22 February. Five days later, he provided a more thorough review of von Bülow's symphonic poem, but had very little to say about Bruckner's work:

Today we can only add that we are truly pleased that this work which we do not totally understand has been successful, if only for the sake of the composer, a worthy and pleasant man.[55]

An article written by Wilhelm Frey and entitled 'Musical Exception' was much more positive. With hindsight, however, we realise that Bruckner was not as 'helpless' and 'uncommonly naive' as Frey suggested:

Anton Bruckner, whose E flat major symphony was presented or, rather, played to a large unprejudiced audience for their judgment the day before yesterday, is a very strange phenomenon. As a productive artist he does not belong to any clique and has absolutely no idea of all the external procedures of what might be called social structure.

---

54 From the review in the *Wiener Allgemeine Zeitung*, 23 February 1881; see *G-A* IV/1, 641-45 for text.

55 From the review in the *Neue freie Presse*, 27 February 1881; see *G-A* IV/1, 646.

As helpless as a child and uncommonly naive, he does not care what the world thinks and says about him but always has a pencil ready to put his ideas down on paper. This man has to compose and everything else must take second place. Like Schubert he has an inner creative urge. He also shares with this prince in the realm of music, however, the fatal characteristic of not knowing when to stop. In spite of this, namely a certain lack of moderation in the outpouring of his musical feelings, his achievements both as a composer and as a performer are astonishing. On one occasion several years ago when an organ competition was arranged in the Josefstadt church to find the artist who most deserved to go to the International Organ Contest [sic] in London, Bruckner was given a theme - only five bars' long - on which he was expected to improvise variations and a fugue. He began without delay to develop the short theme given to him by Gottfried Preyer. The piece grew and grew to undreamt-of proportions and all the listeners were enthralled. Each player was allotted a certain time, but Bruckner had already played twice or three times longer than he should have. The adjudicators approached the organ and reminded him, at first quietly and then more and more insistently, that the time had come to finish, but, lost in the labyrinth of his world of sound, he was deaf to all their exhortations. He knew that he should not play any longer and he knew that he was jeopardising his chances of success by exceeding the time limit in this manner, but there was no way of persuading him to vacate the organ bench. He had made the theme his own and it had to be thoroughly explored. And when he had well and truly exhausted the thematic and fugal possibilities after about twenty-five minutes, he got up without speaking. His face expressed only one thing: 'I have nothing more to say. Now do with me what you will.'

Bruckner the composer is exactly the same. He writes a four-movement symphony... and is not concerned whether the work will ever be performed or even be published. He writes this symphony and thinks to himself, 'Now you can do with me what you will'. The Symphony in E flat is a work whose importance should not be under-estimated. Bruckner is not always able to keep within the bounds of absolute beauty and he frequently sins against the capability of instruments, wind instruments in particular. He often offends our sense of instrumental colour and commits the more reprehensible mistake of not being able to stop at the right time. But this musical heart contains such an abundance of new ideas and this mind effervesces with so many new combinations that one never tires of following them and continually laments that this wealth is so prodigal. The first movement, which begins so auspiciously with the horn motive, seems to me to be the most unified and the most richly endowed. Although one could fill an entire symphony with the numerous ideas which are accumulated in this movement, it is the only one to fuse everything together pliantly into a whole and to lead to a satisfying artistic and musical conclusion. The second movement is already somewhat weaker in its organization of individual motives and there is a disturbing amount of surface glitter. The same could be said of the third movement, a kind of portrayal of a hunt scene, and the fourth movement which is probably the weakest. Nevertheless, there is no denying the abundance of brilliant ideas. But one is aware of a certain lack of feeling for a healthy organism, and if it was conceivable that a type of anthology could be made from this mass of pictures, one could then really begin to enjoy the work.[56]

In an article in the *Wiener Abendpost*, Dr. Hans Paumgartner made the surprising statement, in view of the thematic link between the third and fourth movements, that the final movement 'does not appear to us to belong organically to the preceding three. It is a symphonic poem in itself which we would call "The Last Judgment"'. Paumgartner concluded that, as a result of Bruckner's success, he was now 'one of our most important composers' and 'part of our artistic common property'.[57]

An unsigned article in the *Signale für die musikalische Welt* made further reference to the prodigality of musical ideas in the symphony:

... The concert... ended with a new unpublished symphony by Anton Bruckner. It is the sixth symphony written by this very gifted and highly esteemed court organist in whom the compulsion to write for large forces has a volcanic effect and frequently prevents him from achieving the necessary consistent and logical structure. Another composer would have sufficient material for innumerable symphonies with half of these brilliant ideas. In Bruckner's case it does not need to be underlined that the instrumentation is full of interesting details and can be both powerful and gentle. The first and third movements, the latter a type of hunt rhapsody, proved to be the

---

56 From article entitled 'Musikalischer Ausnahmsfall' in the *Neue Wiener Tagblatt*, 22 February 1881.

57 This article appeared in the *Wiener Abendpost* on 23 February. It is quoted in part in *G-A* IV/1, 650 and more fully in Rolf Keller, 'Das "amerikanische Ehrendoktorat" für Anton Bruckner', *BSL 1992* (Linz, 1995), 90.

most comprehensible.[58]

Although the critical reviews were mixed,[59] Bruckner received a great deal of encouragement and support from his pupils, present and past, and from genuine admirers of his work. One such person was Marie Lorenz, Krzyzanowski's sister-in-law, who presented him with some flowers after the concert and received a belated letter of thanks from the composer in April. Frau Lorenz later recalled Bruckner's 'touchingly beautiful and charming letter', her own enthusiasm for his music at a time when it was still largely misunderstood, and her impressions of a man who found it difficult to trust others but, when his guard was down, would talk at length about his early experiences.[60]

The tentative beginnings of Bruckner's recognition as a composer outside Austria were made with his Fourth Symphony later in the year. In the autumn Franz Schalk, who had just finished his studies at the Conservatory, began his distinguished career as a violinist in the Karlsruhe orchestra.[61] Correspondence between the Schalk

58 From *Signale für die musikalische Welt* (March 1881), 341. Mentioned in *G-A* IV/1, 650f and quoted more fully in Rudolf Louis, *Anton Bruckner* (Munich: Georg Müller, 1918), 311.

59 See also G.W. Gruber, 'Brahms und Bruckner in der zeitgenössischen Wiener Musikkritik', in *BSL 1983* (Linz, 1985), 204 and 215 for reference to Theodor Helm's review in the *Deutsche Musik-Zeitung* 8,55 (20 February); Ingrid Fuchs, 'Bruckner und die österreichische Presse' in *BSL 1991* (Linz, 1994), 92, note 46 for reference to Franz Gehring's review in the *Deutsche Zeitung* (22 February); Rolf Keller, loc.cit., 90 for text of Ludwig Speidel's review in *Fremdenblatt* (26 February). On 18 February Bruckner wrote to Gehring,, who was a lecturer in Mathematics at Vienna University as well as being a music critic, asking for a 'favourable' and 'lenient' reaction to the symphony! Gehring was not usually well-disposed towards the composer. See *HSABB* I, 190; the original of this letter is in Bonn University Library.

60 For Bruckner's letter to Marie Lorenz, dated Vienna, 23 April 1881, see *HSABB*, 192-93; the location of the orginal is unknown; it was first published in *ABB*, 153f. See *G-A* IV/1, 654-56 for her reminiscences of Bruckner.

61 Franz Schalk (1863-1931) was music director in Reichenberg (1888-1890), Graz (1890-95), Prague (1895-98) and Berlin (1898-1900) before returning to Vienna in 1900 where he was involved

brothers towards the end of the year indicates that Franz had persuaded Felix Mottl to perform Bruckner's Fourth Symphony in Karlsruhe. On 31 October, Franz renewed an earlier request to Joseph to 'send the E flat major symphony as soon as possible'.[62]

The following day Franz wrote again to Joseph, expressing his surprise that Bruckner seemed to be reluctant to part with the work:

> I am surprised that Bruckner will not let the symphony out of his sight, as we were entrusted with it in the first place and I certainly knew what I was looking after. You can tell him that the performance was fixed originally for 14 December. Perhaps that will persuade him. Mottl is certainly thinking seriously about performing it. See what you can do...[63]

Later in the month Franz told his brother that he had suggested to Mottl that he

---

with the Opera until his death. See Hans Jancik, 'Franz Schalk' in *MGG* 11 (1963), cols. 1546-47 and Deryck Cooke, 'Franz Schalk' in *The New Grove* 16 (1980), 593.

62 Joseph Schalk (1857-1900), Franz's brother, was a piano professor in the Vienna Conservatory from 1884 until his death. He was artistic director of the *Wagner Society* from 1877 and was extremely active in arousing public awareness of both Bruckner's and Hugo Wolf's music. Wolf's *Eichendorff-Lieder* were dedicated to the Schalk brothers. See Hans Jancik, 'Josef Schalk' in *MGG* 11 (1963), col. 1547.

The Schalk correspondence is located in the *ÖNB*. The shelf no. of the letter dated 31 October is F18 Schalk 158/3/2. Some of the correspondence is printed in Lili Schalk, *Franz Schalk. Briefe und Betrachtungen mit einem Lebensabriss von Viktor Junk* (*FSBB*) (Vienna-Leipzig: Musikwissenschaftlicher Verlag, 1935). For a more comprehensive study of the correspondence, see Thomas Leibnitz, *Die Brüder Schalk und Anton Bruckner* (*LBSAB*) (Tutzing: Schneider, 1988).

63 From letter dated Karlsruhe, 1 November 1881; F18 Schalk 158/3/3 in the *ÖNB*. See also *LBSAB*, 44.

make a personal approach to Bruckner and that the symphony had now arrived.[64]
Bruckner wrote to Mottl on 23 November, enclosing a score of the symphony and
advising him of a change he had made, presumably since the Vienna performance:

> Here it is. The Finale is new. Please observe the cut (that is, in the
> Finale). I have enclosed an obligatory new period (in the full score
> only, at letter O in the Finale). If you should so wish, have it written
> in the parts at my expense.
> Be so good as to ensure that the page is not lost. I will have it
> inserted in the parts later if you do not do it yourself.
> Send it back soon *post festum*.
> I am delighted; you are a genuinely true and great German artist!
> If the symphony is performed well, please send a report to Dr. Hans
> Kleser, Köln am Rhein, Zeughausstrasse12, the editor of the
> *Kölnische Zeitung*. My love to Herr Schalk.
> My Quintet in the *Wagner-Verein* had a huge success. Dr
> Schönaich sends you his greetings. Please take care of my poor
> child!...[65]

At the beginning of the following month Joseph enquired about the symphony,
also mentioning that Bruckner had begun to write his Seventh Symphony 'which,
according to what I have heard, will be one of his most splendid works'.[66] In his
reply Franz informed his brother that the Fourth would be performed the following
Saturday in the third subscription concert and that he and Mottl would provide

---

64 From letter dated Karlsruhe, 28 November 1881; F18 Schalk 158/3/4 in the *ÖNB*. See also
LBSAB, 44.

65 See *HSABB* I, 195 for this letter, dated Vienna, 23 November 1881; the original is in private
possession. It was first published in *ABB*, 155. Hans Kleser had written a short article on Bruckner
in the *Neue Musikzeitung*, Cologne, 1880/ 2, but was not able to persuade Ferdinand Hiller, the
conductor of the Cologne orchestra, to perform the symphony; see *G-A* IV/1, 652-53.

66 Letter from Joseph to Franz, dated Vienna, 2 December 1881; F18 Schalk 158/3/9 in the *ÖNB*.
See also *LBSAB*, 45-46.

Bruckner with a full report of what they hoped would be a successful performance.[67]
But this was not to be. Franz began writing his next letter to Joseph after the first
inadequate rehearsal of the symphony on 6 December when Mottl had difficulties
with the orchestra. He continued his letter on 10 December, the day of the
performance. Franz was now convinced that the symphony would make no impact.
Even Mottl seemed to have lost interest:

> In the meantime I have become so convinced that today's
> performance of Bruckner's symphony will be a failure that I do not
> know how we can break this news to Bruckner. The orchestra is not
> able to meet his requirements. Unfortunately it does not want to
> either... Mottl conducts nonchalantly and is really only performing the
> symphony because he is afraid to send it back unplayed. He is of the
> opinion that the symphony has great weaknesses. I countered briefly,
> 'but much greater strengths!' May God be with Bruckner. His time
> has not yet come...[68]

Unfortunately, Franz's worst fears were realised:

> ...Bruckner's symphony was a complete flop... Much sadder is the fact
> that Mottl did not even begin to understand Bruckner's genius. He
> conducted with a smug expression. His tempi caused the gentle
> motives to become banal. The very intricate thematic working was
> unclearly executed and eluded the listeners. It pains me to write any
> more about it and I am bitterly disappointed that I should have
> encouraged Mottl to give a performance which has done more harm
> than good... You must conceal the failure of the symphony from
> Bruckner as well as you can; it would only depress him to hear that
> one of his most easily understood works had been unanimously
> given the thumbs down. Hardly a pair of hands moved in the entire

---

67 Letter from Franz to Joseph, dated Karlsruhe, 5 December 1881; F18 Schalk 158/3/6 in the
ÖNB. See also LBSAB, 44-45.

68 Letter from Franz to Joseph, begun 6 December and completed 10 December 1881; F18 Schalk
158/3/5 in the ÖNB. See also LBSAB, 46-47.

hall...[69]

The symphony was the last work to be performed in a typically varied programme. It was preceded by Cherubini's overture to *The Water Carriers*, an aria by Haydn, songs by Schubert and Schumann and Gade's Violin Concerto. The critical reviews in the local press were mixed. The reviewer for the *Badische Landeszeitung* had very little of a positive nature to say about the work, lamenting its 'lack of inspiration', 'dearth of ideas' and 'scanty intellectual content' and asking Mottl, 'the tireless, highly talented and skilful conductor' to consider seriously how dangerous it was to make unreasonable demands on the 'good taste of the public' by performing *Die Meistersinger* one day and the 'post-mortem of a musical corpse' the next. The reviewer for the *Karlsruher Zeitung* was more constructive in his criticism, recognizing Bruckner's reputation as an organist and theoretician and his great talent as a composer. While Bruckner's 'feeling for instrumental colour' and 'understanding of large-scale symphonic style' were evident in the work, there was a lack of overall clarity and unity and 'some clumsiness in structure and instrumentation'. If he harnessed his inventive powers and technical resources correctly, he would be able to produce a 'quite outstanding work' in the future.[70]

There is no indication that Bruckner was unduly perturbed about the reception of his symphony. The Schalk brothers were apparently successful in their attempts to 'conceal the failure of the symphony' from him. In addition, he was probably still

---

69 Letter from Franz to Joseph, dated Karlsruhe, 13 December 1881; F18 Schalk 158/3/7 in the *ÖNB*. See also *LBSAB*, 48-49.

70 From reviews in the *Badische Landeszeitung* (17 December) and *Karlsruher Zeitung* (16 December). See *G-A* IV/1, 681ff. for extracts from reviews. See also Andrea Harrandt, '"Ausgezeichneter Hofkapellmeister" - Anton Bruckner an Felix Mottl. Zu Neuerwerbungen der Österreichischen Nationalbibliothek', in *Studien zur Musikwissenschaft* 42 (Tutzing, 1993), 336 concerning a report of the performance in the *Linzer Tagespost* (20 December 1881).

recovering from the shock of being dangerously close to the fire which destroyed the Ring Theatre on 8 December and threatened his apartment in the Hessgasse. He witnessed the fire as he was returning to his apartment, ran through the crowd of people who had gathered, and began collecting his manuscripts. But the fire abated and Bruckner did not need to vacate his rooms. He wrote to his brother-in-law Johann Hueber in Vöcklabruck a few days later, no doubt to reassure him and his sister Rosalie that he was safe. He was still deeply affected, however, by the 'unspeakable suffering of so many people'.[71] Abbot Moser suggested that Bruckner spend Christmas at St. Florian to help him recover from the shock.[72]

Earlier in the year Bruckner was involved in a concert with the *Akademischer Gesangverein*, sharing the rostrum with his friend Weinwurm and possibly appearing as an organ soloist as well. In a letter to an unnamed Kapellmeister he asked if it would be possible to hold a short rehearsal on the morning or afternoon of the concert.[73] Later in the year he had another opportunity of conducting the same choir in the first Viennese performance of *Mitternacht* on 7 December, the evening before the Ring fire. Just over a fortnight later, Bruckner improvised on the organ in the *Musikvereinssaal* as part of a special Christmas charity concert for orphan

---

71 See *HSABB* I, 196 for the text of this postcard, dated Vienna, 11 December 1881; the original is in the *Archiv der Stadt Linz*. For more details of Bruckner's reaction, see his sister's comments as related to Göllerich in *G-A* IV/1, 684ff. Evidently he would have been at the theatre himself had it not been for a change to the programme. Richard Schönberger, the brother-in-law of Josef Vockner, one of his private pupils, stayed with him overnight. On 9 December, the day after the fire, he visited the police morgue to see the bodies.

72 See Simon Ledermüller's letter to Oddo Loidol, *G-A* II/1, 273f.

73 See *HSABB* I, 191 for this letter, dated Vienna, 18 March 1881; the original is owned privately. The 'Hochwohlgeborener H. Kapellmeister' is possibly Joseph Hellmesberger. According to several sources, Bruckner's organ improvisation took place four days earlier. See Scheder, *ABCText*, 370.

relief.[74]

In May Bruckner began to write a choral work - the *Te Deum* WAB 45 - which would later help to establish his reputation as a composer both nationally and internationally. Early sketches of the work in Kremsmünster indicate that he completed preliminary work on 3 May and did further work on the choral parts until 17 May. Amand Loidol, the brother of Bruckner's former pupil Oddo who was now a priest in Kremsmünster, wrote to the latter on 19 May and mentioned that he had met Bruckner on several occasions:

> ... In his apartment he played through the new 'Te Deum', which has still to be written out in fair copy. Bruckner made use of its thematic material for the prelude which he played during the Easter Sunday service in Linz Cathedral. The Linz people, Brava etc., were astonished by his playing. Bruckner is still not able to send you the 'London music piece' because he still does not have it in his possession. Be patient.
> Bruckner has very little free time, and so you should excuse any delay in his writing to you or, perhaps, any failure to do so. He sends his best wishes and is delighted that things are going well for you.[75]

Bruckner spent a good part of his summer vacation at St. Florian. As usual it was a 'working holiday'. After attending the 7.30 am Mass he would work until midday. After a sleep and, often, a walk in the abbey grounds, he would work again until the late afternoon. The Sixth Symphony was his main concern, but the Seventh Symphony was also taking shape in his mind. Indeed, the sketches of the Seventh

---

74 A report of this concert appeared in *Vaterland* on 24 December; see *G-A* IV/1, 687.

75 From letter quoted in *G-A* IV/1, 658-59. Max Brava (1845-1883) was director of the Linz *Musikverein* from 1874 and Alois Weinwurm's successor as chorus master of *Sängerbund* from 1879. The 'London music piece' is probably the Intermezzo from the String Quintet which Bruckner gave Hans Richter to take to London.

were begun in Vienna on 23 September not long after his return from St. Florian. At the beginning of a new Conservatory and University term, a group of young musicians organized by Joseph Schalk rehearsed Bruckner's String Quintet at Schalk's apartment in Jordangasse.[76] Bruckner was invited to the final rehearsals and, after suggesting some tempo changes and other small alterations, declared himself to be very satisfied with their preparation. Both the final rehearsal, which was attended by a few invited critics including Hanslick, and the performance itself - part of a *Wagner Society* musical evening on 17 November - took place in the *Bösendorfersaal*. It has been suggested that the Finale was not performed because Bruckner had given the score of the Quintet, without having a copy made beforehand, to Hans Richter so that he could have it performed and/or printed in England, that Josef Schalk had to reconstruct the parts from his own piano-duet transcription in which only the first three movements were available, and that Bruckner had to reconstruct the Finale later from the original sketches. A letter from Bruckner to Joseph Schalk a week after the performance rules this out, however:

> Dear friend!
>
> Please be go good as to send me the score of the Quintet, the Finale in particular, as soon as possible. (I would like to have made some alterations today.) [77]

Leibnitz suggests that the Finale was not played because it made too many

---

76 The musicians were Julius Winkler (1st violin), Carl Lillich (2nd violin), Hans Kreuzinger (1st viola), Franz Schalk (2nd viola) [later replaced by Desing] and Theodor Lucca (cello).

77 See *HSABB* I, 194f. for this letter, dated Vienna, 23 November 1881; the original is in the *ÖNB*. See also *G-A* IV/1, 678, footnote 2.

demands on both players and listeners and might have jeopardised the undertaking.[78] It is also possible (and the letter above would support this view) that Bruckner, after hearing the work at rehearsals, wished to make changes in the Finale and so held it back from performance. Five days later Joseph Schalk received another letter from Bruckner, in which he was informed that the Finale was now ready.[79] Joseph wrote to Franz about the performance and said that, while it left something to be desired, the dedication of the players had more than made up for any deficiencies.[80] As the performance was only a private one, there were practically no reviews. Eduard Kremser, writing in *Vaterland*, however, described it as an important piece, the Adagio being a movement 'of the deepest feeling'. The reviewer was particularly gratified to observe how Bruckner's reputation as a composer was gradually increasing and was certain that he would finally attain the more widespread recognition that he deserved.[81]

It was in an attempt to obtain this more widespread recognition that Bruckner put the finishing touches to his Symphony no. 6 WAB 106 during the course of the year. The main sources of the work are the autograph score in the *ÖNB* and a copy of the score made by Franz Hlawaczek and with a dedication to Dr. Oelzelt von Newin and his wife Amy which can be found in the *Gesellschaft der Musikfreunde* library.[82]

---

78 See *LBSAB*, 42.

79 See *LBSAB*, 42 for this letter dated Vienna, 28 November 1881; F18 Schalk 151/ 2 in the *ÖNB*.

80 See *FSBB*, 39f. for this letter dated Vienna, 24 November 1881.

81 Review dated 25 December 1881; reprinted in *G-A* IV/1, 679f.

82 The shelf nos. of the autograph score in the *ÖNB* and the copy score in the *Gesellschaft der Musikfreunde* are Mus. Hs. 19.478 and XIII 37.730 respectively. See also Leopold Nowak, *ABSW* VI *Revisionsbericht* (1986), 49f. for a complete list of sources, including two which came to light since the Haas (1935) edition of the score, namely another copy of the score (Mus. Hs. 34.612) and the proofs (Mus. Hs. 29.131) in the *ÖNB*. Nowak also had an opportunity of consulting the copy used for engraving when preparing his edition of Symphony no. 6 (*ABSW* VI) in 1952. This is no longer extant. There is a facsimile of two pages from the Scherzo in the autograph between pages

Dates in the autograph indicate different stages of completion - the first movement was finished in Vienna on 27 September 1880 while Bruckner was in bed suffering from a foot complaint ('im Bette fusskr. liegend'), the second movement was finished at the University on 22 November 1880, the third movement was finished at the University on 17 January 1881, and the sketches of the Finale were completed on 28 June, the string parts were written out by 4 July and the whole was finished in St. Florian on 3 September. More than 40 years ago Nowak wrote that the symphony undeservedly 'lagged behind the others in popularity', no doubt because of various alterations which were made in the first edition without Bruckner's sanction.[83] Today, in spite of its 'verve, happy melodiousness and majestic rhythms',[84] the work has still not attained the popularity of, say, the Third, Fourth and Seventh Symphonies, but it certainly makes more frequent appearances in concert programmes than hitherto. It is shorter and much more compact

---

664 and 665 in *G-A* IV/1, and of a page from the Finale in the autograph in *ABSW* VI *Revisionsbericht*, 53. See also *HSABB* I,196 and 198 for two letters from Bruckner to Josef Maria Kaiser in Linz, dated Vienna, 6 February and 3 May 1882 respectively. Bruckner asked Kaiser to engrave the dedication page of the score and was delighted with the result. The originals of both letters are in the *ÖNB*.

83 Leopold Nowak, *ABSW* VI (1952), foreword. The symphony was first printed by Doblinger (D. 2300) in 1899. See also Georg Göhler, 'Wichtige Aufgaben der Musikwissenschaft gegenüber Anton Bruckner' in *ZfMw* 1(1919), 293, in which the Sixth Symphony is described as a typical example of inaccuracies and inconsistencies which had crept into the scores of Bruckner's works. For more recent discussion, see Harry Halbreich, 'Bruckners Sechste: kein Stiefkind mehr' in *BSL 1982* (Linz, 1983), 85-92; Rudolf Stephan, 'In und Jenseits der Tradition' in *ÖMZ* li/1 (January 1996), 27-32; Benjamin M. Korstvedt, '"Harmonic Daring" and Symphonic Design in Anton Bruckner's Sixth Symphony (An Essay in Historical Analysis)' in *Perspectives on Anton Bruckner* (Aldershot: Ashgate, 2001), in preparation; Timothy L. Jackson, 'The Adagio of the Sixth Symphony and the Anticipatory Tonic Recapitulation in Bruckner, Brahms and Dvorák' in ibid., in preparation.

84 Leopold Nowak, loc.cit.

structurally than the works on either side of it, namely the Fifth and Seventh Symphonies, but there is no corresponding decrease in the wealth of thematic invention.

As Nowak points out in his foreword to the '2nd revised edition' of the F minor Mass, Bruckner made some changes in the autograph of the *Credo* movement in 1881 which 'stand out very well against the brown of the original handwriting' because they were inserted in black ink.[85] Some bars were cut but others were added or doubled by repetition. These changes are part of Bruckner's own re-thinking of the work between 1868 and 1893 which included structural 'scrutinization' in 1876, a few instrumental changes in 1877 and further small but significant alterations in the early 1890s. It was Bruckner's young champion, Joseph Schalk, who was largely responsible for the more extensive changes which were later incorporated in the first edition and which, in Hawkshaw's words, constitute an 'arrangement' of the work rather than an officially sanctioned revision.[86]

Still impelled by a desire to obtain recognition not only in Austria but beyond, Bruckner, no doubt recalling that Cambridge University and Breslau University had conferred an honorary doctorate upon Brahms in 1876 and 1879 respectively, decided to make a formal approach to the same university at the beginning of 1882 and asked Julius Wiesner, the Dean of the Faculty of Philosophy at Vienna University, to provide him with a reference:

---

85 See Nowak, foreword to *ABSW* XVI (1980), as well as Paul Hawkshaw's comments in his 'An anatomy of change: Anton Bruckner's revisions to the Mass in F minor', *Bruckner Studies* (Cambridge, 1997), 19ff. The autograph of the Mass is in the *ÖNB*, Mus. Hs. 2106.

86 See Hawkshaw, loc.cit., 31. Schalk's 'arrangement' was published by Doblinger (D.1866) in 1894. Schalk made use of Johann Noll's copy of the Mass (Mus. Hs. 29.302 in the *ÖNB*) which was specially prepared for performances of the work in the *Hofkapelle* during the 1880s.

In accordance with the wish of Mr. Anton Bruckner, imperial court organist, professor at the Conservatory of Music and lecturer at the University, the deanship testifies that the degree of Doctor of Music is not conferred by the University of Vienna or by any other Austrian university.

With reference to his application for the conferment of a Doctorate of Music by the University of Cambridge, it gives the deanship at this university particular pleasure to be able to confirm herewith that Mr. Anton Bruckner, equally well known as a performer, composer and musical theorist, has been a lecturer in Harmony at the University of Vienna since 1875 and has taught a large number of students each semester with a success that has been universally acknowledged.[87]

There is no indication that Bruckner took this any further at the time..[88] Three years later, however, Bruckner made a similar application, with the help of a Dr. E. Vincent, who translated it into English, to the rector of the University of Philadelphia and then changed the destination to the 'University of Cincinnati'.[89] That Bruckner took his application very seriously is shown by the meticulous way in which he ensured that the English translations of his baptismal certificate, seven certificates from the years 1855-1867, documents regarding his appointments as lecturer at the Conservatory, lecturer at the University and member of the *Hofkapelle*, the confirmation by the deanship of Vienna University that a doctorate of Music could

---

87 This reference is dated Vienna, 12 January 1882. See *G-A* IV/2, 10-11 for the text. According to Friedrich Klose (*Meine Lehrjahre bei Bruckner*, 113), Bruckner envied Brahms's doctorate more than anything else!

88 See Rolf Keller, 'Das "amerikanische Ehrendoktorat" für Anton Bruckner' in *BSL 1992* (Linz, 1995), 73-92. Keller contacted Mrs. E.S. Leedham-Green, the Assistant Keeper of the University Archives, and received the information that there is no record of Bruckner's application ever having been received.

89 The original copy of the application which, with its various appendices, runs to 76 pages, can be found in the *ÖNB* (Suppl. Mus. Hs. 6009 A/Bru 252).

not be conferred in Austria, an evaluation of the D minor Mass by Hellmesberger and several newspaper reviews were verified by Gustav Nathan, the British consul in Vienna. [90] Entries in the *Hochschulkalender* for 1883 indicate that he paid Vincent more than seventy shillings for his assistance.

Bruckner made another appearance as an organ soloist at an *Akademischer Gesangverein* concert in Vienna on 15 March. Nine days later the Schalk brothers gave a concert in the *Bösendorfersaal* which included Joseph's arrangement for piano of the Scherzo from Bruckner's Third Symphony. [91]

Bruckner spent Easter at St. Florian and played the organ on several occasions. Interesting details of his playing, including some of the themes on which he improvised, can be found in four letters sent by Simon Ledermüller at St. Florian to Oddo Loidol at Kremsmünster. [92] At the end of April, Bruckner's F minor Mass was sung in the *Hofkapelle* together with the gradual and offertory motets *Locus iste* and *Os justi*. [93] Albert von Hermann's review of the performance appeared in the *Wiener Allgemeine Zeitung*:

---

90 The appendix of Keller's article (see footnote 88) consists of a comprehensive description of Bruckner's application and the accompanying enclosures. All the translations, with the exception of the Hellmesberger report which was undertaken by Dr. Vincent, were carried out by Dr. Carl Kohn, an official legal interpreter. According to Mark Frazier Lloyd, Director of the Archives and Records Center of the University of Pennsylvania, however, there is no record of any letters 'to or from Anton Bruckner' in the years 1885 and 1886.

91 Franz Schalk had left his job in the Karlsruhe orchestra shortly after the unsuccessful performance of Bruckner's Fourth Symphony. He played works by Goetz, Mozart and Beethoven with his brother.

92 See *G-A* II/1, 275-78 for the texts of these letters.

93 According to Antonicek in *ABDS* 1, Appendix 1, 142. This does not tally with the clearly erroneous information provided in *G-A* IV/2, 32, however - 'as enclaves he performed the *a cappella* chorus *Locus iste* and, for the first time, the fine seven-part *Ave Maria*'. The performance of the Mass and motets was on Sunday 30 April.

It is not surprising that a type of civil war commenced. It would be easy to give a humorous description of the different groups who made up the audience in the chapel and their reaction to the performance, but factual details will suffice. The adversaries of the inspired composer looked at him grimly and, after the *Gloria*, left the church ostentatiously like parliamentary dissidents; the regular attenders shook their heads and gesticulated in all kinds of ways to express their amazement at the 'storm and stress' of the music, while even the court police, who were standing like living pillars, cast anxious glances at the buttresses and had reservations about the mighty brass fanfares proceeding from the choir. The friends of the singers looked at them with equal anxiety, fearing that their voices would not hold out. And that would have been most unfortunate because it would have rendered impossible the performance of a work which must be recognised as important in spite of all faults and misgivings.

Bruckner's work is a large dramatic tone picture. There is dramatic movement in this Mass as in very few compositions of this type. This is most valid in the truly colossal 'Et resurrexit'. It is reminiscent of a famous painting by Führich of the day of resurrection. Similarly in Bruckner's 'Resurrexit' thousand upon thousand of the dead seem to rise from their graves after the usual resurrection sounds. There is no end to the awakening and rising up, and the uniformity of a continually recurring insistent accompaniment pattern produces an aura of immensity. All those who ever lived appear to awaken to a new and better life - now they are all together, and their overwhelming hymn of praise, expressing unshakeable confidence, thunders forth to the Lord who awakens them all. It would be difficult to find a more powerfully effective musical portrayal. The *Benedictus* has an equally large-scale structure. The character of the music produces an atmosphere of blissful peace and delightful happiness. The movement is beautiful from beginning to end and a shimmer of transfiguration hovers over it. The two-part *Agnus* also offers many surprisingly splendid moments. A folk-like motive reminiscent of one of our *Landmesse* song melodies is artistically developed.

The *Kyrie* and *Gloria* are less satisfying than the movements which have already been mentioned in this excellently orchestrated Mass. There are many reminiscences of Wagner, incomprehensible passages and, unfortunately, the ever popular contrast effects such as the alternation of voices. This is particularly true of the *Gloria* where there are musical figures which recall Beckmesser's hopping, fidgeting motive when he first appears. The *Amen* also has something very imposing about it, but the composer is frequently his own worst enemy in allowing a movement which has begun so well to fall away...

Hermann was convinced, however, that the Mass would only achieve its full effect with a large choir in the concert hall. The Viennese public would then appreciate what Bruckner was capable of writing.[94]

On 24 July Bruckner left Vienna to spend a fortnight at Bayreuth, during which time he attended the final rehearsals and the first performance of Wagner's *Parsifal*. On arriving at Bayreuth he had the misfortune of having more than 300 shillings stolen from his travelling bag. Bruckner was in great distress but fortunately some of his friends rallied round and provided him with enough money to see him through. Twenty four years later Wilhelm Tappert, with whom Bruckner had corresponded on several occasions at the end of the 1870s, recalled meeting the composer again:

> In *Parsifal* year (1882) I met the Viennese composer Anton Bruckner on the festival hill on the day of the first performance of the 'festival play'. The composer, a fine man, good-humoured, childlike and unworldly, with whom I maintained a fairly lively correspondence for some time, greeted me at first (in the Viennese manner) as if I was a member of the nobility, continually pronounced the vowel 'a' in my name as an 'o', and gave an animated account of the success achieved by one of his symphonies [the Fourth], conducted by Hans Richter in Vienna. 'There has been nothing like it since Beethoven', Richter said as he embraced the happy composer. 'He got me here, Mr. von Tappert', Bruckner said, pointing to a place on his left shoulder. It was then I learned for the first time that a pickpocket had taken '300 shillings in change' from the outer pocket of the summer coat hung loosely over his shoulders.

---

94 See *G-A* IV/2, 32ff. for complete review.

Bruckner had to borrow some money.[95]

Nine years later Bruckner wrote to Hans von Wolzogen, recalling his 1882 visit to Bayreuth which was the last time he saw and talked to Wagner:

> In 1882 the Master, who was already ill, took me by the hand and said, 'You can be sure that I myself will perform the symphony and all your works'. 'O Master!' I replied. The Master than responded, 'Have you been to Parsifal? How do you like it?' While he held me by the hand, I got down on one knee, pressed his hand to my mouth, kissed it and said, 'O Master, I worship you!' The Master replied, 'Calm yourself, Bruckner - good night!' These were his last words to me. On another occasion I was reproached by the Master, who was sitting beside me at *Parsifal*, because I was applauding so enthusiastically...[96]

A handwritten entry at the end of the *Benedictus* movement in Schimatschek's copy of the E minor Mass indicates that Bruckner stopped off at Linz and Wilhering on his way to Bayreuth; the entry reads 'Restauriert: Wilhering 26 Juli 1882. A.Br.' As Nowak observes, 'it is difficult to say with certainty when exactly Bruckner made his emendations' to the work as there is no noticeable difference in the handwriting between the structural or 'metrical' changes made in 1876 and the alterations made in 1882.[97] Having completed his revision which almost certainly involved the other

---

95 From *Neue Musikzeitung* 20 (1906); quoted in *G-A* IV/2, 39f..

96 See *ABB*, 166ff.; also extract in *G-A* IV/2, 41. In *ABB* it is dated 'probably 1884' because Auer obviously considered it to date from around the same time as another letter to Wolzogen, dated 13 September 1884 - see *HSABB* I, 221. The date of this letter is almost certainly much later, however - probably the end of February or the beginning of March 1891. See Franz Scheder, 'Zur Datierung von Bruckners Brief an Wolzogen (Auer no. 137)' in *BJ 1984/85/86* (Linz, 1988), 65ff.

97 Leopold Nowak, foreword to *ABSW* 17/2, *Messe E-Moll Fassung von 1882* (Vienna, 1959). Schimatschek's copy is in the *ÖNB*, Mus. Hs. 29.301.

movements as well as the *Benedictus*, Bruckner asked Johann Noll, the Viennese copyist, to prepare a new score and parts.[98] There is no known reason why Bruckner should have made alterations to the Mass in 1882, as there is no recorded performance of the work in the *Hofkapelle* at this time. The first performance of the revised version was conducted by Adalbert Schreyer in the old cathedral on 4 October 1885 at the end of the centenary celebrations of the Linz diocese.[99]

On his return from Bayreuth, Bruckner spent some weeks in St. Florian as usual, interrupted by a few days in Vienna when he had to play at the *Hofkapelle*. He gave several concerts, including one on St. Augustine's day (28 August) at the request of several high-ranking prelates who were visiting the abbey. One of his improvisations was based on a theme from *Parsifal*.[100] Another event was a sort of organ contest in the abbey which involved Bruckner and an organ virtuoso from Budapest, Johann Lohr, who had also participated in the organ recital series in London in 1871. Lohr's playing was masterly but Bruckner's even better, according to Josef Gruber's account.[101]

---

98 The date at the end of the first oboe part - 29 September 1882 - indicates that Noll began the process of correcting the original parts, which had been copied by Schimatschek, shortly after Bruckner's return to Vienna from St. Florian. The revised score, Mus. Hs. 6014 in the *ÖNB*, was completed on 24 January 1883.

99 For Schreyer's account of this performance and Bruckner's reaction, as related to Gräflinger, see *GrBL*, 98-99.

100 See Ledermüller's letters to Loidol, *G-A* II/1, 279-80. It is possible that Bruckner visited Ansfelden occasionally during his stays in Upper Austria. On 21 June 1882 he wrote a letter of reference for Ferdinand Albrecht, a schoolteacher in Ansfelden who lived in the house where Bruckner was born. See Rolf Keller, 'Anton Bruckner und die Familie Albrecht' in *BJ 1984/85/86* (Linz, 1988), 53-56, in which the text of this letter and of another letter of reference from Bruckner, dated Vienna, 29 October 1892, can be found.

101 As related to Göllerich, *G-A* II/1, 280f.

During his St. Florian sojourn, Bruckner worked on the Scherzo of his Symphony no. 7, the autograph of which bears the date '12 August 1882, St. Florian'. This movement was completed in Vienna on 16 October. Part of his vacation was spent in Steyr where he enjoyed the company of two keen amateur musicians - Georg Arminger, the parish priest, and Leopold Hofmeyer, a civil servant.[102] Three other friends from Steyr - Carl Almeroth, Isidor Dierkes and Karl Reder - used to meet Bruckner three times a week in Vienna in the 1880s for an evening drink at the *Gause* restaurant in the Johannesgasse.[103]

When Bruckner returned to Vienna there were hopeful signs that the Sixth Symphony would be performed by the Philharmonic in the forthcoming concert season. On 9 September he wrote to his young friend, Joseph Schalk, asking him to contact one of his copyists, Friedrich Spiegel:

> Mr. Spiegel has promised me that he would procure the score of my 6th Symphony from Hans Richter, the Court Music Director, and insert the new alterations. As I cannot find his address, I ask you, dear old friend, to be so good as to convey my request to Mr. Spiegel. If he is able to fulfil my request, I will be pleased to see him tomorrow between 9 and 1 or from 5 or 6 to 8 p.m. in the evening.[104]

During the 1882/83 season, Wilhelm Jahn stood in for Hans Richter as conductor of the Philharmonic concert series. A diary entry - 'Jahn (4.alte)' - suggests that

---

102 Bruckner wrote to Leopold Hofmeyer (1855-1900) on 6 August 1878 to give him advice about his music theory studies; See *HSABB* I, 179; this letter is in private possession in Wels. Hofmeyer was a reliable copyist and later copied the second version of Bruckner's Symphony no. 8.

103 Karl Reder's account of these occasions, which often went on to very late at night because of Bruckner's fondness for freshly-tapped Pilsner beer, can be found in *G-A* IV/2, 62ff.

104 See *HSABB* I, 198f.; the original is F18 Schalk 151/4/1 in the *ÖNB*. Friedrich Spigl (born 1860, Vienna) was one of Bruckner's students at the Conservatory.

Bruckner showed Jahn the original version of his Fourth Symphony perhaps with a view to performance, but it was the Sixth which Jahn chose. After the preliminary run-through, Bruckner wrote to Hofmeyer on St. Theresia's day which, he reminded his friend, was the name-day of his deceased mother and of a young lady friend of his, Therese von Jäger, who lived in Steyr. He continued:

> The Philharmonic have now accepted my 6th Symphony and rejected the rest of the symphonies by other composers. When I introduced myself to the conductor (director of the Court Opera), he said that he was one of my greatest admirers. What do you say to that? (The Philharmonic were so pleased with the work that they applauded vigorously and played a fanfare).[105]

It was thanks to Joseph Schalk and other young friends and devoted students like Ferdinand Löwe, August Stradal and Cyrill Hynais that Bruckner's name was kept before the public to some extent in the early 1880s, albeit in solo piano or piano-duet arrangements of his symphonies performed at 'private musical evenings' of the *Wagner Society* in Vienna. In December 1882 Bruckner planned to have the piano-duet arrangement of his Symphony no. 5 played specially for its dedicatee, Karl von Stremayr. The performers were to be Franz Zottmann and Joseph Schalk. Bruckner asked Schalk to inform Zottmann that Stremayr had suggested Saturday evening. But the performance had to be postponed because of the illness of Stremayr's daughter, and Schalk was asked to pass on this new information to Zottmann.[106]

---

105 See *HSABB* I,199 for this letter dated Vienna, 13 October 1882. It was first published in *ABB*, 156; the location of the original is unknown.

106 Franz Zottmann (1855-1909) was a piano professor at the Conservatory. See *HSABB* I, 200 for Bruckner's original letter to Schalk, dated Vienna, 12 December 1882 and later postcard, dated 15 December 1882; the originals are in the *ÖNB*, F18 Schalk 151/6 and 151/7 respectively.

At the end of the year Bruckner participated as usual in a charity concert for the *Catholic Orphan Relief Society* held in the large *Musikverein* hall on 22 December. The first movement of his Symphony no. 7 was completed a week later, on 29 December. Apart from ongoing work on the symphony Bruckner composed only two short occasional pieces during the year, namely a setting of *Ave Maria* WAB 7 for alto and piano/organ/harmonium accompaniment, and *Sängerbund* WAB 82 for unaccompanied male-voice choir.

Bruckner's third setting of the *Ave Maria* text differs from the other two in its combination of solo voice and instrumental (piano/organ/harmonium) accompaniment. It was written on 5 February 1882 and dedicated to Luise Hochleitner, a young contralto from Wels who had attracted the composer's attention when he visited the town probably during his summer vacation in 1881.[107] The most striking feature of this highly chromatic Marian hymn is the wide range of dynamics employed.

Sängerbund WAB 82 also has a Wels connection. It was composed on 3 February, sent to its dedicatee, August Göllerich sen., on 17 February and its first performance was at a choral festival held in Wels on 10 June 1883.[108] When it was performed again at the 41st anniversary concert of the Steyr *Liedertafel* in 1891, the

---

107 The original manuscript of the work was formerly in the possession of Mrs. Till-Ginzkey, Vienna, but is no longer extant. There is a copy with some insertions by Bruckner in the *ÖNB*, Mus. Hs. 3185. The work appeared in print for the first time in 1902 as a music supplement to the *Neue Musikzeitung* 23. For further information about the work, see *G-A* IV/2, 50-53 and *ABSW* 21/2, 118f. There is a modern edition of the work in *ABSW* 21/1, 118-21.

108 Göllerich was chairman of the Upper Austrian and Salzburg Choral Union. See *HSABB* I, 197 for Bruckner's letter to Göllerich, dated Vienna, 17 February 1882; the original was formerly in the possession of Franziska Göllerich, Hildesheim, and a facsimile was published in the *OÖ. Heimatsblätter* 28 (1974). According to Franz Bayer, Bruckner's friend in Steyr, the original words were provided by Heinrich Wallmann. The work was later furnished with another text by Karl Kerschbaum, edited by Viktor Keldorfer, and first published by Universal Edition (U.E. 3296) in 1911.

reviewer of the *Alpenbote* commented on Bruckner's treatment of the patriotic words:

> ... The first piece, 'Sängerbund' by Bruckner, sounded like their artistic and political creed and in its powerful chords sealed the vow of everlasting faithfulness to German song in every phase of the destiny of the German people.[109]

February 1883 was a momentous month for Bruckner. On Saturday the 10th Joseph Schalk and Franz Zottmann performed Schalk's piano-duet arrangement of the first and third movements of his Seventh Symphony in the *Bösendorfer* hall. On Sunday the 11th the Vienna Philharmonic conducted by Jahn played the two middle movements of his Symphony no. 6 in the large *Musikverein* hall. And, two days later, on Tuesday the 13th, Richard Wagner died in Venice.

Emil Lamberg, one of Bruckner's organ students at the time, remembered the week before the performance when there was a noticeable tension in Bruckner's classes. On the day of the performance Lamberg arrived at Bruckner's apartment at 8 o'clock in the morning and found the composer in an agitated state because his housekeeper Kathi had evidently misplaced the clothes he was going to wear. These were eventually found and Lamberg and Bruckner left for the *Musikverein*:

> ... On the way I noticed to my dismay that the Master was wearing shoes which did not match; this was all the more noticeable as one of the shoes had a shining toe cap of patent leather. Very wisely I took great care not to draw his attention to this in order to avoid a scene and spoil the festival day. The concert was to take place at midday, but we were already in the concert hall before 9 o'clock and found it empty, of course. This appeared to quell his excitement and,

---

109 Review dated 26 July 1891. Quoted by Andrea Harrandt, 'Bruckner und das bürgerliche Musiziergut seiner Jugendzeit' in *BSL 1987* (Linz, 1989), 97. See also *G-A* IV/2, 54ff. for further discussion of the piece.

with the words 'Apprehension ought not spoil our appetite', we retired to a restaurant nearby where he gave me his instructions for the day. The most important was the close observation of Councillor Hanslick whose criticism Bruckner feared. I was to observe Hanslick's facial expression so that I could conclude whether he was favourably or unfavourably disposed towards the work. Then I was to observe the audience closely and report to him what impression his work made.

As far as Professor Hanslick was concerned, it was quite impossible for me to provide satisfactory information as I could see only the back of his large head from where I was sitting and I was unable to draw any conclusion whatsoever. I was able to observe one thing only, namely that he remained seated and was as still, calm and cold as a sphinx during the huge applause. I had no other opportunity of speaking to the Master during the day. He was too preoccupied with his friends. The next day I was able to sweeten the bitter tidings with the information that Brahms had joined in the applause. 'Children, it was truly magnificent yesterday', he said in the class, casting a wicked glance at me.[110]

Auer observes that Jahn 'cleverly placed the two movements in the middle of the programme so that they would receive the maximum attention from the audience.[111]

The reviews of the symphony were mixed. Writing in the Neue freie Presse, Hanslick maintained his sphinx-like attitude and commented in particular on what he regarded as the transference of the Wagnerian style to the symphony:

---

110 From Lamberg's account, as related to Göllerich/Auer in G-A IV/2, 75ff. Emil Lamberg was a student of Bruckner's at the Conservatory and also came to him for private lessons. See HSABB I, 201 for Bruckner's letter to Lamberg's father in Brazil, dated Vienna 5 April 1883, concerning late payment of fees; the original is in the Oberösterreichisches Landesarchiv, Linz.

111 See G-A IV/2, 74. The two movements were preceded by Beethoven's Leonora overture no. 2 and followed by Eckert's Cello Concerto and Spohr's Symphony no. 5.

... This composer, who works only on the large scale, has already written six or seven symphonies, one or other of which, at least in part, have been performed. I find it increasingly difficult to form a proper rapport with these unusual compositions in which ingenious, original and even brilliant details alternate with others which are commonplace and difficult to understand and with empty and dull passages, often without any recognisable connection. Moreover, they are so mercilessly prolonged that there is a danger of both players and listeners running out of breath. In spite of its tiring repetition of the same figures and its immeasurably spun-out *rosalias* which are particularly reminiscent of *Meistersinger* motives, the Adagio was able to win us over because of a certain majestic mood of gentleness. On the other hand, I was completely nonplussed by the grotesque humour of the Scherzo which staggers about wearily and moves from one inexplicable contrast to another. Fortunately, this did not seem to bother others, as one section of the audience applauded the composer tumultuously and called him back innumerable times. Bruckner attracts general goodwill as a result of his integrity and sympathetic personality, the love of his pupils as a result of his teaching activities, and the most powerful support of the 'Wagner faction' on account of his fanatical worship of the composer. The latter would be more beneficial to Bruckner's cause, however, if they could express their support less brusquely.[112]

Max Kalbeck was no kinder in his assessment of the two movements:

... The problems with which we are confronted in the Adagio and Scherzo of Bruckner's Sixth Symphony are as dark as a passage from Jakob Böhme's 'Mysterium magnum'. We are aware that the creative force which seeks to be revealed in this abundance of intricate harmonies is by no means insignificant, and a few flashes of light, which flare up from the chaos and seem to promise the birth of a star, give notice of an original intellect secretly at work. The processes employed in this symphony are similar to those that we have often experienced at times of unusual internal psycho-physical activity, either when we have been in a state of physical or spiritual

---

112 *Neue freie Presse* 6632, 13 February 1883. See Leopold Nowak, *VI Symphonie A-Dur Revisionsbericht* (Vienna: Musikwissenschaftlicher Verlag, 1986), 66.

ecstasy, when we have been asleep or just waking up, or in unusual circumstances when our consciousness is momentarily frozen and paralysed as the result of an unforeseen event. And so we have some idea of the mind-set of a man who confuses the pre-conditions of the creative act with the act itself, the ecstasy of inspiration with the energy of presentation, the subjective will with the objective ability. Anton Bruckner has a dubious propensity towards this. A Jakob Böhme of music, he uses his own terminology of musical mysticism, a concoction of profundity and perversity. Just as Böhme identifies certain minerals with human emotions and divine personalities, so with Bruckner certain chord sequences and series of notes are given a significance which they do not naturally possess. If he were to carry this to its logical conclusion he ought to provide his symphonies with programmes in order to make himself clear to his listeners in another language. The god of music seldom causes him to express what he is thinking and feeling, but rather how he would think and feel if he was able to express the inexpressible. As we know, everyone is a little Shakespeare in his dreams; but we also require a poet to write poetry when he is awake. Bruckner would be one of our leading composers if he was able to give musical realization to his inventive powers and creative energy. His imagination is lacking in logic and his inspiration is not controlled by the inner law according to which the process of artistic creation is accomplished, unaffected by the constraint of external forms. His Adagio in F major sounds like a dream which some composer, the 'Master' himself if you wish, has had of the final duet in 'Siegfried' and 'The Mastersingers'. It is replete with excellent ideas, characteristic phrases, harmonic and instrumental refinements, and we feel that, although one cannot be completely at ease, one can turn a blind eye to its deficiencies. We have not succeeded in obtaining a closer understanding of the Scherzo in A minor. The spectral notes which rush around in it make it far too frantic. There is a wild jumble of stamping, storming, roaring and neighing as if there had been a meeting together of the Wolf's Glen and Walpurgis Night. We wish to be far from the future which is able to enjoy such a distorted piece of music reverberating from a hundred ravines...[113]

In the *Wiener Sonn- und Montagszeitung*, the reviewer had as much to say about

---

113 *Wiener Allgemeine Zeitung* 1063, 13 February 1883, 1f. See Leopold Nowak, op.cit., 66f.

the audience reaction as he had about the work itself:

> If a really great spectacle was the standard of value for a work of art, A. Bruckner would have thoroughly outstripped good old Spohr musically with the Adagio and Scherzo from his Symphony no. 6 and would no longer have any rivals to fear apart from Richard Wagner. However, the different phrases and motives which Bruckner permitted himself to borrow from Wagner without asking his permission virtually guaranteed that the work would be a success with the public and produced the same effect on a 'small but energetic' faction as the proverbial red rag to a bull. There is no denying that the Adagio has many beauties and is a movement of great breadth characterised by interesting motivic development and striking instrumental effects. Although it suffers in places from over-rich orchestration and excessive longueurs, it undoubtedly bears eloquent witness to the presence of a real compositional talent. It is impossible, however, to treat the Scherzo seriously. The public was flabbergasted and when finally, after a critical pause, the 'alpine party' saw danger in the offing, they began to make a very painful howling noise which made those who were impartial think that they were in the presence of schoolchildren playing an unseemly prank on their teacher. We learned afterwards from a reliable source that this was not a prank but in earnest, and the schoolchildren were Wagnerians.[114]

Writing in *Die Presse*, Ludwig Hahn regretted what he perceived as a lack of originality and natural energy in the work:

> The two movements from Bruckner's Sixth Symphony, with which the Philharmonic soothed its conscience as far as contemporary music is concerned, demonstrated a decrease not only in the composer's faults but also, unfortunately, in his virtues. What he has gained in discipline and style on the one hand he has lost in originality and natural energy on the other. What he used to write rushed

---

114 From an article signed 'Florestan' (the pseudonym for Johann von Woerz) which appeared in the *Wiener Sonn- und Montagszeitung* 9, 18 February 1883, 3. See Nowak, op.cit., 68.

by unpredictably like armour-clad Valkyries on steeds which snorted fire amidst claps of thunder. Nowadays he stays closer to the ground and certainly perseveres with a fixed goal in his mind's eye, remaining on the same course for some time - but the effervescent energy, the fascinating impetuosity have been somewhat tempered. There is no doubt that Bruckner possesses both character and skill, but they seem to have departed from him for the time being; will they ever be found again?

It was possible to follow the Adagio with interest and even with pleasure at times, in spite of its peculiarities; but one could only be alienated by the uncouth humour of the Scherzo which evoked the spirit of the Stone Age and Bronze Age. There is no need for Mr. Bruckner, who has sufficient musical inspiration of his own, to live off the food of others, and he should make it his first priority to break free from the tyrannical influence of Wagnerian inspirations and ideas and purge his musical language of its polyphonic excesses. A motive never appears without another accompanying motive springing up alongside it. In a certain sense Bruckner's work has its counterpart in Dvorák's Symphony in D. In the former there is a surfeit of inspired ideas which threatens to sever the taut formal structure; in the latter the quietly felicitous and comfortable structure is able deceptively to contain the true extent of ideas. In the former [there is] an unrestrained fiery soul struggling under its own pain and that of the listener to express dark torment; in the latter an assured, serene imitative spirit making cheerful use of traditional methods with childlike pleasure and displaying an impressive talent with great facility...[115]

The reviewer for the *Signale für die musikalische Welt* was a little kinder but equally lacking in perception:

---

115 *Die Presse* 59, 2 March 1883, 2f. See Nowak, op.cit., 69f. Dvorák's Symphony no. 6 in D, completed in October 1880, was given its first performance in Prague on 25 March 1881. It was performed in Vienna for the first time on 18 February 1883, exactly a week later than the performance of the two movements of Bruckner's symphony, at a *Gesellschaft der Musikfreunde* concert conducted by Wilhelm Gericke.

.. The two symphony movements by Bruckner had the same light and dark sides as this highly valued musician's previous compositions: surprisingly inspired ideas and brilliant instrumentation on the one hand and lack of logical development and exaggerated spinning-out on the other. When this music has come to an end one feels as if one is in the middle of a deep dream, seeking in vain to disentangle the web of bright images.[116]

Dr. Theodor Helm, who was later to become one of Bruckner's staunchest advocates, felt that the composer would have been better served by a performance of one of his other symphonies, either the Third in D minor or the Fourth in E flat major, as he considered the two movements of the Sixth to be unrepresentative of his 'considerable ability':

... The first of the two symphony movements heard recently, an effusive, yearning Adagio of Wagnerian inspiration and modelled on the parallel movement in Beethoven's Ninth, certainly made a predominantly favourable impression on account of its nobility, melodic breadth and colourful instrumentation, even although - as far as one can judge from a first hearing - it seemed to be deficient in well-shaped musical ideas. But the following Scherzo, which contained some typical Brucknerian drolleries and incomprehensible passages as well as conjuring up the Nibelung smiths from 'Rhinegold' and the galloping Valkyries in the concert hall, seemed to us to be far too strident and bizarre, not to say eccentric. The composer, who might have been better served if the regular Philharmonic audience had heard a complete or partial performance of one of his earlier symphonies, the Fifth (sic) in E flat for instance, also received tumultuous acclaim after the aforesaid Scherzo, but the rather too noisy applause eventually provoked opposition.[117]

---

116 Quoted in *G-A* IV/2, 79.

117 *Wiener Signale* 7, 17 February 1883, 52. Helm also provided a similar review for the *Wiener Salonblatt* 8, 18 February 1883, 8. See Nowak, op.cit., 68f.

The most favourable review came, as one might expect, from Bruckner's friend Dr. Hans Paumgartner. Paumgartner praised the conducting and orchestral playing but criticised the decision to play only two movements:

> ... The symphony is an organic whole from which individual limbs can never be detached without endangering the vital force of the whole. Many a movement which produces a disturbing effect when played on its own immediately attains its true significance when it is heard in the context of other movements... Can one conceive of the Scherzo from the 'Ninth' as a separate concert piece? The public would certainly not have lost out if the entire Spohr had been deleted from the programme and replaced by the entire Bruckner...

Paumgartner described the Adagio as 'a piece full of the most solemn feeling' and the Scherzo as 'a piece full of striking features, but ... frequently disturbing', the end of the movement in particular. His final assessment was that Bruckner was a composer 'of great significance' with a 'far above average' artistic personality and whose works would attract 'the undivided interest of all true lovers of art'.[118]

Wagner's death on 13 February came as a hammer blow to Bruckner who, according to the accounts of Göllerich and others, was almost inconsolable. Wagner had been a father-figure, someone who, it seemed, understood his symphonies and had even promised to perform them. Who could take his place? The immediate effect was evident in the elegiac concluding section of the Adagio movement in the Seventh Symphony. When Theodor Helm visited the composer 11 years later, Bruckner recalled these momentous February days, saying that the Adagio had been written partly as a 'premonition of the catastrophe' and partly as funeral music after the catastrophe. He had reached letter W in the score when he heard the grim news

---

118 *Wiener Zeitung* 36, 15 February 1883. See Nowak, op.cit., 67f. for complete review and *G-A* IV/2, 78f. for extracts. The article is also discussed by Norbert Tschulik in his 'Anton Bruckner in der Wiener Zeitung', *BJ 1981* (Linz, 1982), 172.

in the Conservatory on 14 February. The music from letter X to the end was then composed as a coda-cum-funeral music in remembrance of his unforgettable 'Master'.[119]

Bruckner spent most of his Easter break at St. Florian. According to Simon Ledermüller who wrote to Oddo Loidol as usual, providing a full account of Bruckner's activities, he played the organ on Maundy Thursday and at two services on Easter Sunday. Deubler and Traumihler were given the opportunity of hearing parts of his Seventh Symphony.[120] He intimated to Josef Gruber, the St. Florian organist, that he was interested in the vacant organist's post at St. Stephen's cathedral in Vienna. His organ activities also included a recital on the new organ in the *Votivkirche*, during which he improvised on themes from Siegfried's funeral music in *Götterdämmerung*. According to August Stradal, who heard him playing on several occasions in both the *Votivkirche* and the Hofburg chapel, his finger technique was understandably not so good as it had been but his pedal technique was still astonishing and his improvisatory skill outstanding.[121]

At another evening concert promoted by the *Akademischer Wagner-Verein* on 7 May, an entire programme was devoted to Bruckner, namely Symphony no. 3 in Schalk's piano-duet arrangement and the String Quintet played by the Winkler Quartet with Franz Schalk taking the first viola part. Later in the month Dr. Hans Paumgartner wrote a biographical article in the *Wiener Zeitung*, charting Bruckner's progress as a composer to date, pointing out that he had not yet obtained the recognition he deserved, and mentioning the opposition that Hans Richter had

---

119 See *HSABB* I, 201 for Bruckner's undated letter of condolence to Cosima Wagner. The location of the original is unknown; it was first printed in *ABB*, 153.

120 See *G-A* II/1, 281ff.

121 August Stradal (1860-1930) studied with both Liszt and Bruckner. He arranged many of the latter's works for piano solo. See *G-A* IV/2, 84f. for Stradal's account of Bruckner's organ playing.

encountered two years earlier when he performed Bruckner's Fourth Symphony in Vienna. Paumgartner described this symphony as 'one of Bruckner's best works' and 'one of the most inspired pieces in the domain of modern symphonic music', exhibiting both a freshness of thematic invention and a clear and convincing structure. He also showed his own interest in Bruckner's music by mentioning Symphony no. 7, in particular the instrumentation of the Adagio which had only been completed the previous month. It is more than likely that Paumgartner attended Schalk's and Zottmann's piano-duet performance of the first and third movements in February. In this 'preview' of the Seventh, Paumgartner also drew attention to a 'characteristic trait' of the composer, namely that in his symphonies he begins immediately with a 'main theme which is always of great significance, originality and individuality'. He ended his article by expressing a wish that Bruckner would soon complete the Finale and thereby the whole symphony and by recommending his readers to make a thorough and sympathetic study of Bruckner's works so that they could get to grips with his musical language more readily.[122]

A performance of Bruckner's F minor Mass, with *Locus iste* and *Os justi* as Gradual and Offertory motets, conducted by the composer in the *Hofkapelle* on 24 June elicited an extremely favourable and sympathetic review from Johann von Woerz in the *Allgemeine Wiener Zeitung*. It was certainly much more positive than Albert von Hermann's the previous year and perhaps indicated a gradual shift in the climate of opinion:

---

122 *Wiener Zeitung*, 27 May 1883. See Tschulik, loc.cit., 172f.. See also *HSABB* I, 202 for a letter from Bruckner to a 'very dear friend', possibly Paumgartner, in which he congratulates the recipient and his wife on a new position in Bremen, while regretting that they will no longer be in Vienna. The letter is dated Vienna, 9 July 1883; the original is in private possession.

... Today more than ever we had the impression of an unusual and - we certainly choose the right words - undoubtedly inspired work. This Mass is one of the best works that Bruckner has composed. It is written with an understanding for polyphony, an inexhaustible fund of imaginative ideas and a mastery of orchestration that only the greatest composers possess... Bruckner's work is a magnificent religious music drama of thrilling energy and inspiration. The finest part and crown of the Mass is certainly the *Credo*. The 'Incarnatus' is treated with the utmost delicacy, and the 'Passus' and 'Crucifixus est' have an equally effective nobility of expression, but the 'Resurrexit' surpasses everything in this Mass with its colossal power and the impression it gives of overpowering strength. To be sure, if Bruckner had written nothing more than this 'Resurrexit' his name would last for ever! How sublimely the composer has used the first section's affirmation of faith throughout the final section. If the *Credo* is the most powerful movement of the Mass, the beautifully wrought *Benedictus* is the warmest and most tuneful. There is a continual stream of melodic invention and it is as if a thousand birds are warbling and singing! Only someone with a Croesus-like musical imagination can write like this. The *Sanctus* with its delightful 'Hosanna' should be remembered as readily as the *Agnus* which is richly endowed with beautiful things. And when the gradual, *Os justi*, solemn and rich in content, is also taken into consideration, we come to the happy conclusion that we possess in Bruckner, a son of delightful, splendid Upper Austria, a musical talent of the first order, a master whose greatness will only be completely understood by generations to come.[123]

At the same time the Schalk brothers were doing their utmost to increase public awareness of Bruckner. This included attempts to persuade Gutmann, who had published the Third Symphony a few years earlier, to print the String Quintet. During the summer of 1883 Joseph Schalk spent some time at the country house of the composer Adalbert von Goldschmidt. In return for preparing a piano score of Goldschmidt's opera *Heliantus*, Schalk received free food and board. Hoping to arouse Goldschmidt's interest in Bruckner's works, he wrote to his brother Franz on

---

123 Review in the *Wiener Allgemeine Zeitung* 1197, 29 June 1883, quoted in *G-A* IV/2, 87f.

12 July, asking him to send the piano-duet version of the Third Symphony, the Adagio movements from the Fourth and Sixth Symphonies, the Scherzo from the Fifth Symphony and, as soon as it was ready, the Adagio from the Seventh. Franz replied ten days later, saying that he hoped to be able to complete 'the troublesome task of copying and correcting' the Adagio of the Seventh and send it to Joseph in a week's time. Joseph interrupted his stay at Grundlsee to pay a visit to Bayreuth where he saw *Parsifal*. On his return to Grundlsee he wrote to Franz, enthusing about the slow movement of the Seventh; he also encouraged his brother to put more pressure on Gutmann to have the Quintet printed.[124] Goldschmidt was also sufficiently impressed with what he had heard of Bruckner's Fourth to extend an invitation through Joseph to the composer to spend some time at Grundlsee. Because of Court Chapel duties, however, Bruckner had to decline.[125]

In his reply to Joseph's letter Franz was of the opinion that Gutmann would not be prepared to proceed with the printing of the Quintet unless more money was made available.[126] On 28 August Joseph wrote to Gutmann from Grundlsee, expressing disappointment that, the lack of sufficient subscription money notwithstanding, the publication of the Quintet had been unnecessarily delayed. In the meantime, however,

---

124 See *LBSAB*, 56ff. for these three letters in the Schalk correspondence, dated 12 July, 27 July and 30 July respectively; the originals are in the *ÖNB*, F18 Schalk 158/4/13, 158/4/5 and 158/4/17. Also see *HSABB* I, 200f. for two letters from Bruckner to Joseph Schalk, dated Vienna, 9 January and 14 May 1883 respectively. In the former he asks Schalk to lend the piano score of the Fifth Symphony to Moritz von Mayfeld but to ensure that 'the corrections are clearly written out'; in the latter he asks Schalk to send him the score of the Quintet, and mentions that Dr. Paumgartner intends to write something - see above for Paumgartner's article in the *Wiener Zeitung*. The originals are in the *ÖNB*, F18 Schalk 151/7 and 151/8.

125 See *HSABB* I, 202f. for Bruckner's letter to Schalk, dated St. Florian, 10 August 1883; the original is in the *ÖNB*, F18 Schalk 151/9/1.

126 See *FSBB*, 41 and *LBSAB*, 60 for this letter which is dated 1 August 1883. The original is in the *ÖNB*, F18 Schalk 158/4/7.

Franz Schalk had met Gutmann; an undated letter from Franz to Joseph gives an account of this meeting which appears to have ended amicably with Gutmann undertaking to print the work as well as a piano arrangement 'at a convenient time'. At the beginning of September Joseph wrote to Franz, thanked him for dealing firmly with Gutmann, and reminded him that the publisher had promised a fee of 100 florins for the piano arrangement.[127]

Bruckner's summer vacation was spent mostly at St. Florian but there were excursions to Bayreuth where he saw *Parsifal* again and visited Wagner's grave,[128] and a longer stay at Kremsmünster. Oddo Loidol, who was staying at St. Florian at the time, recalled Bruckner's visit:

> Early in the morning of 17 July 1883 Bruckner arrived in St. Florian. He went immediately through the sacristy to the gallery of the church; I [Loidol] was already standing in the sacristy and we greeted each other most heartily. At about 9 a.m. I went to his room (*Prälatengang*, 1st floor, no. 4) where we greeted each other again. In the afternoon he played several movements from his symphonies for me on the piano in the music room, including the Finale of his Seventh Symphony (E) which he had written down but had not yet finished. (He intended to complete it during his stay at St. Florian.)
>
> On another day at 10.30 a.m. he played at my request and 'just for me', as he said on several occasions, for more than half an hour on the great organ - a wonderful Adagio at first, then a symphony-like

---

127 See *HSABB* I, 203f. for Joseph Schalk's letter to Gutmann, dated Grundlsee, 28 August 1883. Count Fürstenberg, one of Bruckner's supporters, had made a contribution of 50 shillings towards the printing costs, but it had been necessary to use this to cover the cost of the *Bruckner evening* on 7 May; see *LBSAB*, 60ff. for the undated letter from Franz to Joseph, and Joseph's letter to Franz, dated 1 September. The originals of all three are in the *ÖNB*, F18 Schalk 147, F18 Schalk 158/4/2 and F18 Schalk 158/4/18.

128 Writing in the *Wiener Musik-Zeitung*, 31 March 1887, Paul Marsop recalled observing Bruckner standing beside the grave praying, with tears running down his face; quoted in *G-A* IV/2, 89f..

movement on full organ in which he incorporated an extended fugue, returning to the first section again when he had finished it. He used the double pedal (obligato) most of the time and employed full organ (10-, 9-, 8-voice). It was a totally free improvisation. He also related that he had composed the Adagio in C sharp minor (from the Symphony no. 7) a week before Wagner's death and he wept as he told me this...

Bruckner said he would go to Bayreuth this year. He stayed at St. Florian from 17 July to 11 August. Then he had to go to Vienna (he also showed me his holiday certificate from Hellmesberger); he returned to St. Florian on 24 August and remained there until 11 September. During his stay at St. Florian he had to play on the great organ on one occasion for Landgrave Vinzenz Fürstenberg.[129]

The last few days of his vacation (11-14 September) were spent at Kremsmünster. Loidol, who had invited him, recalled his visit in some detail. Bruckner played excerpts from his symphonies and from his *Te Deum* in the music room of the abbey, but the highlight of his stay was an organ concert on Wednesday 12 September when he played three improvisations.[130]

Joseph Schalk was invited by Goldschmidt to accompany him on a visit to Germany in the autumn. He saw in this a golden opportunity to create more interest in Bruckner's music.[131] During a visit to Leipzig he made preliminary arrangements to

---

129 See *G-A* II/1, 283f.

130 See *G-A* IV/2, 91-95 for fuller details of this visit, including Loidol's review of the concert in the *Linzer Volksblatt* 214, Wednesday 19 September 1883.

131 See *LBSAB*, 63 for Joseph's letter to Franz, Vienna, 16 September 1883; the original is in the *ÖNB*, F18 Schalk 158/4/19. Bruckner for his part occasionally tried to do what he could to advance the careers of his former pupils. Writing to Joseph on 13 November 1883, for instance, he mentioned that he had recommended him to Professor Zimmermann as a piano teacher for his wife and that he had also had a word with Jahn about a possible conducting engagement for Franz. See *HSABB* 1, 205; the original is in the *ÖNB*, F18 Schalk 151/10.

give a concert later (with Ferdinand Löwe) of his piano-duet arrangement of Bruckner's Seventh Symphony.

Bruckner's connections with Vöcklabruck, where his sister and brother-in-law lived, were strengthened when he was elected honorary member of the *Liedertafel* on 13 November. On 23 December he wrote to Dr. Alois Scherer, a lawyer and patron of the *Liedertafel*, thanking him for this signal honour.[132] On the same day he wrote to his sister Rosalie, thanking her for the Christmas present she had sent and regretting that she was still ill:

> Many thanks for what you sent! But don't send me anything in the future. You need to keep all that you have; give it to the children instead. I am very sorry that your illnesses always last such a long time. Be patient, God will reward you in due course! Don't expect me to write more often - I have little enough time to work.
> My income is still by no means brilliant. I have debts and my students are not always prompt with their payments. I have not been able to have anything copied until now.
> Accept the enclosed fifteen shillings as a small Christmas gift. I wish you all a good Christmas and New Year. I hope especially that you will get well soon!...[133]

In September 1883 the Symphony no. 7 WAB 107, begun two years earlier, was completed at St. Florian. Bruckner put the finishing touches to the Adagio on 21 April, and dates in the autograph indicate the different stages of work on the Finale.[134] On 10 August, the day before he returned to Vienna to fulfil *Hofkapelle* duties, the

---

132 See *HSABB* I, 207 for this letter. The Vöcklabruck *Liedertafel* was founded in 1850. Dr. Alois Scherer (1836-1894) was its president from 1866 to 1876 and 1878 to 1883.

133 See *HSABB* I, 206f. for Rosalie's undated letter to Bruckner and Bruckner's reply; the originals are in the private possession of the Hueber family.

134 The autograph is in the *ÖNB*, Mus. Hs. 19.479.

sketch was completed at St. Florian. The other dates at the end of the manuscript are 'Wien 17.8.1883' and 'St. Florian 3 Sept. 1883, 5.9.1883'. Much of 1884 and the early part of 1885 was spent negotiating the first performance of the symphony conducted by Arthur Nikisch in Leipzig on 30 December 1884 and the more important second performance conducted by Hermann Levi in Munich on 10 March 1885, and correspondence between the Schalk brothers and between Bruckner and Nikisch help us to bridge the gap between the original manuscript and the work as it was performed on these occasions. The symphony was published by Gutmann in December 1885 and dedicated to King Ludwig II of Bavaria.[135] It was to become the most frequently performed of his symphonies and was the first of his works to confirm his growing reputation outside Austria.

Not long after completing the Seventh, Bruckner turned his attention to the *Te Deum* WAB 45 once again. He completed the first draft of the revised version of the work at the end of September and continued working on it until March of the following year, completing it on the 7th of the month. Because there was no space

---

135 Plate number of first edition of full score: A.J.G. 576. The piano-duet reduction was published 11 years later in 1896 (pl. no. A.J.G. 575). The dedication reads: 'Seiner Majestät, dem Könige Ludwig II. von Bayern in tiefster Ehrfurcht gewidmet'. For further information about the symphony, see *G-A* IV/2, 98-120; Leopold Nowak, foreword to *ABSW* VII (Vienna: Musikwissenschaftlicher Verlag, 1954); idem, 'Das Finale von Bruckners VII. Symphonie: eine Formstudie' in *Festschrift Wilhelm Fischer* (Innsbruck, 1956), 143-48, repr. in *Über Anton Bruckner* (Vienna, 1985), 30-34; Robert Simpson, 'The 7th Symphony of Bruckner. An Analysis' in *Chord and Discord* vol. 2 no. 10 (1963), 57-67; Steffen Lieberwirth, 'Anton Bruckner und Leipzig' (*LABL*), *ABDS* 6 (Vienna, 1988); idem, '*Anton Bruckner und Leipzig. Einige neue Erkenntnisse und Ergänzungen*' (*LABLE*), *BJ 1989/90* (Linz, 1992), 277-88; Timothy L. Jackson, 'The Finale of Bruckner's Seventh Symphony and tragic reversed sonata form' in *Bruckner Studies* (Cambridge, 1997), 140-208; Leopold Brauneiss, 'Zahlen und Proportionen in Bruckners Siebenter Symphonie' in *BJ 1994/95/96* (Linz, 1997), 33-46; Graham Phipps, 'Bruckner's free application of strict Sechterian theory with stimulation from Wagnerian sources: an assessment of the first movement of the Seventh Symphony' in *Perspectives on Anton Bruckner* (Ashgate, Aldershot, 2001), in preparation.

in the autograph full score,[136] Bruckner had to write a separate organ part which he finished on March 16. On 3 May Bruckner wrote to Franz Schalk, asking him to make a copy in such a way that the organ part appeared at the bottom of the page:

> ... Therefore, use 24-lined manuscript paper. I must also ask you to make a very exact copy and not to lost anything, as I do not possess a copy. Please ask if there are any problems.[137]

This copy was possibly used for the engraving in 1885 but has not been traced.[138] In revising the work Bruckner concentrated his energy on the final part. He also made some slight changes to the instrumentation and improved the vocal declamation in the earlier sections. Nowak suggests that the cut from letter Q to V in the autograph, indicated by Bruckner himself, 'must have been made at the instigation of Hellmesberger, whose enthusiasm for the *Te Deum* led him to consider performing it in the *Hofkapelle* on the occasion of the conferring of the biretta on Cardinal Ganglbauer on November 22, 1884'. Hellmesberger evidently found the work too long and suggested omitting the 'Te ergo' section. However, 'the cut suggested by Bruckner himself is more comprehensive still, and indeed it would hardly be possible to perform the *Te Deum* at all in so truncated a form'.[139]

---

136 Mus.Hs. 19.486 in the *ÖNB*.

137 See *HSABB* I, 212 for this letter; the original is in the *ÖNB*, F18 Schalk 54/1.

138 The first edition, consisting of full score and parts (T.R. 40b) and piano score arranged by Joseph Schalk (T.R. 40), was published in December 1885 by Theodor Rättig.

139 Leopold Nowak, foreword to *Te Deum. Fassung von 1884. 2. verbesserte Auflage*, *ABSW* XIX (Vienna: Musikwissenschaftlicher Verlag, 1974). For further information, see *G-A* IV/2, 142-55; Dika Newlin, 'Bruckner's Te Deum' in *Chord and Discord* 2/8 (1958); Leopold Nowak, 'Probleme bei der Veröffentlichung von Skizzen dargestellt an einem Beispiel aus Anton Bruckners Te Deum' in *Anthony von Hoboken. Festschrift zum 75. Geburtstag* (Mainz, 1962), 115-21, repr. in *Über Anton Bruckner* (Vienna, 1985), 54-59, which also includes facsimiles of the sketches.

It is not known what prompted Bruckner to write a large-scale sacred work at this stage of his life - sixteen years separate it from the F minor Mass. There is no reason, however, why we should not take at face value his statement that he wished to write it as an act of homage to his 'dear God' for bringing him through all the trials and tribulations he had experienced during his time in Vienna.[140] The *ostinato* character of the constantly recurring descending octave figure with in-filling fifth gives the whole work a compelling inner unity and intensifies its granite-like quality and almost primitive strength and grandeur.[141]

Joseph Schalk and others maintained their efforts to increase public awareness of Bruckner's music throughout 1884. Göllerich and Stradal, who were admirers of Liszt's music, also included piano-solo and piano-duet arrangements of Bruckner's symphonies in their matinees. On 29 January, during a concert which he gave with his brother in the *Bösendorfer* hall, Joseph Schalk played the first and second movements of the Fourth Symphony. A few days earlier Ferdinand Löwe gave his first recital, playing his own arrangement of the Adagio from the First Symphony. The reviewer for the *Deutsche Zeitung*, covering both concerts, remarked that the two movements of the Fourth had made a powerful impression, although performed on the piano rather than the orchestra; what drew his attention in the Adagio was its 'surprisingly passionate upsurge after an over-long contemplative stasis'. In his later recollection of the latter performance, Theodor Helm commented very favourably on both the piano arrangement (specifically its faithfulness to the original orchestral version and Löwe's idiomatic transcription) and Löwe's interpretative

---

140 This statement was made by Bruckner in a letter to Hermann Levi, dated Vienna, 10 May 1885; see *HSABB*, I, 259. The original is in private possession; it was first published in Franz Gräflinger, *Anton Bruckner, Leben und Schaffen* (Berlin: Hesse, 1927), 327f.

141 This descending figure is clearly suggested by the opening of Beethoven's Ninth and is used by Bruckner as early as the 'Et resurrexit' section in the *Credo* of the F minor Mass and the end of the development section in the first movement of Symphony no. '0'.

powers.[142]

A month later, on 27 February, Schalk and Löwe played the former's piano-duet arrangement of Bruckner's Symphony no. 7. Bruckner had written earlier to Joseph Schalk:

> Do you really intend to play two movements with Löwe on two pianos? You must know only too well (as does Löwe) that a symphony like mine cannot produce its proper effect when played with two hands only... And so I would be most grateful if I could hear it once, for the sake of the tempi...[143]

Auer's suggestion that Joseph Schalk had already aroused Arthur Nikisch's interest in the Seventh Symphony when he accompanied Goldschmidt to Leipzig in the autumn of 1883 is contradicted by the Schalk correspondence.[144] Joseph had only prepared the ground for a piano-duet performance which was to be given in Leipzig at about the same time as the performance of Goldschmidt's *Heliantus*. In March 1884 he travelled to Leipzig. Nikisch conducted Goldschmidt's opera with some success at the City Theatre, but the projected piano-duet performance of the symphony seemed at first to be doomed because Löwe was apparently unable to

---

142 The review appeared in the *Deutsche Zeitung*, 7 February 1884. See *G-A* IV/1, 577 for Helm's comments. I am grateful to Dr. Andrea Harrandt of the *Anton Bruckner Institut* for information supplied in connection with her article 'Students and Friends as "Prophets" and "Promoters" - The reception of Bruckner's works in the *Wiener Akademische Wagner-Verein*' in *Perspectives on Anton Bruckner* (Aldershot: Ashgate, 2001), 327-37.

143 See *HSABB* I, 208 for this letter, dated Vienna, 16 January 1884; the original is in the *ÖNB*, F18 Schalk 178a.

144 See *G-A* IV/2, 156-58.

come.[145] On 30 March, however, Joseph wrote enthusiastically to Franz that Löwe's non-appearance had led to an unexpectedly favourable outcome. Joseph had visited Nikisch and they had played through the symphony together, with Nikisch becoming more and more enthusiastic. Nikisch's advice to Joseph was that he should abandon his plans for a piano-duet performance. He (Nikisch) was planning to give a concert in the theatre on behalf of the Wagner memorial fund in April or the beginning of May, and he undertook to prepare the symphony with the utmost care and perform it then:

> ... 'From now on I regard it as my duty to promote Bruckner's cause', he said. After this he wrote a long letter to Bruckner which I will bring with me. We then played through the first movement for the third time!... How pleased I am to be able to convey this news to Bruckner. Under these circumstances I will be returning to Vienna early on Tuesday.[146]

---

145 See *HSABB* I, 209 for a letter from Goldschmidt to Joseph Schalk, dated Leipzig, 10 March 1884. Goldschmidt reassured Schalk on two counts: (a) that his plan to give a piano-duet performance of the Seventh would meet with no difficulty; (b) that he should be able to find a publisher for Bruckner in Leipzig. Also see *LBSAB*, 66 for a letter from Franz Schalk to his brother, dated 28 March 1884. The originals of both letters are in the *ÖNB*, F18 Schalk 152a/1 and F18 Schalk 158/5/5 respectively.

Arthur Nikisch (1855-1922) had a distinguished career as a conductor. He was involved with many of the leading orchestras of the time (Leipzig Gewandhaus, Berlin Philharmonic, Hamburg Philharmonic, Boston Symphony Orchestra, Budapest Opera). For further information, see Manfred Schuler, 'Arthur Nikisch' in *MGG* 9 (1961), cols. 1531ff., and Hans-Hubert Schönzeler, 'Arthur Nikisch' in *The New Grove* 13 (1980), 244f.

146 See *HSABB* I, 209-10 for Nikisch's letter to Bruckner, dated Leipzig, 29 March 1884, and Joseph Schalk's letter to Franz, dated Leipzig, 30 March 1884; the originals of both letters are in the *ÖNB*, F18 Schalk 185a and F18 Schalk 158/5/6 respectively. In his letter to Bruckner, Nikisch confirmed that he intended to perform the Seventh in Leipzig within the next two months, adding that it was a 'matter of honour' for him to achieve public recognition for Bruckner's works. There

On 5 April, just before Easter, the Winkler Quartet gave another performance of Bruckner's String Quintet in an *Akademischer Gesangverein* concert. Writing in the *Deutsche Zeitung*, Theodor Helm described the Adagio as one of the 'noblest, most inspired, most gentle and most euphonious pieces that has been written in modern times', adding that it 'has the same effect as would a truly inspired piece dating from Beethoven's last period and only just discovered among his unpublished compositions'.[147] A fortnight later, Hans Paumgartner, writing in the *Wiener Abendpost*, regarded it as a 'grave injustice that this work is still not played by our established Quartets', an obvious thrust at the Hellmesberger Quartet.[148]

In the course of the year the Winkler Quartet gave another private performance of the Adagio from the Quintet in the *Votivkirche*. This was for the benefit of Duke Maximilian Emanuel of Bavaria to whom Bruckner dedicated the work. After the publication of the Quintet, Bruckner sent a dedication copy to the Duke. According to Lucca, the cellist in the Winkler Quartet, the Duke 'did not appear to be particularly musical' but he let it be known through his secretary, Count Ritterstein, that the performance in the *Votivkirche* was 'one of his most enjoyable musical experiences' and sent Bruckner a diamond pin.[149]

As Bruckner had been invited to play the new organ in the *Rudolfinum* and to attend an organ convention in Prague, he was unable to spend Easter at St. Florian as usual. According to Franz Marschner who happened to be staying with his parents in Prague at the same time, Bruckner met the leading church musicians in the city as well as Hermann Langer, a fine organist from Leipzig. His

---

is a facsimile of this letter in *LABL*, 24.

147 Review of 8 April 1884; see *G-A* IV/2, 159f.

148 Review of 22 April 1884; see *G-A* IV/2, 159.

149 See *G-A* IV/2, 160ff. for Lucca's recollection of the *Votivkirche* performance, and *HSABB* I, 224 for Ritterstein's letter to Bruckner, dated Schloß Biederstein (Schwabing, near Munich), 29 October 1884; the original of this letter is in the *ÖNB*.

improvisational facility was as fine as ever but he was 'less successful in his organ playing during High Mass in the cathedral on Easter Sunday'.[150]

During a year which was largely taken up with negotiations with Nikisch concerning the first performance of the Seventh Symphony, Bruckner had time to compose two short sacred pieces - *Christus factus est* WAB 11 and *Salvum fac populum* WAB 40 - as well as a *Prelude* in C major for harmonium or organ *WAB* 129.

Christus factus est, for four-part mixed-voice choir *a cappella*, is Bruckner's third setting of the text normally associated with the Maundy Thursday liturgy and was written in Vienna on 28 May and dedicated to his young friend Oddo Loidol in Kremsmünster. Not surprisingly, given the date of the piece, there are several motivic connections with the Seventh Symphony, the *Te Deum* and the Eighth Symphony.[151]

We do not know for what purpose Bruckner wrote his *Salvum fac populum*, a setting of lines from the *Te Deum* for four-part mixed-voice choir *a cappella* composed in Vienna on 14 November. It is possible that he intended it for inclusion in a Caecilian publication or for performance at either St. Florian or Kremsmünster. Plainchant-like phrases for bass, short sections in a fauxbourdon-type homophony

---

150 See *G-A* IV/2, 165. Dr. Franz L.V. Marschner (1855-1932) was a composer, organist and music theorist. He was educated and worked in Prague and Vienna, and was a student at the Vienna Conservatory from 1883 to 1885. His reminiscences of Bruckner can be found in *G-A* IV/2, 129-32 and *passim*.

151 The autograph of this motet is in the private collection of Dr. Arthur Wilhelm, Basel-Bottmingen. The engraver's copy, used for the first edition in 1886, namely no. 1 of *Vier Graduale* published by Theodor Rättig (pl .no. T.R. 41), is in the *ÖNB*, Mus. Hs. 37.281, and the dedication copy is in Kremsmünster music library, D7/320. For further information, see *G-A* IV/2, 169-72, *ABSW* XXI/2, 119-23 and Timothy Jackson, 'The Enharmonics of Faith: Enharmonic Symbolism in Bruckner's "Christus factus est" (1884)' in *BJ 1987/88* (Linz, 1990), 7-20. A modern edition of the piece can be found in *ABSW* XXI/1, 22-25.

and equally short polyphonic enclaves alternate.[152]

On his return from Prague after Easter, Bruckner wrote to Nikisch to thank him for his interest in the Seventh Symphony:

> Having just returned from Prague (where I made the acquaintance of Professor Langer from Leipzig), I am taking this opportunity of expressing my deepest thanks for your kindness. Once again I breathe a sigh of relief at your words of approval and think 'at last you have found a true artist'. I pray that your favourable attitude towards me will continue and that you will not abandon me - for you are certainly the only one who can and, praise God, also wants to come to my aid. Mr. Seidl has also expressed similar sentiments and will perhaps imitate your noble example in the future. If it is necessary for me to attend the final rehearsal, I will ask for a couple of days' leave of absence. I will be deeply indebted to you for as long as I live and you will have my greatest admiration for your artistry and your noble endeavour. Three cheers for an artist of real distinction!...[153]

At the end of April and beginning of May Bruckner wrote two letters to Anton Vergeiner in Freistadt who had asked the composer to supply him with some

---

152 For further information, see *G-A* IV/2, 200f. and *ABSW* XXI/2, 123-26. The work first appeared in print in a facsimile of the autograph, Mus. Hs. 6022 in the *ÖNB*, between pages 496 and 497 in *G-A* IV/2 (1936). There is a modern edition in *ABSW* XXI/1, 126-28. On page 129 of the same volume is a modern edition of *Veni Creator Spiritus* (c.1884), Bruckner's harmonization of a plainchant melody for voice and organ. It was first published in *G-A* IV/1, 524.

153 See *HSABB* I, 211 for this letter, dated Vienna, 16 April 1884; the original is privately owned. Anton Seidl (1850-1898) was one of the finest Wagner conductors of his generation. He was conductor of the Leipzig Opera (1879), Bremen Opera (1883), New York Metropolitan (1885) and New York Philharmonic (1891) and gave the first American performance of Bruckner's Fourth Symphony on 4 April 1888. For further information, see Reinhold Sietz, 'Anton Seidl' in *MGG* 12 (1965), cols. 472f., and Hans-Hubert Schönzeler, 'Anton Seidl' in *The New Grove* 17, 113.

biographical information for an article which he intended to write for publication later in the year. In the first letter Bruckner drew Vergeiner's attention to articles which had already appeared in other newspapers and mentioned Nikisch's interest in his Seventh Symphony which he hoped to perform in May.[154] Vergeiner must have asked for more specific information because, in the second letter, we have answers to five questions. The most revealing is the information about Hanslick, or rather Bruckner's almost paranoid fear of the man:

> ... 3rd question: Apart from Herbeck Hanslick used to be my most important and greatest supporter. He will never write about me again in the same way as he did up until 1874 (when I was appointed lecturer at the University); he had even very flattering things to say about me as a composer and conductor.
>
> Above all, please do not criticise Hanslick on my account because he has a terrible temper; he has the power to destroy. There is no point in fighting against him. One can only plead with him. And I cannot even do that, because he always refuses...
>
> Opposed to me are Hanslick (*freie Presse*) and his two lieutenants, Kalbeck (*Presse*) and Dömpke (*allgemeine Zeitung*). These two have to write to order; the other papers are favourably disposed towards me.[155]

Around the same time Bruckner wrote to his former pupil Rudolf Krzyzanowski in Starnberg, bringing him up to date about his recent compositions:

---

154 See *HSABB* I, 211f. for this letter, dated Vienna, 25 April 1884. The location of the original is unknown; it was first published in *ABB*, 159f. Anton Vergeiner (1858-1901) was a lawyer and highly gifted amateur musician. He attended some of Bruckner's lectures while he was pursuing law studies at Vienna University. His brother, Hermann Pius Vergeiner (1859-1900), was one of Bruckner's organ students at the Conservatory and was a prizewinner in the 1880-81 semester.

155 See *HSABB* I, 213f. for the complete letter, dated Vienna, 9 May 1884; the original is privately owned.

... Apologies!!! Congratulations! Where will this letter find you? My 7th Symphony is completed, as well as a large *Te Deum*. Nikisch in Leipzig is absolutely delighted with the 7th and wants to perform it soon at a concert for the Wagner memorial fund.

Here in Vienna nothing has been performed apart from the String Quintet in an *Akademischer Gesangverein* concert. Hans Richter performs nothing [of mine] anywhere. He plays the same tune as Hanslick!

As I shall probably be spending a longer time in Munich and surrounding area this year, I could see you there. It would be a great joy for me to be able to speak to my old favourite.

Send me your proper address...

My congratulations to your wife!

My compositions have not earned me a kreuzer.

The Quintet is dedicated to Max Emanuel in Bavaria.[156]

The projected performance of the Seventh in Leipzig was postponed at first from May to June, and Bruckner wrote to Nikisch on 11 June asking him for further information:

... Above all my warmest congratulations on your engagement! May God grant you the happiest of futures!

May I ask you once again: is the concert now going to take place? On the 21st of this month? And if so, when are the two final rehearsals which I would so very much like to attend? Perhaps I will hear this work only once in any case, as I am not having any success in Vienna. Therefore it is all the more important for me to hear it, unless you think I should not come.

If you should wish me to be present I will have to request leave of absence from my various superiors; so could I have a prompt reply, please!

I would be overjoyed to see my youngest child brought into the world by the leading German conductor! I am very excited already. Marvellous things have been written recently in the *Deutsche Zeitung*, the *Bayreuther Blätter* and German papers!

---

156 See *HSABB* I, 213 for this letter, dated Vienna, 5 May 1884; the original is privately owned. The congratulations may refer to the birth of a child.

I repeat my urgent request and commend myself and my child to you in the hope of a favourable response...[157]

In his reply Nikisch said that insurmountable difficulties had caused the premiere of the work to be postponed until September:

Unfortunately, on account of serious obstacles, we have had to postpone the concert which should have been given on the 27th of this month. At first I thought that it would only be a matter of a few days, but now we see that we will have to postpone it until September. Although I am sorry that I have not yet been able to introduce the Leipzig public to this marvellous E major symphony, I am convinced that the performance is guaranteed a full attendance in September when all the Leipzig people have returned from their Summer travels and, as a result of its undoubted success, will prompt other concert-giving bodies to perform it. As you are still on holiday in September, dear Master, I am certainly reckoning on seeing you here. You will be pleased with Leipzig. I have already given you so much publicity through piano performances and have won so many friends for your marvellous symphony that the success of the performance is assured!...[158]

Three days before the beginning of his Summer vacation Bruckner wrote another letter to Nikisch. Expecting the conductor to be in touch with him, he gave him some idea of where he would be while away from Vienna. He had also had second

---

157 See *HSABB* I, 215 for this letter; the original is privately owned.

158 See *HSABB* I, 215f. for this letter, dated Leipzig, 16 June 1884; the original is in the *ÖNB*. Notices in two Leipzig papers, the *Musikalischer Wochenblatt* (19 June) and the *Leipziger Nachrichten* (20 June), indicated a forthcoming concert for the benefit of the Bayreuth fund in which the chief work was to be a Bruckner symphony. Two days later, on 18 June, Bruckner wrote to Joseph Schalk, addressing him as his 'honourable partner in the struggle' and asking him if he knew of any particular reason why the concert had been postponed until September. See *HSABB* I, 216; original in the *ÖNB*, F18 Schalk 151/12.

thoughts about the tempo of the Finale:

> At Wolzogen's request I have just become a member of the *Allgemeiner Deutsche Musikverein.* On the 20th I go to Bayreuth, then to Munich, and later to my native Upper Austria where I will remain until 1 September. My letters will be re-directed to St. Florian abbey near Linz. Recently Messrs Schalk and Löwe played the Finale of the Seventh Symphony for me on two pianos and I realised that I must have chosen too quick a tempo. I became convinced that the tempo should be a very moderate one and frequent changes of tempo would be required. With a gifted conductor like you in charge, all of this will no doubt happen automatically. My earnest request to you, my most generous supporter, is that I should be present at the last two rehearsals so that I can hear the work three times. I will not trouble anyone here in Vienna - Hellmesberger, the court music director, is so delighted with my new *Te Deum* and wants to perform it at court...[159]

In his next letter to Nikisch, written during his stay at St. Florian, Bruckner requested that the first performance of the Seventh be put back until the beginning of the University term:

> I am now at St. Florian abbey in Upper Austria and all letters are being re-directed to me here. In Bayreuth Hans von Wolzogen and the German students recommended that I ask for the concert not to take place until the beginning of the University term, so that the German student body can also be involved. I submit this request herewith to the relevant authority, adding in all humility that I put myself completely at your disposal. As Hans v. Wolzogen is going

---

159 See *HSABB* I, 217 for this letter, dated Vienna, 17 July 1884; the original is in private possession. Bruckner had already asked Pius Richter if they could agree on some kind of division of holiday arrangements so that he could travel to Bayreuth with the *Wagner Society* on 20 July - see *HSABB* I, 216 for Bruckner's letter to Richter, 2 July 1884; also *HSABB* I, 222 for another letter from Bruckner to Richter, dated Vienna, 18 September 1884, in which he informs him of his return to Vienna and expresses his gratitude; the original is in the *ÖNB*.

to write to the German student body I expect to gain many supporters among the young people. 'Gaudeamus igitur'. I have begun my Eighth Symphony. Highly esteemed artist, do not lose patience with me and please continue to honour me with your invaluable help!...[160]

Bruckner's request was granted and the date of the performance was put back to November. On the same day he wrote to Nikisch Bruckner also informed Joseph Schalk about Hermann Levi's wish to perform at least the Adagio of the Seventh in Munich the following March and asked for his assistance in sending a copy of the score to Munich:

Dear friend!
Baron Ostini, president of the *Allgemeiner Wagnerverein* in Munich, would like to obtain the score of the Seventh Symphony for H. Levi either in the near future or in the autumn. Should we not ensure that it is copied either completely or partially?
I must leave this now to your judgment. I would not be happy to part with this autograph score unless there was a very good reason. I believe you have it. Did we not want to make some improvements? Perhaps a couple of movements could be written out.
As soon as Ostini writes to me we must send them to him. His address: Baron Ostini, Munich / Burgstrasse 12/3.
And so, as soon as I write to you again please be so good as to forward the score (a copy, if possible, but without mistakes - otherwise music director Levi will send it back immediately.)
Please write to me, Mr. Schalk, and tell me if you are in Vienna and are going to remain there. If you intend to go away, please send the score to me at St. Florian near Linz as soon as possible.[161]

---

160 See *HSABB* I, 218 for this letter, dated St. Florian, 6 August 1884; the original is privately owned.

161 See *HSABB* I, 218-19 for this letter, dated St. Florian, 6 August 1884; the original is in the ÖNB, F18 Schalk 151/13/1. Hermann Levi (1839-1900) was court music director in Munich from 1872 to 1890 and was appointed general music director there in 1894. He conducted at Bayreuth several times, including the first performance of *Parsifal* in July 1882. He was also a fine interpreter

During the summer of 1884 Joseph Schalk was working on an article on Bruckner which was to be published in the October issue of the *Bayreuther Blätter* and, like Vergeiner's, was intended to commemorate the composer's 60th birthday in September. A few articles appeared earlier in pro-Wagnerian journals. Joseph Schalk alluded to one of these by a certain Dr. Schuster, which appeared in the *Kunst-Chronik* in August, when he wrote to Franz regretting that his own article would not appear until October.[162]

In his letter to Nikisch on 17 July Bruckner outlined his itinerary during the holiday months. After his annual visit to Bayreuth, he spent some time in Munich where he met Baron Ostini and, with a letter of introduction from Landgrave Fürstenberg, was received by Archduchess Gisela, daughter of Emperor Franz Josef, and Karl Freiherr von Perfall, intendant of the court theatre. He obviously regarded this as a necessary preliminary to his request that King Ludwig of Bavaria be the dedicatee of his new symphony. In a letter to Perfall in September Bruckner enclosed copies of Wagnerian keepsakes, remarking that they would be of 'great use in achieving my purpose'.[163]

One of Bruckner's travelling companions on his visit to Bayreuth was a leather merchant and Wagner enthusiast called Josef Diernhofer. He promised to compose a piece for harmonium and, on 20 August, wrote to Diernhofer enclosing a short Prelude in C major WAB 129:

---

of Brahms. For further information, see Richard Schnal, 'Hermann Levi' in *MGG* 8 (1960), cols. 680ff., and Friedrich Baser, 'Hermann Levi' in *The New Grove* 10 (1980), 702f.

162 See *LBSAB*, 70-71 for this letter dated Vienna, 10 August 1884; the original is in the *ÖNB*, F18 Schalk 158/5/11.

163 See Franz Gräflinger, *Anton Bruckner. Leben und Schaffen* [*GrBLS*] (Berlin: Hesse, 1927), 355f. for this letter dated St. Florian, 13 September 1884. During his visits to Bayreuth from 1884 onwards Bruckner regularly visited Wagner's grave. As a memento of his visit in 1884 he took three ivy leaves and placed them in an envelope with the inscription '1884. Drei Blätter aus Bayreuth v. des + Meisters Grabe'. The original of this letter is privately owned.

At present I am in Kremsmünster where I have written out the little piece composed at St. Florian. I shall be delighted if you are pleased with it.

My D minor symphony (dedicated to Richard Wagner) is published in both full score and piano score by Rättig in Vienna. And my Quintet by Gutmann in Vienna (Opera Theatre).

You deserve to be greatly honoured for your fine taste and enthusiasm for art.

I imagine that you have a family? My warmest greetings to all!

In Leipzig I have requested that the concert, in which my Seventh Symphony is to be performed for the benefit of the Wagner memorial, be postponed until the beginning of the University term. Today I received a third letter from the enthusiastic music director in which my request is granted.

The symphony will probably go to Munich after Leipzig.

Duke Max Emanuel and Princess Gisela received me most graciously.[164]

The Prelude in C major is only 27 bars' long and is essentially a microcosm of several of the techniques employed by Bruckner in his larger compositions.[165]

Bruckner spent just over a week at Kremsmünster (17-25 August) and his friend Oddo Loidol left a written record of his movements during this time:

---

164 See *HSABB* I, 219 for this letter, dated Kremsmünster 20 August 1884; the original is in private ownership in Linz.

165 The Prelude was first published by Universal Edition (U.E. 8752) as a music supplement in *Musica divina* xiv (1926). For further information, see *G-A* IV/2, 187ff., Altman Kellner, *Musikgeschichte des Stiftes Kremsmünster* (Kassel/Basel, 1956), 762; Martin Vogel, 'Bruckner in reiner Stimmung. Eine Analyse des Orgelpräludiums in C-dur' in *BJ 1981* (Linz, 1982), 159-66 where the piece is also printed on p.160; Kevin J. Swinden, 'Bruckner's *Perger* Prelude: A Dramatic Revue of Wagner?' in *Music Analysis* 18/1(March 1999), 101-24; and Erwin Horn, ed. *Werke für Orgel*, *ABSW* XII/6 (Vienna, 1999), vii-viii. This *Complete Edition* volume includes both the fair copy of 20 August (p. 16) and a transcription of an earlier sketch (p. 17).

Bruckner normally spent the forenoon composing in the music room; he composed *inter alia* the second part of his Seventh [sic] Symphony (C); one evening when he was in room no. 2 he wrote the Prelude for harmonium for Diernhofer, the leather merchant from Perg, and send it to him from here. In the afternoons he went on walks with my brother Amand and me. In the evenings he always remained in the refectory with the clergy.

He showed me the letter from music director Nikisch in Leipzig and told us that the students had given him such a welcome in Munich and that he had been invited to visit Archduchess Gisela etc. etc.

On 21 August he gave a great organ concert; on 22 August we had an excursion to Wartberg accompanied by my brother Amand and Georg, the music director. On 24 August he played the organ brilliantly at High Mass...[166]

Loidol's review of Bruckner's organ concert on 21 August appeared in the *Linzer Volksblatt* a week later. According to Loidol, Bruckner played this new Prelude as his first piece and then developed it further. He also improvised on a pedal theme which Loidol notated on the sketch of the Prelude.[167] Later in the year Loidol asked Bruckner to write out the complete fugue and, indeed, more of his improvised organ compositions so that the musical world would have a permanent record of works other than his symphonies. But Bruckner was unwilling to do this. Like other fine improvisers, with the possible exception of Franz Liszt, he found it difficult to recapture on the paper the inspiration of the moment.

Bruckner was based at St. Florian for the rest of his summer vacation but visited Linz, Steyr and Vöcklabruck where he celebrated his 60th birthday on 4 September and was serenaded by the local choral society and military band.[168] While in Vöcklabruck he also found time to complete the sketches of the first movement of

---

166 See *G-A* IV/2, 189f.

167 See *G-A* IV/2, 193 for this theme.

168 See *G-A* III/1, 584 for further details.

his Eighth Symphony.

The Seventh Symphony was still foremost in his mind, however. On 13 September he wrote not only to Perfall concerning the dedication of the symphony but to Hans von Wolzogen as well:

> ... The German students applauded me vigorously. In accordance with their wishes and my request, the concert in Leipzig on behalf of the Wagner memorial, which included the performance of my Seventh Symphony, has been postponed until the University lectures have begun. In a recent (third) enthusiastic letter, Nikisch granted my request. (The new tubas and the funeral music for our unforgettable Master are in the second movement.)
>
> Max van de Sandt and the gentlemen from Weimar are full of enthusiasm for the D minor symphony. Baron Ostini will make every effort on behalf on my symphony in Munich...[169]

In September Franz Schalk took up his first appointment as conductor - assistant conductor in the Moravian town of Olomouc. In one of his letters to Franz, Joseph sends Bruckner's greetings, looks forward with some envy to his younger brother being in a position to conduct one of Bruckner's works, and provides up-to-date information about the Eighth Symphony:

> ... The first movement is complete in sketch form. There are some marvellous things in the theme and its excursions. He has played it through for Hirsch and me...[170]

---

169 See *HSABB* I, 221 for this letter dated St. Florian, 13 September 1884. It was first published in *ABB*, 165f.; the original is not extant. Max van de Sandt (1863-1934) was a pianist and composer and one of Liszt's pupils in Weimar.

170 See *LBSAB*, 72 for this letter dated Vienna, 23 September 1884; the original is in the *ÖNB*, F18 Schalk 158/5/19. Richard Hirsch was a member of the *Wagnerverein* in Vienna and a friend of Hugo Wolf.

On 26 September Anton Vergeiner's article on Bruckner appeared in the Linz *Tagespost*. Vergeiner attempted to draw a clear distinction between Brahms and Bruckner and castigated the Viennese and their most prominent music critics for their failure to give proper recognition to the composer. Hanslick was described as a 'grumpy gatekeeper of the musical Parnassus', that is the critic who determined what was acceptable in Viennese musical life. When Bruckner sent a belated letter of thanks to Vergeiner on 5 November, he alluded to this particularly apt description of Hanslick and added some details of his current musical activities:

> ... So long as the gatekeeper does not lift the ban, all is lost! Truly a hard, but certain fate. While those who are in favour have received 30,000 marks and even more for a symphony, those who are not in favour are not even able to have a work printed. The Leipzig concert will take place soon. On Sunday (9 Nov.) I will be conducting my 3rd Mass in the *Hofburgkapelle*...[171]

Nearly three weeks later Bruckner sent another short letter to Vergeiner who had apparently asked to see the score of one of the composer's works:

> Your kindness brings me great pleasure!
> The score has just been returned to me. I am usually at home until 12.00 on Wednesday and Friday mornings. I will be pleased to make your acquaintance. Mr. Hanslick has been very cross with me (recently).
> NB It would be certainly be of great help if you were the critic of

---

171 See *HSABB* I, 224-25 for this letter dated Vienna, 5 November 1884; the original is in private ownership. Vergeiner's article in the *Linzer Tagespost* on 26 September is paraphrased in *G-A* IV/2, 194f. For further information about Vergeiner and the increasingly German national and antisemitic tone of the *Tagespost* during the 1880s, see Uwe Harten's contribution to the round table session 'Bruckner und die österreichische Presse', *BSL 1991* (Linz, 1994), 97f.

the *Freie Presse.*[172]

Joseph Schalk's article on Bruckner appeared in the *Bayreuther Blätter* in October
and helped to prepare the way for the reception of his works outside Austria. Schalk
stressed the connection with Wagner, the obvious 'Germanness' of his music and the
'sublime' qualities of the symphonic movements which had been misconstrued:

> ... Forged by pure, unadulterated musical strength, these movements
> rose up boldly like rocks but there were no meandering and well-
> trodden paths leading to them. There was a change from hedges and
> bushes to wild trees of gigantic size and they were passed by. It was
> certainly conceded that there were 'inspired traits' but they were
> lacking in 'any kind of form'. The important reputations which critics
> were able to claim for themselves by stressing 'form' intimidated their
> readers to such an extent that none of them even dared to venture the
> question what 'form' was supposed to mean, but preferred to
> maintain a comfortable attitude of respect for an unknown quantity
> and to have unconditional faith in the authority of its source... What
> is described as form in a limited sense, the arrangement of periods in
> a musical paragraph, is to be understood only in the context of and
> simultaneously with a complete understanding of the content, as the
> determining factor here is certainly not the law of symmetry but
> another more fundamental law which is apparently related to it but
> cannot be grasped by mere theoretical speculation. And so very soon
> that section of the Viennese musical public which would have been at
> all capable of remaining uninfluenced by the superficially impressive
> for a longer time was not given the opportunity of taking a lively
> interest in Bruckner. One is all the more ashamed never to have
> experienced public apathy to the same degree.
>   Bruckner himself saw only one way of salvation - the 'way to Him'
> [that is, Wagner]. He alone could reassure him - he, whose greatness
> had filled his soul with glowing enthusiasm for a long time; he

---

172 See *HSABB* I, 226 for this letter dated Vienna, 24 November 1884. It was first printed in *ABB*,
170f; the original is not extant. The identity of the score referred to is unknown.

wanted to run to him and spread out his work under the penetrating eye of his illustrious master... Childlike purity and uninhibitedness, inexplicable disregard for and ignorance of each and every practicality characterise him as a master and as an artist. The possessor of a fiery temperament and a deep and thoroughly gentle warm-heartedness which is pervaded by that purely German humour, gentle but strong, that is unfortunately seldom encountered, he makes his lonely way through life. He has never gone out of his way to find a publisher for his works and, regrettably, only his Wagner Symphony and Quintet have appeared in print so far...

Turning to Bruckner's symphonies in general, Schalk was at pains to point out that they 'find the law of their development within themselves', that is they are not dependent upon extra-musical factors, and he added that it should not be held against Bruckner if he availed himself freely of the advances made in the Wagnerian music drama in the realms of harmony, modulation and thematic and contrapuntal development.[173]

In October Nikisch assured Bruckner that he was still making every effort to arouse interest in the Seventh in Leipzig:

Today I have played through the Symphony in E major to Mr. Oskar Schwalm, the music critic of the influential Leipzig newpaper, the 'Leipziger Tagesblatt'.
He was beside himself with delight and asked me to inform you that he was truly filled with enthusiasm for your magnificent masterpiece and that he considers it his duty to use all of his influence to work in the press on your behalf and to ensure that you are not deprived of the public recognition which you so richly deserve. He asked me to lend him the piano score for some time so that he could become better acquainted with the magnificent work, and so I must request your friend Schalk, who has asked for the score back, to leave it for me so that I can play through the symphony to a few other critics.

---

173 See *LBSAB*, 225ff. for extracts from this article which appeared in the *Bayreuther Blätter* 7/10, 329-334. The article contains music examples from the Seventh Symphony.

I am taking an almost childlike delight in the performance, as it will undoubtedly have an enormous success![174]

In October Bruckner lost a dear friend, the St. Florian music director Ignaz Traumihler, who had been very ill during the composer's stay at the abbey the previous month. Mozart's *Requiem* was performed at Traumihler's funeral on 15 October and Bruckner played the organ, improvising on the themes of the double fugue from the *Agnus Dei*.

At the end of October, Liszt wrote to Bruckner to thank him for the dedication of the Symphony no. 2 in C minor. He had read it through with interest, but would have preferred to hear it played by an orchestra. He wished the composer every success with his 'unwavering efforts'.[175] Liszt intended to take the dedication score with him to Weimar but apparently left it in his apartment in the Schottengasse. When Bruckner got to know about this by chance a year later he regarded Liszt's seeming carelessness in leaving the score unattended as an indication of a lack of interest in the work and withdrew the dedication. Apart from this episode his relationship with Liszt was reasonably cordial given the obvious differences in their personalities and lifestyles. He admired the *Faust* symphony, without understanding the programmatic basis of the work, and thought highly of the *Gran Festival Mass* and the *Coronation Mass*. His response to the two oratorios, *Christus* and *St. Elisabeth*, was less enthusiastic. He knew and played Liszt's Fugue on B-A-C-H for organ. Although well aware of Liszt's reputation as a piano virtuoso, he personally

---

174 See *HSABB* I, 223 for this letter dated Leipzig, 15 October 1884; the original is in St. Florian.

175 See *HSABB* I, 223 for this letter dated Vienna, 29 October 1884. The location of the original is unknown; it was first published in *ABB*, 329, and there is a facsimile of the original between pages 272 and 273.

preferred Rubinstein's playing.[176]

At the beginning of November Joseph Schalk played his arrangements of two Bruckner symphony movements - the Adagio from the Seventh and the Scherzo from the Fourth - at a *Wagnerverein* concert in the *Bösendorfersaal*.[177] A few days later, nearly 18 months after the previous performance of the F minor Mass in the *Hofkapelle*, Bruckner conducted the work again, together with the first performance of the new motet, *Christus factus est*, as gradual and *Os justi* as offertory. Once again Dr. Theodor Helm, writing in the *Wiener Allgemeine Zeitung*, was full of praise for the work:

> Bruckner's inspired work was performed brilliantly and tastefully under the composer's personal direction. In spite of its great length this significant and impressive composition was listened to with great attention. We must also repeat this year what we were able to say last year. Whoever is not able to discover Bruckner's genius in this work, whoever cannot sense that a divinely inspired composer has written it, has slept through the last decades of musical development and so there is no point in arguing with him. As far as we are concerned, however - in spite of a few features which militate against the work and in spite of the enormous demands it makes on the singers - we are always very pleased when it is in the repertory, we can have heartfelt enthusiasm for this splendid piece, and we feel that deep devoutness and the pure naivety of true genius had an equal share in its creation. We also have the same admiration for the two enclaves,

---

176 See *G-A* IV/2, 166-69 and 471ff; August Stradal, 'Franz Liszt und Anton Bruckner. Eine vergleichende Studie' in *Allgemeine Musikzeitung* 38 (1911), 783ff.; idem, *Erinnerungen an Franz Liszt* (Bern and Leipzig, 1929); Wilhelm Kurthen, 'Liszt und Bruckner als Messenkomponisten' in *Musica sacra* 55 (1925), 265-71; Othmar Wessely, 'Bruckner und Liszt' in *BS 1986* (Linz, 1989), 67-72; Rudolf Stephan, 'Bruckner und Liszt. Hat der Komponist Franz Liszt Bruckner beeinflusst?' in *ibid*, 169-80; Constantin Floros, 'Diskussionsbeitrag zum Thema Bruckner und Liszt' in *ibid*, 181-88. See also Stephen Johnson, op. cit., 145-50.

177 The concert took place on Tuesday 4 November and was reviewed in the *Deutsche Zeitung* on 6 November.

'Os justi' and the new and surprisingly beautiful 'Christus factus'. There is no 'if' and 'but' about the 'Resurrexit' of the Mass. Friend and foe alike are so emotionally moved that they forget about criticism and analysis. The colossal over-all impression certainly leads to self-reflection and true religious exaltation! And, in my opinion, that is the greatest praise that can be given to church composers at any time.[178]

In the meantime, there had been more correspondence concerning the Seventh. On 5 November Bruckner wrote to Nikisch, acknowledging his letter of 15 October, mentioning Levi's interest in the work, and asking when the performance would take place. His main concern, however, was that the work should be understood:

> Hans v. Wolzogen would like to know the day of the performance well in advance... You cannot imagine how delighted I am with your fine letters. Please convey my deepest respects to Mr. Schwalm and tell him what great pleasure his kindness has given me. Mr. Levi, the Munich music director, wants to see the score of the Seventh Symphony. Will the concert now take place in November? In any event could I ask you, when you reply, to state that I 'must be present at the two final rehearsals' so that I can request leave. In the score there are actually a lot of important details apart from tempo changes which have not been marked. Will the Seventh Symphony, the Adagio in particular, not be too difficult a work for the public to grasp as an introduction to my music? (The Fourth 'Romantic' Symphony would probably have been an easier introductory work.)
> In our *Wagnerverein*, people began to understand the Adagio of the Seventh only after repeated playing (on the piano). Perhaps the most important people should attend the rehearsals so that they will understand the work better? I am pleased with the tuba passages. I am longing for things to happen and looking forward with excitement to the performance. I hope that several rehearsals have taken place already. Have the parts been written well and correctly? How does the work sound when played by orchestra? With my heartfelt request for many rehearsals...
> N.B. I am not able to send Mr. Grünberg the parts of the Quintet

---

178 See *G-A* IV/2, 198f..

because they are not ready yet. I have given Mr. Gutmann his letter. Greetings![179]

Bruckner could hardly disguise his disappointment that the Leipzig performance had been postponed, but at least there was now the prospect of another performance of the Seventh in Munich. Hermann Levi had made Bruckner's acquaintance at Bayreuth and, according to Auer, had already studied one of his symphonies, describing it as 'an extremely significant work'.[180] Bruckner sent a copy of the score of the Seventh to Baron von Ostini who in turn passed it on to Levi. The composer was delighted to receive the following letter from Levi:

I have read through with great interest the symphony passed on to me by Mr. von Ostini. At first the work displeased me, then it gripped me, and finally I have acquired an immense respect for the man who could produced something as individual and important as this. But, in spite of my sincere admiration, I - as the person responsible for directing our concerts here - have a few reservations about introducing our public to the work. If I myself have had difficulty in getting into the work - (I am still not able to grasp the final movement) - how much more disconcerted the Munich public will be, even although its response to new works is no less than friendly. And so I would ask your permission to perform the Adagio only in one of our future (royal) concerts. This movement is the easiest and the most gripping. I have no doubt that it will be very successful, and I would be able to build on that success by performing the whole work later. Please tell me honestly what you think of this proposal! In the meantime, preparations are going well. I am playing the Adagio and - as far as it is possible on the piano - the first movement to every musician who comes to me, and experience in every case the same mounting response from astonishment to admiration which I had myself. By the day of the concert half of the town will know already who and what Bruckner is. Hitherto - to our shame, let it be said -

---

179 See *HSABB* 1, 225 for this letter dated Vienna, 5 November 1884; the original is privately owned.

180 Auer conjectures that it was the Sixth rather than the Seventh Symphony; see *G-A* 4/2, 203.

no one, myself included, knew this.[181]

Two months after Traumihler's death Bruckner was mourning the loss of the man who had been his strict but patient and understanding employer in Linz and had maintained a close interest in his career in Vienna, Bishop Franz Josef Rudigier. Oddo Loidol accompanied Bruckner to Rudigier's funeral in Linz on 4 December, and Bruckner played the organ in a performance of Mozart's Requiem.[182]

On 8 December Bruckner replied to Levi's letter. From a letter written on the same day to Mrs Judith Pfeiffenberger, née Bogner, the daughter of his former superior in St. Florian and one of the children he had taught during his time there, we learn that Levi sent a second letter to Bruckner between 30 November and 8 December:

> ... I take this opportunity of sending you some piano pieces. Please accept them as a small and insignificant token of my true admiration; postage has been pre-paid. I have received letters from Leipzig and Munich which have brought tears to my eyes! They honour me in calling me Beethoven's successor. The court music director in Munich has even put his house at my disposal and has offered to refund my travelling expenses when I travel there in March for a performance of my symphony. Remarkable! Richard Wagner wanted to perform all seven of my symphonies. Unfortunately he is dead!
>
> I offer you my deepest sympathy belatedly. May the passage of time heal the terrible wounds or at least alleviate the pain which is the unfailing consequence of such misfortune! May God be with you and

---

181 See *HSABB* 1, 227 for this letter dated Munich, 30 November 1884; the original is in St. Florian. Levi seems to indicate here that he had not seen any of Bruckner's symphonies - which contradicts Auer's statement; see previous footnote.

182 See *G-A* III/1, 588.

your dear children...[183]

In his reply to Levi's two letters, Bruckner began by describing his relationship with Wagner:

> For some years now, my dear Sir, I have admired you as one of the leading artists in the world. Your letter, which does me such great honour, increases my respect for you a thousandfold, however. This letter is a veritable gem. I will never part with it, and it will always bring me solace during the many times I have to endure insults. Our dear departed Master knew only the D minor symphony (no. 3). He said to me once as he embraced me: 'Dear friend, it's right that you should dedicate this work to me. It has given me immense pleasure'. He frequently called for its performance in Vienna. Mr. Seidl also said that he had heard the most flattering things from the Master about this symphony. About six months before his death the dearly departed said to me, 'You can be sure that I will perform your symphonies myself'. Now it appears as if the dearly-loved, deceased master found a guardian, as it were, for me before he passed away, one in whom he could put his greatest trust.

Levi, of course, was the 'great artist', the guardian who would ensure that Bruckner's works would reach a larger audience. Bruckner agreed with Levi that the Adagio of the Seventh was the most gripping movement while the first movement was the most easily understood. He then drew Levi's attention to his other symphonies, the Fourth in particular:

> I have two other approachable symphonies - the Second in C minor (Herbeck's favourite) and the Fourth in E flat major (the 'Romantic')

---

183 See *HSABB* 1, 227-28 for this letter; the original is in the *ÖNB*. The piano pieces referred to are perhaps copies of the two pieces dedicated to her, namely the *Lancier-Quadrille* WAB 120 and *Steiermärker* WAB 122, which both date from the St. Florian period. Judith Pfeiffenberger's father had died in 1879. It is possible that she had lost her husband recently.

which Richter has performed with huge success. I recommend the 1st and 3rd movements in particular. In the 1st movement day is announced by the horn during the perfect silence of night. 2nd movement: song. 3rd movement: Hunt Trio. Mealtime music for the hunters in the wood. Permit me, most noble patron, to send you the score of my 4th Symphony for your perusal.

Should you abide by your decision and perform only the Adagio [C sharp minor] of the 7th Symphony in E major, I would make only one sincere request, namely that the public is informed that it is not because of any weakness in the work that the other movements are not being played.

I have just found your second exceptionally nice letter at home. A thousand apologies for not replying earlier. I was in Linz at the bishop's funeral. I wept like a child over the second letter. There are no words to describe your generosity. Everything is all right as far as I am concerned! Should I follow your sensible advice, I will very probably come with Landgrave Fürstenberg who asks me to convey his respect and admiration to you. Mr von. Grün also sends his very warm greetings.

I am still waiting to hear whether you wish to perform anything from the 4th Symphony, the 1st and 3rd movements for instance. If you consider the 2nd movement (Adagio) from the 7th Symphony in E major to be more effective, please let me know and I will write to Leipzig immediately and ask for the parts to be returned. Court Director Nikisch is very enthusiastic about the 7th... I am delighted with your kind invitation and with the [offer of] travelling expenses. But the greatest honour for me will be to visit you and to be with you, even for such a short time. My dear court director, I ask you humbly not to forsake me. All my hope and pride are in you, my highest and most noble artistic patron...[184]

After more than a month had elapsed, Nikisch replied to Bruckner's letter of 5 November and explained that it had been necessary to give rehearsals for the production of Wagner's *Tristan und Isolde* precedence over the projected performance of the Seventh Symphony in November:

---

184 See *HSABB* 1, 228f. for this letter dated Vienna, 8 December 1884. The originals of both this letter and the second letter mentioned by Bruckner are not extant; this letter was published for the first time in *GrBLS*, 320ff.

As a result of the many strenuous rehearsals for 'Tristan' which we performed with huge success the day before yesterday, the concert could no longer take place in November as projected. It will now be performed definitely on 30 December and I repeat my request that you give us the pleasure of your presence at the performance and, if possible, at the two final rehearsals as well.

Now to a matter of conscience: in your last letter you informed me of your concern that, as the first work of yours to be performed here, the Seventh Symphony might be too difficult for a foreign public to grasp and deemed the Fourth (Romantic) more suitable for this purpose. Should you still be of this opinion today, in other words should you prefer us to introduce the Leipzig public to the 7th in a later concert and perform the 4th now, I would have to ask you to send the score and parts of this work immediately. I also have to point out that we have no tubas available for the Seventh and will have to use 4 horns instead.

As soon as you receive this letter could you wire me immediately to let me know which symphony you have chosen...[185]

Bruckner had made up his mind that the Seventh Symphony should be performed. He made official application for leave from his *Hofkapelle* duties from 27 December until 1 January and asked Pius Richter to stand in for him.[186] He was able to inform Nikisch that leave had been granted when he wrote to him on 19 December, but there is no mention of the bronchial condition which was causing him trouble and which he alluded to a week later when he wrote to Richter:

I have my leave 'in the bag' already and intend to travel by North-West Railway's courier train on the evening of the 26th and arrive in Leipzig at 11.00 am on Saturday 27 December (unless you should say to me, 'it is better to stay at home'.)

---

185 See *HSABB* 1, 229f. for this letter dated Leipzig, 10 December 1884; the original is in St. Florian.

186 See *HSABB* 1, 231and 234 for the application to the *Hofkapelle* dated Vienna, 16 December 1884, and the letter to Pius Richter dated Vienna, 26 December 1884. The originals of both letters are in the *ÖNB*; there is a facsimile of the autograph of the former in *LABL*, 25.

Are there no military tubas which can be used?
Have there been any rehearsals so far?
How does the symphony sound?
Please be so kind as to write to me, as I am very excited already.
(If the work is unsuccessful, I will return home at dead of night.)
Many congratulations on the excellent 'Tristan' success. I hope that everything is going well already. I am certain that the players who perform 'Tristan' so well will also play my Seventh Symphony superbly..
If you should have any further requests, you have only to let me know. It is a pity that the Universities are on vacation just now. Levi's letters from Munich are splendid...[187]

Nikisch replied by return of post:

I am delighted that you have been able to get some leave. The performance will take place definitely on the 30th. There have been rehearsals already; as the work is very difficult it must be rehearsed carefully. We will have five rehearsals altogether for the symphony; I believe that will be sufficient. You will have to change the orchestration of some passages as it does not work and does not sound good. If you are coming on Saturday we will certainly have enough time to make the changes.
Tristan und Isolde is being performed here on Saturday! Is your friend Schalk coming with you? I would be very pleased to see him. I am going away for the Christmas holiday tomorrow and don't return to Leipzig until Friday evening. If you should have anything important to communicate to me in the meantime, write to me at the following address: Arthur Nikisch, Cassel, Weinberg 2...[188]

Joseph Schalk did not accompany Bruckner to Leipzig. He had already asked his brother Franz, who was now working as a conductor in Dresden, to go to the

---

187 See *HSABB* 1, 231f. for this letter dated Vienna, 19 December 1884; the original is privately owned.

188 See *HSABB*, 232f. for this letter dated Leipzig, 21 December 1884; the original is in St. Florian.

Leipzig performance and send back a report to Vienna.[189]   He also arranged a 'Bruckner evening' in the *Bösendorfersaal* on 22 December.   It consisted of the whole of the First Symphony (in Löwe's arrangement) played on two pianos by Löwe and Schalk, the first movement of the Fourth played by Löwe, the third movement of the Third played by Schalk, as well as Wotan's monologue from Act 2 of *Die Walküre* in which the soloist was Richard Hirsch. Bruckner mentioned the success of this concert, the forthcoming Leipzig performance of the Seventh and Levi's friendly interest when he wrote his annual Christmas letter to his sister Rosalie in Vöcklabruck.[190] He also wrote to Joseph Schalk, describing the concert as 'the greatest success he had experienced in Vienna' but voicing his concern that there had been no newspaper reviews of the performances.[191] Bruckner was in fact mistaken. Theodor Helm reviewed the concert in the *Deutsche Zeitung* and wrote that the Scherzo of the First had made the greatest impact.[192] There was a very positive review by Emil v. Hartmann in the *Deutsche Kunst- und Musikzeitung*, a journal which was sympathetic to the 'new German' direction in general and the *Wagner Society* in particular. Hartmann commended Schalk and Löwe for:

... at least salving the honour of musical Vienna, which has so terribly ignored its native composer who is the most important among living composers for the future of the symphony, by providing superb, finely-conceived interpretations of a few of his orchestral

189 See *LBSAB*, 74-75 for this letter dated Vienna, 13 December 1884; the original is in the *ÖNB*, F18 Schalk 158/5/22.

190 See *HSABB* 1, 233 for this letter dated Vienna, 24 December 1884. The original is in the *Museum für Geschichte der Stadt Leipzig*, and there is a facsimile of the autograph in *LABL*, 26.

191 See *HSABB* 1, 234 for this letter dated Vienna, 26 December 1884; the original is in the *ÖNB*, F18 Schalk 151/2/2/1.

192 *Deutsche Zeitung* 4660 (24 December 1884).

works.[193]

Another review in the *Allgemeine Kunst-Chronik* described Schalk and Löwe as 'artistic apostles', young men who were 'working with touching devotion and enthusiasm for the revered Bruckner'.[194]

Perhaps the most interesting review was that of the young Hugo Wolf in the *Wiener Salonblatt.* Wolf had possibly heard earlier piano and two-piano performances of Bruckner's works. Although by no means an uncritical admirer of the older composer, he took the musical authorities to task for not giving more frequent orchestral performances of Bruckner's symphonies:

> ...Bruckner, this Titan in conflict with the gods, must be content with trying to communicate his music to the public from the piano. It's a miserable business, but better than not being heard at all. And when our unlucky fellow has the good luck to find such enthusiastic interpreters as Löwe and Schalk, then we must count him at least partially compensated for the unjust procedure of our fashionable musical institutions.
>
> I have just spoken of Herr Bruckner as a Titan in conflict with the gods. I could not, in truth, think of a more appropriate metaphor with which to characterize this composer, combining as it does both praise and disparagement in equal portions: raw material forces against the predominance of the intellect. Translated into the terminology of art, it reveals an extraordinary native artistic endowment in all its freshness, incompatible with the musical sensibility, the intelligence, the manifestations of a level of cultivation, characteristic of our time. These are the principal elements in the work of this composer, and they find themselves, unfortunately, at loggerheads. Had Bruckner ever succeeded in achieving their reconciliation, he would have become, without doubt, a great figure approaching the significance of Liszt...
>
> Thus he wavers, rooted halfway between Beethoven and the new

---

193 *Deutsche Kunst- und Musikzeitung* xii (1 January 1885), 3. Quoted in *LBSAB*, 77f.

194 *Allgemeine Kunst-Chronik* (17 January 1885).

advances of the moderns, the latter represented most successfully and vividly in Liszt's symphonic poems, unable to decide for the one or the other. That is his misfortune. I do not hesitate, however, to describe Bruckner's symphonies as the most important symphonic creations to have been written since Beethoven...

It would certainly be rewarding, then, to give this inspired evangelist more attention than has been accorded him hitherto. It is a truly shocking sight to see this extraordinary man barred from the concert hall. Among living composers (excepting Liszt, of course) he has the first and greatest claim to be performed and admired.[195]

While in Leipzig Bruckner demonstrated his skill as an organist by improvising on the *Gewandhaus* organ. The performance of the Seventh Symphony at the Town Theatre in Leipzig on 30 December had a mixed response. Indeed, as Leibnitz points out, there seem to be two conflicting versions of what actually happened.[196] On the one hand, there is the version in the Göllerich-Auer biography in which some displeasure among the public is conceded but the overall impression is one of great success, with 30 December being described as the 'birthday of Bruckner's world fame'.[197] On the other hand there are Franz Schalk's two reports, the first to his brother Joseph which has been lost,[198] and the second to his friend Richard Spur in Vienna in which he mentions lack of receptivity among certain members of the

---

195 Extract from review which appeared in the *Wiener Salonblatt* (28 December 1884). Quoted from Henry Pleasants, *The Music Criticism of Hugo Wolf* (New York: Holmes and Meier, 1979), 98f.

196 See *LBSAB*, 79.

197 See *G-A* IV/2, 213.

198 In a letter to Franz, written over two days (30 and 31 December 1884), Joseph renewed an earlier request for a report of the performance. On 3 January 1885, Joseph acknowledged receipt of Franz's report and asked him for more details, for instance the effect of the Finale. See *FSBB*, 44f. and *LBSAB* 78ff. for these two letters, the originals of which are in the *ÖNB*, F18 Schalk 158/5/24 and F18 Schalk 158/6/1.

public and indeed Bruckner's 'desperation' after the performance.[199]

In spite of Schalk's reservations, the critical reaction appears to have been favourable on the whole. Writing in the *Leipziger Neueste Nachrichten*, which had prepared its readers for the premiere of the symphony in two earlier articles,[200] Bernhard Vogel first congratulated Nikisch on having the courage of his convictions in performing the work of a composer who was already 'standing on the threshold of old age' and had still not attained 'the degree of general recognition which he certainly would have found under normal circumstances'. He then discussed the work in more detail:

> The work itself deserves the highest admiration. In closely following models provided by Berlioz and Liszt in their symphonic poems rather than the example of Beethoven, Bruckner presents us with musical tone pictures in which glowing colour vies with the white heat of inventive power, so that the listener is gripped as if with invisible chains from beginning to end.
>
> Perhaps here and there the symphonic threads become too entangled, with the result that the composer finds it difficult to establish the starting- and finishing-points at the right time; perhaps in other passages he may proceed too aphoristically and pay homage to an unusual and remarkable musical logic which frequently bars the way to a clear understanding and a convenient overview of the whole process of musical thought... But of what importance is that in view of the high level of artistic integrity recognizable in all four movements, in view of an almost youthful freshness of musical invention and a genuine, natural empathy with Berlioz, Liszt and, above all, Wagner, by virtue of which he stands out like a giant above the crowd of those pygmies who believe that they have

---

199 See *HSABB* 1, 236f. for this letter dated Dresden, 19 January 1885; the original is in the *ÖNB*, F18 Schalk 36a.

200 These appeared in the paper on Wednesday 24 December and Tuesday 30 December 1884 respectively. See *LABL*, 38.

achieved something splendid when they repeat parrot-fashion what these composers have already said more strikingly and powerfully. Anton Bruckner is a self-contained and highly individual artist. If one were to desire anything different from him one would be asking him to be untrue to himself; and he will never do that either now or at any other time. And so we can only express the wish that we will be able to get to know his other symphonies at some time or another in order to learn and appreciate from comparable works the stature of the symphonist who has made such an imposing first appearance here.[201]

The reviewer in the *Neue Zeitschrift für Musik* had more to say about one of the other works in the programme, Liszt's symphonic poem *Les Préludes*, than Bruckner's symphony which he described as 'too spun out' with a mixture of good and 'many really trivial' ideas.[202]

Ernst W. Fritzsch, writing in the *Musikalisches Wochenblatt*, was more complimentary. After praising Nikisch's choice of programme which was much more progressive in outlook than usual, he turned his attention to Bruckner's work:

> ... The symphony was of great interest and its 2nd and 3rd movements, the Adagio and Scherzo, excited our warmest admiration. This composer knows how to say something truly original and impressive and his work is distinguished by an unusual originality of musical ideas. He is at his most profound in the Adagio, a most beautiful movement which reveals truly Beethovenian sublimity in the invention of its main themes and keeps the listener in suspense right to the end of the solemn funeral hymn at the close. The Scherzo, a model of fluent productive energy and orchestrally conceived through and through, is equally original. In the first and fourth movements the listener has the impression in a few places that the logical thread of development has been interrupted, that the individual sections

---

201 From Vogel's review in the *Leipziger Neueste Nachrichten*, 1 January 1885. See *G-A* IV/2, 214ff. and *LABL*, 48f.

202 From Johann F. Schucht's review in the *Neue Zeitschrift für Musik* 81 (9 January 1885), 17.

are only superficially connected and the symphonic flow has come unstuck. As far as content is concerned, both these movements are of great interest; indeed they have a wealth of ideas for which the composer is to be envied. The expressive power of this symphony is heightened by its brilliant instrumentation. Mr. Nikisch, the conductor, had rehearsed the new work admirably.

The performance was immensely successful and the orchestra deserves the highest praise. The composer, who was present, was called out at the end of the Finale of his most striking work and received two laurel wreaths, an honour that was highly deserved...[203]

Hans Merian, the critic for the *Leipziger Tageblatt und Anzeiger*, was less impressed:

The performance of this work, the composer's Seventh Symphony, did not really fulfil expectations, and the public which consisted for the most part of those sympathetic to the Wagnerian direction, responded rather coolly. While it must be said primarily in its praise that it is orchestrated with care and great skill, it is lacking, nevertheless, in unity of thought. The work is shot through with numerous reminiscences of Wagner's compositions, an almost unavoidable feature of Wagnerian imitations.

The first movement, for instance, ends with music which reminds us of the 'fire magic' from *Die Walküre*. But it lacks the strictly logical thematic development and the true polyphonic texture which is peculiar to the works of the Bayreuth master. Bruckner, in common with the majority of the Wagner imitators, has to be reminded continually of the maxim: many parts sounding together do not constitute polyphony. The character of the entire work is more theatrical-dramatic than symphonic and the impression it makes is as if someone is sitting at the piano indulging in a free fantasia on well-known themes which are developed and interwoven without any purpose. The sound is beautiful but there is no clear objective.[204]

---

203 See *G-A* IV/2, 216ff. and facsimile of original in *LABL*, 46f.

204 From Hans Merian's review in the *Leipziger Tageblatt und Anzeiger* 79/1 (1 January 1885). See *LABL*, 45.

There were more factual reports of the concert in the *Deutsche Zeitung*, the *Deutsche Kunst- und Musikzeitung* and the *Kölnische Zeitung*. The report in the *Deutsche Kunst- und Musikzeitung* was provided by Franz Schalk and signed by him although it was largely the work of Joseph Schalk who edited it for publication. In his letter to Spur on 19 January, Franz explained:

> I must decline the praise of my review - no matter how difficult I find it. My brother deserves it. I wrote only a few lines (because I did not enjoy the task) and they can only be regarded as the embryo of an article.[205]

The review reported a considerable success and Leibnitz remarks that this was probably a deliberate attempt to suppress anything negative and, in a sense, to manipulate a favourable reaction in Vienna:

> We encounter here that characteristic mentality which is a distinguishing feature, like a leitmotiv, of the Schalk-Bruckner relationship. Bruckner had to be helped to success, if necessary, through personal interventions (made with the best of intentions) which extended later not only to reviews but also to the works themselves.[206]

Schalk was at pains to underline the great originality of the symphony:

> ... On first hearing this work one cannot fail to be astonished by the power and magnitude as well as by the nobility and originality of the ideas. By understanding the content we will be guarded from the error of describing the work superficially as Wagnerian, and the boldness of harmony and modulation may easily mislead us into

---

205 See page 426, footnote 199.

206 See *LBSAB*, 80.

believing this to be true. But these are achievements of the modern period in general and t heir artistic value is determined primarily by the way in which they are used. Right at the outset the first theme of the opening movement begins with long-held breath and rises up as if out of a new, undreamt-of world. Its true character, like that of the majority of Bruckner's most beautiful ideas, is one of sublime peace, a peace replete with the deepest emotion which immediately causes us to feel truly liberated as only the most genuine art can do. Radiance and melodiousness surround the musical soul of this song and lift us up gradually to that realm of cheerful heavenly serenity which is occupied by the second theme and even more by the third...

A realm of the most solemn mourning is disclosed to us in the second movement (Adagio). Begun full of foreboding in January 1883, this Adagio was completed under the shattering influence of the report of Richard Wagner's death. It has been said of the second theme - and justifiably so - that it can only be compared with Beethoven's greatest inspirations. A brilliant *fortissimo* chord insistently repeated in a biting rhythm appears to guard the gates of this paradise like the flaming sword of the cherubim, and we are allowed only a moment to tarry blissfully in these Elysian fields.

It is easier for us to give verbal expression to our feelings in listening to the first two movements. In the Scherzo we are confronted with the inexplicable, incomprehensible side of the musician who is continually drawing up new things from the deepest depths when our poetic imaginative faculty threatens to abandon us. And it is so much in evidence in this movement that the rhythmical and dynamic effect is quite baffling. The rhythm is truly orgiastic, but it should be noted that this is the result of simple basic elemental power, not the artificial combination of syncopations of which we have had a surfeit in the modern period...

Suffused with the same all-powerful rhythm, the first theme of the Finale now strides boldly forth, and it gives us pleasure to be made aware of its relationship with the main theme of the first movement. In this transformation it seemed to join with us, as it were, in the deep experiences of the Adagio and Scherzo, and now it storms through all the regions of this ocean of sound with intensified spiritual power and freedom. Very little space is given to a gentle second theme and this makes us more calmly aware of the new power. An unceasing climactic process reaches its victorious peak by means of the entry of the opening motive of the first movement in brilliant *fortissimo...*[207]

Elisabeth Herzogenberg seems to have been the spokeswoman for those in Leipzig who reacted against the favourable publicity given to Bruckner at the time. She and her husband found the Seventh Symphony a dreadful and insignificant work and had no sympathy for the composer[208]. As a keen Brahms devotee she wrote on more than one occasion to Brahms, asking him what he thought of Bruckner. He refused to say anything about his music, except to point out that one of Bruckner's symphonies and his Quintet had been printed and that she should form her own opinion. About Bruckner the person:

> He is a poor crazy man whom the St. Florian priests have on their conscience. I don't know if you have any conception of what it means to have spent your youth with priests. I could tell you one or two things about Bruckner. But I should not even be talking about such nasty things with you.[209]

The day after his review appeared in the *Deutsche Kunst- und Musikzeitung*, Joseph Schalk reported to his brother that he and Löwe had recently gone through the score of the Seventh with Bruckner in order to make a few alterations and improvements. He also mentioned his delight that Nikisch had approved of their suggestion that a cymbal clash be added at the climactic point in the Adagio (C

---

207 Extract from review ('Musikbrief aus Leipzig') as printed in *G-A* IV/2, 220-24 and *LBSAB*, 83-86.

208 This information was provided in a letter from Konrad Fiedler to Adolf Hildebrand; see *G-A* IV/2, 278.

209 From Brahms's letter to Elisabeth Herzogenberg, 12 January 1885. See Max Kalbeck, ed., *The Herzogenberg Correspondence* (London, 1909). See also *G-A* IV/2, 240f.

432

major chord 6/4 chord also involving triangle and timpani).[210]

Unaware that Joseph had been largely responsible for the article, Bruckner wrote to Franz, thanking him profusely and mentioning a second performance of the Adagio and Scherzo movements in Leipzig. He also took the opportunity to send his belated congratulations:

> As you have almost certainly taken up your position in the *Residenztheater* by now, please permit me to offer you my heartiest congratulations!
> My apologies for delaying my departure from Leipzig until 10 in the evening and not taking the early train - perhaps you had a fruitless wait for me. I was trying to find a publisher, but without success.
> I can find no words to describe the *most splendid* article that has ever been written about me! It was inspired to the highest degree! I embrace you a thousand times for it, my noblest of friends! It's a pity that this article did not appear in the *Deutsche Zeitung*!!
> Next Wednesday, the 28th, the two middle movements will be performed for a second time. I hope you don't think it impertinent of me to ask you to be so good as to send perhaps a short extract from the most recent article in the *Deutsche Kunst- und Musik-Zeitung* of 9 January or else something entirely new to Dr. Helm for the *Deutsche Zeitung* which is widely read - but only if you feel inspired to do so, my dearest Franz. This is a very sincere request; it doesn't matter how brief it is...[211]

Leading representatives of the main publishing houses, Peters and Breitkopf &

---

210 See *FSBB*, 48ff. and *LBSAB*, 81ff. for this letter dated Vienna, 10 January 1885; the original is in the *ÖNB*, F18 Schalk 158/6/2.

211 See *HSABB* 1, 237f. for this letter dated Vienna, 23 January 1885; the original is in the *ÖNB*, F18 Schalk 54/2. The second performance of the middle movements of the symphony took place in Leipzig on 27 January 1885 in the presence of King Albert and Queen Carola of Saxony who were visiting Leipzig.

Härtel, had been invited to the Leipzig performance. In spite of Nikisch's recommendation and Bruckner's own visits to the publishing houses before he returned to Vienna, no interest was shown.

When Franz told his brother that he was embarrassed by Bruckner's effusive praise, Joseph replied that it was better to leave Bruckner in the dark about the true authorship of the article, particularly as others were just as unaware of what had happened.[212]

In the meantime, as Joseph informed Franz on 10 January, the Hellmesberger Quartet had given the first major performance of Bruckner's String Quintet in the large *Musikverein* hall on 8 January. The Viennese critics on the whole were well disposed towards Bruckner. Even Max Kalbeck was able to muster up some enthusiasm for the Adagio movement:

> ... We do not begrudge the good old man his fine success and only wish that the friends of his music had as honourable intentions towards him as we do. However, our personal feelings must not tempt us to use other yardsticks to measure him by than his brothers in counterpoint. When we see the well-rounded man, his face aglow with unfathomable happiness, standing before us and compare this reassuring picture with the violent outbursts of his art, we are disconcerted and ask how it is possible for this devout and upright person to be able to express such an ambiguous truth which can scarcely be distinguished from a lie... To be sure, Bruckner is by far the most dangerous of today's composers, his ideas cannot be fathomed, and that which cannot be construed possesses a magical, seductive power which causes greater damage than the refined and laboriously entangled sophistries of others. What he provides is music of pure revelation, as he has received it from above or below, without any profane addition of worldly logic, art and good sense. According to legend it is said of St. Chrysosthomus that the apostles John and Peter visited him in the form of two angels and handed to him the

---

212 See *LBSAB*, 87f. for this letter dated Vienna, 25 January 1885; the original is in the *ÖNB*, F18 Schalk 158/6/4.

keys of the secrets of scripture as well as power over the hearts of the faithful. Our composer may have had a rare visit of that kind from time to time. And if it was not always two of God's messengers who came down to him, perhaps it was an angel and a demon who quarrelled for his soul. Too weak to make a decisive choice between them, he lent them both his ear and their insinuations were conscientiously recorded on the five-line system - the only one that Bruckner knows. His music smells of heavenly roses and reeks of infernal sulphur; just a little connecting incense in between and we would have a ready-made mystic.

The F major Quintet is a mixed sequence of musical hallucinations, an apocalypse in four chapters the unravelling of which would require a new subsidiary work. If Bruckner was in the position to compose this explanatory work he would possibly be one of the greatest composers. Bright ideas spring up everywhere but most of them fizzle out like sheet lightning at night and do not emerge from the darkness. The Moderato of the first movement displays only an outward moderation in the prescribed rhythm; all the elements of music are to be found in the wildest turmoil here. The harmony disowns any connection with the tonal basis and the tonality's only proof of identity is the key-signature and the final cadence. As soon as it reaches its second step the declamatory main theme falls into an abyss and the rocking subsidiary theme begins cheerfully, as if nothing has happened, in F sharp major after the bass has 'mistakenly' slipped down a semitone from its C major cadence. The dynamics change just as capriciously and arbitrarily. There is hardly a bar in which the composer has not stipulated a new quantity or quality of sound, from *ppp* to *fff*. In between we find not only the Italian abbreviations in general use but also special markings like 'ohne Aufschwellung' ['without swelling'], 'gezogen' [drawn out], 'langgezogen' ['long drawn out'], 'breit gestrichen' ['with long bow-strokes'], 'sehr zart' ['very soft'], 'hervortretend' ['prominent'], 'markirt' ['accented'], 'ohne jede Markirung' ['without any accent'] and 'sanft hervortretend' ['gently emphasised']. Of what help is all this signalling and indicating if the relevant passages do not emerge naturally and speak for themselves? We could do without the development section - insofar as one can give this name to such a jumble of asthmatic recitatives and thematic sighs, either 'drawn out' or 'with long bow-strokes'; its music seems to us to be - to make use

of a German turn of phrase - rough-hewn and untidy.[213]
We can cope much better with the Scherzo. The sweet Trio
recompenses us for the bitter humour of the main movement which
provides us with vinegar in place of wine; it has a short but richly
sonorous melody, full or spirit and good humour. The Finale begins
with a dance of unclean spirits which assaults the listener like a swarm
of melancholy ideas: doubt and care for nothing and against nothing;
useless mosquitoes which blot out the light of the sun. How it spins
and surges, gives off a lot of smoke and dust and becomes bloated
with ephemeral importance. Deceptive organ points add a dissonant
droning bass. A quaver figure, a sequence of major sixths, appears as
both a melody- and subsidiary part and, after it has been prolonged by
means of the most varied harmonic events, a hulking great fugato
stumbles in and gives the signal for a universal contrapuntal
bloodbath. Woe to the poor melody which is subjected to these
sharply whetted, blindly raging, murderous violins bows! It is hung,
drawn and quartered, cut into pieces...
　　If these three movements have their origin in hell, the Adagio (3rd
movement) comes directly from paradise. Pure light in a thousand
colours and nuances streams forth from it. It is the reflection of an
ecstatic vision reaching to the seventh heaven. We think of these
terze rime of Dante sweeping upwards to the 'eternal circles', of that
wonderful, profound passage which Goethe may have had in mind in
his *Chorus mysticus*: the poet sees Beatrice who looks up at the sun
with a steadfast gaze and receives the heavenly light through the eye
of her lover; a new day breaks for him and, lost in contemplation of
her radiant countenance, he ascends to the delights of paradise. To
experience its luminous power to the full, one must hear the broadly-
flowing radiant song as played on Hellmesberger's violin. The much
experienced quartet leader cleverly moved the Adagio forward to the
second movement so that it came just at the right time to recompense
the listeners handsomely for the torments suffered in the Allegro...[214]

Writing from an equally conservative standpoint in the *Wiener Allgemeine Zeitung*,
Gustav Dömpke referred first of all somewhat dismissively to the obvious points of

---

213 'nicht gehau'n und nicht gestochen'.

214 From review in *Die Presse* (12 January 1885), as printed in *G-A* IV/2, 250-55.

contact between Bruckner's Quintet and the music of the 'New German School' in terms of 'unnatural harmonic sequences and formal structure' but conceded that there were many fine passages, particularly in the Adagio:

If the Bruckner F major Quintet had succumbed to the Wagnerian influence completely, we could have written a short obituary notice. But it contains phrases, passages and sections which provide evidence of such an unmistakably independent, individual and significant talent that their combination with so many of a contrary nature constitutes one of the most remarkable problems in contemporary music. What was the clearest testimony against the validity of its success with the public, however, was the almost equal volume of applause after all four movements, even although everyone who studies the work a little more closely will find that the Adagio is superior in every respect to all the other movements. The first movement begins immediately with a theme which could easily lead anyone who has not heard any other Bruckner composition to make the mistake of regarding it as a pointless exercise as early as the tenth bar. However, this forced thematic structure, without any trace of a firm harmonic basis, and these weakly dissolving opening sequences are so characteristic of the new school's conception of tonality, paradoxical as they may be in the context of a movement which has yet to be developed, that every hope of any further communication is apparently ruled out. And yet the same Moderato contains not only this theme which takes up half of the movement and only has to show itself to guarantee torment and boredom, but also a gentle and rather unusual subsidiary theme (F sharp major as opposed to F major) which unfortunately gets caught up too soon in pointless modulations. Also in the bridge passages between these two themes there is occasional evidence of a special, if somewhat muddled, mind at work. As each of his movements must traverse more or less all twenty-four keys and that these are by no means sufficient to express his inner feelings goes without saying as far as Bruckner is concerned; the boldest manoeuvres, as they appear occasionally in particular places in late Beethoven, are a small thing to him.

Hellmesberger did well to follow this morbid opening movement with the Adagio and not the Scherzo as originally conceived. Recuperation was certainly necessary. But this Adagio in G flat major is far more than a small dose of medicine, a temporary source of relief for the feverish. It is the cure itself. Indeed it seems to me to be a piece of music which excels all the other instrumental compositions of the present time in invention and deeply-felt ensemble writing (with the exception, of course, of the one great composer who is incomparable). There is only one ill-sounding passage in it (bars 91-95, p. 39 in the score) which is no less violent harmonically than the other movements. These few bars sound as if the composer of the Adagio had written them in a dream or as if he was not responsible for them at all. On the other hand, of course, this entire Adagio sounds as if it has been composed by a composer other than that of the Allegro movements. So much maturity and refinement are intertwined here in the boldest and most unusual ways. When one hears the first expansive, magnificently-formed theme, how it unfolds in quiet majesty for twelve bars, how it rises to a splendid climax and then sinks to the depths again, one can scarcely believe one's ears; one is even more surprised when the movement maintains the same high level, with a few minor exceptions, almost from beginning to end. After a long stretch of development, it comes to a beautiful and majestic conclusion with a noble figure in the second violin. There is truly something of the divine spark in this Adagio.

It is difficult to do justice in a few words to the last two movements which again plunge down precipitously, but without sinking quite so low as the opening Moderato. Although offensive on the whole, not only do they contain many noticeably positive sections, the Trio of the Scherzo and the lovely second theme of the Finale, for instance, but, even with their droll impudence, there is something strangely different about them. As in the first movement they are at their most unbearable in betraying almost from beginning to end the bad influence of Wagner, namely his harmony and so-called dramatic polyphony. The first theme of the Finale is also directly reminiscent of the Fight Scene in *Die Meistersinger*.

It is obvious that the work as a whole, which is without precedent in chamber music, can only be compared with one or two of Bruckner's symphonies of which, not without reason, only a small number have become known. It would be absurd to hope for a purification process to take place in Bruckner's works, because he is 60 years of age and turning grey in the admiration of his ideal [composer]. We cannot measure what contribution he would have made to music if he had followed less untrustworthy stars...[215]

Ludwig Speidel's review in the *Wiener Fremdenblatt* and Theodor Helm's in the *Deutsche Zeitung* were much more appreciative. According to Speidel, many in the audience were pleasantly surprised by the work which was given a superb performance by Hellmesberger and his quartet:

> The Quintet was not entirely new to us. We had already heard the two middle movements, the Scherzo and the Adagio, and these two movements have remained our favourites now that we know the whole work. In the first movement the principal theme with its triplet tailpiece lets us know right away in what direction Bruckner is marching, and in the Finale we are confronted with the seven-league boots' motive from Richard Wagner's 'Faust' overture. The detailed working-out is masterly, of course, but we wish that the different sections of the composition were drawn together more tightly and, in particular, the structure was more open and pliable, especially in those places where the significance of the motives in no way compensates for the lack of coordination. Modulatory freedom is pushed to the limit throughout the work. Indeed the last movement, which is obviously intended to be in F minor (with the exception of the final bars where there is a return to F major) does not declare itself to be in this key at any point but travels *incognito* and in disguise like a great lord. (This movement also oscillates enharmonically between A flat minor and E major in places.)
>
> The Scherzo, which benefits from a more tightly-knit structure, is a most interesting and charming movement with an original bass - a minor-major scale which strides through two-and-a-half octaves - , melodious part-writing and a pleasantly tuneful Trio. The Adagio is an outpouring of pure song - heartfelt and yearning but with bitter interludes. The movement begins in G flat major, the key most distant from F major according to the circle of fifths. But the whole work is, of course, pervaded by a system of harmonic changes, a device used by Bruckner frequently and always with characteristic effect. The

---

215 From review in the *Wiener Allgemeine Zeitung* (17 January 1885) as reprinted in Louis, *Anton Bruckner*, 313-17; there is also an extract in *G-A* IV/2, 255-59.

relationship between G flat and F is naturally the same as that between E flat and D in the Trio. The originality of invention and an equally original technique compensate for this harmonic licence and boldness which, in any case, is no longer too drastic for a generation trained in dangerous musical procedures. We cannot compare Bruckner's Quintet with any other contemporary composition; it is quite unique. (Bruckner's Quintet has appeared in print, in a beautifully-produced edition published by Gutmann in Vienna, and in dedicated to Duke Max Emanuel of Bavaria)...[216]

Helm had no compunction in describing the Quintet as 'indisputably one of the most important works to have appeared in the realm of modern chamber music', and confessed that he had been 'completely overwhelmed' by the performance:

... The crown, or rather the musical heart, of the whole work is the Adagio in G flat major. Can one name a slow movement written by any other living composer which is superior to this one in spontaneous warmth and melodic intensity, in solemnity, nobility of soul, gentleness and enchanting sonority? When this heavenly instrumental song begins with the great melody on first violin, an almost inexhaustible fountain of the noblest feelings is opened up to us, and when the piece finally evaporates atomically, as it were (how beautiful the voice-leading in the second violin!), we feel that we ourselves have been 'dissolved' and have been removed from all earthly tribulation. This Adagio in G flat can be compared only with Beethoven's most sublime (in his last quartets), with Schubert's sweetest and with Wagner's most transfigured (for instance, in the Prelude to the Third Act of *Die Meistersinger* to which it is related in mood). But the other movements of the Quintet are full of individual charm, in other words the thematic invention is most successful throughout...
      We wish to make a formal apology here for treating the Finale somewhat harshly after our first hearing of it. It is not only the equal of the earlier movements in musical importance but also contains some of the finest pages in the score. Bruckner's contrapuntal skill,

---

216 From review in the *WienerFremdenblatt* (17 January 1885) as reprinted in Louis, op.cit., 312f. and in *G-A* IV/2, 259ff.

displayed in the combination of broadly-bowed crotchets and a triplet motive, is triumphant here; it achieves the most superb climactic processes.

We know only too well all the objections that can be raised to Bruckner's Quintet, or at least its outer movements. The composer's rich inventive and masterly creative powers do not wholly correspond to his artistic understanding and his logical method. From time to time he gives too much scope to his unusually vivid imagination which often erupts in sudden flights of fancy. No doubt aware of his unusual contrapuntal skill he also pushes polyphony to its limits and has far too great expectations of the receptive ability of his listeners. How good it is, however, to meet once again a naive composer, in the best sense of the word - one who does not brood but creates out of inner necessity, who speaks his own language, a language in which we hear not only an imposing individual personality but also the musical achievements of our century, a real and genuine development. Only those people who were really narrow-minded would take it amiss that Bruckner has availed himself not only of the Classical composers, in particular Beethoven whom he worships, but the rich harmonic language of Wagner and other modern composers as well, and that he creates Wagnerian storm and stress both in his symphonies and in his Quintet...

The success of Bruckner's Quintet in Hellmesberger's soirée was a splendid one, perhaps surpassing all the expectations of the composer and his friends. There was repeated tumultuous acclaim for the composer as early as after the first movement, and this applause, which was unanimous and not just the response of a few enthusiasts, increased after the wonderful Adagio and at the end of the work.

The splendid Scherzo, which is always structurally the most lucid and rounded movement in Bruckner's works, was unusually the least successful. It seems that the public was not able fully to appreciate Bruckner's harmonic boldness in moving impetuously towards the final D major cadence by way of the notes a - e - f sharp. However, as has been mentioned already, the overall success of the new work was the most splendid imaginable and, since by a stroke of good fortune our inspired compatriot won a no less glorious victory in front of the less receptive Leipzig public a few days earlier, we no longer give up hope of seeing the name 'Anton Bruckner' firmly established in our regular concert repertoire.

In any case Bruckner can no longer be ignored even by the very conservative critics in Vienna after the memorable performance of his Quintet on 8 January 1885.[217]

There were further reviews, more or less favourable, in other Viennese journals as well as a report of the concert by Count Ferdinand P. Laurencin d'Armond, a Wagner and Liszt enthusiast, which appeared later in the *Neue Zeitschrift für Musik* and, while praising the Adagio movement, was critical of Bruckner's 'stumbling around from one thematic embryo to another'.[218]

Reviewing recent performances of Bruckner's works in Vienna, namely Löwe's and Schalk's piano-duet concert in the *Bösendorfersaal* and the Hellmesberger Quartet concert, Hans Paumgartner criticised the 'learned musicians of the Court Opera Orchestra' for their inability to evaluate the true worth of Bruckner's symphonies and for forcing him to 'eat the bread of artistic exile' as a result of their refusal to perform his works. He compared them unfavourably with their fellow musicians in Leipzig and Munich, particularly as there was a great barrenness of symphonic art in Vienna at the time and the 'living fountain of Bruckner's creations would be doubly welcome'.[219]

Helm's hope that Bruckner's works would now be played more regularly in

---

217 From review in the *Deutsche Zeitung* (14 January 1885) as reprinted in *G-A* IV/2, 261-65. On 24 January, Bruckner wrote Helm a letter of profuse thanks, thanking him for supporting him in these 'so sad times', describing his words as 'precious jewels' and asking him to include a short report of the performance of the two middle movements of the Seventh in Leipzig on 28 January which, he hoped, Franz Schalk would send from Dresden; see *HSABB* 1, 238 for this letter, the original of which is in the *ÖNB*.

218 See Louis, op.cit., 319 and *G-A* IV/2, 266f. for this review which appeared originally in the *Neue Zeitschrift für Musik* 81 (29 May 1885), 244. Count Ferdinand Peter Laurencin d'Armond (1819-1890) was a musicologist and music critic. He worked for the *Neue Zeitschrift für Musik* where his articles often appeared under the pseudonym 'Philokales'.

219 Paumgartner's report in the *Wiener Abendpost* (13 January 1885); see Tschulik, op.cit., 173f.

Vienna as a result of the successful performance of the Quintet took some time to be fulfilled. On the other hand, more and more interest was being shown in his works in Germany and beyond. In letters to his sister Rosalie and to Dr. Prohaska, the president of the Linz *Musikverein*, Bruckner mentioned the two Leipzig performances and the forthcoming Munich and Hamburg performances of the Seventh Symphony as well as a recent performance of the Third Symphony in The Hague, Holland.[220] The performance in The Hague on 4 February 1885, which marked the beginning of a strong Dutch connection with Bruckner's works, was conducted by Johannes Verhulst, but the men responsible for stimulating interest in Bruckner's works in Holland were Dr. W.L. van Meurs, a librarian by profession, and H.A. Simon, an Austrian who was a member of the *Musikverein* in The Hague. In February Bruckner wrote an appreciative letter to van Meurs in which he provided details of recent performances of his works, particularly the Quintet, but lamented the general lack of recognition of his music:

> ... Hellmesberger, the court music director, wants to perform it [the Quintet] again in November. He has asked me to write another work for him, called the Quintet a 'revelation' and described me as '*the modern composer*'. 'Vienna could be proud etc. etc.' The Quintet has been published by Gutmann in Vienna (Opera House). Otherwise I am frowned upon by the entire music clique in Vienna (with the exception of the *Deutsche Zeitung, Fremdenblatt, Tageblatt, Morgenpost* and the music journals). No doubt you will understand why. None of my works has been published apart from the Third Symphony and the Quintet. If only I could find a publisher! I am writing my Eighth Symphony at the moment. Mr. Brahms treats me almost with disdain...

---

220 See *HSABB* 1, 238f. and 240 for the texts of these letters, both dated Vienna, 9 February 1885; the original of the former is in the *Gesellschaft der Musikfreunde* library, Vienna, and that of the latter is in the Linz *Singakademie, Frohsinn* archive.

As a postscript, Bruckner provided the additional information that he had 'written nothing for the organ'! Perhaps he meant 'nothing significant'.[221]

In spite of Bruckner's complaints in this letter there was a growing wave of support for him in Vienna. On 22 January 1885 he was elected an honorary member of the *Akademischer Richard-Wagner-Verein*.[222] While he continued to devote most of his non-teaching hours to composition, he played the organ much less frequently except as part of his *Hofkapelle* duties and in church-based performances. Indeed he declined invitations to play the organ in Vienna, Graz and Linz as part of the Bach and Handel bicentenary celebrations in 1885, recommending in his place the blind organist, Joseph Labor, and another Upper Austrian, Joseph Reiter.[223]

The one critic who was conspicuous by his absence from the many reviews of the Quintet in January was Hanslick. Hanslick took the opportunity of combining a review of the work with a review of the performance of Bruckner's male-voice chorus, *Mitternacht* WAB 80, by the *Akademischer Gesangverein* conducted by Rudolf Weinwurm on Sunday 22 February:

> ... To be sure Heuberger [one of whose works was also performed in the second concert] is still a modest spendthrift even in the moments

---

221 See *HSABB* 1, 239f. for this letter dated Vienna, 9 February 1885. The original, which was printed for the first time in *ABB*, 175f., is privately owned. A letter from Ferdinand Löwe to Franz Schalk, dated February 1885, indicates that it was written in response to a letter from van Meurs which has been lost; the original of Löwe's letter is the *ÖNB*, F18 Schalk 97.

222 See *HSABB* 1, 242f. for a letter, dated Vienna 26 February 1885, from the *Akademischer Richard-Wagner-Verein* (signed by the chairman, Dr. Viktor Boller, and the secretary, Prof. Alois Höfler) to Hermann Levi, expressing appreciation of his decision to perform the Seventh in Munich, and mentioning Bruckner's election as an honorary member of the *Verein*; the original is in the *ÖNB*.

223 See, for instance, his letter to Prohaska (footnote 220) in which he declined an invitation from the Linz *Musikverein*.

of most wanton wastefulness when compared with Anton Bruckner who surprises us the most when he remains in the same key for three bars. That is certainly the case in his new [sic] choral piece, *Um* [sic] *Mitternacht*, and consequently we have been pleasantly surprised. The limited vocal range of the male-voice choir has unquestionably curbed Bruckner's roving imagination. The first strophe, by no means long-winded or immoderate in spite of its breadth, has the pure, warm, golden tone of a poetic mood picture. It is a pity that in the very next strophe he sets the words 'die Glockenklänge ferner Dome' ['the bell sounds from the distant cathedral'] very powerfully in a noisy *ff* and, by revelling in this grandeur, has difficulty in bringing his setting of this short and simple poem to a conclusion. Bruckner has become the flavour of the moment and, while I am delighted for this modest artist who has remained unrecognized for many years, I am unable to enjoy this flavour. It remains a psychological puzzle how this gentlest and most peaceable of all men - he is no longer young - becomes, in the act of composition, an anarchist who pitilessly sacrifices everything that is called logic and clarity of development and structural and tonal unity. His music rises up like a shapeless, burning pillar of smoke assuming now this and now that form. It is not without its sparks of genius and there are even some longer passages of beauty. But can one extract the most profound ideas from *Hamlet* and *King Lear* and, to my mind, a few from *Faust* as well, combine them in the most random fashion possible with a variety of flat, confused, interminable speeches and then ask oneself whether it adds up to a work of art?

A most interesting book by Ludwig Nohl, *The historical Development of Chamber Music*, has appeared almost at the same time as Bruckner's F major Quintet published by Gutmann and performed by Hellmesberger to enthusiastic applause. We can help Mr. Nohl; he should have a look at Bruckner's Quintet. He will find there a string quintet 'reduction' of the pure Wagnerian style, the endless melody, the emancipation from all natural laws of modulation, Wotan's pathos, Mime's will-o'-the-wisp humour and Isolde's ecstasy consuming itself in inexhaustible climactic processes. What was sadly missing in Mr. Nohl's book has now been found, and a second edition of his *Development of Chamber Music* can have a closing chapter of glowing transfiguration without which 'development' and 'chamber music' would certainly remain nothing but an 'illusion'...[224]

The first three movements of the Quintet were played again by the Hellmesberger Quartet in a concert in the Linz *Redoutensaal* on 8 March 1885. By this time, however, Bruckner's thoughts were directed elsewhere - to Munich where Levi was to perform his Seventh Symphony two days later, on 10 March.[225] On 25 February he had written to Nikisch in Leipzig, thanking him once again for the December performance and enthusing about Bernhard Vogel's review in the *Leipziger Neueste Nachrichten*. He was not sure if Levi had received the corrected parts:

> ... Mr. Levi still has the corrected score of the 4th Symphony (Romantic). What is the position with the Seventh? Have you been good enough to see to the correction of the parts? Please send the bill. Have you sent them to Hamburg or will you do so later? Does Mr. Levi already have them. I am as ignorant as a child. The 3rd Symphony in D minor was performed in The Hague (Holland). I received marvellous letters. Can a publisher not be found?... I don't know anything about Munich. How were the two movements [the Adagio and Scherzo of the Seventh] received recently?...[226]

Levi had changed his original intention of performing only the Adagio of the Seventh. The successful performance of the work in Leipzig and his own growing appreciation of it had persuaded him that he should rehearse and perform the work

---

224 From Hanslick's review in the *Neue Freie Presse* (26 February 1885) as reprinted in *G-A* IV/2, 270ff.

225 Bruckner wrote to his brother Ignaz in St. Florian on 27 February, asking him to make it known that the Hellmesberger Quartet would be performing his Quintet in Linz on 8 March and that he would be travelling to Munich on Saturday 7 March. See *HSABB* 1, 243 for this letter; the original is privately owned.

226 See *HSABB* 1, 242 for this letter; the original is privately owned.

in its entirety. He informed Bruckner with great enthusiasm that he knew the first and second movements by heart and that he 'hurried from one friend to another' to introduce them to his music.[227] On 27 February Bruckner wrote to Baron von Ostini, the president of the *Munich Wagner Society*, and made specific requests about accommodation, rehearsals and a possible meeting with members of the *Wagner Society*:

> ... As the symphony is to be performed on 10 March, I will arrive in Munich early in the morning of Sunday the 8th and will be staying again at the 'Vier Jahreszeiten'. I have asked the Court Music Director for a couple of rehearsals because there are very many hidden difficulties and such like in the work. There could very well be a rehearsal on the Sunday if Mr. von Levi was agreeable. Could I ask you, Baron Ostini, to intercede on my behalf? A few corrections have also to be made in the score.
> The Landgrave is now better and sends hearty greetings. He also supports my request. In addition he suggested I mention to you that it would be very good if I made the acquaintance of members of the Wagner Society at a special gathering before the concert. If I also met members of the 'Holy Grail' I would make many friends. And so I would be most grateful for your help in this very important matter. I would certainly not put the gentlemen to so much trouble if I did not consider the situation to be so important...[228]

Levi was happy to comply with Bruckner's request for two rehearsals:

---

227 This letter is mentioned in *G-A* IV/2, 273. Its date is not known, but it was probably written during January or February 1885.

228 See *HSABB* 1, 243f. for this letter. It was first published in *GrBLS*, 356f; the original is in private possession. The Landgrave referred to is Landgrave Fürstenberg, and the 'Holy Grail' presumably another Wagner association in Munich with links to the Munich branch of the *Akademischer Richard-Wagner-Verein*.

... In accordance with your wish I have arranged a rehearsal (in the *Odeon Hall*) on Sunday at 10.30 a.m. The final rehearsal will take place on Monday at 10 in the morning. I rehearsed the symphony the day before yesterday. The orchestra was naturally hesitant and didn't understand anything. People here are unbelievably reactionary, of course. But that doesn't matter, provided that they play well - and they will do so. It is just the same with Wagner. (I don't believe that there are as many as 3 Wagnerians in the orchestra!) Take heart and trust me!

I still do not know where to begin with the final movement. But that will come soon, I hope...

Baron Ostini told me of your letter. I will make sure that one or two friends join us on Monday evening...[229]

Although Levi had offered Bruckner accommodation in his own house, the composer and Friedrich Eckstein, who accompanied him from Vienna, decided to stay in a hotel called 'Vier Jahreszeiten', as Bruckner pointed out to Baron von Ostini. His early arrival enabled him to explain one or two difficult passages in the Finale to Levi before the Sunday rehearsal. Consequently the work was well rehearsed both on the Sunday and on the Monday prior to the performance on Tuesday 10 March.

As well as Eckstein, three of Bruckner's young friends - Joseph Schalk, Ferdinand Löwe and Carl Almeroth - came to Munich for the performance which was, by all accounts, most successful. Joseph wrote to Franz enthusiastically about it as well as providing some interesting snippets of information about Bruckner's time in Munich:

... The success was truly splendid. Levi showed a remarkable amount of understanding and care. Unfortunately we did not attend any of the rehearsals. We were very pleased with the performance. The first

---

229 See *HSABB* 1, 244 for this letter from Levi to Bruckner dated Munich, 4 March 1885; the original is in St. Florian.

movement was taken too fast for my liking, however, and, as a result, was the one least understood by the audience. Many of the Munich musicians are really enthusiastic, particularly Porges who wrote a very fine review for the *Munch'ner Nachrichten*. Bruckner is overjoyed. Everything is going well as far as the planned dedication to the king is concerned. Intendant Perfall has assured Bruckner of his special goodwill on several occasions. All in all, the whole Munich affair looks like a triumphant procession for Bruckner. He has been honoured to a surprising extent in all artistic circles (banquets, laurel wreaths). Kaulbach has painted his portrait, Hanfstängl has taken his photograph and Leipzig has receded very much into the background as a result of all this. Nikisch did not bring the work to life in any way whatsoever. The fact that the orchestral parts of the symphony were still teeming with mistakes in Munich casts a strange light on the entire Leipzig performance. The Finale made a very great impression on me here. The wind produced an overwhelming effect. Bruckner has fallen in love with the tubas and their players. The day after the performance we also heard an excellent performance (without cuts) of *Die Walküre*. After the opera finished the wind players were most happy to comply with Bruckner's wish that they play the funeral music from the Adagio once again in the theatre as soon as the audience had left. He did not give up until they had played the passage three times altogether. That they did it at all after the exertions of the evening is the finest testimony to their respect and admiration for Bruckner...[230]

In his review in the *Münchner Neueste Nachrichten*, Heinrich Porges went so far as to claim that the work took a place of pre-eminence among the symphonic

---

[230] See *FSBB*, 50f. and *LBSAB*, 88f. for this letter dated Vienna, 16 March 1885; the original is in the ÖNB, F18 Schalk 158/1/11. Hermann Kaulbach (1846-1909) was a Munich artist who specialized in genre and historical paintings. His portrait of Bruckner, signed 'H. Kaulbach 11 März 1885' can be found in the *Oberösterreichisches Landesmuseum*, Linz (Sign. G297). See Renate Grasberger, 'Bruckner-Ikonographie Teil I: Um 1854 bis 1924', *ABDS* 7 (Linz, 1990), 26 and 118 for reproductions. Franz Hanfstängl (1804-1877) was official photographer to the Prussian court. His son Edgar took over his photography business in 1863. Copies of Edgar Hanfstängl's photograph of Bruckner can be found in the *Oberösterreichisches Landesmuseum*, Linz (Sign. PF III 18/6) and the *Historisches Museum der Stadt Wien* (I.N. 57.079). See Grasberger, op.cit., 26 for reproductions.

compositions of the last 20 years and that Bruckner had successfully combined the essential features of the Beethovenian symphony with the new developments made by Berlioz, Liszt and Wagner and fused them into a style distinctively his own. He described Bruckner as a composer 'who does not have to try to be clever in order to make something great out of small, trifling themes, but whose original conception already shows an instinctive feeling for the truly great':

> What speaks to us from the broadly flowing songs of the Bruckner symphony and almost compels us to join sympathetically in the experience is the breathing of a musical soul which is striving to embrace the universe. With the Adagio, a truly inspired funeral song, Bruckner has written his name for ever in the golden book of music.
> The vigorous themes of the genuinely Beethovenian Scherzo are filled with the elemental power of true Germanic humour. The structure of the first movement is surprising. It does not conform to any stereotype and yet there is a logical consistency about its development. There is a great freshness about the Finale. Here as in the other movements Bruckner demonstrates his masterly organization and control of large-scale periodic structure...[231]

In the first part of his review in the *Süddeutsche Presse*, Fritz von Ostini, Karl's son, reminded his readers how little-known Bruckner had been in Munich prior to the performance and how astonished a large part of the public were at the end when they saw not a young man coming to the front to acknowledge the applause but 'an unpretentious older man with sparkling eyes and beaming face receiving it and then transferring it modestly and gratefully to our fine orchestra and its excellent conductor'. In discussing the symphony, Ostini was just as concerned as Porges to underline the high quality of musical invention throughout:

---

231 From Porges's review in the *Münchner Neueste Nachrichten* (12 March 1885); see *G-A* IV/2, 289ff.

... And what an abundance of feeling, spirit and life is contained in this symphony! Nothing is contrived, everything is felt in the most profound musical soul. No meagre thoughts are treated, turned and twisted in skilful fashion in order to prolong proceedings. No small sentimentalities are moulded into broad forms. No 'song without words' is padded out to make an Adagio and no elfin dance to make a Scherzo. The opening movement is introduced by a very unusual but magnificently-shaped motive for cellos and basses which soon gives way to a large number of others but returns repeatedly to participate in an extensive process of contrapuntal development. The second movement, the Adagio, has a magnificent, serene stillness. It moves forward in large, broad steps. In its emotional content, sense of struggle and almost Classical voice-leading, this composition can be compared only with Beethoven's finest works. This impressive movement would be sufficient to place Bruckner in the foremost rank of composers and among the immortals. The next movement is an original and quite gruff Scherzo - no silly teenage joke, but genuine, robust, divine humour. The Finale crowns the whole symphony in a fitting and splendid manner and here it is largely the trumpets, bass tubas and horns which produce a striking effect. The instrumentation in general is impressive... thanks to Bruckner's ability to employ and master all the possibilities of the modern orchestra at his disposal with Wagnerian understanding and Berliozian skill.

That such a composition should be written in our time when inspired works are conspicuous by their absence, that its creator should have to experience such a brilliant success after a long life full of struggles, disappointments and privations, and that we were able to find here in Munich not only the forces but also the lively, sympathetic interest in such a performance - these are facts which should compensate for contemporary musical life, for the period of imitation lacking in originality at the beginning of which we may perhaps find ourselves, and should give real satisfaction to the true friend of music...[232]

The prestigious *Berliner Tageblatt* also reported the performances of the Seventh in Leipzig and Munich. The review of the Munich performance was provided by Dr.

---

232 From Ostini's review in the *Süddeutsche Presse* (14 March 1885); see *G-A* IV/2, 291-94.

Paul Marsop who commented on the closely-knit formal structure of the first three movements, in spite of 'the occasional glimpses of the dramatic style', and the masterly polyphonic style throughout, but felt that the final movement was not on the same high level as the other movements, that its themes were not so 'symphonically malleable' and their working-out not sufficiently coherent. Nevertheless, no symphonic work had made such an impact in Munich for many years.[233]

Joseph Schalk also provided two reviews of the performance in the *Deutsche Kunst- und Musikzeitung* and the *Wiener Allgemeine Kunst-Chronik*. In the latter he acknowledged that the Munich orchestra had been equal to the task of 'fulfilling the composer's most stringent requirements' and that the powerful effect of the trombones and tubas in the Finale could be compared only with the final scene of Wagner's *Götterdämmerung*.[234]

The notable success of the Munich performance of the Seventh, particularly when compared with the earlier Leipzig performance, is confirmed by Dr. Konrad Fiedler, a financier and writer on music and the arts, who was present at both. He met Bruckner at a dinner party in Munich and was soon on cordial terms with the composer. Although he had reservations about the symphony after the Leipzig performance, he distanced himself from those who, like the Herzogenbergs, were so pro-Brahms that they could see no good in Bruckner. After the Munich performance, however, he wrote enthusiastically to his friend Adolf Hildebrand about the 'colossal success', adding that 'incidentally, there was no comparison between its performance here under Levi and the Leipzig performance'. In a separate letter,

---

233 Marsop's review appeared in the *Berliner Tageblatt* on 13 March; the review of the Leipzig performance was signed 'H.E.' (= Heinrich Ehrlich). See *G-A* IV/2, 294ff.

234 The review, which appeared in the *Deutsche Kunst- und Musikzeitung* XII (22 March 1885), 139, included quotations from Porges's article. See *LBSAB*, 89-92 for extracts from both reviews and *G-A* IV/2, 287ff. for reprint of the article in the *Allgemeine Kunst-Chronik*.

he mentioned that Bruckner had played the organ in a church on 12 March 'and that is his strong point'.[235] Before Bruckner returned to Vienna on 14 March Fiedler arranged a private performance of his Quintet played by members of the court orchestra.

The Munich episode was a timely morale-booster for Bruckner. Not only had he been present at an extremely successful performance of his Seventh and given an organ recital to some of the leading artists in Munich; he had also been introduced by Levi to Princess Amalie of Bavaria, the cousin of Archduchess Marie Valerie, youngest child of Emperor Franz Josef. He could not contain his joy when writing to Nikisch and Wolzogen shortly after his return to Vienna. In both letters he mentioned public acclaim, favourable reviews, the possibility of another performance in Munich in the autumn, and the Munich court intendant's promise to speak on his behalf to King Ludwig to whom he wished to dedicate the symphony. But he did not want the 'Leipzig connection' to be severed:

> ... Mr. Levi will send you the 4th Symphony should you wish it. Please convey my respects to my supporters, particularly the director and Mr. Vogel, and my affectionate regards to the ladies. I embrace you a thousand times as the fount of all goodness for me. Eternal thanks!
> I am enclosing only one review - from the 'Neueste Nachrichten'. When you have read it, please be so good as to pass it on to Mr. Vogel with my sincerest request that he publish it, if possible. Perhaps this will make a good impression on the publisher...[236]

---

235 These extracts are taken from the Fiedler-Hildebrand correspondence originally published by Wolfgang Jess in Dresden and reprinted as a footnote in G-A IV/2, 278f.; see also Oskar Lang, 'Anton Bruckner im zeitgenössischen Briefwechsel' in *Zeitschrift für Musik* 99 (October 1932), 880f.

236 See *HSABB* 1, 245 for this letter dated Vienna, 15 March 1885. It was first published in *ABB*, 179f; the original is privately owned.

In his letter to Wolzogen Bruckner contrasted Levi's high opinion of his work with some remarks Hans Richter had reputedly made recently:

... Mr. Levi proposed a toast during the artists' get-together [after the performance]: 'to the most important symphonic work since Beethoven's death!' And he went on to say that the performance of this magnificent work (his own words) was the crown of his artistic achievement!... What a difference from Mr. Richter who is alleged to have called me a lunatic without [any sense of] form only a fortnight ago. These same witnesses declared that he declared Brahms's Third Symphony (which was evidently a flop again on Sunday) to be the new *Eroica* (to please Hanslick, of course). My symphony will stay in Munich. Mr. Levi will not allow it to be my ruin in Vienna. He will take care of the printing. He and the intendant will submit a report to the king, and the symphony is to be performed again in November. On 11 March my friends from Vienna and I attended the performance of *Die Walküre* in Munich. It was splendid - I had not heard this magnificent work in its entirety since 1876. After the audience had left, Mr. Levi agreed to my request that the tubas and horns play the funeral song from the second movement of the Seventh Symphony three times in memory of our blessed and much-loved immortal Master. Countless tears were shed. I cannot begin to describe the scene in the darkened court theatre. Requiescat in pace!!! The reviews are all excellent and many have marvellous things to say. The finest are those in the *Neueste Nachrichten* (by Mr. Porges, as I discovered later) and the *Süddeutsche Presse*. God be praised, Munich is now on my side. I have sufficient [support] there for the rest of my life! I am taking the liberty of sending you only one review - the one in the *Neueste Nachrichten*.

My deepest respects to the baroness. I beg you to continue to be favourably disposed towards me!

I have also your article to thank for the performance in Holland (The Hague) as well as countless others. Eternal thanks!... In Holland they want to have all my symphonies.[237]

---

237 See *HSABB* 1, 246 for this letter dated Vienna, 18 March 1885. It was first published in *ABB*, 180ff.; the original is privately owned. Brahms's Third Symphony was played at a Philharmonic concert in Vienna on 15 March.

Probably on the strength of his Munich success Bruckner thought it opportune to renew his attempts to secure an honorary doctorate from a foreign University. At the end of the quaintly and often unidiomatically translated 'petition', Bruckner requested that 'the University of Philadelphia [Cincinnati]... graciously accept the dedication of my Romantic Symphony and may perhaps... confer on me as a boon the Doctorship of Music, which I shall always know to appreciate...'[238]

On the same day as this 'petition' an important article written by Theodor Helm appeared in the *Deutsche Zeitung*. Helm bemoaned the fact that Robert Franz's songs and Franz Liszt's orchestral works were not performed often enough in concerts. As far as Bruckner's works were concerned, the Philharmonic players in general and Hans Richter in particular should be ashamed of their reluctance to perform anything - in view of the reports of the composer's recent successes in Leipzig, The Hague and Munich. Bruckner himself had provided a fitting reply in one of his University lectures to the criticism that he was a musical anarchist and that the principle of tonality did not exist for him -

> When I permit myself a few bold deviations here and there in my works, I always return to the main tonality and never let it out of my sight completely. I am like a mountaineer who wants to climb higher in order to obtain a clearer view and yet remains with the same area.[239]

---

238 The 'petition' is dated Vienna, 24 March 1885. For further information, see earlier in the chapter (page 395 and footnote 89). For the complete text, see *G-A* IV/2, 296-99 and Rolf Keller, 'Das "amerikanische Ehrendoktorat" für Bruckner' in *BSL 1992* (Linz, 1995), 82ff. The University of Philadelphia is now the University of Pennsylvania. According to information received from Dr. Benjamin Korstvedt, there is no record of Bruckner's petition in the University archives. In addition, the archivist pointed out that it 'was unheard of for someone to petition for an honorary degree'.

239 From Theodor Helm's article in the *Deutsche Zeitung* (24 March 1885). Reprinted in *G-A* IV/2, 311ff.

On 11 April Paumgartner, writing in the *Wiener Zeitung*, echoed Helm's comments. He quoted from the two important Munich reviews of the performance of the Seventh and made use of the opportunity to argue that it was a matter of artistic and national honour for this work to be included in the following season's Philharmonic programme.

In a letter to Wagner's youngest daughter, Eva, Bruckner also referred to the successful performance of his symphony in Munich and made a point of adding that the funeral music from the slow movement was 'played three times by the tubas and horns in the darkness of the court theatre after a performance of *Die Walküre*... in memory of the dearly-loved immortal Master of all Masters'.[240]

Three weeks after the performance of the Seventh Symphony, the Walter Quartet gave a public performance of Bruckner's String Quintet in Munich. About a fortnight later Bruckner wrote to Levi to thank him for his assistance and described him as the 'greatest conductor in the world' and Munich as his 'artistic home'. In addition he invited him to spend some of his summer vacation with him in Steyr and St. Florian. He then continued:

> ... I received from Munich only the *Süddeutsche Presse* review of the Quintet. It was certainly not so good as the review of the Symphony. Baron Ostini was probably not at the performance.
> Mr. Greif sent me the orchestral parts - no doubt by mistake.

---

240 See *HSABB* 1, 250 for a draft of this letter, dated Vienna 10 April 1885 and written in response to a letter from Eva Wagner. It was first published in *ABB*, 202f. and the original is possibly in private possession. Bruckner also refers in this letter to a letter he had received from Wagner on 31 January 1868, a copy of which he had sent in September of the previous year (i.e. 1884) to Adolf von Groß, a government official in Bayreuth and a close friend of the Wagner family, and another copy of which he encloses. Cf. letters to Perfall and Hans von Wolzogen, 13 September 1884 (see footnotes 163 and 169) concerning Wagner mementoes. See also Egon Voss, 'Wagner und Bruckner' in Christoph-Hellmut Mahling , ed., *Anton Bruckner. Studien zu Werk und Wirkung. Walter Wiora zum 30. Dezember 1986* (Tutzing: Schneider, 1988), 221 and 232.

Should I send them back? If the King were to request another performance, as you mentioned earlier, the orchestral parts would have to be available. Mr. Frei (sic), editor of the *Tagblatt*, sends his respects. Mr. Richter has spoken to me about the 7th Symphony. I have said that it cannot be performed in Vienna until it has been printed. I am not going to allow the work to be played by the court music director now and be ruined by Mr. Hanslick etc. He should perform an already ruined symphony in the meantime.

(The Quintet has to be played more slowly, particularly the answering phrases for viola in the second subject of the first movement; and then the second part of the Scherzo up to the repeat of the opening is to be taken almost *Andante*)...

N.B. I had to laugh at the preview of the Quintet in the *Cöln'sche Zeitung* in which I am described as the most adventurous and inspired of the living composers and can only be compared with Beethoven. Priceless![241]

The performance of the Quintet in Munich on 31 March was another notable success. Once again Porges provided a perceptive review in the *Münchner Neueste Nachrichten*, and, Bruckner's slight disappointment notwithstanding, commented favourably on Bruckner's artistic handling of string textures and his ability to combine broadly flowing melodies, rich harmonies and complex rhythms into a satisfying whole.[242]

Levi responded to Bruckner's letter on 13 April, providing details of the performance and thanking him for his invitation to spend a couple of days' holiday with him. The matter of the symphony's dedication was also being pursued:

---

241 See *HSABB* 1, 248f. for this letter dated Vienna, 10 April 1885; the original is in the Music Section of the *Staatsbibliothek Preußischer Kulturbesitz*, Berlin. Wilhelm Frey (1833-1909), the editor and music reviewer of the *Neuer Wiener Tagblatt*, was a keen Bruckner advocate. Bruckner gave the same directions concerning passages in the first movement and the Scherzo in a letter to Benno Walter, the leader of the quartet, dated Vienna, 27 March 1885. See *HSABB* 1, 247; the original is also in the Music Section of the *Staatsbibliothek Preußischer Kulturbesitz*, Berlin.

242 See *G-A* IV/2, 301ff. for a reprint of the complete review.

... Many thanks for your delightful letter! If it is at all possible, I will arrange to spend a couple of days with you in the country this summer. I am going to Florence at the beginning of May (where I will meet up with the Fiedlers and rehearse your Quintet with the local Quartet Society), then to Rome to visit my friend Lenbach, and then to Switzerland at the beginning of June. I am worn out and long for a rest!

The performance of the Quintet here was really good. The Fiedlers invited the players to their house the day before the performance, and I went through the work thoroughly with them. (They had five rehearsals already before this!) I believe that the tempi were correct. (The first movement *molto moderato*!) The public responded very enthusiastically. I have not read the *Süddeutsche Presse* (Ostini was not present), but Porges wrote a very fine and warm-hearted review in the *Neueste*. I will ask him to send you a copy.

It will be another fortnight before I can write to you about the matter concerning the king. I have sent a long report to the intendant and he has passed it on to the court secretary's office. It appears that things move slowly there. There is no doubt that the king will accept the dedication, but there must be something in it for you. This matter will certainly be settled before my departure.

Wüllner in Cologne has announced the 7th Symphony for next winter; Müller in Frankfurt has also approached me. Gutmann should speed things up a little, so that the score and parts are ready before the beginning of the winter season.

Could you perhaps meet me in Florence at the beginning of May? That would be splendid!

I did not arrange for the parts to be sent back to you. But hold on to them for a while!...[243]

After the excitement of the previous three months Bruckner took the opportunity of his Easter break of about a week (1-7 April) in the quiet surroundings of St. Florian to refresh himself physically and spiritually. He played the organ at some of the services, continued working on his Eighth Symphony and, according to the abbey organist, Josef Gruber, asked the prelate Ferdinand Moser if he could be buried

---

243 See *HSABB* 1, 250f. for this letter dated Munich, 13 April 1885; the original is in St. Florian. The letter is dated incorrectly in both *ABB*, 315f. (3 April) and *G-A* IV/2, 316 (8 April).

458

in the vaults of the abbey beneath the great organ.[244]

On his return from St. Florian Bruckner received a telegram from Eckstein in Cologne - 'Quintet performed here by Heckmann. Most brilliant success. Letter follows'. In the following letter Eckstein commented on the excellent performance and the prolonged applause.[245] Dr. Hans Kleser, who had provided a preview of the performance in the *Kölnische Zeitung* on 8 April, wrote to Bruckner on 9 April to confirm that the reception of the work (first three movements only) in a concert which also included performances of a quartet by Wolfrum and a quintet by Svendsen had been favourable in spite of the conservatism of the public - 'we are still suffering here from the after-effects of Hiller'. Franz Wüllner had been present and the performance had 'encouraged him even more to perform a symphony next winter'.[246]

On 23 April Bruckner's loyal young friends, Joseph Schalk and Ferdinand Löwe, gave another piano-duet performance of the first movement of Symphony no. 3 and the second and fourth movements of Symphony no. 1 in the *Bösendorfersaal*. A detailed review of the concert appeared in the *Deutsche Kunst- und Musikzeitung* on 1 May, and the critic observed that both pianists played 'with such astonishing

---

244 See *G-A* II/1, 287ff. and *G-A* IV/2, 303f.

245 The telegram was presumably sent on 8 April and the letter on 9 April. Both have been lost; they are mentioned by Bruckner in his letter to Levi of 10 April (see earlier and footnote 241). See also *G-A* IV/2, 304.

246 See *G-A* IV/2, 305f. and *HSABB* 1, 247 for this letter, the original of which is no longer extant. Ferdinand Hiller (1811-1885) was one of the leading figures in the musical life of Cologne from 1850 until his retirement in 1884. He founded the Cologne Conservatory in 1850 and was its director for many years. He was also conductor of the Gürzenich Concerts in Cologne and made several trips to Vienna, St. Petersburg and England as a guest conductor. Franz Wüllner (1832-1902) was a pianist, conductor and composer who held conducting positions in various German cities, including Munich, Dresden, Berlin and Cologne; he succeeded Hiller as conductor of the Gürzenich Concerts in Cologne and gave the first Cologne performance of Bruckner's Seventh in the winter season of 1887/88.

technical assurance that they and the composer who was present were received with acclamation at the end of each movement'.[247]

Bruckner spent most of the second half of April preparing for the first performance of his *Te Deum*. He rehearsed the choir painstakingly himself and, because no orchestra was available, made use of a piano-duet accompaniment, the piano parts played by Joseph Schalk and Robert Erben.[248] Bruckner had received some advice earlier from the opera singer Rosa Papier-Paumgartner, Dr. Hans Paumgartner's wife, about the vocal writing and had thanked her profusely in a letter.[249] The performance took place in the small *Musikverein* hall on Saturday 2 May in a concert which included another performance of the Quintet given by the Hellmesberger Quartet as well as some Liszt and Wagner songs.

The review of the concert in the Linz *Tagespost* highlighted the harmonic and contrapuntal boldness, the clear structure and the 'genuinely religious nature' of the new work and looked forward to the performance with full orchestral accompaniment scheduled for the 1885-86 *Gesellschaft* series.[250] Hugo Wolf, writing in the *Salonblatt*, regretted that lack of space prevented him from discussing the concert in any detail but noted that 'the impression made upon the listeners by this work [the *Te Deum*] was utterly overwhelming, even without the supporting

---

247 See *LBSAB*, 96ff. for this review. The reviewer was possibly Emil v. Hartmann who was present at the concert.

248 Robert Erben (1862-1925), who had recently graduated from the Vienna Conservatory, took the place of the indisposed Löwe.

249 See *HSABB* 1, 241 for this letter dated Vienna, 18 February 1885. It was first published in *ABB*, 176f; the original is privately owned.

250 See *G-A* IV/2, 309f. for the full report.

460

orchestra'.[251]

At about this time Johann Burgstaller, the music director of Linz Cathedral, asked Bruckner to provide a work for the diocesan centenary in October, specifically a sacred composition to accompany the procession of the bishop into the cathedral. Bruckner wrote his *Ecce sacerdos magnus* WAB 13 for double choir (SSAATTBB), three trombones and organ at the end of April and send it to Burgstaller together with an accompanying letter on 18 May.[252] A performance of his E minor Mass was also being contemplated and Bruckner took the opportunity to inform Burgstaller that the Mass was dedicated to Bishop Rudigier and was the property of the Cathedral Chapter. As he had made some alterations since its first performance in 1869, he suggested that these should be copied into the parts 'now that we have a new bishop':

> ... The Mass is for choir with woodwind and brass accompaniment but without strings. I rehearsed it in 1869 and conducted it at the consecration of the *Votivkapelle*, one of the finest days of my life... Although 'Sicut erat' was not given to me, I have used the words in the plainsong section [of *Ecce sacerdos*].[253]

Ecce sacerdos was not performed at the centenary celebrations and had to wait another 27 years for its first performance. It comes from the same spring as the *Te Deum*, and the bare fifths at the opening, the rapid harmonic transitions, the modal

---

251 Hugo Wolf's report appeared in the *Salonblatt* on 10 May 1885. See Pleasants, op.cit., 143. Other reviews appeared in the *Deutsche Zeitung* (3 May), the *Neue Wiener Tagblatt* (5 May) and the *Deutsche Kunst- und Musikzeitung* XII (9 May), 214. See *LBSAB*, 98f. for extracts from the latter.

252 The dates 20 April 1885 and 28 April 1885 are at the end of the autograph score which is located in the library of the *Wiener Männergesangverein*.

253 See *HSABB* 1, 264 for this letter, dated Vienna 18 May 1885; the original is in the *Dombauverein*, Linz. See also Chapter 3, pp. 174-75.

tendency of the harmonies, the mediant relationship of keys and the majestic, ceremonial mood all point to that work.[254]

Success breeds success and Levi's performance of the Seventh in particular encouraged other German conductors to programme the work. Preparations were also in train for the printing of the symphony, and Levi kept his promise to use his influence in the Munich court to expedite the dedication to King Ludwig II. When he wrote to Levi on 16 April, Bruckner mentioned some difficulties he was experiencing with his Viennese publisher, Gutmann:

> ... I am extremely surprised that I have heard nothing from Mr.
> Gutmann. Does he have a score? Can no publisher be found in Mainz
> then? Perhaps if we wait another year? I will never receive a penny
> here. There are difficulties with Schalk's piano score. Schalk is
> unwilling to give it to Gutmann because he did not receive any
> payment from him for the Quintet, the printing costs of which were
> covered by subscription. I believe, however, that an artist of your
> great understanding would be the best person to act in this matter -
> and that is very encouraging. My young friends are of the opinion
> that any publishing house in Germany would be better. They believe
> that Gutmann would have to pay in any other situation. Or should we
> wait?
> I will follow your advice and will put my trust in you, my illustrious
> patron! There is rarely any harm in waiting...[255]

Earlier in this letter Bruckner referred to the possibility of the Adagio from the Seventh being performed in Karlsruhe during the music festival organized by the

---

254 The first recorded performance of *Ecce sacerdos* was on 21 November 1912 at a concert in Vöcklabruck conducted by Max Auer. The work was first published in 1911 by Universal Edition (U.E. 3298), edited by Viktor Keldorfer. For further information, see *G-A* IV/2, 313-16 and *ABSW* XXI/2, 129ff. There is a modern edition of the piece in *ABSW* XXI/1, 130-40.

255 See *HSABB* 1, 251f. for this letter, dated Vienna 16 April 1885. It was first published in *GrBLS*, 326f.; the original is privately owned.

Allgemeiner Deutscher Musikverein at the end of May. But he was in two minds:

> ... It is very risky to allow the piece to be conducted by an unknown conductor who is perhaps unsympathetic to the new direction. Only those who believe in the work could perform it. What should I do?

Bruckner itemised his reservations in more detail when he wrote to his 'dearest old young friend' Felix Mottl in Karlsruhe the following day:

> ... 'That must be Bruckner', you will say - and you are correct, it is he. Listen: Professor Riedel from Leipzig has offered me the opportunity of having the Adagio from the 7th Symphony performed at the *Allgemeines Deutsches Musikfest*. Liszt and Dr. Standthartner also recommended that I take up the offer. However, you now play the leading role in this:
> 1. Is the orchestra not too ill-disposed towards me?
> 2. Do you have the new tubas which are used in the *Ring* or, if not, can you get them?
> 3. Do you wish to be like Levi and Nikisch and put all your artistic support at the disposal of your old teacher, who has always been fond of you, by rehearsing and conducting the Adagio with the tubas and funeral music in memory of our dear-departed Master as if it was your own work?
> If you, a renowned conductor, can tackle it with enthusiasm, you are the right artist for the task!
> Three cheers, my dear Mottl, if you can give me your true German word of honour! The matter is then settled and I can send the parts to Leipzig.
> NB. The four [Wagner] tubas are very important; also the bass tuba. I reckon that both of us could get some enjoyment out of it.
> My decision lies in your hands...[256]

---

256 See *HSABB* 1, 252f. for this letter, dated Vienna 17 April 1885; the original is in the *ÖNB*. Josef Standthartner (1818-1892), director of one of the main hospitals in Vienna, was one of the directors of the *Gesellschaft der Musikfreunde* and a friend of both Wagner and Bruckner.

Five days later Bruckner wrote to Mottl again to send his condolences on the death of his brother Fritz, with his regrets that he would not be able to attend the funeral because of teaching commitments at the Conservatory.[257]   At the end of April Bruckner sent the orchestral parts to his young friend and provided some performance directions:

> ... I enclose the orchestral parts. You will receive the score from Mr. Levi. At [letter] X in the Adagio (funeral music for tubas and horns) I implore you to increase the *cresc.* three bars before Y to *fff* in the next bar and then decrease it again at the third crotchet one bar before Y. Be sure to use tubas. (Under no circumstances substitute horns for tubas.) Would it not be desirable to perform the Scherzo and Trio as well? (Particularly for the audience's benefit)...[258]

When Liszt, the president of the *Allgemeiner Deutscher Musikverein*, was in Vienna at the beginning of May he invited Bruckner to his apartment in the *Schottenhof* in order to discuss the projected Karlsruhe performance.   Bruckner seized the opportunity to suggest a performance of the complete work rather than the Adagio only. As the programme had already been arranged, Liszt was not keen to make any changes but promised to do what he could. When Bruckner wrote to Mottl again on 9 May, he repeated his earlier suggestion that the Scherzo and Trio be played after the Adagio and reiterated his earlier performance directions:

> ... My friends here are of the opinion that, as the Adagio is very solemn, it would be desirable to follow it with the Scherzo and Trio for the sake of applause! Do you not agree?...
> Please adopt a very slow and solemn tempo. At the funeral music at the end (in memory of our deceased Master), *think of the one who*

257 See *HSABB* 1, 254 for this letter, dated Vienna 22 April 1885; the original is in the *ÖNB*.

258 See *HSABB* 1, 256 for this letter, dated Vienna 29 April 1885; the original is in the *ÖNB*.

was our ideal. Please do not forget the *fff* at the end of the funeral music.[259]

In spite of Bruckner's (and Liszt's?) efforts, only the Adagio was played during the Festival on 30 May.

As far as the dedication and the printing of the symphony were concerned, Levi was able to provide Bruckner with excellent news at the end of April:

> After frequent conversations with Captain Gresser, the king's court secretary, I can inform you that His Majesty will certainly accept the dedication of your Seventh. You will receive in due course - in the next few days, I hope - an official communication from the cabinet or the intendant, to which I would ask you to respond immediately (directly to the king). In this letter of thanks, make the request that His Majesty have your symphony or just the Adagio played at a special performance. Neither the intendant nor the cabinet secretary can recommend this to the king. (It would take too long to explain this more fully to you. No one can make a recommendation regarding 'extraordinary' performances of plays and operas. The king does this on his own initiative.) In your letter of thanks, make full use of phrases like 'your most obedient servant' and 'your most gracious Majesty' etc. as the king sets great store by such formalities. How is it now with Gutmann? I have not heard anything else whatsoever. Between ourselves (no one else needs to know about it!) I have offered him 1,000 marks as a contribution towards the costs. (Fiedler, a certain Count Oriolla and I are the members of this *Allgemeiner Anton-Bruckner-Verein!*) And I would think that he could quite easily provide Mr. Schalk with a fee from that! If he didn't, I would certainly find a publisher in Germany. But it would be good if he could give a categorical 'No' or 'Yes'. If you are absolutely against Gutmann, write to me. My only reason for approaching him was that he published the Quintet.
> I am leaving on May 1ˢᵗ or 2ⁿᵈ. Unfortunately I cannot come to Vienna (Dr. Boller has invited me to the Bruckner evening). I have a travelling companion and I made him a firm promise a long time

---

259 See *HSABB* 1, 258-59 for this letter, dated Vienna 9 May 1885; the original is in the *ÖNB*.

ago that I would go directly to Italy with him...[260]

Bruckner was overwhelmed with Levi's generosity and thanked him profusely in his reply. He enclosed Gutmann's contract and confirmed that he had 'nothing against Mr. Gutmann', describing him as 'the most active businessman in the world'. He mentioned that he had sent the orchestral parts of the Seventh to Mottl in Karlsruhe and asked Levi to forward the score of the work and convey some instructions:

> ... Would you be so good as to indicate to Herr Mottl that the 5 tubas (not horns as in Leipzig) are of the utmost importance. If the *fff* is not marked in the score (for tubas and horns) at the end of the funeral music in the Adagio, please insert it in the manner in which it was played three times after *Die Walküre*. Regarding his Majesty, I will do exactly as you suggest... As soon as the contract is returned to me I will hand over the score to Gutmann...[261]

Levi's suggestion that Bruckner use such formal styles of address as 'your most obedient servant' and 'your most gracious Majesty' when writing to the king makes amusing reading, as for Bruckner it was second nature to adopt submissive terms like these when writing to anyone in authority. His letter of thanks to the king is liberally sprinkled with them:

---

260 See *HSABB* 1, 254f. for Levi's letter to Bruckner, dated Munich 26 April 1885; the original is in St. Florian.

261 See *HSABB* 1, 255f. for this undated letter. It was first published in *GrBLS*, 329f; the original is privately owned. It was clearly written as a response to Levi's letter of 26 April and was intended to reach Levi before his departure for Italy - hence the surmised date of 29 April in *HSABB*. See also *HSABB* 1, 257 for a letter from Levi to Joseph Schalk, dated Munich 1 May 1885, in which he mentions that he has returned the contract and regrets the lack of communication between them; the original is in the *ÖNB*, F18 Schalk 153/1.

... Your Majesty, the true royal patron of the immortal Master
[Wagner], has always been for me the ideal German monarch! The
illustrious and marvellous portrait of Your Majesty has always been
at my side! And now I bow down before Your Majesty with the
utmost deference and subservience and thank the Almighty that He,
in His everlasting wisdom, has granted the world a heavenly guardian
and protector of German art in the person of His Supreme Majesty,
the King...[262]

Bruckner referred to this letter when writing to Marie Demar on 11 May - 'I have
just thanked the King of Bavaria for accepting the dedication'. Marie Demar was a
young lady whom he had met several times at the Opera House in Vienna. He sent
her a photograph of himself on 2 March with the request that she in turn send her
photograph to him! Bruckner was delighted when she complied with this request.
He was less successful, however, with his proposal of marriage and intention to
dedicate his Eighth Symphony to her, both of which she graciously declined. Yet
another abortive 'affair of the heart'![263]

In his next letter to Levi, Bruckner was able to provide him with a substantial
amount of information:

... I trust that you arrived in Rome safely. I received the supreme
resolution from the king's intendant and yesterday, 9 May, sent the
letter of thanks to the king via the ministerial councillor, von
Schneider. Absolutely everything is your work! Eternal thanks! May
God bless you! Thousand upon thousand hurrahs! I am very happy

---

262 See *HSABB* 1, 257f. for this undated letter. From references to it in other letters written at the
same time, however, we can assume that it was sent to the king on either 8 or 9 May 1885; there is
an autograph draft of the letter in the *ÖNB*.

263 See *HSABB* 1, 260f. for Bruckner's letter to Marie Demar, dated Vienna, 11 May 1885; the
original is in the *ÖNB*. Marie Demar (1865-1946) married William Blaschek in 1890.

with the whole affair.

Mr. Gutmann is already making plenty of noise and is also very pleased with the outcome. Friend Mottl has written to me several times and I received a card a few hours ago in which he says he is really delighted with the 'marvellous piece', as he calls it, and will do his utmost etc. The Te Deum was performed with indescribable jubilation, the Quintet as well (again played by Hellmesberger).

Wetzler of Vienna wants to publish the Te Deum, which I have written for choir and orchestra and dedicated to God as a thanksgiving for surviving so much suffering in Vienna. Mr. Richter is to perform it in London when he receives his doctorate!!

It is my sincere wish that you obtain all the rest and recreation you need and that your nervous system in particular will be refreshed in Switzerland. Once again I thank you from the bottom of my heart and pray that you will continue to be favourably disposed towards me! I only wish that I could see you sometime in Upper Austria...[264]

In this letter and in other letters written at the same time, Wetzler is mentioned as the potential publisher of the Te Deum.[265] In fact, thanks to the generosity of his pupil, Friedrich Eckstein, who undertook to defray a large part of the expenses involved, it was Theodor Rättig, the publisher of the Third Symphony, who

---

264 See *HSABB* 1, 259 for this letter from Bruckner to Levi, dated Vienna, 10 May 1885. It was first published in *GrBLS*, 327f.; the original is privately owned. Levi's itinerary, as outlined in his letter of 26 April to Bruckner, was Florence (until 6 May) and Rome (6-16 May). Hans Richter did not perform the *Te Deum* in London, but gave the first British performance of a Bruckner symphony - no. 7 - in May 1887.

265 See *HSABB* 1, 261ff. for four letters: (1) to Theodor Helm (in which he encloses copies of Munich reviews), dated Vienna, 11 May 1885; original in private possession; (2) to Johannes P. Hupfauf, director of Munich at Salzburg Cathedral, dated Vienna, 11 May 1885; original in the *ÖNB*; (3) to Eduard Rappoldi, a well-known violinist based in Dresden, undated; first published in *ABB*, 186, original not extant; (4) to Moritz von Mayfeld, dated Vienna, 12 May 1885; original in the *Archiv der Stadt Linz*, Linz.

266 Full score T.R. 40b; piano score (ed. J. Schalk), T.R. 40.

eventually published the work later in the year.[266]

The performance of the Adagio from the Seventh Symphony in Karlsruhe on 30 May made a considerable impact on many of the professional and knowledgeable amateur musicians present. The reviewer for the *Weimarer Zeitung* was amazed that Bruckner's name had been completely unknown outside Vienna until recent months,[267] and Richard Pohl, a music journalist in Weimar and a personal friend of Liszt and Wagner, and Professor Ludwig Nohl from Heidelberg University were particularly impressed. The latter wrote to Bruckner from Heidelberg on 3 June, saying that the Adagio had given him 'renewed comfort and hope for the future of our heavenly art' and no other music apart from Bach, Beethoven and Wagner had affected him in this way. A nervous illness prevented him from writing any more fully at the time, but he hoped to visit Vienna in the near future and express himself more fully to Bruckner.[268] Bruckner was so delighted with Nohl's letter that he sent it to several of his friends, suggesting that it be published as a kind of anti-toxin to the poisonous utterances of Hanslick and others. On 20 June, for instance, he wrote to Wolzogen:

> ... A veritable antidote to the persecutions of Hanslick and his gang.
> There are much more honourable men in Germany! Please be so
> good as to have this letter published in the [*Bayreuther*] *Blätter*.
> Your famous paper gave me an opening in Holland. I thank
> you from the bottom of my heart, most noble patron - you are an

---

267 See *G-A* IV/2, 331 for an extract from this review which appeared in the *Weimarer Zeitung* on 3 June 1885.

268 See *HSABB* 1, 264f. for this letter, dated Heidelberg, 6 June 1885; the original is in the *ÖNB*.

269 See *HSABB* 1, 268 for this letter, dated Vienna, 20 June 1885. It was first published in *ABB*, 191; the original has been lost.

aristocrat in the true sense of the word and brilliantly gifted![269]

Wolzogen replied to this letter on 12 July, apologizing for not writing earlier because he had been away from Bayreuth. He promised Bruckner that he would quote Nohl's letter at the earliest possible opportunity and suggested that the Adagio of the Seventh could be performed at one of the well-attended 'popular concerts' in Berlin.[270]

Apart from Nohl's letter, however, Bruckner had received very little news about the performance and, understandably, was surprised at the lack of communication. He wrote to Mottl on 17 June:

Dearest friend! Superb court music director!

A few days ago I received a very enthusiastic and honourable letter from Professor Nohl in Heidelberg and realised that there must have been a very successful performance. I waited in vain for a report from Dr. Schönaich and for the Karlsruhe papers - but to no avail! They must have been really bad!

I have heard nothing else, apart from through Göllerich who is too enthusiastic in these matters for my liking. (I read something in the *Frankfurter [Zeitung]* and the *Elsas-Lothringer Zeitung* for the first time a few days ago.) Apart from that, nothing! My authority is Mr. Nohl who is really enthusiastic - and he would not have been if he had not heard the movement played so brilliantly!

Please accept my most deeply-felt gratitude and admiration for your kindness and friendship! I will never forget it! And, now that you are such a great artist, please continue to be my 'old-young' friend and brother and put your brilliant artistry at the disposal of my works...

---

270   See *HSABB* 1, 272 for this letter, dated Bayreuth, 12 July 1885; the original is in St. Florian.

Gutmann has been asking for the orchestral parts...[271]

Bruckner was also none too pleased with his young friend Göllerich who had promised to send a report of the Karlsruhe performance to Theodor Helm for publication in the *Deutscher Zeitung* but had failed to do so. In order to ensure some kind of report in a Viennese newspaper Bruckner wrote to Helm, enclosing Göllerich's enthusiastic letter about the performance, in the hope that it would be a viable substitute, but Helm did not make use of it.[272] Bruckner's tone was distinctly cool when he wrote to Göllerich on 24 June:

To Mr. A. Göllerich,
Composer, at present in Weimar

Dear friend,

Many thanks for your letter. Unfortunately, I have to inform you that you have disappointed me greatly by not keeping your promise to write to Dr. Helm. Consequently Helm has not written anything, as both Dr. Schönaich and Mottl have also failed to send a report.
I certainly provided Dr. Helm with your letter but he returned it to me without comment. Once again I confirm my great disappointment that important people received no reports from my friends...
Helm wrote today that he waited in vain until the deadline.[273]

---

271 See *HSABB* 1, 266f. for this letter, dated Vienna, 17 June 1885. The review in the *Frankfurter Zeitung* was published on 1 June.

272 See *HSABB* 1, 267f. for Bruckner's letter to Helm, dated Vienna, 19 June 1885. The original is in the *Wiener Stadtbibliothek*, and there is a facsimile in **Plate 4**. Göllerich's letter to Bruckner is not extant. Although Helm did not make use of this letter, Gutmann used Nohl's letter in an advertisement in the *Deutscher Zeitung* (14 June 1885) concerning the forthcoming publication of Symphony no. 7.

273 See *HSABB* 1, 268f. for this letter, dated Vienna, 24 June 1885; the original is privately owned.

He was on more friendly terms when he wrote to Göllerich again a fortnight later. He began by asking Göllerich to pass on his 'deepest respects' to Liszt, and continued:

> My dear, good friend,
>
> You will find it wholly understandable that it would mean a great deal to me if Dr. Helm were to print in the *Deutscher Zeitung*, albeit belatedly, what the German musicians have to say about me - 'nothing like this written since Beethoven', 'can only be compared with Beethoven in feeling and Wagner in compositional facility'. He [Helm] is staying at the *Hahn* inn in Nonnthal, Salzburg. He appears to be somewhat difficult to persuade, in spite of your fine words. But you can do it, my highly esteemed friend and dear biographer, particularly if you give him no peace. So please do what you can. It is certainly the first public festival in Germany in which my name has appeared...
>
> Gutmann told me that von Bülow had recommended the 7th Symphony to Berlin. I go to Steyr at the end of this week...

Repeating his request that Helm be given no peace, Bruckner suggested that Göllerich send the following paraphrased extracts from a review of the symphony by Ernst Wilhelm Fritzsch, the editor of *Musikalisches Wochenblatt* which had 'marvellous things to say about me':

> 'Who among living composers has written anything similar or who can be believed capable of doing so; how far back in the past must we search to find anything of equal value? Honour where honour is due! - but this *Adagio* is unique among the works of the post-Beethovenian period'...
>
> 'It remains for the Viennese to pay homage to their distinguished fellow-citizen particularly when cultural backwaters have at last been persuaded to recognise Anton Bruckner'...
>
> 'As soon as time allows, we will look out for a French or Hungarian countess who may be persuaded to act as Bruckner's

patron'...[274]

On the same day (7 July), Bruckner wrote to Arthur Nikisch, his 'great and noble patron and friend' and the 'first apostle to proclaim my unknown word in Germany with the utmost energy and dignity' to congratulate him on his forthcoming wedding. He also supplied the information that he would be going soon to Steyr in Upper Austria where he would be working diligently [on his 8th Symphony].[275]

A month earlier, on *Corpus Christi* day (4 June) Bruckner and Eckstein travelled to Klosterneuburg where he played the organ at High Mass. Later in the day they joined the Schalk brothers, Löwe, Hynais, Julius Mayreder and Hugo Wolf. Bruckner was no doubt very pleased to meet (for the first time) the young man who had spoken so highly of his works in the *Salonblatt*. Eckstein reports a time of great conviviality and a wide-ranging conversation touching on, among other subjects, Brahms, Hans Richter, the Seventh Symphony and the choice of a suitable opera libretto![276]

Bruckner spent most of his summer vacation as a guest of Father Aichinger, the parish priest in Steyr. Although he was based there for seven weeks (9 July - 27 August), he visited Kremsmünster for four days (1-4 August) as well as calling on his sister and her family in Vöcklabruck. He was a guest at St. Florian for the final part of his holiday (27 August - 4 September) and had to return to Vienna earlier than

---

274 See *HSABB* 1, 270f. for this letter, dated Vienna, 7 July 1885; the original is privately owned.. Göllerich was one of Liszt's pupils and was acting as his secretary at the time.

275 See *HSABB* 1, 271 for this letter; the original is privately owned.

276 See Friedrich Eckstein, 'Die erste und die letzte Begegnung zwischen Hugo Wolf und Anton Bruckner' in Karl Kobald, ed., *In memoriam Anton Bruckner* (Zurich-Vienna-Leipzig, 1924), 51-56, and Günter Brosche, 'Anton Bruckner und Hugo Wolf' in O.Wessely, ed., *Bruckner-Studien* (Vienna, 1975), 175. See also Stephen Johnson, op.cit., 142f. The year is given as 1886 in *G-A* IV/2, 480-85.

usual because his *Hofkapelle* duties re-commenced on 6 September.[277] He no doubt availed himself of the special concession of 50% reduction in rail fares for all court employees which was ratified in June.[278] To spend so little of his vacation at St. Florian was certainly a departure from the norm. There was a written invitation from Bernhard Deubler, the new choir director, to which Bruckner replied on 17 June:

> ... It is also a joy for me to be able to come to St. Florian, because it is the quietest place for me to work. I have continual difficulty with only one thing - being a burden to the abbey. If I could pay for my own accommodation, I would be much more settled and could stay there without any embarrassment. There is really a limit to all kindness! I also wish you a really good holiday...
> Please pass on my greetings to Oddo [Loidol] and Ignaz.[279]

We do not know if Bruckner's 'embarrassment' concealed another reason for not spending more time at the abbey during the summer of 1885. Perhaps, as Auer suggests, there was a combination of circumstances - a positive response from Aichinger to Bruckner's request to stay at his residence in Steyr, new personnel at the abbey, including Moser, the new prelate, with whom Bruckner was not on such

---

277 On 28 June Bruckner wrote to Pius Richter informing of the dates of his duties over the summer and asking him if he would be able to act as his substitute. The dates he gave were 26 and 31 July, 16, 18 and 22 August, 6,7,8 and 12 September. Richter was clearly able to help with the July and August dates but not with the September ones. See *HSABB* 1, 269 for this letter; the original is in the *ÖNB*.

278 See *ABDS* 1, 101f. for Hellmesberger's circular letter to the members of the *Hofkapelle*, dated Vienna, 5 June 1885.

279 See *HSABB* 1, 266 for this letter; the original is in St. Florian. Deubler's letter to Bruckner is not extant.

familiar terms, and genuine embarrassment, as mentioned in the letter.[280]

Steyr may not have been such a quiet place to compose as the peaceful surroundings of St. Florian, but it provided Bruckner with the opportunity of continuing preparatory work on his Eighth Symphony. During the few days he spent at Kremsmünster he played the organ on several occasions and discussed future performance possibilities with Oddo and Amand Loidol.[281]

During his short stay at St. Florian, Bruckner played the organ as usual during the morning service on 28 August (St. Augustine's day). The sung Mass was Liszt's *Missa choralis* and the gradual his own *Os justi*. In the afternoon he gave an organ recital which was attended by many of his friends and admirers. In his report of the recital in the Linz *Tagespost*, Carl Almeroth described the scene as a sort of 'mini-Bayreuth to which Bruckner's admirers made a pilgrimage, using every conceivable form of transport - coach, cycle, train, on foot - so as to hear the sublime music which Master Bruckner would produce from the fine instrument'. The themes which he used for improvisation purposes were taken from *The Ring* and from his own Seventh and Eighth Symphonies.[282]

The day before he left St. Florian to return to Vienna, Bruckner wrote one of his finest short sacred works, *Virga Jesse floruit* WAB 52, for *a cappella* mixed-voice choir. This setting of a text taken from the Feast of the Blessed Virgin was

---

280 See *G-A* II/1, 289ff. and IV/2, 342. Although there was a verbal promise, there appears to have been no written promise that Bruckner's wish to be buried under the great organ would be fulfilled. See later in Chapter 6 for the content of Bruckner's will and the provision that he be buried in Steyr if his wish to be buried in St. Florian was not granted. Bruckner wrote to Aichinger on 1 July, asking for accommodation and offering to pay. All he required was a quiet, cool room and a small piano, if possible, as he had to work 'very industriously on his 8th Symphony'. See *HSABB* 1, 269f.; the original is privately owned.

281 See *G-A* IV/2, 343ff. for further details.

282 See *G-A* II/1, 292ff. for a reprint of Almeroth's report of 1 September 1885.

dedicated posthumously to Ignaz Traumihler and was possibly intended originally, like *Ecce sacerdos*, for the centenary of the Linz diocese in October 1885.[283] Its first performance, however, seems to have been as an enclave in a performance of the F minor Mass in the court chapel later in the year, on 8 December.

Bruckner's young friends were by no means unoccupied during the summer months, thanks to Levi's generous offer of 1000 marks to cover the printing costs of the Seventh which included a fee for Joseph Schalk for preparing a piano score and supervising the printing. Joseph sent the piano score to his brother Franz who made some alterations which were extensive enough for the score to be regarded as at least a joint venture. On 14 July Joseph wrote to his brother:

> ... The corrections in the piano score of the Seventh have already come. Gutmann told me that it would be impossible, now that my name has already appeared in all the publicity, to substitute your name; I persuaded him to make a partial change. It should now read: 'Piano score by Franz and Joseph Schalk'. If you do not agree with that, write to me so that I can speak to him again. Löwe and I have had a lot of work with the first proofs and, as a result of your sketchy notation, particularly in the Finale, still have a considerable amount to change and correct. Schuch in Dresden wishes to perform the work next year. Bruckner is already away from Vienna in Steyr. I am sending you a cutting from the *Tagblatt*; please return it. I hope that you have heard from Nikisch why he is upset with Bruckner. If he should still be there, tell him in any case that he has offended me by not replying to my letter. I don't think much of fly-by-night enthusiasts. I have recently got to know a nice example in Mottl whom we (Bruckner, Löwe and I) met in Hietzing.[284]

---

283 According to Max Auer, *Anton Bruckner als Kirchenmusiker* (Regensburg: Bosse, 1927), 30. The autograph of the work has been lost, but the engraver's copy used for the first edition in 1886 - no. 4 of *Vier Graduale* , publ. Rättig (T.R. 42) - is in the *ÖNB*. For further information, see *G-A* IV/2, 346-49 and *ABSW* XXI/2, 131-34. For a modern edition of the motet, see *ABSW* XXI/1, 141-45.

284 See *FSBB*, 52-53 and *LBSAB*, 100-01 for this letter, dated Vienna 14 July 1885; the original is in the *ÖNB*, F18 Schalk 158/6/10. We have no information about the mysterious breakdown in

A fortnight later Joseph wrote to Franz again, this time concerning the proofs of the full score of the Seventh, in particular a detail of instrumentation at the end of the first movement. As Leibnitz points out, this highlights for the first time 'the problem which has beset Bruckner research into the Bruckner-Schalk relationship: the question to what extent the brothers intervened in the preparation of Bruckner's works for publication either through advice or independent decision-making'[285]

> ... The engraving seems to be very accurate. If you can remember what was actually decided regarding the organ point at the end of the first movement (whether with or without double bass), write to me immediately, as Bruckner's manuscript - in which no alteration has been made and only the timpanist has the E - has been used as the printer's copy. Perhaps you would prefer to see the proofs yourself. I will send them to you, if you wish. Bruckner is in Steyr.[286]

Bruckner wrote to Franz from Steyr on 16 August to report that he had just finished sketching the Eighth Symphony. He referred to the Finale as the 'most significant movement of my entire life' and hoped that he might be able to show it to Franz when he returned to Vienna [on 5 September].[287]

Bruckner also mentioned a 'colossal article' about him which had appeared in the *Deutscher Montagsblatt* on 10 August. Its author was Paul Marsop, who had sent a report of the Munich performance of the Seventh to the same paper earlier in the year. Writing to Franz, Joseph Schalk expressed some surprise that Marsop, a

---

the relationship between Bruckner and Nikisch to whom Bruckner had written a very friendly letter on 7 July; see earlier and footnote 275.

285 *LBSAB*, 101.

286 See *LBSAB*, 101f. for this letter, dated Vienna, 27 July 1885; the original is in the ÖNB, F18 Schalk 158/6/11. The organ point referred to is in bars 391ff. in the score.

287 See *HSABB* 1, 272f. for this letter; the original is in the ÖNB, F18 Schalk 54/3.

well-known Wagnerian but also an admirer of Brahms, should write such a lengthy article.[288]

In this article, Marsop begins by describing Bruckner as the only living composer, apart from Brahms and Robert Franz, that future historians would have to take seriously. Beside him even such important symphonists of the post-Schumann period as Joachim Raff and Robert Volkmann appeared insignificant. And yet he was comparatively unknown outside his own country. Wagner's recommendation had been as much a hindrance as a help, given the conservative musical climate. As a result of the performance of the Seventh in Leipzig and Munich, however, his importance was gradually being recognised. There was a marked contrast between Bruckner the man 'who stood in his modest attire in front of the excited audience and bowed helplessly and awkwardly' and his music which possessed that one constituent factor conspicuously lacking from contemporary works - 'die Kraft' ('power'):

> ... At last, at last someone who again puts his whole being into the creative process and is not one of those who, if only God had granted them the precious heavenly gift of originality, would then know where to begin. At last someone who not only mixes his colours because it seems good to him that others have done likewise but who gives life and colour to the product of his creative mind as soon as his imagination takes flight!

Marsop goes on to say that the majority of Bruckner's themes have two assets - a broad melodic sweep and a genuine symphonic character. Although his ability to

---

288 See *LBSAB*, 103 for this letter, dated 18 August 1885; the original is in the *ÖNB*, F18 Schalk 158/6/13. In a later letter to Levi (see below), Bruckner made further reference to his article which, he said, had appeared in the *Berliner Tageblatt*. It is possible that this was merely a reprint. The article was certainly reprinted in the Linz *Tagespost* 204 on 6 September 1885.

achieve great musical climaxes demonstrates 'the assiduous study of Wagner', he is 'sensible and tells himself that the rules of the dramatic style cannot be applied to absolute music'. Moreover, he is 'sufficiently gifted for it not to be necessary for him to have his imagination stirred initially by a "poetic" programme'. And, in spite of the many differences between them, Brahms and Bruckner have one thing in common, namely that they 'do not wish to have anything to do with the Berlioz-Liszt movement away from the mainstream' but lean much more strongly on Beethoven. While Brahms reaches back to the *Eroica* and the first three movements of the Ninth by way of Schumann's *Manfred* overture, Bruckner does so by way of *Die Meistersinger*. Both methods are understandable and justifiable. Marsop pursues the comparison further:

> ... In all fairness it must be stressed that Brahms, who displays a considerable mastery of symphonic style in the opening parts of his C minor and F major symphonies, has never been able to write a majestic, broadly flowing Adagio of the kind that we find in Bruckner's Seventh Symphony and in his String Quintet. To find comparable passages in modern music one has to point to the slow movements in Beethoven's C sharp minor Quartet and the *Hammerklavier* sonata. There is also another respect in which Bruckner is in advance of Brahms; he possesses something of that Beethovenian or, if one prefers, Schumannesque humour which turns a small part of the world upside down, plays tag with it for a few minutes and then puts it back in its place nice and neatly. In the Brucknerian Scherzo, Mercutio improvises and Prospero waves his wand. Caprice and imagination are at work alternately and, although there is such a unique admixture of the reasonable and the fantastic, the rational person again feels, nevertheless, how completely a divine folly driven by the malice of method represents the conciliatory middle way between wisdom and madness.

Marsop ends by recalling Bruckner's visit to Wagner's grave which he observed unnoticed the previous year:

... Now quiet and hesitant steps could be heard. In order not to disturb the peace of the great dead composer, a man came near the grave, his head already covered with the silvery-grey hair of approaching old age. He made his way reverently to the foot of the memorial stone, took of his hat, folded his hands and began to pray with such warmth and fervour until tear upon tear ran down his cheeks and the feeling of pain was relieved in sighs of the deepest devotion. The wood-bird was silent - and the Wanderer would also have heard nothing more; his eyes would have been filled with tears as well and, in compassion for the suffering of another, he may have remembered his own grief. Then the first shafts of sunlight pierced through the branches and tinged with gold the name that was engraved on the stone. The face of the devout man, engrossed in prayer, lit up with what was like the revelation of a higher power; all sadness vanished and there was a brightening of his features which were now filled with a new hope and confidence. It was the reflection of the greatness of Beethoven on the countenance of Anton Bruckner.[289]

Bruckner mentioned Marsop's 'splendid article' once again when he wrote to Levi shortly after his return to Vienna. While there was growing interest in his work in Germany, he still had reservations about subjecting his Seventh to the onslaughts of the Viennese critics:

> ... Two days later [i.e. after receiving a copy of Paul Marsop's article] Bote and Bock, the leading publishing house in Berlin, contacted me concerning the publication of my symphonies, with the request that I send them the score of my Fourth (Romantic) Symphony in E flat. If you intend to use this score for performance purposes, I will immediately send them my autograph score, which I do not want to be used for printing. Where is the score of the 7th Symphony which you sent to Karlsruhe? I have had to use the autograph score for printing purposes - and it looks shocking, of course. Mr. Richter told me yesterday that he wishes to perform the *Te Deum*. He is not going to get the Seventh - Hanslick!!! I told Mr. Richter that, if he wishes to perform one of my symphonies at any time, he should choose one

---

289 Marsop's lengthy article is reprinted in *G-A* IV/2, 350-61.

that Hanslick has already ruined anyway; he can destroy it even more. I have finished composing the Eighth. I wish that the detailed working-out was complete. If only I had more time! You will be pleased with it one day. Now to the most important matter. Are you completely restored to good health? This is my dearest wish, indeed my daily prayer...[290]

It was at about this time that August Göllerich (junior) was beginning to plan a biography of Bruckner. He asked the composer for a few days of his time so that he could obtain the background biographical information he required. In his reply Bruckner mentioned Marsop's article and Bote and Bock's request, but suggested that Göllerich spare himself the expense (of travelling?) involved. He did not have the time, as the Conservatory term was about to begin. So, 'the biography can wait'.[291]

A few days later Bruckner wrote to his young friend Oddo Loidol in Kremsmünster and sent him the score of *Christus factus est* 'in memory of 2 August 1885' as well as giving him the news about Marsop's article and Bote and Bock's approach. He was also concerned that Father Georg Huemer, the director of music at the abbey, have the F minor Mass copied as soon as possible and ended his letter

---

290 See *HSABB* 1, 273f. for this letter, dated Vienna, 7 September 1885. It was first published in *GrBLS*, 328-29; the original is not extant. On 19 September, Bruckner also wrote to his Berlin acquaintance, Wilhelm Tappert, asking him to return the score and parts of the Fourth which he had lent him in 1876 with a view to a possible performance. He pointed out that he had completely revised the symphony since then and that Richter had performed the 'new version' with great success in Vienna. See *HSABB* 1, 274 for this letter. It was first published in the *Allgemeine Musikzeitung* 67 (1940), 410f.; the original is not extant.

291 See *HSABB* 1, 274f. for this letter from Bruckner to Göllerich, dated Vienna, 20 September 1885; the original is privately owned.

by saying that he hoped to be in Linz on 4 October.[292]

Bruckner was referring here to his participation in the centenary celebrations of the Linz diocese. On 4 October his E minor Mass was given its second performance in Linz, 16 years after its successful premiere. The score used for this performance had been prepared by Johann Noll, the *Hofkapelle* copyist, in January 1883 and incorporated the various alterations Bruckner had made in the intervening years, particularly in 1876 and 1882. Adalbert Schreyer, who was asked by Johann Burgstaller to prepare and conduct the performance, later recalled some details:

> ... Bruckner would have liked the Sanctus, which begins with an unaccompanied and strictly polyphonic passage in the manner of Palestrina, to be performed even more slowly. But he had to admit that I had good reasons, in particular the risk of losing pitch, for not taking it any more slowly...

Schreyer also remembered Bruckner standing near the organ 'with his eyes raised ecstatically to the vaulted roof, his lips moving in silent prayer' during the performance. On 28 October Bruckner wrote to Schreyer to thank him for his 'heroic artistic deed' in conducting the Mass.[293] On the same day he wrote to Burgstaller, thanking him for his efforts in ensuring a successful performance of the Mass and asking him to accept the dedication of his *Afferentur* motet. He enclosed

---

292 See *HSABB* 1, 275 for this letter, dated Vienna, 25 September 1885; the original is in Kremsmünster Abbey. 2 August was the date of Loidol's ordination ceremony in Kremsmünster; Bruckner played the organ at High Mass. Bruckner possibly wanted the Mass copied quickly so that it could be returned to Vienna in time for a *Hofkapelle* performance.

293 See *GrBL*, 98f. for Schreyer's reminiscences, and *HSABB* 1, 277f. for Bruckner's letter to Schreyer; the original of this letter is in the *Oberösterreichisches Landesmuseum*, Linz. See also Chapter 3, pp. 174-75.

a copy of the Mass together with a sheet of alterations which he asked him to enter in his own copy of the work.[294] A diary entry in the *Krakauer Schreibkalender* - 'Messe Nr. 2 Hl.Riedel in Leipzig' - suggests that he also considered offering the work to the Leipzig choir director for performance in the course of the year.

In spite of his reservations about a performance of the Seventh Symphony in Vienna, the Philharmonic decided to include it in their programme for the 1885/86 season. On 18 October Hans Paumgartner reported in the *Wiener Zeitung* that the symphony had been scheduled for performance. A few days before this, however, the reluctant composer wrote to the Philharmonic committee to express his reservations in view of the 'sad local situation so far as influential criticism is concerned' which could only be exacerbated by his recent German successes.[295] On 6 November Bruckner gave another reason for his disquiet when writing to Mayfeld in Linz:

> ... I made a protest against the performance of my Seventh Symphony because it is futile in Vienna on account of Hanslick and his gang. If the Philharmonic take no heed of my protest, let them do what they want. There is no point in performing it before January as the parts have not yet been printed.
>
> As far as I know, the score etc. (piano arrangement) will not be published until even later than that. 20 orders from abroad, including three from America, have been received.

He then went on to touch on another subject, perhaps in response to a question

---

294 See *HSABB* 1, 277 for this letter; the original of the letter, together with the sheet of alterations (which is not in Bruckner's handwriting) is in the *ÖNB*. See also Chapter 3, p. 175.

295 See *HSABB* 1, 275f. for this letter, dated Vienna, 13 October 1885; the original of this letter is in the library of the Vienna Philharmonic. In a letter to Aichinger, also dated Vienna, 13 October 1885, Bruckner complained that the Philharmonic appeared to be turning a deaf ear to his protestations. See *HSABB* 1, 276; the original of this letter is in Steyr.

raised by Mayfeld in an earlier letter:

> So far as marriage is concerned, I still do not have any bride-to-be. If only I could find a really suitable dear girl! I certainly have many lady friends. A large number of the fair sex have been pursuing me recently and think that they have to be treated idealistically! It's terrible when one is not feeling well! Totally desolate!...[296]

Towards the end of the year there were three performances of Bruckner's Third Symphony outside Austria. On 6 December Walter Damrosch conducted the work in the Metropolitan Opera House, New York. Both the open rehearsal and performance were reported in *The New York Times*, and there were further reviews of the performance in the New York *Evening Post* and the *New York Daily Tribune*. Both the *New York Times* and *Evening Post* reviews were patronizing, the former praising the distinctness and fluency of the motives, the masterful thematic treatment, and the rich and vivid instrumentation but regretting the lack of 'a spark of inspiration or a grain of inventiveness', the latter commenting that the symphony was well constructed but ponderous and 'void of inspiration' for the most part. The review in the *Daily Tribune*, on the other hand, was complimentary if not overly enthusiastic:

> ... The likeness between this symphony and the ninth of Beethoven is accentuated by the circumstance that both are in the key of D minor. But it might be said here that the resemblance stops with the key and the subject matter of the first movements. Of the tremendous emotional power of Beethoven's crowning work there is no trace in the work of the modern writer, which sounds pedantic and uninspired...Of the four movements the Scherzo alone makes an unqualifiedly pleasing impression. It is fluent, fresh and vigorous in

---

296 See *HSABB* 1, 278 for this letter, dated Vienna, 6 November 1885; the original is in the *Archiv der Stadt Linz*, Linz.

its rhythms and altogether such a piece of music as can be heard at any time with pleasure. The symphony is laid out on a liberal scale, but it is in no respect as revolutionary as might have been expected from so profound a devotee of Wagner as Herr Bruckner. It was given a respectful hearing, but the Scherzo alone called out an emphatic expression of pleasure from the listeners.[297]

Two performances of the Third in Germany, the first in Frankfurt conducted by Karl Müller, the second in Dresden conducted by Ernst Schuch helped to make 1885 a year in which there were positive and encouraging signs of Bruckner's long-delayed recognition as a leading composer.

The Frankfurt performance on 4 December received mixed reviews. The local *Kleine Presse* attributed its lack of impact not only to the renowned conservatism of the Frankfurt public but, more importantly, to the lack of structural unity and thematic cohesion in the symphony. The reviewer detected 'a potpourri of themes from Wagner's last works' in the final movement. The report in the Leipzig *Musikalisches Wochenblatt*, on the other hand, was more encouraging. The symphony was hailed as 'one of the most significant symphonic works of the last decades' and its perceived lack of impact was attributable not to inherent weaknesses but rather to deficiencies in the performance. The reviewer referred to specific parts in the score where clarity had been marred by the conductor's failure to observe

---

297 From review in the *New York Daily Tribune* (7 December 1885). See Thomas Röder, *III. Symphonie D-Moll, Revisionsbericht, ABSW* zu 3/1-3 (Vienna, Musikwissenschaftlicher Verlag, 1997), 400ff. for the reports in *The New York Times* (5 and 6 December 1885), *The Evening Post* (7 December 1885), *The New York Daily Tribune* (7 December 1885) and an extract from Walter Damrosch, *My Musical Life* (New York 1923, repr. 1972), 352, in which the conductor recalls the performance and his later meeting with Bruckner in Berlin. Röder also provides the German translation of the *The New York Tribune* article which appeared in the *Wiener Zeitung* on 22 December 1885. An abbreviated version of the same translation appeared in the *Linzer Volksblatt* 298 on 30 December 1885. See also *G-A* IV/2, 368f.

the written dynamic and performance marks.[298]

On 23 November, Bruckner wrote to Ernst Schuch, and asked him to avoid over-quick tempi when conducting the symphony in Dresden.[299]   As in Frankfurt, public and press reception of the Dresden performance on 11 December was less than enthusiastic. Writing in the *Dresdner Anzeiger*, Carl Friedrich Niese acknowledged Bruckner's ability to conceive large-scale structures but regretted his inability to articulate them with 'clarity and lucidity'. Bernhard Seuberlich, the reviewer for *Dresdner Nachrichten*, praised Schuch's assured handling of the work and the orchestra's virtuoso playing but felt that the Seventh, which had already been performed successfully elsewhere, would have been a better choice; the symphony was marvellously scored and there was an abundance of original ideas but the 'nervous composer' preferred to move suddenly from one to another without giving any sufficient clarity and shape; only the third movement displayed the symmetry and unity one would expect from a symphonic movement. Similar sentiments were expressed in a short report of the Dresden performance in the Leipzig *Musikalisches Wochenblatt* in January 1886.[300]

---

298 See Röder, op.cit., 398f. for reprints of the reviews in the *Kleine Presse* (5 December 1885) and the *Musikalisches Wochenblatt* (7 January 1886). Röder also quotes from a letter from Clara Schumann to Brahms (Frankfurt 15 December 1885) in which she comments unfavourably on the symphony. See also Berthold Litzmann, *Clara Schumann. Ein Künstlerleben. Nach Tagebüchern und Briefen* III (Leipzig 1909), 473.

299 See *HSABB* 1, 278f. for this letter; the original is privately owned. Ernst (von) Schuch (1847-1914) was a pupil of Otto Dessoff. He was appointed court music director in Dresden in 1873 and became general music director in the city in 1889. He had obviously written to Bruckner for information about other works, including the D minor Mass (a copy of which Bruckner enclosed with his letter), the Te Deum and the Fourth Symphony.

300 See Röder, op.cit., 402ff. for reprints of the preview in the *Dresdner Anzeiger* (11 December 1885) and the reviews in the *Dresdner Anzeiger* (13 December 1885), *Dresdner Nachrichten* (13 December 1885) and *Musikalisches Wochenblatt* (28 January 1886). Röder also quotes a passage

Early in the New Year Bruckner's former teacher, Otto Kitzler, wrote to him to congratulate him on the Dresden 'success' and to offer his apologies in advance for not being able to attend the performance of the *Te Deum* in Vienna a few days later:

Dear old friend,

My brother in Dresden who visited me for a few days at Christmas told me that he had heard your Symphony in D minor there and had witnessed an outstanding success. I offer you my heartiest congratulations and am sincerely pleased that you are receiving at last the honour and recognition you deserve.

It has certainly taken a long enough time! I also read fine things about a performance of one of your Masses (is it a recent composition?) in the *Hofkapelle*. I have been deprived of a great pleasure as a result of the unfortunately necessary postponement of our Music Society concert from today until next Sunday, as I wanted to come to Vienna on this day (the 10th) to attend the performance of your *Te Deum*. I have bought myself the score and will perform it next autumn. The programmes for this season are already fixed, unfortunately, but the relevant musical material has already been purchased. A grand majestic current flows through the *Te Deum*. My warmest congratulations - I am already anticipating the reception keenly.

I will be with you in spirit on Sunday. To end with something prosaic. I spent a very pleasant time with my family in Waidhofen last summer. I was in Linz on 1 August and asked Zappe about you, but he was not able to tell me where you were. If you had been staying

---

from a letter from Emil Naumann to Ernst Klinger (in response to Klinger's query why Naumann had not given due recognition to Austrian composers like Bruckner and Johann Ev. Habert in his *Illustrierter Musikgeschichte*). Naumann, who had been present at the Dresden performance of Bruckner's Third, said that the symphony was devoid of structural proportion and organic unity and displayed nothing of the 'inner soundness, truthfulness and beauty of tone [found in the works] of our great symphonists Haydn, Mozart, Beethoven, Fr. Schubert, Spohr, Mendelssohn and Robert Schumann'. See also *G-A* IV/2, 373f.

at St. Florian I would certainly have looked you up...[301]

Recalling that King Albert of Saxony had enjoyed the performance of the two middle movements of Symphony no. 7 in Leipzig at the end of January 1885, Bruckner hoped that Schuch's performance of the Third in Dresden might make a sufficient impression on the king for him to give sympathetic consideration to a request for financial help towards the printing of the Eighth Symphony. We gather that Schuch was either unable or unwilling to act as a 'go-between' from the first of three letters which Bruckner sent to Elisabeth Kietz, the daughter of Gustav Kietz, the sculptor commissioned in the early 1870s to make a bust of Cosima Wagner. She came to Vienna in the autumn of 1885 as a guest of Dr. Hermann Behn who was one of Bruckner's pupils at the time. Bruckner met her and was charmed both by her winning personality and her love of music:

> ... A young lady has never acted on my behalf so pleasantly and generously as you have! A thousand thanks! I will never forget it. How often my thoughts turn longingly to you and your noble nature which I greatly admire. And your lovely letter! Councillor [Schuch] is not so well-disposed towards me as a man like Levi etc. etc. He still hasn't written to me and he has not fulfilled my request concerning the king, which he promised he would be sure to do...[302]

At the end of 1885, on 30 December, Ferdinand Löwe and Joseph Schalk played the first and third movements of the Seventh Symphony at one of the *Wagner Society*'s musical evenings. By means of such concerts Bruckner's devoted friends

---

301 See *HSABB* 1, 282f. for this letter, dated Brno 6 January 1886; the original is in St. Florian. Bruckner's F minor Mass was performed in the *Hofkapelle* on 8 December 1885. The first performance with orchestra of the *Te Deum* was conducted by Hans Richter on 10 January 1886.

302 See *HSABB* 1, 304 for this letter, dated Vienna 16 June 1886. It was first published in *GrBB*, 162f; the original is not extant

and pupils were attempting to increase his public profile, and they continued to do so even when the strong bastions of conservatism in Vienna appeared to be slowly crumbling in the late 1880s and early 1890s. There was evidence, however, that music critics and journalists were beginning of take greater note of the composer. Two letters sent in December - to Theodor Helm and Carl Ferdinand Pohl, secretary of the *Gesellschaft der Musikfreunde* - include a brief *curriculum vitae* and indicate that Bruckner had been asked to provide this as the basis for future articles.[303]

The measure of Bruckner's increasing success as a composer can be gauged from a brief review of works performed during 1886. The Seventh Symphony was, understandably, the most frequently performed - on 7 January at one of the Gürzenich concerts in Cologne, conducted by Franz Wüllner; on 19 February in Hamburg by the Philharmonic Orchestra conducted by Julius Bernuth; on 14 March in Graz by the orchestra of the *Steiermarker Musikverein* conducted by Dr. Karl Muck; on 21 March in Vienna by the Philharmonic conducted by Hans Richter; on 29 July in Chicago by an orchestra conducted by Theodor Thomas; on 12 and 13 November in New York by an orchestra conducted by Theodor Thomas (Thomas also conducted the work in Boston during the year); and on 18 November in Amsterdam at a *Caecilian Society* concert conducted by Daniel de Lange. The Third Symphony was conducted by Richard Hol in The Hague on 17 March and Utrecht on 20 March, and the first and third movements of the Fourth Symphony were performed by the *Tonkünstlerverein* of Sondershausen conducted by Karl Schröder on 4 June. The first choral and orchestral performance of the *Te Deum* in Vienna on 10 January, conducted by Hans Richter, was followed by performances in Munich

---

303 See *HSABB* 1, 280f. for Bruckner's letter to Helm, dated Vienna, 1 December 1885, and *HSABB* 1, 282 for his letter to Pohl, dated Vienna,, 31 December 1885; the originals of both letters can be found in the library of the *Gesellschaft der Musikfreunde*. An article on Bruckner by Helm appeared in the Leipzig *Musikalisches Wochenblatt* in five instalments (30 December 1885, 7, 14, 21 and 28 January 1886).

(conducted Levi, 7 April), Linz (conducted Floderer, 15 April, in a *Frohsinn* concert which also included performances of *Germanenzug* and the Adagio from Symphony no. 3) and Prague (conducted Friedrich Heßler, 23 or 28 November). The String Quintet was performed again in Vienna by the Hellmesberger Quartet on 7 January and in Sondershausen by the Halir-Grützmacher Quartet in early June. In Leipzig, Karl Riedel directed a performance of the Gloria and Credo movements from the E minor Mass (with organ accompaniment) on 3 July. The *Akademischer Gesangverein,* conducted by Rudolf Weinwurm, included *Trösterin Musik* in a choral concert in Vienna on 11 April and gave an outdoor performance of *Germanenzug* in Meidling at the beginning of May.

The performance of the Seventh in Cologne on 7 January received a favourable review in the *Neue Musikzeitung* from Hans Kleser who began, as many other reviewers had begun, by expressing surprise that the composer had taken such a long time to become recognised outside his own country. He continued by outlining what he perceived to be the main characteristics of Bruckner's style - 'unusually fine thematic invention', the masterly development of a 'grand leading idea' and a control of the whole orchestra both technically and dynamically.[304]

On the same evening (7 January), the Hellmesberger Quartet gave another performance of Bruckner's String Quintet in their concert series. Hugo Wolf reviewed the performance in the *Wiener Salonblatt* on 10 January:

> Anton Bruckner's Quintet is one of these rare artistic phenomena blessed with the capacity to utter a profound secret in a simple,

---

304 See *G-A* IV/2, 392-94 for an extract from this review in the *Neue Musikzeitung* VII/2 (January 1886). There was another review of the performance in the *Schweizerische Musikzeitung* 26 (1886), 27.

sensible way, in contrast to the usual procedure, much favoured by our modern 'masters', of clothing simple, everyday thoughts in the enigmatic utterances of oracles. Bruckner's music flows full-bodied and rich from the clear fountain of a childlike spirit. One can say of any of his works: 'It sounded so old, and was yet so new'.[305] This is thanks to a strong, popular strain that emerges everywhere in his symphonic compositions, sometimes overtly, sometimes hidden. How charming, for example, is the Ländler-like Trio of the Quintet! How well the composer, for all his earthiness, knows how to play the gentleman of distinction, sometimes by a harmonic deviation or a bit of ingenious counterpoint, by a more richly coloured instrumentation or a surprising inversion of themes etc.

But Bruckner's harmonic and melodic language was neither banal nor contrived. His musical structure, on the other hand, could be criticised for a certain lack of cohesion:

His thematic invention is the product of an extraordinarily fertile fantasy and a glowing perceptiveness, hence the lucid imagery of his musical language. The sentence structure, however, seems too dependent upon rapid progress, well-ordered periods and a certain well-rounded formal equilibrium... Granted, one can elaborate a subject just as well, and just as exhaustively, in chopped-off sentences as in a long caravan of the best-ordered periods. Epigrammatic brevity of form can allow thoughts to emerge more powerfully and more plastically, but also in a more one-sided and often less clear manner. Here, in every case, a happy medium is preferable to either extreme...[306]

Three days later, on 10 January, the Te Deum was given its first performance with full orchestral accompaniment in the third concert of the Gesellschaft subscription series. Bruckner's vivid setting of the Latin text won him great public acclaim and

---

305 Hans Sachs's words in his Act 2 monologue in Die Meistersinger as he recalls Walther's singing.

306 From review as translated by Pleasants, op.cit., 179f.

the critical reaction was generally favourable.

Writing in the *Wiener Fremdenblatt*, Ludwig Speidel made the usual reference to the musical influences of Beethoven, Liszt, Wagner and Berlioz, but highlighted the profound religious inspiration behind the work:

> In his enthusiasm the gifted former choirboy has courageously stepped out of the confines of the Catholic church whose humble servant he has been for many years. He praises his God with voices and strings, timpani and trumpets, completely unconcerned about the possibility of his being somewhat excessive in his treatment of the great subject. He bears his Lord aloft as in a storm, as in a whirlwind. But then, after such 'storm and stress' for the portrayal of which no device is too strong, the depths of heaven and the whole gamut of feelings are laid open. It is a joyful seeing and hearing of the mysteries of faith, their heights and depths. The human voice moves into the foreground as the one organ endowed with the ability to convey such mysteries, whereas one seems to hear in the orchestra the creature longing for salvation. The passage 'Non horruisti virginis uterum' [bars 133-37] has never been set to music with such fervour and passion and, in the following passage, comforting and blissful voices speak to us about victory over death and the opening up of the kingdom of heaven...[307]

Theodor Helm remarked that even those who were usually inclined to ridicule Bruckner or to maintain a stubborn silence when one of his works was being performed joined in the tumultuous applause,[308] while Hans Paumgartner said that the *Te Deum* had guaranteed the composer a worthy place beside Bach and

---

307 From Ludwig Speidel's review in the *Wiener Fremdenblatt* (19 January 1886), as reprinted in *G-A* IV/2, 401f.

308 From Theodor Helm's review in the *Deutsche Zeitung* (13 January 1886), as quoted in *G-A* IV/2, 402.

Beethoven.[309] Emil von Hartmann's review in the *Musikalische Rundschau* drew
attention to the combination of 'inspired invention' and 'enormous musical learning'
in the work, as well as the 'religious feeling' which inspired it and prompted the
dedication 'Omnia ad majorem Dei gloriam'.[310]

The other two works in the concert were Schubert's *Miriams Siegesgesang* and
Schütz's *Die sieben Worte*. Kalbeck, writing in *Die Presse*, made some comparisons
between the latter and Bruckner's *Te Deum* before adopting his normal position of
regarding Bruckner as no more than an imitator of Wagner. But there were also
some words of praise:

> Apart from *Miriams Siegesgesang*, the third *Gesellschaft* concert
> brought us two very singular works which, although separated by a
> time-gap of centuries, nevertheless have a kind of spiritual
> relationship: Heinrich Schütz's *Die sieben Worte* and Anton
> Bruckner's *Te Deum*. While one does not seem to be music as yet,
> the other is nearly music no longer. But both produce a highly
> individual impression and we have sympathy on the one hand for the
> dry old historian who cocoons himself reverently in the grey
> monotony of Schütz's gospel setting, and on the other hand for the
> modernist seeking unusual stimulants whose wishes are abundantly
> satisfied by the arbitrary and fantastic kaleidoscope of colours. Both
> works lack the variety of hues and the light and shade which, to our
> mind, belong to a good painting. They exist as if in a vacuum... We
> do not know with the latter [Bruckner] where the devout musician
> ceases and the seeker after effect begins. Nevertheless, the *Te Deum*
> is by far the most unified, self-contained and effective work by the
> musical mystic known to us and gives evidence of his outstanding

---

309 From Hans Paumgartner's review in the *Wiener Abendpost* (14 January 1886), as quoted in *G-A* IV/2, 403. Paumgartner's report also contains a review of the recent performance of the String Quintet which would also, in his opinion, occupy a permanent place of distinction in the chamber music repertoire.

310 From Emil von Hartmann's review in the *Musikalische Rundschau* (20 January 1886), as quoted in *G-A* IV/2, 403f.

talent.

Bruckner goes back to Beethoven and Wagner shows him the way. Of course, this is not the universally known Beethoven, the master *in extenso* as our lay understanding comprehends him, but that quite special Beethoven, rediscovered after his death, who begins at the very place where he really finishes. The *Te Deum* could be called an offspring of the Ninth Symphony, if it was not at the same time an offshoot of the Nibelung trilogy. A violin figure which pervades the work with the persistence of a steam engine is nothing more than the bare fifths' figuration from which the Allegro of the Ninth is developed. What with Beethoven was an original idea, whose musical and aesthetic justification was clear to everyone, appears to be more like the result of a misunderstanding when Bruckner uses it, although there is no reason to doubt that it still retains its profound significance. It is possible that the microcosm finds its place in the ascending and descending quavers. We readily concede that this hollow-sounding surge of voices and instruments has a surprising effect of elemental force. At the place where the voices begin to expand harmonically and contrapuntally we believe that we see Wotan rather than the God in whose honour the *Te Deum* was written - an unpleasant coincidence for the orthodox Christian, but one which does not disturb us! Bruckner's polyphony is a law unto itself; it belongs to the realm of the haphazard and avails itself of mortar when the rising sap of the musical cell-tissue and the blood running through the veins of the artistic organism are beginning to dry up... The crumbling fugue of 'In te, Domine, speravi' is shored up but does not develop. It is certainly possible that Bruckner, whose profound understanding of counterpoint and all related skills is universally praised, intended to give appropriate prominence to doubt with which hope is normally tinged, and that consequently he preferred to hide his light under a bushel than resolve to expose even a minuscule part of his greater ability. In the choral passage preceding the fugue there is a - perhaps intentional - reminiscence of the final duet from *Siegfried*. And perhaps in his final 'Non confundar in aeternum' the composer is interceding with his dear God not to allow the trilogy to fall into disrepute but to preserve the Bayreuth festival and its building for ever. Indeed anything is conceivable... We have no reservations, however, in praising the deeply felt 'Te ergo' and its repetition in 'Salvum fac' with its unidiomatic but appealing violin solo. Both movements are enclosed by choral and orchestral movements of tremendous drive and energy, like gently rolling meadows surrounded by a dark forest whose towering tree-tops sway in the storm. It is to be hoped that even those who disagree will infer from our honest remarks that we consider Bruckner's *Te Deum* to be an interesting and estimable work of its kind which we have no hesitation in ranking above the normal run-of-the-mill type which observes all the rules...[311]

Hanslick was also grudging in his muted praise of the work:

... In contrast to the old Schütz is the almost violent modern effect of Anton Bruckner's *Te Deum*. This praise of God comes storming along with thunderous power - full organ, roaring trombones and drum beats, the whole choir *fortissimo* and in unison. In comparison with other Bruckner works, however, his *Te Deum* seems more clear and more unified. Of course, it is not lacking in jarring transitions and contrasts and in undisguised Wagnerian reminiscences. But the *Te Deum* possesses more musical logic than we are accustomed to from Bruckner who takes pleasure in placing the most heterogeneous ideas side by side and in warming us up with some longer beautiful passage only to thrust us in ice-cold water immediately afterwards...[312]

In a later report of this concert which appeared in the *Neue Zeitschrift für Musik*, Count Laurencin d'Armond praised the uncommon richness of musical ideas in the work but criticised the patchwork nature of the whole.[313] Nevertheless the general feeling was that Bruckner had achieved a notable success with his choral work.[314]

---

311 From Max Kalbeck's review in *Die Presse* (17 January 1886), as reprinted in *G-A* IV/2, 404-08.

312 From Eduard Hanslick's review in the *Neue freie Presse* 7658 (19 January 1886), as quoted in *G-A* IV/2, 408f.

313 This review appeared in the *Neue Zeitschrift für Musik* 82 (16 July 1886), 321f. See extract in Louis, op.cit., 320f. and *G-A* IV/2, 409.

314 Other reviews of the performance appeared in the *Illustriertes Wiener Extrablatt* (23 January 1886) and in Kastner's *Wiener Musikalischer Zeitung* 1 (24 January 1886), 292f. The latter also includes a review of the performance of the Quintet on 7 January. See Gerold W. Gruber, 'Brahms

It was the most frequently performed of his choral compositions during his lifetime and it has retained its position in the repertoire ever since. Many of Bruckner's colleagues and friends were at the performance and several sent letters of congratulation afterwards. Rudolf Weinwurm's generous and warm-hearted sentiments must have brought particular pleasure to the composer. Weinwurm prefaced his letter with a musical quotation from the beginning of the *Te Deum* and went on to say how strikingly the orchestral performance had confirmed the earlier impression made by the performance with piano accompaniment the previous year.[315]

As well as refining and orchestrating the first version of his Eighth Symphony during 1886, Bruckner composed a short choral piece, *Um Mitternacht* WAB 90. He completed it on 11 February and made use of the same text by Robert Prutz which he had set 22 years earlier.[316] It was written specifically for a special Bruckner concert in Linz on 15 April planned by the *Frohsinn* choral society. Earlier in the year the choir committee wrote to Bruckner to inquire what music of his was available for performance, and he replied on 2 February:

> ... The *Te Deum* and the 3rd (D minor) symphony are published by Gutmann (opera house). The publisher holds the performance rights, however, and the music cannot be hired or even copied. All that I could do to help you would be to send you , for example, the 1st and 3rd (Hunt) movements of the 4th (Romantic) Symphony which is not

---

und Bruckner in der zeitgenössischen Wiener Musikkritik' in *BSL 1983* (Linz, 1985), 210.

315 See *HSABB* 1, 283f. for this letter, dated Vienna, 13 January 1886; the original is in St. Florian. See also *HSABB* 1, 283ff. for other congratulatory letters from Countess Anna Amadei (Vienna, 11 January 1886; original in St. Florian), 'old friends' from Linz including Wilhelm Floderer and Karl Kerschbaum (Linz, 18 January 1886; original in St. Florian) and Betty von Mayfeld (23 January 1886; original in St. Florian).

316 Namely *Um Mitternacht* WAB 89 for male voices with piano accompaniment (1864).

yet in print (but I am afraid that Munich may want this symphony; in which case, I would have to send you another for the Linz performance)...[317]

Bruckner's response to the textual imagery is just as keen as it is in his first setting of *Um Mitternacht*. The second and third verses are set for tenor solo and evocative humming accompaniment for choir which provides a rich, frequently shifting harmonic background.[318]

Another choral piece, written at about the same time as *Um Mitternacht* - *Ave regina coelorum* WAB 8 - can be mentioned here, as it demonstrates Bruckner's continuing involvement, albeit sporadic, with sacred music. The work takes the form of a unison vocal line, accompanied by organ chords. The melody is plainchant-like but is Bruckner's own.[319]

The performance of the Seventh Symphony in Hamburg on 19 February had a mixed reception. While the conservative Hamburg public reacted coolly,

---

317 See *HSABB* 1, 286 for this letter, dated Vienna, 2 February 1886; the original is in the library of the *Linzer Singakademie*.

318 The work is discussed fully in *G-A* IV/2, 410ff. It was dedicated to the Strasbourg Male Voice Society which published a facsimile edition of the piece in 1886. It was later edited by Viktor Keldorfer and printed by Universal Edition (U.E. 2927) in 1911. See also Renate Grasberger, *Werkzeichnis Anton Bruckner* (Tutzing, 1977), 215 and idem, *Bruckner Ikonographie. Teil 1: Um 1854 bis 1924, ABDS* 7 (Vienna, 1990), 27 for a facsimile of the first page.

319 The autograph of the piece is in the *ÖNB* and there are sketches in the Kremsmünster Abbey library. It was written for Klosterneuburg and was first published (1910) in the *Jahrbuch des Stiftes Klosterneuburg* III, 132. For further information, see *ABSW* XXI/1, 186 and *ABSW* XXI/2, 135-39. There is a modern edition in *ABSW* XXI/1, 148-49. A facsimile of the first page of the autograph can be found in *ABSW* XXI/2, xxviii. The piece is dated 1886 by Renate Grasberger in her *Werkzeichnis*, 12, 'between 1885 and 1888' by Leopold Nowak in *ABSW* XXI/2, 135 and '12.2. 1886 (?)' by Franz Scheder, *ABC Textband*, 491 on account of the fact that the sketch in the Kremsmünster library is written on the same sheet as sketches for the Finale of the Eighth Symphony.

connoisseurs were much less guarded in their response. One of these was the critic Wilhelm Zinne who wrote to Bruckner the day after the performance:

Yesterday your Seventh Symphony filled me with an enthusiasm which I have not experienced to the same degree before, except with Beethoven's Ninth. Never before last night have I been filled with so much admiration when confronted with the work of a genius. This enthusiasm has remained and the overwhelming impression it has made on me is proof that I have found in your symphony that ideal symphonic work which I have been longing for with uncertainty. I have laid aside those scores which I have been intending to study so that I can become acquainted with your incomparable work as soon as possible. That I am not the only one who hopes to profit from its universal value is demonstrated by the number of those who approached the conductor immediately after hearing the work, in order to obtain the score. Within the circle of musicians there is unanimous agreement about the worth of the Seventh. That a public like the Hamburgers would react coolly and negatively to such a flow of ideas could only be expected by anyone who encounters this extremely stupid crowd every day and who knows the favourite meal of this most noble species with its super-blasé attitude. But that will give you less cause for concern, dear Master, in view of the great impact your work made yesterday on the large number of your friends and enthusiastic admirers.

Although you might already have the reviews in two of the daily papers here - 'Hamb[urger] Correspondent' (Sittard) and Hamb[urger] Nachrichten' (A.F. Riecins) - I am sending them to you because it is just possible that you did not receive them from anyone else. I do not wish to send you the review in another usually very popular paper because the reviewer in question clearly approached your work without the enthusiasm the event deserved and with a great lack of understanding of the symphonic genre. You must ascribe the constant reference to Brahms in the other two papers (I would gladly exchange his four symphonies for your 'Seventh' alone) to the fact that a significant degree of local patriotism is at stake and, as a result, objective judgment often suffers because things are viewed through 'rose-tinted spectacles'.

I am also able to submit a report of the performance of the symphony yesterday to the new 'Musikalische Rundschau' in Vienna. But I have an overwhelming desire to express my boundless admiration and respect to you - and the fact that I, like you, was once a 'village organist and schoolteacher' can only add to my appreciation, if that is possible...[320]

In acknowledging Zinne's letter, Bruckner expressed surprise that his friend Sucher had not conducted the symphony, but was delighted that Zinne had understood the work so well, particularly as the performance seems to have been less than ideal - certainly in comparison with the Leipzig and Munich performances. Perhaps a 'lack of rhythmical energy' was to blame.[321]

In a second letter written shortly afterwards, Zinne gave Bruckner the surprising news that Eduard Marxsen, Brahms's old teacher, had attended the concert and was full of praise for the symphony:

> ... I was asked by our director of music, Professor v. Bernuth, to pass on the score of the 7th Symphony to Eduard Marxsen, Brahms's teacher, as he was very keen to get to know it. My conversation with Marxsen centred almost entirely on the new symphony. The old man, still in excellent spirits, did not stop praising the beauty of the Bruckner symphony for an entire half-hour. He had gone to the

---

320 See *HSABB* 1, 287 for Zinne's letter, dated Hamburg, 20 February 1886. The letter was first published in *ABB*, 385f; the original is not extant. Carl Wilhelm Zinne (1858-1934) became one of Bruckner's staunchest supporters in North Germany. Further information about him is provided by Kurt Blaukopf in Herta Blaukopf, ed., *Mahler's Unknown Letters* (London: Gollancz, 1986), 227ff. For further information about Josef Sittard, see below. A. F. Riecins = August Ferdinand Riccius (1819-1886) who was a composer, conductor and music critic resident in Hamburg from 1864 onwards.

321 See *HSABB* 1, 288 for this letter; no date given, but the date 'nach dem 20. Februar 1886 is surmised'. There is a copy of the letter with the original envelope in the *Öffentliche Bücherhallen*, Hamburg. Josef Sucher (1843-1908), a former pupil of Sechter's, musical director of the Hamburg Opera from 1878 and of the Court Opera in Berlin from 1882, had evidently promised to conduct the symphony. Bruckner may have been unaware that he had moved to Berlin.

concert with few expectations, but he declared the symphony not only the greatest of modern times but one of the most outstanding that we possess. He had made this judgment before getting to know the score. Everyone who has ears to hear must be of the same opinion. He was evidently very annoyed about the reception of the work on 19 February (there was some hissing after the Adagio in C sharp minor, for instance!) and went home thinking that he was the only one who was enthusiastic about it, only to be disabused of this notion when he read the papers a few days later. He made no mention at all of his pupil Brahms throughout the entire conversation. When a member of the Philharmonic committee said to him, 'We have made real fools of ourselves with the symphony', Marxsen retorted, 'To make a judgment like that is proof of your ignorance. At best you could say "it is not to my taste"'.[322]

Joseph Sittard's intelligent review in the *Hamburger Correspondent* dwelt on the structural expansiveness of the symphony:

No matter how one approaches Bruckner's works, even those who are unable to appreciate them will have to concede that an artist of genius speaks to us from this Seventh Symphony. He certainly cannot be reproached for formlessness and lack of contrapuntal knowledge and skill, nor can a considerable creative power in thematic invention be denied him. The structural conventions are most strictly observed in all four movements. Bruckner even allows himself the luxury, which an artist endowed with the divine power of strong vivid imagination is certainly at liberty to do, of supplementing the usual two main themes in the first movement, for example, with a third of equal importance and of adding yet another contrasting theme. The structure is certainly expanded by this means but it is an expansion which, to borrow a legal expression, is effected on thoroughly judicial and legitimate grounds. Bruckner's themes are designed on the large scale; all of them are filled with a significant content and are of an outstanding melodic beauty. These are not expressionless miniature motives made up of intervals put together at random,

---

322 See *HSABB* 1, 289 for this letter; no date given, but 'zwischen 20. und 26. Februar 1886' is surmised. It was first published in *ABB*, 384f.; the original is not extant.

but large, bold and powerful ideas that could only be conceived by a man of stature. The way in which he develops these ideas is novel and unusual, even bizarre at times. His imagination often works fitfully and moves along in seven-league boots. But it does not follow that the legitimacy of his artistic creativity should be called into question. If we adopt such a puritanical standpoint, we can then place a full-stop at the end of Beethoven's works and say: thus far and no further. Intellectual development does not stop, however, and the inspired artist has always appeared at the appropriate time to point art along new paths. When Brahms appeared with his larger works they were all found to be abstruse and artificial. The greatest arbitrariness was discovered in them and nothing but cold reflection could be seen. But the worst criticism was that the melodies could not be retained and taken back home. And today? Today Bruckner has to listen to the same criticisms, but intensified, and he is accused of the deadly sin of Wagnerianism. However, he has not copied the advances for which we have the composer of *The Ring* to thank, but simply accepted the greater wealth of expressive means acquired by music during the past fifty years, transferred them to symphonic form and developed them in a completely independent way. In a word, Bruckner is no mannerist, but a stylist, an artist who possesses such a superabundance of musical riches that he does not need to obtain a loan from anyone else.

Sittard described the Adagio as 'a movement the like of which has not been written since the funeral march in Beethoven's *Eroica*... a funeral march of the most noble kind', and continued:

The principal theme is in two parts. Five tubas together with violas, cellos and double basses begin a mournful motive in the lugubrious minor key. The string orchestra continues with a moving song in E major in the rhythm of a solemn funeral march. The mourning is transfigured, as it were, by the recollection of the deeds of a great man or hero who was snatched from the world. With this theme, which is made up of two contrasting parts, the composer has already prepared the foundation for a vivid dramatic development, but a subsidiary theme now appears. It has a beautiful consolatory character and lifts the spirits of those who are mourning. And how the composer proceeds to develop these themes! A drama of the most shattering kind enfolds before our mind's eye. The first mournful motive again gives way to the march-like theme in the major and then also appears in the friendly major key at the greatest climactic point where it is joined by the violins descending from the heights. But the sounds of mourning still appear, albeit fleetingly, and the movement ends quietly and comfortingly with a heavenward glance, as it were. The composer who was able to write such a work of art as this movement belongs among the immortals...[323]

On 24 February Bruckner wrote to Sittard to express his gratitude. He mentioned the successes of the earlier Leipzig and Munich performances and added that it was vital that the Scherzo was played 'very quickly; the changes of tempo are imperative'.[324]

Another Hamburg musician with whom Bruckner corresponded at the time, E. Schweitzer, wrote him a very encouraging letter on 20 March and confirmed what Zinne had already said about the great impact made by the Seventh:

> ... My dear Professor, I cannot avoid writing you a few lines in response to your very charming letter. First of all I have to convey to you warmest greetings from Professor Bernuth and Director Marxsen. Both are still completely full of the powerful impression that your magnificent symphony made on them. How badly Bruch's *Odysseus* fared in comparison, and how superficial, even trivial at times, and boring for the most part it seems in contrast to your work! There has been a great swing of opinion in your favour here in Hamburg partly as a result of all the critics enthusiastically taking your side and,

---

323 From Sittard's review in the *Hamburger Correspondent* (20 February 1886), as reprinted in *G-A* IV/2, 417-20. Josef Sittard (1846-1903) was a music journalist who was based in Hamburg from 1885 onwards and who, like Wilhelm Zinne, was an eloquent advocate of Bruckner's music in North Germany. A.F. Riccius's review also appeared in the *Hamburger Nachrichten* on 20 February 1886.

324 See *HSABB* 1, 288f. for Bruckner's letter to Sittard: the original is in the *Bayerische Staatsbibliothek*, Munich.

it must also be said, largely on account of Marxsen standing up for you so energetically. The so-called Brahmsians had not expected that. These fellows are Brahms supporters in name only. In actuality Brahms serves them only as a cover so that they can fire their poisoned arrows at the newly-emerging fine, first-rate composers. In fact, they treat Brahms in the same way, and even wounded him in the not too distant past in a manner similar to what they are saying now about your great work. Marxsen has told me so many times how one day when Schumann had presented the young Brahms with a testimonial - 'New Paths' - which did him [Marxsen] the greatest credit, Brahms's father came to him in great sadness because all the musicians had told him that, as a result of such a stupid article about Johannes, his son's whole career had been destroyed!

You mention Sucher in your letter. Now, between ourselves, it is fortunate that he was not the first to perform the symphony here - it would not have been possible for a long time. In the first place, the Municipal Theatre orchestra is the most overworked in the world. Each month it is required to play at least 29-30 times in the Hamburg or Altona or Theatiner theatres and, during the summer months, to give performances in the zoo each evening from 7 to 12 for Director Tottini. It is quite clear that the necessary time and, as far as the conductor is concerned, the necessary freshness are not available to rehearse a masterpiece such as yours.

And it must be said that Mr. von Bernuth rehearsed the symphony very carefully and it was given a very good performance. Between ourselves, there is a particular reason why he is criticised in the Hamburg papers. He will not allow a lady friend of Dr. H., the chief editor of [one of] the above papers, to sing in the Philharmonic concerts! That is an open secret here!...[325]

The first Austrian performance of the Seventh was given not in Vienna but in Graz. On 14 March, Dr. Karl Muck, a young music director at the beginning of a

---

[325] See *HSABB* 1, 292f. for this letter, dated Altona, 20 March 1886. It was first printed in *ABB*, 360ff. The originals of both this letter and Bruckner's earlier letter to Schweitzer are not extant.

distinguished career, conducted the orchestra of the *Steiermärkische Musikverein.*[326] Preparations for the concert were meticulous. No less than 14 rehearsals were held and Muck had to correct many copyist's mistakes in the parts. Bruckner attended the final rehearsals and, according to Eckstein, had to make a detailed search of some of the popular Graz watering-holes in order to find the tuba players from the Vienna Philharmonic who were supposed to be engaged in playing rather than drinking! But Muck's painstaking rehearsals paid dividends. Bruckner received a standing ovation and the review in the leading Graz paper, the *Tagespost*, was complimentary on the whole. The critic, Karl Maria von Savenau, had strong reservations, however, about 'those passages in Bruckner's score where too many dissonances, indeed whole sequences of dissonances destroy the euphony, and the supreme principle of beauty in all art is violated', adding that 'exuberance in art is the signature of the modern era - we are living in a dithyrambic epoch'.[327]

Muck enclosed a copy of this review when he wrote to Bruckner the day after

---

326 Karl Muck (1859-1940) studied at Würzburg and Leipzig and held posts as music director in Zurich, Salzburg and Brno before going to Graz. He moved to Prague in 1886, Berlin in 1892, and took up an appointment as conductor of the Boston Symphony Orchestra in 1912. After the 1914-18 war, during which he was interned, he became a guest conductor in Europe and America but was based in Hamburg from 1922 to 1933. For further information, see Kurt Stephenson, 'Carl Muck' in *MGG* 9 (1961), cols. 842-43, and Hans Christoph Worbs, 'Carl Muck' in *The New Grove* 12 (1980), 757.

327 See *G-A* IV/2, 424-27 for a reprint of the complete review which appeared in the Graz *Tagespost* on 16 March 1886. Earlier, on 12 March, the evening edition of this paper printed a biographical article on Bruckner. See Ingrid Schubert, 'Wagner und die Neudeutschen in Graz' in *BSL 1984* (Linz, 1986), 36f. for further information and for extracts from another review which appeared in the Graz *Morgenpost* 61 (also 16 March 1886). The young Siegmund von Hausegger also provided a report for the *Deutsche Zeitung* (16 March 1886). It was his first contact with Bruckner and his music. The concert was held in the Graz *Stephaniesaal*. After the concert, Bruckner gave an organ recital in the hall.

504

the performance:

> Once again my sincere thanks for the unforgettably beautiful hours
> which I spent studying your work. You can rest assured that I will
> seize every opportunity to renew my acquaintance with it in the
> future! The period of your stay passed too quickly, and I was always
> surrounded by idle or tiresome people, with the result that I did not
> have the opportunity of telling you properly how much your work
> meant to me and how I did my utmost to do justice to your high
> intentions. I trust that I was successful in providing you with at least
> some proof of this through the performance.
>
> I enclose the 'review' from Savenau, our Beckmesser-in-chief. The
> others have still not reported anything. As soon as their concoctions
> appear, I will send them to you.
>
> In accordance with your wish, I am also sending you my portrait.
> I would be extremely pleased if you could send me a picture of
> yourself very soon; but please do not forget to add the appropriate
> dedication by writing a couple of lines.
>
> Have you already read Hausegger's review in the *Deutsche
> Zeitung?*..[328]

Finally, on Sunday 21 March, the symphony was given its first orchestral
performance in Vienna. Bruckner had already written to Bernhard Deubler in
St.Florian inviting him and Ferdinand Moser to what he undoubtedly regarded as a
major event in his career.[329] In spite of his earlier reservations about a Viennese
performance of the Seventh, Bruckner described it afterwards as the best performance
he had heard of any of his works and was full of praise for Richter and the
Philharmonic players. At a reception given in Bruckner's honour by the *Wagner
Society* after the concert, Richter spoke very graciously of a change of attitude

---

328 See *HSABB* 1, 290-91 for this letter, dated Graz, 16 March 1886; the original is in St. Florian.

329 Not only did he send them an invitation, but he also undertook to procure tickets for them! See
HSABB 1, 290 and 291 for his two letters to Deubler, dated Vienna, 16 and 19 March 1886
respectively; the originals are in St. Florian.

towards Bruckner on the part of the Philharmonic players. There had been misunderstanding and distrust in the past, but now there was complete acceptance. Bruckner would never again have to hear the first performance of any of his works outside Vienna.[330]

On 24 March Bruckner wrote to Josef Sittard in Hamburg to provide details of the very positive reception of the symphony in Vienna, in spite of the normal lack of enthusiasm expressed by the triumvirate of Hanslick, Dömpke and Kalbeck![331] The following day he sent almost identical letters to Levi and Wolzogen, informing them of the successful performances of the work in Graz and Vienna:

> ... All struggling and striving were to no avail. The 7th Symphony was performed by the Philharmonic on the 21st. Richter put his whole heart into it. The jubilant reception was indescribable. 5-6 tumultuous recalls even after the 1st movement; and so it went on - after the Finale unceasing tumultuous enthusiasm and recalls. A laurel wreath from the *Wagner Society* and a bouquet. The picture of the Master with my wreath round his neck was so marvellously apt. I also received the bust of the 'immortal' one from Dresden the following day, and I embraced it warmly and tearfully.
> On 14 March I was in Graz for a performance of the same work

---

330 On 25 March Bruckner wrote officially to the Philharmonic Society to congratulate Richter on his 'excellent and most inspired conducting' and to express his 'deepest admiration' of the orchestral players' excellent performance. See *HSABB* 1, 295 for this letter; the original is privately owned.

331 See *HSABB* 1, 293f. for this letter; the original is in the *Bayerische Staatsbibliothek*, Munich. See also *HSABB* 1, 296f. for a letter from Friedrich Eckstein to Sittard, dated Vienna, 3 April 1886; the original is also in the *Bayerische Staatsbibliothek*. In his letter, Eckstein says that he has arranged for Rättig to send Sittard the scores of the Third Symphony and the *Te Deum*, but laments the fact that so much of Bruckner's music - 'perhaps a thousand written pages' - still remains unpublished. Enclosed with his letter are some of the reviews of the Vienna performance of the Seventh. When Bruckner wrote to Sittard later in the year (probably in August), he enclosed some details of his compositions and mentioned that Rättig had sent him the scores requested. See *HSABB* 1, 312 for this undated letter; the original is also in the *Bayerische Staatsbibliothek*.

directed by Dr. Muck, a brilliant conductor from Würzburg. An equally great success! Could you possibly arrange for a short report to appear in a Munich paper? I would be most grateful.

Bote and Bock have withdrawn and I no longer have a publisher [for the Fourth Symphony]. I felt I had to make you, my artistic father, aware of this. Please convey my deepest thanks and respects to Dr. and Mrs. von Fiedler. My kindest regards to your wife.

The king should now have the score...

N.B. I have just seen the *Morgenpost* of 23 March and the *Deutsche Zeitung* of 25 March which are splendid. Speidl (*Fremdenblatt*), Frei (*Tagblatt*) and the *Wiener Zeitung* should also be good.[332]

In his letter to Wolzogen Bruckner apologized for not being at home when Wolzogen visited him and thanked him for his letter which contained a poem that could possibly be set to music - St. Francis's 'Hymn to the Sun'. Bruckner was delighted with the 'splendid poem' but had other demands on his time:

... Unfortunately I am submerged in the 8th Symphony and have almost no time to compose. On 14 March I was in Graz for the performance of my 7th Symphony. The performance, directed by Dr. Mück, a brilliant conductor from Würzburg, was excellent (14 rehearsals) and the reception was indescribably magnificent. I was greeted with fanfares after the Finale.

On 21 March the performance of the same work in Vienna by the Philharmonic under Richter was truly excellent...[333]

---

332 See *HSABB* 1, 294 for this letter to Levi. It was first published in *GrBLS*, 331; the original is not extant. Bruckner refers here to the dedication score of the Seventh which he had sent to King Ludwig II on 5 March (according to a diary entry of that date); Ludwig Klug, the Bavarian court secretary, forwarded the score to the king in Hohenschwangau on 10 March. See also *HSABB* 1, 295 for Bruckner's letter of thanks to the *Wagner Society*, also dated Vienna, 25 May 1886; the original is in the Vienna *Stadtbibliothek*.

333 See *HSABB* 1, 295f. for this letter to Wolzogen; the original is in the Vienna *Stadtbibliothek*.

Bruckner must have been thrilled to receive the congratulations of many of his Conservatory colleagues after the Vienna performance. He was apparently even more surprised and delighted to find a telegram awaiting him when he returned home. It was from Johann Strauss - 'I am completely overcome. It was one of the greatest experiences of my life'.

As Bruckner had anticipated, the critical reviews of the Seventh polarized quite clearly into pro- and anti-Bruckner groups. Hanslick was at least honest enough to confess that his first impressions made it impossible for him to arrive at an objective assessment of the work:

> ... Bruckner's new Symphony in E major was the *pièce de resistance*. The public certainly did not display much resistance. Some already fled as early as the end of the second movement of this symphonic boa-constrictor and a large number departed after the third, so that only a small number remained to enjoy the Finale. However, this plucky Bruckner legion applauded and cheered with the might of thousands. It has certainly never happened previously that a composer has been recalled four or five times after each single movement. Bruckner is the newest idol of the Wagnerians. It cannot exactly be said that he has become fashionable, because the public will in no way follow this fashion. But Bruckner has become a military command and the 'second Beethoven', an article of faith for the Wagner community. I confess frankly that I would find it difficult to judge Bruckner's symphony fairly as it seems to me to be so unnatural, overblown, morbid and pernicious. As in all of Bruckner's larger works, the E major symphony contains inspired ideas, interesting and, indeed, beautiful passages, six bars here and eight bars there; but between these flashes there are stretches of interminable darkness, leaden monotony and feverish over-excitement. In a letter to me, one of Germany's most respected musicians describes Bruckner's symphony as the chaotic dream of an orchestral musician overtaxed by twenty *Tristan* rehearsals. That appears to me to be apt and to the point. This is as much as I can say with any honesty after my first disturbing impression...[334]

---

334 From the review in the *Neue freie Presse* 7755 (30 March 1886), as reprinted in *G-A* IV/2, 436f.

The like-minded Gustav Dömpke took Bruckner to task for his lack of architectural sense and deficiency in long-term harmonic planning:

... Bruckner lacks the feeling for the basic elements of any musical structure and for the combination of a series of integral melodic and harmonic parts; it has forsaken him if he ever possessed it. His imagination is so incurably diseased and fractured - and we know what tutor and 'healer' was responsible - that it does not recognize anything which resembles the necessity for regularity in chord sequence and periodic structure. The top and bottom of his view of art is that creative spirits ignore all laws and rules usually followed to some extent by others. What seems to us momentarily to be great and pure in Bruckner must be a chance occurrence or a deception. Perhaps we should give up the attempt once and for all to seek an explanation for the abnormalities of a 60-year-old which a 20-year-old could not eliminate quickly enough. Bruckner composes like a drunkard. He is a past master in deception, and his imagination is swamped by the most heterogeneous dregs of Beethoven's and Wagner's music without the balance of an intellect which is capable of sifting these influences according to their value and essential ingredients and, above all, without the artistic power of assimilating them and forging them into a separate and independent individuality. In Bruckner's modulatory and periodic structures we find the most purposeless breadth as well as the most startling rashness and lack of reason. Verbose repetitions of a motive by means of so-called *rosalias* are of such frequent occurrence in each of his symphony movements that one must marvel at the self-deception of those who admire such passages. A new-fangled *rosalia* differs from the old honourable one in its pronounced predilection for remote keys whose cunning accumulation makes such a strong impression on the listener and keeps him so occupied that he forgets the *rosalia* and is not so bored as he should be. Unfortunately, after the measured, impressive opening which is reminiscent partly of Wagner and partly of Beethoven (the best part of the entire symphony), the rest of the first movement goes downhill. The main theme of the Adagio undeniably makes a strong outer impression when one first hears it, but it is no more than an effective combination of constituent parts, albeit original and deeply-felt. Comparison with the Adagio theme of a true master in the Haydn-Brahms tradition will also make the difference gradually clear to those who allow themselves willingly to be deceived at the outset. At the end of the first section the composer mixes bass tubas and horns and has them play the most gruesome and chromatically divergent passages possible. We truly tremble at the musty smell that assaults our noses from the discords of this decay-addicted counterpoint.

Scherzo and Finale do not trail far behind the first two movements. The former certainly has a lot of temperament and a cheerful theme (influenced by Beethoven's Ninth) but there is a far too ugly mixture of roughness and over-refinement as it progresses.

There is unanimous agreement that the Finale is the weakest and most chaotic part of the symphony. Even the eulogists tend to agree. Its motto ought to be: 'Parturiunt montes, nascetur ridiculus mus'. Not only the opening but the movement as a whole appears to have been swept together by a broom. The same is true of the piercing instrumentation in which the composer has a predilection for sudden alternations of *pp* and *ff*. Otherwise the orchestration is the attractive part of the work, but even it ceases to be interesting when pure nonsense is being scored.[335]

Although illness prevented Max Kalbeck, the music critic of *Die Presse*, from attending the concert, he provided a review of the work based on a perusal of the score and, possibly, attendance at one of the rehearsals:

... If only the E major symphony was the first orchestral work of a 20-year-old. Then we would not need to ask, 'What has happened to your other works, old man?' And the fermenting juice, which behaves just as absurdly here as it does in Bruckner's other compositions, would finally give us the promise of a good wine. If Mr Hans Richter is as serious as he appears to be in his admiration for the composer who has been unjustly ignored during his lifetime, he will have unenviable obligations to fulfil. There remains nothing else for him to do but perform Bruckner's six earlier symphonies one after the another as soon as possible. The composer, crowned with

---

335 From Dömpke's review in the *Wiener Allgemeine Zeitung* 2186 (30 March 1886), as reprinted in *G-A* IV/2, 438-40. The Latin motto is from Horace: 'The mountains are in travail, an absurd mouse will be born'.

laurels as 'German symphonist', his faithful admirers, and the critics have a right to make this demand. If Bruckner is the inspired successor of Beethoven that we are supposed to recognize and admire, he should take charge of the Philharmonic concerts and show the world what he is capable of doing! He who has said A must also say B, and he who brings the E major symphony must also bring the Symphonies in A major, B flat major, E flat major, D minor and C minor at the risk of filling the empty seats in the hall by proclaiming the message of the new gospel. We believe in the future of the Bruckner symphony as little as we believe in the victory of chaos over the cosmos. But that is a matter of opinion and a question of taste about which there is no need to argue, as far as we are aware. Bruckner treats the orchestra like an instrument upon which one can improvise at pleasure. His Seventh Symphony is no more than an impromptu comedy with stock characters which is partly attractive and partly repellent, a picture painted in a variety of colours and modelled on Beethovenian and Wagnerian motives. Ideas coruscate and glimmer in the simmering broth-like mass of orchestral sound, but these ideas are the dead and mutilated remains of an old world doomed to destruction, not the fruitful seeds of a new world struggling to come into being. Nevertheless, something could be done with even these ideas if they were manipulated by a master who had control over the over-all structure. But the sizzling flames fizzle out, fading away just as they are at their most bright, and the outer shell is destroyed.

The most successful movement of the work, relatively speaking, is the slow movement in C sharp minor, a scrupulously schematic copy of the Adagio of Beethoven's Ninth Symphony with the free use of Beethovenian and Wagnerian melodies. Siegfried's obsequies from *Götterdämmerung*, the Funeral March from the *Eroica*, the 'Cry to the Saviour' from *Parsifal* and thematic elements borrowed from the Adagio of the Ninth are woven together with great skill to form a tone-painting whose predominantly dark colour and timbre make a strong impression on the listener. Two pairs of tenor and bass tubas and a contrabass tuba dig a pitch-black grave into which one peers with ecstatic trembling. But this Adagio, praised to the skies by its over-zealous admirers, also suffers from the same basic malady that afflicts all Bruckner's works and is due to the absolute inability of the composer to think and act according to the laws of musical logic. With a predictability bordering on the comic Bruckner invariably places his rehearsal letters at the points where he has run out of breath, and he has to go to all the trouble of using all 24 letters of the alphabet.

How proudly he begins his Allegro. The theme for horns and cellos rises heavenwards above tremolando violins. But how pathetic is the end of this bold ascent! It was no shooting star, no flying eagle, only a rocket that disintegrates in the air. And, at the end, the entire symphony peters out like a musical firework.

Bruckner's thematic and contrapuntal endeavours are touching in their clumsiness. In the first movement he introduces an awkward quaver figure with upward-leaping semiquavers as an independent motive. No one can say where it comes from and where it is going to - but it comes from the 'Nibelungs' and goes to the devil. It is provided with a melody to comfort it in its abandoned state, and when everything finally comes together it is certainly there as well. Empty chromatic scales, dry sequences and cruel harmonic jokes which make one's hair stand on end - these are all Bruckner's stock-in-trade. Many a military trumpeter will envy him his ability to achieve contrapuntal miracles with broken chords which are played rhythmically in the manner of the 'Urmotiv' in *Das Rheingold*.

The third movement of the symphony, which is too strictly modelled on the Scherzo of Beethoven's Ninth, has as its main theme a trumpet signal which would be of excellent use in the first major fire that we have. Above all, this Scherzo shows very conspicuously that Bruckner is of necessity one of those modern composers who are dissatisfied with the established order of things only to the extent that they are unable to find their own place in the latter. The 'bold' composer makes up his inventory pedantically and with the anxiety of an accountant, and produces one four-bar period after another with the sweat of his brow so that no mistake occurs!

The Finale begins with the same tremolo as the Allegro and finishes also with the same theatrical apotheosis in which the Bengal light undeniably produces applause but does not leave a particularly pleasant fragrance. In between there is a large stretch consisting of a partly alarming, partly amusing mixture of bravado and wretchedness, and this ambitious expanse of music attempts in vain to replace the depth that is lacking. The confusion that this more than problematical work, which exists only by the grace of its great predecessor, is said to cause in otherwise entirely rational people results *inter alia* from the fact that the music publisher, Mr. Albert Gutmann, has considered the highly unfavourable response of the famous critic, Eduard Hanslick, to be a recommendation of his most

512

recent product and has added a report of the same as an advertisement.[336]

More thoughtful and discriminating reviews were provided by Hans Paumgartner and Robert Hirschfeld, both writing in the *Abendpost*. Paumgartner provided a lengthy article, part of which was a criticism of a section of the audience and critics like Hanslick who were unable to entertain the possibility of admiring a work like Bruckner's Seventh as well as maintaining their obvious preference for Brahms's works. As far as Bruckner's symphony was concerned, Paumgartner praised the composer's 'symphonic thinking' as reflected in the character of all the themes, their presentation and development, the orchestral conception of the themes (as compared with the themes in the orchestral works of Mendelssohn, Schumann and Brahms which, he considered, were pianistically inspired) and Bruckner's boldness in expanding traditional symphonic form and adapting it so that it had become 'an independent means of expression for his inner thoughts'. Although the Finale in particular had a novel structure, its motivic content was so impressive that it would soon become a favourite piece for every musician.[337]

Hirschfeld's article a few days later was pleasantly free of 'point-scoring' and contained a well-balanced, objective comparison of Brahms's and Bruckner's styles:

> To all appearances the Viennese are not lacking in artistic taste but only in enough space to exercise it. We have a lot of enthusiasm but little room for monuments. It is no doubt simply because no space could be found for Bruckner's symphonic works in the Philharmonic

---

336 From Max Kalbeck's review in *Die Presse* (3 April 1886) as reprinted in *G-A* IV/2, 441-50 and Manfred Wagner, *Bruckner* (Mainz, 1983), 169-74. In Gutmann's defence, it should be pointed out that his other advertisements for the symphony included favourable reports of the work!

337 From Paumgartner's review in the *Wiener Abendpost* (27 March 1886) as reprinted in *G-A* IV/2, 450-55. See also Tschulik, op.cit., 174f.

programmes that it has been impossible to perform anything other than fragments of his symphonies up to now. And it has been the enthusiasm aroused by numerous performances of the Seventh Symphony in Germany which seems to have opened up a space for the most recent symphony of our native composer in the Philharmonic programme-plan.

And now for once Bruckner has found not only a place but even a place of honour. And this place of honour is of such importance that the ridicule of adverse critics no longer affects him. In the *Neue freie Presse*, Ed. Hanslick dares to offend good taste by declaring that Bruckner composes like a drunkard.[338] We live in sorry times when men dare to say such things about a composer who has had a long and honourable life as a productive artist, an esteemed teacher, a highly regarded church composer, and our most brilliant organist. People of this ilk who dare to serve art have never contributed strong and original deeds, serious and sincere words, and noble teaching. Where these men sense an artistic spirit who is to be feared as something of a rival of Johannes Brahms in any musical sphere, he is suppressed and silenced in all sorts of ways. It has to be said that the incontestable reputation of such an important man as Brahms does not need to be protected by such critical nightwatchmen. Nevertheless, I have more empathy with Brahms as a symphonist than with Bruckner who can now claim to be his equal as a result of his 'Seventh'. The sturdy and dour strength of Brahms seems to me better suited to the symphonic style than Bruckner's prodigal and superabundant inventive powers. If many of Brahms's symphonic themes are lacking in the necessary succinctness, Bruckner's freely- and expressively-unfolding themes often possess too much, with the result that one has difficulty in avoiding dramatic ideas which really have nothing to do with the symphony. I would prefer to focus some attention on Brahms's methods of handling the symphonic style as bequeathed by Beethoven than to be concerned with Bruckner's attempts at greater breadth and display of colour. The introduction of dramatic accents, and the dynamic style in particular, to the symphony lends it an unsettled, rhapsodic character, a type of freedom which seems to me to be unsuited to symphonic form as it leads without fail to the dramatic symphony and to programme music which signifies the disintegration of absolute music.

---

338 It was not Hanslick, but Gustav Dömpke, writing in the *Wiener Allgemeine Zeitung*, who made this comment. See earlier.

I am not sure if a step which really leads to disintegration can be counted as progress in the truest sense. These typically rhapsodic features were most noticeable in the last movement of the E major symphony. The excellent conclusion of the first movement also seems to me not to be an organic part of the whole structure. One has the feeling here that a theatre curtain suddenly drops with a loud noise and separates the listener from an important dramatic scene.

But of what importance are such aesthetic reservations beside the truly overpowering and inexhaustible richness of imagination, the amazing structural strength and the deep-seated warmth of feeling which seem to be combined so felicitously in Bruckner's artistically skilful and yet so naive creative spirit and give the E major symphony the unmistakable stamp of a master work? These extraordinary assets are combined with Bruckner's entirely excellent art of instrumentation which presents the most intricate musical combinations and the boldest contrasts in the brightest and clearest light. As a result, each idea in the symphony is carefully introduced and shown to full advantage...[339]

Theodor Helm was convinced that the performance of the Seventh in Vienna marked a definite breakthrough in Bruckner reception in the city and could think of no other symphony since Beethoven which had such an arresting and majestic opening. After a thorough analysis of the first movement, in which he praised the originality of all three main ideas, the wealth of motivic development in the middle section, and the triumphant coda which reminded him of the end of Wagner's *Das Rheingold* as the gods process into Valhalla, Helm described the Adagio with its 'most shattering funereal sounds' as 'perhaps the greatest written since Beethoven' and 'certainly without any comparison the most sublime symphonic Adagio of modern times'. Not only was it a memorial to Wagner, but Beethoven, 'another composer deified by Bruckner', had given his 'heavenly blessing' in inspiring the 'consolatory second main theme' which was reminiscent of the 'equally soulful,

---

339 From Robert Hirschfeld's review in the *Wiener Abendpost* (1 April 1886), as reprinted in *G-A* IV/2, 463-66.

equally transfigured D major and G major episodes in the Adagio of the Ninth Symphony'. Other suggested Beethovenian models for the movement were the funeral march from the *Eroica* symphony and, in terms of the 'gigantic plan of the formal dimensions', the F sharp minor Adagio from the Piano Sonata in B flat op. 106. The applause for the 'much more complex' first movement was much greater than that for the second movement probably because many in the audience 'lost the thread' of the extended periodic structure of the latter.

Helm also detected a 'Beethovenian spirit' in the A minor Scherzo and described the F major Trio as a 'veritable melodic pearl'. In the Finale, he was full of praise for the orchestra which coped admirably with Bruckner's occasional 'unconventional [melodic] leaps' and 'flashes of lightning' and communicated the ringing sonority and rhythmical elan of the movement with enthusiasm.[340]

Finally, Hugo Wolf, writing in the *Wiener Salonblatt*, was pleased to report the successful performance and the public's belated recognition of the composer:

> ... Bruckner has not been spared the age-old painful experience of the prophet without honour in his own land. Struggling for decades in vain against the obtuseness and the hostility of the critics, rejected by the concert institutions, pursued by envy and ill will, he was already an old man when fortune kissed his brow and the thankless world pressed laurel wreaths upon his head. Not even Berlioz had so bad a time of it as Bruckner. Berlioz was denied by his countrymen, but abroad he enjoyed successes, and in his creative prime, too, that must have brought a measure of consolation for his misadventures in Paris. For Bruckner the doors of foreign concert halls were first opened late in his life, and the transient attention given his works under Herbeck's influence was neither serious nor thorough enough to reveal his full worth in the spotlight it deserved. Only most recently, thanks to the efforts of some young musicians and the Academic Wagner Society, has there been a favourable turn in the public attitude toward

---

340   From Theodor Helm's review in the *Deutsche Zeitung* (25 March 1886), as reprinted in *G-A* IV/2, 455-62.

his works. His Te Deum was performed to applause in the concerts of the Society of Friends of Music, and now the Symphony no. 7 in E, so jubilantly received in Germany. The ice of our concert institutions' severe reserve has been broken. The great success enjoyed by our countryman abroad could no longer be contemplated with the indifference heretofore most generously accorded Bruckner's works by our Philharmonic Orchestra...[341]

Wolf's thinly-veiled sarcasm notwithstanding, Bruckner thanked Richter and the orchestra for their contribution to the success of the work.[342] Richter for his part thought highly enough of the symphony to take it with him to England the following year when he gave a series of concerts with the London Philharmonic in St. James's Hall. Bruckner's pleasure in Johann Strauss's acknowledgment of the significance of the symphony was increased when a social evening was arranged for the two composers and the sculptor, Viktor Tilgner, who was later to make a bust of Bruckner.

Between the Graz and Vienna performances of Symphony no. 7 there were two performances in Holland of Symphony no. 3, both conducted by Richard Hol, the first in The Hague on 17 March, the second in Utrecht on 20 March. The critical response was lukewarm; the reviewer for *Caecilia* found much that was beautiful and original in the work but criticised the composer for his 'unfortunate insertion of a trivial, meaningless motive' in the Finale.[343]

---

341 From the review in the *Wiener Salonblatt* (28 March 1886), as translated by Pleasants, op.cit., 201ff.

342 See page 505 and footnote 330.

343 Reviews appeared in two issues of *Caecilia* (The Hague, 1 and 15 April), the first covering the performance in The Hague, the second the performance in Utrecht. See Thomas Röder, *III. Symphonie D-Moll Revisionbericht*, 405f. for extracts from these reviews. See also Cornelis van Zwol, 'Holland: ein Brucknerland seit 1885' in *BJ 1980* (Linz, 1980), 135. Richard Hol (1825-1904) was organist at Utrecht Cathedral, director of the local Music School and director of the town

Munich had witnessed a momentous performance of Bruckner's Seventh in March 1885. A year later, on 7 April 1886, Hermann Levi directed an equally successful performance of the *Te Deum*. The music-loving Princess Amalie was present at both the afternoon rehearsal, during which Bruckner improvised on the organ, and the evening concert, and spoke to the composer.[344] Writing in the *Münchner Neueste Nachrichten* on 10 April, the reviewer detected similarities, stylistically and motivically with Liszt's compositions but singled out the 'structural succinctness and conciseness' and the 'warmth of feeling' for special mention:

> With this work Bruckner has come alongside the great composers Berlioz and Liszt who, for their part, have drawn inspiration from Beethoven's great Mass and produced a number of sacred and oratorio-like works which in their totality represent a rebirth of the true sacred-religious style. In these works ardent and passionate feelings and the attempt to produce precise poetic and musical expression lead of necessity to individual and characteristic melodic shapes. Although the contrapuntal element is by no means completely in the background it is no longer regarded as an end in itself.
>
> The essence of Bruckner's *Te Deum* is that it occupies a unique intermediate position between the styles that prevail in Berlioz's and Liszt's religious works. Bruckner has structural objectivity in common with the former... whereas the type of feeling is more reminiscent of Liszt. The composer reveals himself to be a master of the contrapuntal style. Particularly fine are the rhythmically independent voice-leading and the extremely detailed development of the 'in te speravi' fugue with its enormous upswing at 'non confundar in aeternum'...[345]

---

concerts.

344 See *G-A* IV/2, 470f. for her recollection of the meeting.

345 From the review in the *Münchner Neueste Nachrichten* (10 April 1886), as reprinted in *G-A* IV/2, 471ff. See also Uwe Harten, 'Zu Anton Bruckners vorletzten Münchener Aufenthalt' in *Studien zur Musikwissenschaft* 42 (Tutzing 1993), 325.

On 11 April Rudolf Weinwurm conducted the *Akademischer Gesangverein* in a performance of Bruckner's *Trösterin Musik* WAB 88. But the original words, written specifically in memory of Josef Seiberl in St. Florian in 1877 (*Nachruf* WAB 81), were changed and a new text supplied by August Seuffert, editor of the *Wiener Zeitung* and a member of the choir. Hans Paumgartner provided an appreciative review of the choral piece in the *Abendpost* on 30 April. Bruckner also had the opportunity of hearing another of his choral pieces, *Germanenzug*, performed by the same conductor and choir at an open-air concert in Meidling shortly afterwards.

It is not known if Bruckner spent Easter at St. Florian.[346] He had invited Deubler, the choir director, and Moser, the abbot, to the Vienna performance of his Seventh Symphony, and it is possible that Deubler at least was also present at a special concert given in the composer's honour in Linz on 15 April. On 12 April Bruckner wrote a brief note to Göllerich in Wels to inform him that he would be taking the express train from Vienna to Linz on Wednesday 14 April, and on 13 April he asked Wilhelm Floderer, the conductor of *Frohsinn*, to book a room for him at the *Kanone* hotel and added that there was a possibility that one of his young German students would be accompanying him.[347]

The concert consisted of performances of *Germanenzug*, *Um Mitternacht*, the

---

346 He was certainly there on 24 April, the date of a letter sent to the German Railway Company in which he reported the loss of a winter hat during a train journey between Vienna and Munich on 5/6 April, possibly taken mistakenly by a young army lieutenant. See *HSABB* 1, 300; the original is privately owned.

347 See *HSABB* 1, 297f. for these two letters. The letter to Göllerich was first published in *ABB*, 210 and the letter to Floderer was first published in the *Neue musikalische Presse* 14/3 (1905); neither of the originals is extant. The young German student was almost certainly Friedrich Klose, who began private lessons with Bruckner in 1886. See *HSABB* 1, 298-99 for a letter from Klose to Göllerich, dated Vienna 16 April 1886. Klose also provides details of the Linz stay in his *Meine Lehrjahre bei Bruckner.*

Adagio from Symphony no. 3 and the *Te Deum*, and Bruckner's many fellow Upper Austrians who attended made a point of demonstrating their esteem by giving him a standing ovation at the end. In a short speech of thanks, Bruckner recalled the various trials and tribulations of his career, including the 'great humiliation' he had been subjected to by 'three Viennese newspapers', remembered with affection the encouragement and support of Wagner, acknowledged the recent help provided by Nikisch in Leipzig, Levi in Munich, Mottl in Karlsruhe and Richter in Vienna, and considered the present day as one of the greatest in his life. To end the proceedings, a special chorus written in his honour - 'An Meister Bruckner' (with music by Floderer and text by Kerschbaum) - was sung.[348]

Bruckner was so convinced that Hanslick (and Brahms) were inflicting further 'great humiliation' on him by ostensibly putting pressure on Richter not to perform his Seventh Symphony in London at the end of May that he asked Levi to intercede on his behalf and persuade Richter not to renege on his alleged promise.[349] There is no indication that Levi carried out this rather unusual request; perhaps he felt that it would be professionally unethical to do so. On the other hand, he did what he could to gain greater recognition for Bruckner in his native Austria. Shortly after the

---

348 See *G-A* III/1, 593 for further details. The text of Bruckner's speech is printed in *ABB*, 208-09. Bruckner also sent a special letter of thanks to *Frohsinn* on 20 April. He thanked all those who had helped to make the occasion so memorable, particularly as it had taken place among his 'family' in Linz. See *HSABB* 1, 299 for this letter which was first printed in the *Linzer Zeitung* on 30 April. Although Bruckner mentioned Mottl among those who had helped to create interest in his works outside Austria, he was disappointed to learn that his former pupil had directed a performance of the *Te Deum* in Karlsruhe in April with piano accompaniment only. He wrote to Mottl to express his disappointment and disapproval, pointing out that the *Te Deum* had now been performed with orchestral accompaniment in Munich, Vienna and even Linz! See *HSABB* 1, 303 for this letter, dated Vienna 4 May 1886; the original is in the *ÖNB*.

349 See *HSABB* 1, 300 for this letter, dated Vienna, 29 April 1886. It was first published in *GrBLS*, 332.

performance of the *Te Deum* in Munich, Levi wrote to the music-loving Princess
Amalie in the hope of securing her help:

> ... Bruckner's life has been a series of failures and disappointments up
> to now; a few works performed in his native country... have certainly
> been very successful with the public but the very powerful Viennese
> press - under the leadership of the philistine Hanslick who is opposed
> to any progress in the realm of music - has always treated Bruckner
> as a man who is by no means to be taken 'seriously', as a madman
> who has only the occasional lucid moment. Bruckner enjoyed his first
> real success with the performance of his 7ᵗʰ Symphony here last year.
> He had introduced himself to me in Bayreuth two years ago (hitherto
> even his name had been unknown to me!) and had asked me at least
> to take a look at one of his works. I promised him that I would look
> through his work thoroughly. On my return to Munich I found the
> score of his 7ᵗʰ Symphony, and the more I studied the work the more
> astonished I was that a man like this could have been ignored for such
> a long time. At the first rehearsal of this very difficult and unusual
> work I had to contend with the opposition of almost the entire
> orchestra. The opinion was that it was not music at all, and the
> committee of the Music Academy even put pressure on me to drop
> the work from the repertoire. But I refused to be put off and
> consequently had the pleasure of observing the musicians become
> more interested with each rehearsal (I held five) and finally become
> really enthusiastic at the performance. The majority of the public
> were also thrilled, and this evening was the first shaft of light in the
> life of this much neglected man. With the assistance of a few friends
> I then collected a small sum of money which I made available to a
> Viennese publisher as a contribution towards the cost of printing the
> symphony. I also supported Bruckner's most humble request that His
> Majesty, our most gracious King, accept the dedication of the
> symphony. Eventually, as a result of his success here, other concert-
> giving bodies took notice of Bruckner. In short, it appeared as if
> good fortune would finally work a little in his favour. But,
> unfortunately, this has still made no difference to Bruckner's parlous
> material situation. In order simply to make ends meet, he has to
> teach for five-seven hours each day. The majority of his works
> lie unpublished in his cupboard, and official circles in Vienna either
> show their disapproval or constantly ignore him. He is thoroughly

disheartened and, under these circumstances, it is doubtful whether he will be able to complete his newest and, according to his friends, most significant symphony.

My most humble request to Your Royal Highness is this: would it be possible for you to put in a good word for Bruckner? The Austrian State has to atone for some earlier sins of omission. Mozart was left to struggle with life's necessities, and Schubert was allowed to become the victim of poverty. Even Beethoven was not able to enjoy any support whatsoever from the court or from the state. Far be it from me to rank Bruckner alongside these immortals. Nevertheless among composers alive today he is the most important and the one most deserving of support. Perhaps Your Royal Highness could take the opportunity of making your imperial cousin, Archduchess Valerie, aware of Bruckner's position! A small annual stipend from the Emperor's private purse would restore Bruckner's creative spark, rescue him from the compulsory labour of teaching and, as a result, perhaps enrich the world with some important masterworks. And as Bruckner is already 62 years of age, that should probably not be too great a sacrifice to make!

In order to provide Your Royal Highness with further information I take the liberty of enclosing a letter from one of Bruckner's friends and pupils, as well as a review of the symphony referred to above.

I ask Your Royal Highness to pardon me for approaching you in this manner. But the deep interest which Your Royal Highness takes in our art and the confidence that I have in your great kindness causes me to hope that your response to this letter will be a friendly one...[350]

On 4 June Bruckner wrote to Levi to thank him for his support and to give him the news that the first and third movements of his Symphony no. 4 and his String Quintet were to be performed during the Composers' Festival of the *Allgemeiner Deutscher Musikverein* held in Sondershausen from 3 to 6 June.[351] Liszt, who was the driving force behind the Festival, was by no means a 'Bruckner enthusiast' and had reservations about the Seventh, but he did concede admiration for parts of the

---

350 See *HSABB* 1, 301f. for this undated letter; it was first published in *G-A* IV/2, 486-90.

351 See *HSABB* 1, 303 for this letter. It was first published in *GrBLS*, 333.

Quintet. He had already played a piano-duet arrangement of the Adagio with his cousin, the Countess Henriette von Liszt.[352]

King Ludwig of Bavaria, the dedicatee of Bruckner's Seventh Symphony and a potential influential patron of his music, died tragically on 13 June. There was still strong support for Bruckner in the Munich court, however. Levi's letter to Princess Amalie no doubt exaggerated Bruckner's 'perilous material situation' but it had the desired effect. Princess Amalie evidently wrote to the Emperor and received a reply from him on 28 June, indicating that something would be done for Bruckner. On 1 July the Lord Chamberlain received an official letter, signed but not written by Hellmesberger, with the recommendation that Bruckner be awarded a minor decoration - the 'Knight Cross of the Franz Josef Order' - and granted an increase in salary of 300 florins per annum. Attention was drawn to Bruckner's 'commendable performance of duties' as a court organist, as well as his prominence as a composer of symphonies and church music, two of his Masses being among the most striking of the *Hofkapelle*'s repertoire:

> ...Several of his great symphonies, the number of which has reached eight so far, have had sensational successes in the Vienna Philharmonic concerts and in performances in Munich, Leipzig etc. etc. The same is true of a String Quintet which has had an enthusiastic reception from the public in several recent performances.
> Bruckner's compositions have an abundance of inventiveness, inspiration and high artistic quality and will undoubtedly bring the

---

352   See August Stradal, 'Erinnerungen aus Bruckners letzter Zeit' in *Zeitschrift für Musik* 99 (1932), 974 and Lisa Ramann, *Lisztiana. Erinnerungen an Franz Liszt (1873-1886/87)* (Mainz, 1983), 337-45. See also *HSABB* 1, 302 for Bruckner's letter to Hermann Behn, Vienna 1 May 1886; the original is in the Music Division of the New York Public Library.

composer widespread recognition...[353]

The Lord Chamberlain, Prince Hohenlohe-Schillingsfürst, supported Hellmesberger's recommendation, and the Emperor gave his official approval on 8 July.[354] Bruckner received the decoration on 9 July and there was an official notice in the *Wiener Zeitung* the following day.[355] On 9 July Bruckner took Levi's advice and used Princess Amalie's name-day as an opportunity to send both his best wishes and his profound thanks for the active part she had played in interceding on his behalf with the Austrian royal family.[356] He received several messages of congratulation, including two letters from St. Florian, the first from Moser, the second from the abbey choir.[357] His friend of many years, Rudolf Weinwurm, also wrote to him to say that, as 'the most significant of our native composers', he richly deserved the honour.[358]

Bruckner's letters to Hermann Levi, Adolf Obermüller of the Linz *Musikverein* and Moritz von Mayfeld also refer to this honour. He expressed his profound

---

353 From transcript of official letter in *ABDS* 1, 50 and 102ff. Further information about the Franz Josef medal can be found in *ABDS* 1,112f.

354 See *ABDS* 1, 51-54 and 104-110. The salary increase came into effect on 1 August.

355 *Wiener Zeitung* 155 (10 July 1886).

356 See *HSABB* 1, 306 for the texts of both Levi's letter to Bruckner, dated Munich, 6 July 1886, and Bruckner's letter to Princess Amalie, dated Vienna, 9 July 1886; the original of the former is in St. Florian, and that of the latter is not extant.

357 See *HSABB* 1, 308 for Provost Ferdinand Moser's letter, dated St. Florian, 11 July 1886, and *HSABB* 1, 310 for the letter from the choir, dated St. Florian, 15 July 1886 and signed by some of the members; the originals of both are in St. Florian.

358 See *HSABB* 1, 307 for this letter, dated Vienna, 9 July 1886; the original is also in St. Florian.

gratitude to Levi for the important part he had played.[359] Mayfeld was informed that the Emperor had evidently offered to pay for any 'artistic journeys' Bruckner might wish to undertake in the future. Another interesting piece of information in this letter suggests that the immediate problems concerning Richter's performance of the Seventh Symphony in London had been resolved. These had been highlighted in an earlier letter to Levi at the end of April and in a letter to Wilhelm Zinne in June.[360] Now, however, it was a question of the performance having to be 'postponed' because Richter had taken ill.[361]

In the meantime, the British musical public was made aware of both Bruckner and his Seventh Symphony in an article written by C.A. Barry which appeared in the *Musical Times* on 1 June:

> Readers of German musical papers will have noticed that during the last few months their columns have teemed with biographical and critical notices of the composer whose name heads this article and who, on all sides, has been heralded by them as presenting the rare phenomenon of a man who, after the attainment of his sixtieth year, has suddenly burst upon the world with his Seventh Symphony, and wherever it has been performed has been at once recognised as a composer of extraordinary genius and acquirements. In England the name of Anton Bruckner, which is not to be found in any biographical musical dictionary, either English or foreign, that we have been able to consult, will probably only be familiar to a few from the fact that on the occasion of the opening of the Royal Albert Hall, in 1871, he

---

359 See *HSABB* 1, 307 for Bruckner's undated letter to Levi which was first published in *GrBLS*, 333f., and *HSABB* 1, 309 for the letter to Obermüllner, dated Vienna, 13 July 1886, the original of which is in the *Linzer Singakademie*.

360 See *HSABB* 1, 304f. for Bruckner's letter to Zinne, dated Vienna, 16 June 1886, in which he enclosed three photographs of himself for his Hamburg friends - one for Zinne, one for Marxsen and one for Bernuth; the original is in Hamburg Public Library.

361 See *HSABB* 1, 311 for Bruckner's letter to Mayfeld, dated Vienna, 23 July 1886; the original is in the *Archiv der Stadt Linz*.

was one of a number of foreign organists who, by invitation, repaired to this country with the view of exhibiting their skill upon the newly created organ of the Royal Albert Hall and that of the Crystal Palace. As a performance of Herr Bruckner's Seventh Symphony, which has created so great a stir of late in musical Germany, is promised at a forthcoming Richter Concert, the name of this composer, if his Symphony meets with the same reception that it has had elsewhere, will be in everyone's mouth. We propose therefore to advance a few particulars of his artistic career, so far as we have been enabled to cull them from German papers which we have at hand, and from other sources.

During his biographical sketch, Barry recalled Bruckner's exploits as an organ virtuoso:

In 1869 he visited France where, as a virtuoso of the organ, he secured a series of veritable triumphs, especially at Nancy and Paris. In 1871, as already stated, he came to England on a similar mission. Here it may be recalled that, on one occasion of his improvising at the Crystal Palace, he played in so inspired a manner, and was so carried away by his feelings, that the blowers were unable to supply the necessary amount of wind that he required.

Later in the article Barry discussed Bruckner's compositional output in general and the Symphony no. 7 and *Te Deum* in particular:

As only four of Bruckner's larger works - viz. his Symphonies nos. 3 and 7, his Te Deum, and a String Quintet - have as yet been published, it is impossible to speak of his compositions generally, except on hearsay. In preference to this, therefore, we confine ourselves to furnishing a few particulars of those of his works, the scores of which lie before us - viz. the Symphony no. 7 in E and the Te Deum. But preparatory to this it may be remarked that in the very early days of the 'Richter' Concerts, Hans Richter brought the score of Bruckner's 'Wagner' Symphony with him to London, with the view of performing the Scherzo therefrom - an intention which, however, was not realised. An opportunity was then accorded the present writer of cursorily examining the score of this Symphony, but all that at the present date he can recall respecting it is the fact that in outward appearance it was a work of gigantic proportions... A hasty glance at the score [of the Seventh Symphony] is sufficient to prove at once that we are in the presence of a composer who has something important to say, and has his own peculiar mode of expressing himself. But so polyphonic is it in its structure, and so important and independent a part is assigned to the wind instruments that, without further study than we have been able to give to it, it would be rash to predict how it will come out in performance. In regard to the predominance of the wind instruments, it may, however, be said that in its external aspect it more nearly resembles the score of 'Die Meistersinger' than any other which we can call to mind. Of the work generally it may be said that though it conforms to the usual four-movement symphonic plan, it is laid out on a grand scale. Bruckner requires a large canvas for his picture, a goodly stock of brushes for the delineation of his subjects, both in mass and in detail, and a pallet furnished with the most vivid and brilliant colours. To drop metaphor, it may be said that his themes are of a strikingly bold and impressive character, and that both contrapuntally and orchestrally they are treated with consummate skill and effect. A strong family likeness exists between the first and last movements, a modification of the first subject of the former forming the principal basis of the latter, and thus serving to impart a sense of unity to the entire work. The Scherzo will probably be the most readily accepted of the four movements, but the Adagio is undoubtedly the most important. This was written soon after Wagner's death, avowedly as an Elegy in memory of the great master, and a most elevating and impressive Elegy it certainly is. Overwhelmed with grief at the death of his friend, Bruckner has here interpolated a motive from his Te Deum, which is therein associated with the words: 'Non confundar in aeternum', and thus comes very appropriately as a prayer both for the deceased master and for his survivors...

The Te Deum, which is laid out for chorus, a quartet of soloists, organ *ad libitum* and orchestra, by its greater simplicity and rugged grandeur contrasts strongly with the elaborateness of the Symphony... By maintaining for the most part a diatonic tonality in the purely choral portions of this work, by unison singing, by the admission of so-called ecclesiastical progressions, by the use of triads without their thirds, and by keeping the distinction between praise and prayer well in view, Bruckner has produced a work of an eminently religious character, and one for which the epithet 'sublime' does not seem too strong...[362]

Nikisch's performances of the Seventh Symphony and of two movements from the same work in Leipzig at the end of 1884 and beginning of 1885 had one interesting repercussion. The *Riedel-Verein*, a choral society founded and conducted by Professor Karl Riedel, sang two movements from Bruckner's E minor Mass in St. Peter's Church, Leipzig on 3 July 1886. In a preliminary notice which appeared in the *Leipziger Tageblatt* on the morning of the concert, Riedel described the principal features of the *Gloria* and *Credo* movements, referring erroneously to the Mass in question as 'an unprinted Mass in C major which is in regular use in the liturgy of the imperial court chapel in Vienna and which has also been performed in Linz'. After the concert there were reviews of the performance in the main Leipzig papers. The reviewer of the *Leipziger Zeitung* considered that the acoustics of the church hindered a true appreciation of the music with its frequent modulations and chromatic passages.[363] Writing in the *Leipziger Nachrichten*, Bernhard Vogel praised the initiative of Riedel and his choir but regretted that the work had been accompanied by an organ instead of wind instruments as in the original:

...However, if we accept this as a necessary expedient and concentrate on the vocal parts, we have to concede that there is an abundance of striking individual features and bold ideas in surprising harmonic garb. Just as Bruckner in his symphonies appears to be a contemporary of Berlioz, so here the frequent bold changes of key are most clearly reminiscent of the Frenchman's great Requiem. In Bruckner's work,

---

362 From C.A. Barry's article in *The Musical Times* xxvii / 520 (1 June 1886), 322ff. A German translation of the first paragraph of this article can be found in *G-A* IV/2, 529f.

363 See *LABL*, 65 for this review of 5 July 1886.

just as in Berlioz's, the abundance of important individual ideas seems oppressive and unclear to us at times, and just as it can happen that one is unable to see the wood for the trees, many will look in vain for the desired unity and the large, all-encompassing main idea in the coincidental fusion of clever details.

But how these individual features astonish us! The 'Amen' fugue, although suitably more subdued in character than the bright Gloria, is a veritable masterpiece of modern counterpoint.[364]

Martin Krause, the critic of the *Leipziger Tageblatt*, also regretted the lack of the original wind accompaniment and would have preferred to hear the two movements in the context of the whole Mass rather than sandwiched between various sacred pieces.[365] Intonation problems in the Credo reduced its impact but the Gloria had many strikingly beautiful passages:

... the 'Qui tollis peccata mundi' and the great upswing after the 'Quoniam tu solus sanctus' can only come from the mind of a composer of genius. Another performance will no doubt give us a clearer understanding of the remarkable 'Amen' which has a strange physiognomy that is probably without parallel.[366]

The performance was also reviewed in two music journals, the *Musikalische Wochenblatt* and the *Neue Zeitschrift für Musik*. In the former the reviewer was impressed by the demonstration of harmonic and contrapuntal skill but was critical of the 'many profane and secular sounds emanating from this music, reminiscent of the theatre rather than the house of God.' In the latter the reviewer commented that the stirring effect produced by the Gloria had been weakened by the final 'Amen'

---

364 See *LABL*, 65f. for this review of 6 July 1886.

365 The concert included motets by Palestrina, Victoria, Eccard, Bach and Franck, arias/songs by Handel, Beethoven and Hiller, and organ pieces by Frescobaldi, Huber and Liszt.

366 See *LABL*, 66 for this review of 5 July 1886.

which was too long-drawn-out. In his opinion, the Credo did not reach the same heights.[367]

Bruckner set off on his annual Bayreuth trip on 24 July. He informed Wilhelm Zinne of his imminent departure when writing to him on 22 July. Zinne had written to Bruckner on 12 July, enclosing a photograph of himself and passing on the good wishes of Bruckner's other Hamburg acquaintances, Marxsen and Bernuth.[368] On 31 July Franz Liszt died in Bayreuth. Bruckner played at his funeral service on 4 August, improvising on themes from Wagner's *Parsifal*. According to both Göllerich and Stradal, he was very self-critical and was upset by the lack of imagination and invention in his playing.[369] On the journey back from Bayreuth, however, Bruckner seems to have been in better humour (in spite of his hopes of seeing the *Grossglockner* being dashed!) and talked to Stradal and a travelling companion, Taborsky, a music publisher from Pest, about his Eighth Symphony:

> ... He mentioned... the death knell which is imitated at the end of the first movement, the German 'Michael' who dances in the Scherzo, the Cossacks (beginning of the final movement) and the powerful brass theme which is meant to portray the two Emperors...[370]

---

367 See *LABL*, 67 for extracts from these two reviews, dated 15 July and 9 July 1886 respectively.

368 See *HSABB* 1, 308f. for Zinne's letter to Bruckner. It was first published in *ABB*, 389ff.; the original is not extant. This letter is also mentioned by Blaukopf in Herta Blaukopf, op.cit., 227. See *HSABB* 1, 311for Bruckner's reply, dated Vienna, 22 July 1886; the original is in the Hamburg Public Library.

369 See August Stradal, 'Erinnerungen...' in *Zeitschrift für Musik* 99 (1932), 976. There were reports of the funeral in the *Fränkische Kurier* (4 August), *Bayreuther Tagblatt* (4 August) and *Oberfränkische Zeitung* (5 August). See *G-A* IV/2, 494ff., Stradal, op.cit., 977f. and Franz Scheder, 'Frühe Bruckner-Aufführungen in Nürnberg', *BJ 1989/90* (Linz, 1992), 260.

370 From Stradal's account, as reported to Göllerich; see *G-A* IV/2, 496f.

After spending some time with his sister and brother-in-law in Vöcklabruck, Bruckner travelled to Steyr on 17 August. He had been invited to stay at the presbytery again, and was met at the station by his young friend, Franz Wiesner. The following day he played the organ in the parish church during High Mass.[371] Bruckner probably spent some time at St. Florian, but dates at the end of the Adagio and at the beginning of the Finale of the Eighth Symphony clearly indicate work on these movements in Steyr at the end of August and beginning of September.

On his return to Vienna Bruckner had organ commitments at the *Hofkapelle* on 17 and 19 September. An audience with the Emperor on 23 September at 11.00 a.m. provided him with an opportunity to thank him personally for the decoration he had received. It appears that Bruckner also used some of the time at his disposal to raise once again the question of financial support for the increasing expense incurred in travelling to venues outside Austria where his works were being performed. Franz Josef's response was sympathetic.

Bruckner took an almost childlike pleasure in hearing reports of performances of his Seventh Symphony in America (Chicago, New York and Boston) and Amsterdam. In a letter to his young friend, Elisabeth Kietz, in February 1887, he referred back to these successful 1886 performances and hoped that the symphony would make a similar impression in Dresden.[372]

---

371 Wiesner relates how Bruckner was translated 'into another world during his organ playing' in his account which appears in *G-A* IV/2, 500f.

372 See *G-A* IV/2 for an extract from this letter to Elisabeth Kietz, dated Vienna, 23 February 1887. See also *HSABB* 1, 304 for an earlier letter to Kietz, dated Vienna, 16 June 1886. The original is not extant; it was first published in *GrBB*, 162f. Elisabeth Kietz was the daughter of the sculptor, Gustav Adolph Kietz whom Bruckner got to know in Bayreuth in 1873. She stayed in Vienna as a guest of Hermann Behn during the autumn of 1885 and met Bruckner then. There were two performances of Bruckner's Seventh Symphony in Dresden during 1887. The first on 15 March was conducted by Jean Louis Nicodé, and the second in April was conducted by Ernst von Schuch.

Bruckner was invited by the *Deutscher Singverein* in Prague to play the organ part in a performance of his *Te Deum* to be conducted by Friedrich Heßler on 28 November. He was offered a sum of 50 florins for travelling expenses; there is no indication that he responded to this invitation.[373]

In any case, the dissemination of his works by means of the printed score was in the forefront of Bruckner's mind at this time. After two movements from the Fourth Symphony had been performed in Sondershausen, Bruckner had asked Karl Riedel to send the score to Schott in Mainz. Schott, however, had declined to print the work and had returned the manuscript to him in August. Bruckner offered it to Gutmann whose response was more favourable but who, as the composer indicated in a letter to Levi, had suggested that the composer request a grant of 1000 florins from the court towards the cost of printing. Bruckner was unwilling to do this. Evidently nothing had changed in Vienna:

> ... Everything is as it always has been in Vienna (It seems that Schönaich has turned against me again.) Without the support of Hanslick everything is doomed to failure in Vienna! I have been aware of this since 1874 (when I was appointed lecturer at the University). I lose patience sometimes. I still do not know when the 8th Symphony will be finished, but at least I have another seven. To Mrs von Fiedler I send my warm greetings and to Dr. Fiedler and you, my artistic father, I send my deepest respects and thanks for everything...[374]

373 See *HSABB* 1, 314 for the letter of invitation to Bruckner from the *Deutscher Singverein*. It is dated Prague, 17 November 1886 and is signed by the secretary, Heinrich Weiner, and the president, Prof. Dr. A. Weiß; the original is in St. Florian.

373 See *HSABB* 1, 313f. for this letter from Bruckner to Levi, dated Vienna, 16 November 1886. It was first published in *GrBLS*, 334f.; the original is not extant. See also *HSABB* 1, 313 for Levi's letter to Joseph Schalk, dated Munich, 14 November 1886, regarding difficulties in finding a publisher for the Fourth; the original of this letter is in the *ÖNB*, F18 Schalk 153/2.

In December Bruckner was granted another audience at the Hofburg. On this occasion he was received by Archduchess Valerie, the Emperor's daughter, and Princess Amalie of Bavaria who was visiting Vienna at the time. Princess Amalie provided the following report of the meeting:

> ... I got to know for the first time Bruckner's truly droll personality, this child-like naivety and simplicity combined with such stature and talent which he was aware of himself because he related how Wagner had said to him, 'Bruckner, you are a great composer', and had promised him that he would perform his symphonies. But there was no trace of self-importance in his words - only the justifiable pride of the divinely-gifted artist. Bruckner was working on the final movement of his Eighth Symphony at the time and said that the Scherzo was the 'German Michael'. In the final movement there was a funeral march where all the motives, including the German Michael, came together like friends gathering round a death-bed with great grief. He wanted this symphony to be performed, not in Vienna because of anxiety about malicious criticism, but in Munich. He did not appear to see eye-to-eye with court music director Levi about the symphony at this point in time. I heard later that Bruckner had given way in this difference of artistic opinion. Bruckner had a truly touching devotion for his Emperor. He told me that it was the finest day of his life when he spoke to the Emperor for the first time and that he was so delighted with the Franz Josef decoration precisely because it bore the Emperor's signature. Although he had been offered extraordinary support, he said, that, on this occasion, he did not wish to ask for anything and 'rob' the imperial coffers which had so many demands made on them. As an Upper Austrian he would not do such a thing.[375]

Nevertheless, Bruckner appears to have persuaded Princess Amalie that he would benefit from an annual pension of some kind. To obtain it was far from a simple matter, however. Bruckner explained this when he wrote to Levi again on 3 January

---

375 Princess Amalie's account appears in *G-A* IV/2, 504f. The 'difference of artistic opinion' between Bruckner and Levi came a year later.

1887:

... I was granted an audience by Princess Amalie in the Hofburg recently; (like everything else, I have you to thank for this). Both the Princess and Archduchess Valerie, who was also present, were extremely gracious. I spent a long time with their Royal Highnesses who appear to have been well entertained by my company. I shall tell you everything when I next see you. Nitsch, a senior civil servant, wanted to take the initiative and grant me a fixed salary from the Emperor's private purse (so that I would not have to ask continually for the Emperor's financial support) to enable me to give up private teaching and have more time for composing. The 8th Symphony, which is still not finished, is, unfortunately, the most glaring evidence that I do not have as much time and money as my superior, Hellmesberger, is disposed to maintain. This situation appears to be a great obstacle. Princess Amalie is in complete agreement with me and has promised most graciously to speak to His Royal Highness on my behalf.

I learned today from Prelate Mayer, the court priest who also took my side earlier, that Baron Mair, the general director of the imperial private bank, is just as opposed to a fixed income as Hellmesberger!!! That is certainly the most shocking news! Perhaps Princess Amalie has already heard this from the mouth of the Emperor himself and has informed you. Nothing can be done if the Emperor does not make a direct recommendation himself.

In Leipzig the King of Saxony has expressed great enthusiasm for the 7th Symphony (which, according to reports, is said to have had great success in Amsterdam and, particularly, New York). Princess Amalie was there recently. Perhaps a knock on that particular door would not be in vain. In my opinion, help from abroad is all the more reliable, because enemies at home fall by the wayside. Judging by what has happened already, I know that you, court music director, who have been responsible for all that I have attained so far, have been unceasing in the past in your efforts to draw the king's attention to my situation. Consequently I have been bold enough to pour out my heart to you in this manner. Please do not be annoyed. You are my only supporter.

My kindest regards and respects to Mrs von Fiedler and her husband, Dr. Fiedler. If it is possible and permissible, please convey my deepest respects and most humble thanks to His Royal Highness. I thank you again, court music director, for all your kindness up to now, ask you for your continued goodwill, and remain respectfully yours...

N.B. I will gladly give Herr Gutmann the 1000 marks towards printing (the 4th 'Romantic' Symphony in E flat).[376]

Bruckner was apparently unsuccessful in his attempts to obtain a fixed pension. Auer comments:

... Above all it was court music director Hellmesberger who opposed it, his reason being that there were so many poor and needy people in Austria who had a greater claim to financial support than Bruckner. While one courtier was well-disposed towards him, another opposed him. And so, in spite of, indeed perhaps because of, his direct approach to the high nobility and royalty, he was not able to obtain a larger fixed income which would have allowed him to give up his regular occupation and concentrate on his activities as a composer.[377]

Nevertheless, Bruckner's financial situation was by no stretch of the imagination parlous. In the meantime, his young friends were continuing to help and, even at this stage, 'advise' him. Hostile criticism from a particular section of the Viennese press seems to have made him more ill-humoured and even suspicious of his friends at times, however. While his relationship with Franz Schalk remained on a good footing - perhaps a case of absence making the heart grow fonder - his relationship with Joseph became cooler. Bruckner was certainly somewhat jealous of Joseph's

---

376 See *GrBLS*, 335ff. for this letter. Extracts can also be found in *G-A* IV/2, 504, 507ff. and 523. Felix Nitsch was one of the Imperial treasurers. 'Prelate Mayer' = Dr. Laurenz Mayer (1828 - 1912) who was a chaplain at the court; 'Baron Mair' = Friedrich von Mayr. Levi and his friends raised the money required for the Fourth to be published by Gutmann. See also Levi's letter to Joseph Schalk (footnote 373) concerning the money raised. The full score appeared in 1889 (A.J.G. 710) and the parts and Löwe's piano-duet arrangement in 1890 (A.J.G. 712).

377 *G-A* IV/2, 506f.

enthusiasm for and promotion of Hugo Wolf's music from 1887 onwards; and yet Joseph remained an extremely active promoter of Bruckner's music. As we shall see, Bruckner's self-confidence was shattered by Levi's negative reaction to the original version of the Eighth Symphony in the autumn of 1887. Leibnitz comments lucidly on one of the most knotty problems of Bruckner research:

> ... Now began the years of agonizing self-criticism and self-revision, the revision of Symphonies VIII, III and I. Bruckner's pupils and friends, particularly the Schalk brothers, were involved in this revision process. The entangling of the complex interrelationship between Bruckner's own willingness to make alterations and the interference of his pupils and friends is one of the most interesting albeit impenetrable problems of Bruckner research.[378]

On 6 December 1886, Joseph Schalk sent Franz, now music director of a theatre in Czernowitz, his piano reduction of the first movement of the Eighth Symphony so that he could take a critical look at it. He asked him to make sure that he returned it promptly and 'well packed', adding:

> ... Bruckner sends his greetings and wishes to inform you about his trials and tribulations in the composition of the Finale. In the meantime, Löwe has assumed the position of musical adviser.[379]

Bruckner was still in communication with his friends in Hamburg. On 13 December Eduard Marxsen wrote to him from Altona to thank him for replying so quickly to an earlier letter and for assisting his efforts to establish a charitable

---

378 See *LBSAB*, 110.

379 See *LBSAB*, 111. The original of this letter is in the *ÖNB*, F18 Schalk 158/7/8.

foundation.[380]

Shortly before setting off to spend his Christmas vacation at St. Florian, he wrote to his copyist, Leopold Hofmeyer in Steyr, enclosing 10 florins for some work with which he was extremely pleased and sending seasonal greetings.[381] Johann Aichinger, the parish priest of Steyr, was the recipient of another letter written at the same time. Bruckner, obviously grateful for being able to spend time in Steyr during the summer, took the opportunity of Aichinger's name day to send him some bottles of Klosterneuburger wine![382] On the same day he wrote to Aichinger he informed Bernhard Deubler in St. Florian that he would be leaving Vienna early on the morning of 24 December and asked him to ensure that his brother Ignaz made arrangements for a coach to pick him up at Enns station.[383] He returned to Vienna on 28 December.

1887 was another year of mixed fortunes for Bruckner. There were mixed critical reactions to performances of his Seventh Symphony in Berlin, Dresden, Budapest and London. On the other hand, his *Te Deum* was well received in Linz. After much effort the Eighth Symphony was finally completed.

---

380 See *HSABB* I, 315 for this letter. It was first published in *ABB*, 340; the original is not extant. A sum of money was sent from the *Gesellschaft der Musikfreunde* to the foundation on 23 December 1886.

381 See *HSABB* I, 315f. for this letter, dated Vienna, 17 December 1886; the original is in private possession. See also *HSABB* I, 315 for Hofmeyer's reply which is erroneously dated Steyr, 29 November 1886 (perhaps 29 December was intended?); the original of this letter is in St. Florian.

382 See *HSABB* I, 316 for this letter, dated Vienna, 22 December 1886; the original is in Steyr. Bruckner also mentioned his audience with Princess Amalie and Archduchess Valerie in the Hofburg earlier in the month.

383 See *HSABB* I, 317 for this letter, dated Vienna 22 December 1886. It was first published in *ABB*, 295; the original is not extant.

Bruckner once again expressed his gratitude to Nikisch in one of four letters written at the beginning of the year. He had found it difficult to bid farewell to his friend in Bayreuth the previous summer. He asked Nikisch to pass on a card to Mahler and to convey his thanks to Bernhard Vogel.[384] In replying to a letter from Friedrich Klose, Bruckner reciprocated his New Year greetings and added the interesting piece of news that the performance of Brahms's Symphony no. 4 at a concert in Vienna on 2 January had been a 'disastrous flop'.[385] It is not difficult to detect a mood of despondency in the other two letters. Franz Schalk had presumably spent part of his Christmas vacation in Vienna. In sending seasonal greetings to his young friend, Bruckner congratulated him on his 'artistic successes'. Since Franz's departure, however, he had returned to his former lonely existence, relieved occasionally by the unpredictable 'comet-like' appearances of Joseph![386] Bruckner also sent New Year greetings to Theodor Helm, thanking him for his support and describing him as the 'only one who has spoken up openly and honourably on my behalf'. Unfortunately, the others had 'fallen asleep' and some had even proved to be 'false friends now firmly ensconced in the enemy camp'. Bruckner asked Helm to mention favourable reports he had received of performances of the Seventh in New York and Amsterdam in 'a small article'. He looked forward to an early opportunity of becoming better acquainted with his 'most honourable supporter - the

---

384   See *ABB*, 215f. for this letter, dated Vienna New Year 1887; the original is in private possession. Mahler worked as assistant conductor at the *Neue Theater* in Leipzig from 1886 to 1888.

385   See Friedrich Klose, *Meine Lehrjahre bei Bruckner* (Regensburg, 1927), 149 for the text of this letter, dated Vienna, 3 January 1887; the original is in the Universitätsbibliothek Basel, Nachlaß Klose. Klose's letter to Bruckner has been lost. Bruckner also mentioned the apparent failure of Brahms's symphony in his letter to Levi, also dated Vienna 3 January; see page 533f.

386   See *FSBB*, 71 for this letter, dated Vienna, New Year 1887; the original is in the *ÖNB*.

538

only one'.[387]

Bruckner's Seventh Symphony was performed by Karl Klindworth and the Berlin Philharmonic Orchestra in Berlin on 31 January in a concert which also included Mozart's Symphony no. 41 and Brahms's Violin Concerto.[388] The reviewer for the *Deutsche Tageblatt* commented on the phenomenon of a 63-year-old composer one of whose works had been performed in Berlin for the first time. Many other composers had written seven or even more symphonies which had never been performed - without any loss to the world. But this was a different matter altogether:

...In this symphony a giant clad in armour from head to foot has stood before us, and our response can only be one of astonishment. How is it possible that a man such as this could remain unknown right to the end of his life, thus sharing the fate of so many by not coming alive until after his death? He stands before us, half-Beethoven, half-Wagner, and yet more Wagnerian than Beethovenian. Nevertheless, he is neither of these two, but a unique phenomenon. It is of no consequence that we can find no parallels to his treatment of ideas. It is entirely up to you if you are reminded of the Ninth in this place and of *Die Walküre* in another, because in the next instant it becomes only a fleeting play of shadows which immediately reveals the individuality of its own appearance. The symphony has the customary four movements, an Allegro in E major, an Adagio in C sharp minor, a Scherzo in A minor and a Finale in E major; but these are only the approximate fundamental tonalities to which Bruckner is not essentially bound. The structure of his melodies, his modulations and even his instrumentation are all Wagnerian, but they are handled in such an eminently unique way that Bruckner can undoubtedly be said to be one of the few who have truly understood the Bayreuth master. And so he has been able to transfer his style to another genre. Those who wish to talk about reminiscences are at liberty to do so, and one

---

387 See *ABB*, 197, 216f. for this letter, dated Vienna, 9 January 1887; the original is probably in private possession.

388 The concert and Bruckner's attendance were previewed in editions of the *Vossische Zeitung* and the *Neue Preußische Zeitung* from 27 January onwards.

person will no doubt have discovered the Valkyries in this place, a second will have discovered Fafner in another place, while a third will have found the 'magic fire' elsewhere. These reminiscences seem to us to be only apparent similarities which are self-evident, so to speak. The work, a gigantic work incidentally, made a very powerful impression on us, so powerful that it seems downright presumptuous of us to venture a review after hearing it for the first time. We wish this to remain a provisional judgment. It is to be hoped that there will be an opportunity of hearing more than one repeat performance of this amazing colossus as soon as possible, and then we could take a closer look at it. We were not entirely surprised that so many of our colleagues had experienced enough of Mr. Bruckner after the first movement. The majority, however, were honourable enough to wait until the end and then several of them came to me in complete amazement and asked, 'What was that?' There is no doubt that it was unexpected and splendid. As we have just said, we hope soon to be able to come to a clearer understanding of the 'how' and 'why'.[389]

Other reviews, including Alexander Moskowski's in the *Deutsches Montagsblatt* on 7 February, were less friendly, and there seems to have been something of the same anti-Wagner animosity directed towards Bruckner in Berlin as there was in Vienna.[390] On 13 February, however, Hans v. Wolzogen wrote to him to apologize on behalf of his fellow-Berliners:

> ... I fear that you have seen my dear native city of Berlin in a bad light and, as a Berliner, I am doubly sorry about this. The Berliners are considered to be irreverent, hyper-critical people and raving modernists. But the opposite is the case. On the contrary, they maintain a touching reverence for the old, have hardly any critical

---

389 Review of 2 February 1887, signed 'w', as reprinted in *G-A* IV/2, 518-21.

390 See *G-A* IV/2, 521 for further details. Other reviews appeared in the *Börse-Courier*, the *Musikalische Rundschau*, the *Vossische Zeitung*, the *Neue Preußische Zeitung* and the *Allgemeine Musik-Zeitung*.

faculties of their own and are most tenaciously opposed to true progress. They are the most good-natured simpletons in the world and have the misfortune always to behave in such a distrustful manner towards what is foreign to them. But when they become well-acquainted with the foreign and the modern becomes old, they cling on to it with the same touching reverence and with unshakeable Nordic faithfulness. This future also awaits you and is anticipated and sensed already by the best of those serious musicians who felt ashamed of and vexed with their fellow-citizens on the evening when your symphony was performed. My information about this comes from respected sources who are of more value than all critics and ruling majorities. An important writer said that pearls had been cast before swine. Another renowned literary figure, who has a fine musical talent, expressed himself thus: 'Up to now, *faute de mieux*, I have considered Brahms to be a pretty decent symphonist. Now the good Doctor shrivels into insignificance when placed alongside this giant, as in this concert'...[391]

Wilhelm Zinne tried to arrange a meeting or interview with Hans v. Bülow in the hope that the latter would lend some support to the Bruckner cause in Germany. Bülow agreed to the meeting but expressed surprise that Zinne should be an admirer of the 'musical or, rather, anti-musical nonsense of the crank Bruckner'.[392] Bruckner obviously had some inkling of Bülow's opinion of him, because he mentioned him by name when replying to Wolzogen's letter:

> ... v. Bülow has terrible things to say about me; also, it must be said, about Berlioz, Liszt and even Master Wagner. This is extremely sad! He declared that only Master Brahms had revealed real music to him!!! etc. Together with Hanslick he makes life very difficult for me! Hans Richter complies with his (Hanslick's) every wish, and everything in Vienna is just as it has always been and always will be...

---

391 See *ABB*, 381 and *G-A* IV/2, 521f. for this letter, dated Bayreuth, 13 February 1887; the original is in St. Florian.

392 See *ABB*, 394 and *G-A* IV/2, 518 for the text of this letter, dated 13 February 1887.

NB. The Berlin 'Deutsche Tageblatt' of 2 February (2nd edition)
had some fine things to say.[393]

The mixed reception of the Seventh Symphony in Berlin did not prevent Louis
Nicodé from giving its first performance at a Philharmonic concert in Dresden on 15
March. Nicodé wrote to Bruckner on 11 March, introducing himself as one of the
'most enthusiastic devotees of your splendid work (E major symphony)'.[394] Bruckner
was profuse in his thanks, regretted that he would not be able to attend the
performance, and drew Nicodé's attention to an improvement in the scoring of a
passage in the Adagio:

NB. At the end of the 2nd movement (Adagio) in the tuba passage
(the actual funeral music), four horns blown fff produce a much better
effect than two horns three bars before Y.[395]

In Vienna the first anniversary of the performance of the Seventh Symphony did
not pass entirely unnoticed. An article in Kastner's *Wiener Musikalische Zeitung*
upbraided the Viennese for their unwillingness to programme the symphony again
during the previous 12 months and reprinted Paul Marsop's prophetic article in the
Berliner Tageblatt 18 months earlier.[396]

---

393 See *ABB*, 217 (also extract in *G-A* IV/2, 517) for this letter, dated Vienna, 23 February 1887;
the location of the original is unknown. Bruckner also voiced the same grievances about the
difficulty of life in Vienna and Bülow's desire to ruin him in a letter to Theodor Helm four months
later - on 2 June. See *ABB*, 219; the location of the original is unknown.

394 See *ABB*, 335 (also extract in *G-A* IV/2, 523f.) for this letter; the original is in St. Florian.

395 See *ABB*, 218 (also extract in *G-A* IV/2, 524) for this letter, dated Vienna, 13 March 1887; the
location of the original is unknown.

396 This article appeared in the *Wiener Musikalische Zeitung* 22 on 23 March 1887. For Marsop's
article (16 August 1885), see page 477 and footnote 288.

The performance of the symphony conducted by Sándor Erkel in Budapest at the beginning of April was reported in the *Pester Lloyd* on 5 April:

> ... Although not unaware of the great weaknesses which can be found in this gigantic work of superhuman dimensions, we cannot fail to recognise at the same time the composer's great aspirations and tremendous expressive powers. This feeling would increase to one of genuine admiration if we saw individual parts of the work detached from the whole, were no longer confused by the formlessness of the two outer movements, but could examine the two inner movements, the Adagio and the Scherzo, purely on their own merits and become absorbed without prejudice in their musical beauties which undoubtedly secure them a place among the most important musical works of today. If a heroic decision had been made to reduce the entire symphony to these two movements in which Bruckner has given of his best, the effect would certainly have been drastic but the end result would have been indisputable. But the immeasurable longueurs and repetitions of the Finale are downright unbearable in the context of the overall duration of the symphony which exceeds one hour, particularly when the work is the last piece in the concert programme. Our Philharmonic played the symphony with all the devotion of which it is capable and the conductor, Sándor Erkel, who was an eloquent advocate for the greatly misunderstood and persecuted composer, can take the chief credit for the excellent performance.[397]

On 23 May Hans Richter gave the first English performance of a Bruckner symphony when he conducted the Seventh in St. James's Hall, London. Charles Barry, who had provided an introductory article the previous year, recorded his impressions:

> At the fourth concert... Mr. Richter satisfied the long-standing curiosity of amateurs about Anton Bruckner's Seventh Symphony -

---

[397] Extract from the review of the concert on 4 April in the *Pester Lloyd* (5 April 1887), as reprinted in *G-A* IV/2, 527f.

a work that has gone the round of applauding Germany, and was promised in London last year, but, for some reason or other, then withheld. We confess to some disappointment of hopes not unnaturally raised by reports from abroad. It was, we regret to say, outside our cognisance that Bruckner is the protégé of a particular school. We thought that his work has been judged on its merits, whereas it now appears that personal sympathy had more to do with the verdict. There is reason for unfeigned regret at the failure of the much-vaunted Symphony, since every man with a heart in him must desire success for a composer of sixty-three who has vainly struggled after fame all his life. Yet fail it did, at any rate for the time, the audience listening with unmistakable coldness, or else going away. Reasons for this may be found in extreme length - a fault substantially aggravated by lack of proportionate interest -, in an exaggerated and spasmodic matter only allowable when the composer follows the changing and contrasted sentiments of a poetic text, and in an extraordinary mixture of scholasticism with the freedom of the Wagnerian school. Listening to this symphony one might suppose that the orchestral part of a Wagner opera is being played by itself, yet each movement closely follows established form, and the melodies in each movement are largely made by the process known as 'inversion by contrary motion'. We do not say that the last-named feature is of great consequence as affecting the popularity of the work, because the bulk of an average audience would not recognise the inversions, but it shows the curious state of Bruckner's mind as that of a man brought up on the dry bones of counterpoint, and endeavouring to pose as one who can reconcile Wagnerian methods with those of a past age. There are some fine passages in the slow movement - a sort of elegy for Wagner - and the trio of the Scherzo is pleasing. Each movement, indeed, contains something for admiration, but it is swamped by the abounding product of striving to reconcile various things, and by the results of pretentious endeavour. Mr. Richter may not accept the verdict of a first audience. In that case we shall be ready to hear the work again, and to modify our opinion should there be reason.[398]

Barry was evidently not entirely honest about his reaction to the work when he wrote to Bruckner after the performance. Bruckner informed Theodor Helm:

---

398 From article 'Richter Concerts' in *The Musical Times* xxviii / 532 (June 1, 1887), 342f.

Mr. Barry from London wrote to tell me that Richter conducted a masterly performance of my 7th Symphony in front of a large audience on 23 May and that the work had given him enormous pleasure and aroused his deepest admiration. There is no indication in his letter of how the public responded. I have not been informed of any reviews up to now...[399]

Bruckner's initially more favourable reception in Holland resulted in his being elected an honorary member of the *Maatschappij tot bevordering van Toonkunst* in Amsterdam on 10 June. The secretary of the Society who was probably responsible for nominating Bruckner was Daniel de Lange, the conductor of the successful performance of Bruckner's Seventh in Amsterdam in November 1886.[400]

At the same time as his Seventh Symphony was being performed outside Austria, Bruckner's male-voice chorus *Um Mitternacht* WAB 90 and Joseph Schalk's two-piano arrangement of his Fifth Symphony were heard in Vienna for the first time. Writing to Theodor Helm on 22 April, Bruckner provided some details of the choral piece but made a point of recommending the symphony the performance of which had been arranged at Helm's request.[401] Eduard Kremser directed the *Wiener*

---

399 See *ABB*, 219 and extract in *G-A* IV/2, 536 for Bruckner's letter to Helm, dated Vienna, 2 June 1887; the location of the original is unknown. The originals of Helm's letter to Bruckner, to which this was a response, and of Barry's letter to Bruckner are not extant.

400 This 'Society for the Promotion of Music' in Amsterdam was founded in 1829. For further information about Bruckner's music in Holland, see Cornelis van Zwol, 'Holland: ein Brucknerland seit 1885' in *BJ 1980* (Linz, 1980), 135-41. There is a copy of the Society's letter to Bruckner in the *Gemeente Archief Amsterdam*; see Nico Steffen, 'Die Bruckner-Tradition des Königlichen Concertgebouw-Orchesters' I in *Mitteilungsblatt der IBG* 39 (December 1992), 25, note 5. On 25 August, Bruckner wrote to the Society from St. Florian and thanked them for the 'magnificent diploma'. The original of this letter is in the *Gemeente Archief Amsterdam*, and there is a facsimile of the final page in Cornelis van Zwol, op.cit., 140.

401 See *ABB*, 218-19 and extract in *G-A* IV/2, 526; the original is in the Vienna *Stadtbibliothek*.

Männergesangverein in two performances of the choral piece, on 27 March and 6
April respectively. The context of the latter was a 'spiritual concert' and Auer
comments that Bruckner played the organ on this occasion - his 'last public
appearance as an organ improviser in Vienna'.[402]

We have more information about the preliminary rehearsals for the Fifth Symphony,
not least a considerable amount of ill-humour (some of it no doubt understandable)
on Bruckner's part, from Friedrich Klose's detailed description in *Meine Lehrjahre*
and correspondence between Bruckner and Joseph Schalk. As Bruckner had been
very much involved in the rehearsals preceding the cancelled performance of the Fifth
Symphony five years earlier, Schalk thought that Bruckner's presence would not be
necessary at any rehearsals apart from the final one. Bruckner, however, thought
otherwise and Klose reported what turned out to be a major confrontation between
the composer and his well-meaning erstwhile pupil at Gause's restaurant, with
Bruckner demanding a postponement of the concert and Schalk saying that this would
be impossible. Eventually, according to Klose, Schalk gave way, promised to
postpone the concert, and agreed to have as many rehearsals as Bruckner deemed
necessary.[403]

Three letters written within a few days of each other towards the end of March
document the situation more clearly. Writing to Joseph on 25 March, Bruckner was
adamant that he attend more rehearsals of the Fifth before he could give his
permission for the performance to go ahead. In replying to Bruckner's letter two
days later, Schalk reminded him that he and the second pianist, Franz Zottmann, had
spent weeks carefully rehearsing the work. However, he invited Bruckner to attend

---

402 See *G-A* IV/2, 526f. In the edition of the *Wiener Zeitung* for 8 October 1887, however, there
is an announcement that Bruckner is to play the organ after the service in the parish church of Alser-
Vorstadt the following day.

403 Friedrich Klose, op.cit., 140ff. See also Stephen Johnson, op.cit., 123-26.

two rehearsals the following weekend and was prepared, if Bruckner was not satisfied, to postpone the performance even although this would be a great disappointment to his friends. There was no question of another of Bruckner's works being substituted because there would be insufficient time to rehearse from scratch in time for the concert originally scheduled for 12 April. Joseph was also concerned that the enthusiasm of that part of the Viennese public well-disposed towards Bruckner should be maintained. Another winter without a performance of a Bruckner work, albeit on two pianos, would by no means help the Bruckner cause.[404]

Bruckner was not to be moved, however, although his attitude had softened a little - he addressed Schalk as 'dearest, most honourable friend':

> I made up my mind most firmly yesterday that I would most resolutely decline with thanks all performances of my works if they were not preceded by several weeks of thorough rehearsal - and, moreover, rehearsals in my presence. I ask you, therefore, to be so good as to choose something else in place of my 5th Symphony. But, if it is convenient, please tackle my 5th during April and May and inform me of the rehearsal dates. I appeal to our long-standing friendship in asking you to comply with my wishes.[405]

This letter does not have Schalk's address, only the mark 'loco', and this suggests that it was sent by internal mail within the Conservatory. That Bruckner chose to write a letter rather than speak to Joseph personally suggests tension in the relationship. As Klose reports, a compromise was finally reached after both calmed down at the end of a furious argument in Gause's restaurant. The Fifth Symphony

---

404 See *LBSAB*, 113f. The originals of both Bruckner's letter and Joseph Schalk's reply are in the *ÖNB*.

405 See *LBSAB*, 114f. for this letter, dated 28 March 1887; the original is in the *ÖNB*, F18 Schalk 151/2/3/1.

would not be replaced but the concert would be put back until 20 April. Bruckner attended all the rehearsals leading up to the final performance. He was in a bad mood most of the time, a large part of his ill-humour being directed at Schalk rather than Zottmann. He found fault with all manner of things, for instance lack of balance between the parts, lack of contrapuntal clarity, and too little prominence being given to an important inner part. It was not until Schalk's and Zottmann's performance received an ovation at the end of the concert on 20 April that his resistance was finally broken down:

> ... Suddenly his face lit up as if it had been touched by a magic wand. He sprang from his seat, pushed forward to the front through the wave of applause and bowed a number of times with his hands crossed over his heart and his face beaming. And so: 'all's well that ends well'.[406]

The concert, which began with a performance of Liszt's B minor sonata by Schalk, was previewed in the *Neue freie Presse* and by Max Kalbeck in *Die Presse*.[407] The programme book of the concert contained an explanatory note on the symphony by Schalk who drew attention to its polyphonic character and its fusion of symphonic and fugal techniques in the final movement which reminded him of the parallel movement in Mozart's *Jupiter* symphony.[408]

In his review of the performance Theodor Helm congratulated Schalk and Zottmann for giving the symphony a hearing but considered that the time had not yet come for it to be properly appreciated in an orchestral performance:

---

406 Klose, op.cit., 142ff.

407 *Neue freie Presse* 8128 (14 April 1887), 5; *Die Presse* 107 (14 April 1887), 1.

408 See *ABSW* V *Revisionsbericht, Anhang nr.1*, 75 for complete programme note.

... Of the composer's seven symphonies, this, the Fifth, is the one that is least known. Not one note of it has been heard in public before, whereas the others (with the exception of the Seventh) have all had single performances, without finding a place as yet in the general orchestral repertoire.

But Bruckner has kept his Fifth Symphony (composed in the years 1878 to 1880) hidden away in his work-desk, giving only his most intimate friends a glimpse of the score. And now that we have heard the work, albeit only in a piano transcription, we understand why. In no other work, perhaps, has the composer allowed his Pegasus to rush headlong and unrestrainedly through the clouds and has he been so unconcerned about conventional aims and proportions and the receptive ability of normally endowed listeners. Everything is on a large, enormous scale, but it must be said that there is also a slight degree of the abnormal. This symphony, which lasts one-and-a-half hours, provides very clear evidence of both the virtues and the weaknesses of Bruckner's magnificent talent. Veritable strokes of genius, colossal climactic surges of a kind not found in the works of any other composer living today, and, cheek-by-jowl with these, a sudden break in the thread of musical thought, strange ideas which baffle the listener.

In a thoughtful explanatory note appended to the programme, Professor Schalk describes Bruckner's 'Fifth' as the most specifically contrapuntal of his symphonies. In fact, the work, its final movement in particular, demonstrates a very powerful contrapuntal energy and an unlimited mastery of polyphony in which the composer is seen to be a worthy disciple and heir of Sebastian Bach. But the comparison with Mozart's Jupiter Symphony and its famous closing fugue seems somewhat off-the-mark. If Mozart, the man of symmetry and of fine proportions, were to come down today, he would probably shorten Bruckner's colossal Finale by half. Only then would its gigantic climax, from the point where the bold main theme of the first movement triumphantly joins the head motive of the principal theme of the Finale, achieve its full effect. As is so often the case with Bruckner, the Scherzo is the most convincing and the most compact movement. It is a splendid piece, Beethovenian in inspiration, concealing the most unusual contrasts of mood within itself and yet so gigantic in size that another composer could have made three or four movements from it. In spite of its excessive length, the Scherzo is effective enough to be performed on its own. For the time being, however, we would deem it inadvisable to play the whole symphony without cuts to an average audience like the Philharmonic's. Nevertheless it was to their great credit that Mr. Schalk and Mr. Zottmann provided us with a glimpse of our highly gifted Bruckner's most subjective work, and they also proved to be the right guides through this symphonic labyrinth...[409]

Joseph was not impressed with Helm's review. Writing to his brother Franz, who was now music director in Carlsbad, he declared himself satisfied with the 'great artistic success' of the whole undertaking, however; but, as usual, he had just managed to break even financially:

> ... In my next letter I will enclose Helm's review from which you will see clearly his lack of understanding of the 5th Symphony. However, the applause - such an important factor for Bruckner, as you know - was really enormous, and so he was extremely satisfied with the whole undertaking. We are already planning something big and bold for next year. I will speak to you about it later when we have made good progress.

In this letter, Joseph also referred to Ferdinand Löwe's involvement in the revision of Bruckner's Fourth Symphony, with the composer's permission, before it went to print:

> ... The unbelievably painstaking punctiliousness, not to say pedantry, has resulted in the task being extremely protracted, with the result that Gutmann, who is publishing it, did not receive the first movement until a few days ago.[410]

---

409 From Helm's review in the *Deutsche Zeitung* 5501 (Morning Edition, 26 April 1887), 1. See *ABSW* V *Revisionsbericht, Anhang nr. 2*, 75-76 for complete review entitled 'End of the Concert Season'.

410 See *LBSAB*, 118 and 127 for these extracts from Joseph Schalk's letter to his brother, dated Vienna, 9 May 1887; the original is in the *ÖNB*, F18 Schalk 158/8/4.

The printer's copy of the Fourth Symphony discovered in 1939 among the effects of Hans Löwe, Ferdinand Löwe's son, reveals that Bruckner himself not only checked Ferdinand's work but also made revisions of his own.[411]

From 1887 onwards Joseph Schalk devoted just as much energy to his activities as a Wolf 'propagandist' as he did to furthering the Bruckner cause. The *Wagner Society* evenings provided opportunities for Wolf's songs to become better known. Franz Schalk was aware of the possibility that Bruckner could feel 'left out in the cold' but was certain that he would rise above any jealous feelings he might have.[412]

Bruckner spent his summer vacation in Upper Austria as usual, some of it in Steyr and some of it in St. Florian. On 23 July he wrote to the *Hofkapelle* to request holiday leave.[413] On the same day he contacted Nikolaus Manskopf in Frankfurt who had written to him seeking information about those works of his which had been printed. Bruckner was extremely optimistic in surmising that the Fourth Symphony would be in print 'by October or November'.[414]

During his stay at St. Florian Bruckner played the organ for services as usual. On 28 August, St. Augustine's Day, Palestrina's *Missa Papae Marcelli* and Bruckner's own *Os justi* were sung. Deubler wrote later to thank Bruckner for his help and to ask him where he could obtain copies of the *Requiem* parts. Bruckner had left his full score at St. Florian and Deubler intended to perform the work there on *All Souls*

---

411 Bruckner referred to revision work on the Fourth as well as alterations made to the Eighth in a letter to Hermann Levi, dated Vienna, 27 February 1888. See *GrBLS*, 340f. and *G-A* IV/2, 589; the original is in private possession.

412 Franz hinted as much in a letter to Joseph on 18 December 1888. See *LBSAB*, 119f.; the original is in the *ÖNB*, F18 Schalk 158/9/43.

413 See *ABDS* 1, 114.

414 See *GrBB*, 79 for this letter. Bruckner's Third Symphony had been performed in Frankfurt in December 1885. The Seventh was performed there for the first time in December 1895 and the Fourth during the winter season of 1896/97.

Day at the beginning of November.[415]

Although Bruckner began sketching his Ninth Symphony during the summer and, on his return to Vienna, began to flesh out his ideas in score form, most of his energy was devoted to the completion of the Eighth Symphony with which he had been engaged since the summer of 1884. Dates on the surviving autograph sketches and eventual full scores of each movement provide us with a timetable of Bruckner's work on the first version of the symphony.[416]

---

415 See *G-A* II/1, 300f. for Deubler's letter to Bruckner, dated St. Florian, 15 October 1887; the original is in St. Florian.

416 The material is located in the Music Section of the *ÖNB* under the shelf numbers. Mus.Hs. 6001-02, 6040-55, 6065, 6070-71, 6083-84, 19.675, 28.234-35, 28.241-42, 28.244-45 and Cod. 19.480. See also *G-A* IV/2, 531-57 and Leopold Nowak, foreword to *ABSW* VIII/1 (Vienna: Musikwissenschaftlicher Verlag, 1972). For further information about both the first and second versions of the symphony, consult the following representative literature: Franz Gräflinger, 'Bruckners 8. Symphonie' in *In Memoriam Anton Bruckner* (Vienna 1924), 100-13; Robert Simpson, 'The Eighth Symphony of Bruckner. An Analysis' in *Chord and Discord* 2/6 (1950), 42-55; Leopold Nowak, 'Die VIII Symphonie Anton Bruckners und ihr zweite Fassung' in *ÖMZ* 10 (1955), 157-60, repr. in Nowak, *Über Anton Bruckner* (Vienna 1985), 27ff.; Paul Dawson-Bowling, 'Thematic and Tonal Unity in Bruckner's Eighth Symphony' in *The Music Review* 30 (1969), 225-36; Rudolf Klein, 'Präsentation der Urfassung von Bruckners Achter' in *ÖMZ* 29 (1974), 152f.; Manfred Wagner, 'Zu den Fassungen von Bruckners Achter Sinfonie in c-Moll' in *Der Wandel des Konzepts. Zu den verschiedenen Fassungen von Bruckners Dritter, Vierter und Achter Sinfonie* (Vienna: Musikwissenschaftlicher Verlag, 1980), 39-52; Constantin Floros, 'Die Fassungen der Achten Symphonie von Anton Bruckner' in *BSL 1980* (Linz, 1981), 53-63; Cornelis van Zwol, 'Bruckners Achte Symphonie - Ende und neuer Anfang' in *BSL 1982* (Linz, 1983), 41-58; Erwin Horn, 'Evolution und Metamorphose in der Achten Symphonie von Anton Bruckner' in *BJ 1989/90* (Linz, 1992), 7-33; Bryan Gilliam, 'The Two Versions of Bruckner's Eighth Symphony' in *19th-Century Music* xvi/1 (1992), 59-69; Manfred Wagner, 'Zur Rezeptionsgeschichte von Anton Bruckners Achter Symphonie' in *BJ 1991/92/93* (Vienna, 1995), 109-15; Erwin Horn, 'Metamorphose des Hauptthemas der Achten Symphonie im Scherzo-Thema' in *BSL 1992* (Linz, 1995), 123-27; Gernot Gruber, 'Zum Verhältnis von Strukturanalyse. Inhaltsdeutung und

After his successful direction of the Seventh Symphony in Munich in March 1885, Hermann Levi had monitored progress on the Eighth with interest. As early as February 1886 he wrote to Joseph Schalk concerning the printing of the work which he had not yet seen:

> .. When the 8th is ready for printing, the Emperor will pay the costs - he has promised as much in a letter to Princess Amalie - and then Bruckner must also receive a fee, of course.[417]

After working painstakingly on the Finale from 26 October 1886 until 22 April 1887 and continuing to put finishing touches to this movement right up to the middle of August, Bruckner wrote jubilantly to Levi on 4 September, the day of his 63rd birthday:

> Hallelujah! The Eighth is finished at last and you, my artistic father, must be the first to hear the news. Should I have the orchestral parts copied in Vienna or, at my own expense, in Munich?... First of all, I want to ask you if you will perform the Eighth. Then, after the holidays, I want to ask His Majesty the Emperor if he will accept the dedication... Please forgive me for troubling you. I am returning to Vienna, I District, Hessgasse 7 on the 15th, and will commence the twentieth year of my employment there...[418]

---

musikalischer Rezeption. Exemplifiziert an Bruckners Achter Symphonie' in *BSL 1992* (Linz, 1995), 129-42; Mathias Hansen, 'Persönlichkeit im Werk. Zum Bild Anton Bruckners in der Analyse seiner Musik' in *BSL 1992* (Linz, 1995), 187-93; Benjamin M. Korstvedt, *Bruckner: Symphony no. 8* (Cambridge: CUP, 2000); Joseph C. Kraus, 'Musical Time in the Eighth Symphony' in Howie, Jackson and Hawkshaw, eds., *Perspectives on Anton Bruckner* (Aldershot: Ashgate, 2001), in preparation.

417 See *LBSAB*, 129 for this letter, dated Munich, 2 February 1886; the original is in the *ÖNB*, F18 Schalk 153/2.

418 See *GrBLS*, 338 for full text and *G-A* IV/2, 558f. for extract; the original is in the *ÖNB*.

Levi replied warmly on 8 September, asking Bruckner to send the score as soon as possible and adding that he would like to have the parts written out in Munich. He saw a performance at the end of November or beginning of December as a realistic possibility and invited the composer to stay with him when he came to the rehearsals.[419]

On 19 September Bruckner complied with Levi's request and sent the score of the Eighth with an accompanying letter:

> ... May it find grace! I really cannot describe my joy at the prospect of a performance under your masterly direction! I have also so much to say to my eminent artistic father. May you keep in excellent health - then the days of rehearsal and of the performance will hardly be days of suffering, as is often the case with me. May God give his blessing![420]

Unfortunately, Levi's initial enthusiasm turned to disappointment as he discovered that he was unable to get to grips with the score. Unwilling to hurt Bruckner's feelings, he wrote diplomatically to Joseph Schalk, expressing his reservations and seeking his advice:

> ... Not knowing where else I can get help, I must seek your advice and your assistance. In short, I cannot get to grips with the Eighth Symphony and do not have the will to perform it.
> I am absolutely certain that it would meet with the greatest resistance from both orchestra and public. That would make no difference if I was totally convinced by the work, as I was with the Seventh, and could again say to the orchestra, 'You will certainly like it after the fifth rehearsal!' But I am terribly disappointed. I have studied the work for days on end but cannot really get into it. Far

---

419 See *ABB*, 319; the original of this letter is in St. Florian.

420 See *GrBLS*, 339 for full text and *G-A* IV/2, 559f. for extract; the original is in the *Gesellschaft der Musikfreunde* library.

be it from me to wish to pass judgment - it is, of course, quite possible that I am mistaken and too stupid or too old - but I find the instrumentation impossible. What has particularly alarmed me is the great similarity with the Seventh and the almost stereotyped form. The beginning of the first movement is splendid but I don't know where to start with the development section. And the entire final movement - it is a closed book to me. What do I do now? I shudder at the thought of how this news will affect our friend! I cannot write to him. Should I suggest that he listens to the work at a rehearsal here sometime in the future? In my predicament I gave the score to a good musician who is a friend of mine, and he too was of the opinion that a performance would be impossible. Please reply immediately and advise me how I can approach Bruckner. If he simply shrugged it off by calling me an ass or, worse, a faithless friend, I would be quite content. But I fear a much worse reaction. I am afraid that he will be totally crushed by this disappointment.

Do you know the symphony well? And can you understand it? Help me, I am at a total loss![421]

Schalk's reply was clearly helpful, because Levi was able to say in a second letter that it had brought him some peace of mind.[422] In the meantime, however, he had plucked up the courage to write to Bruckner and he was concerned about Bruckner's possible reaction, as he had not yet received a reply. In this very honest letter, which he must have found extremely difficult to write, Levi attempted to explain his feelings about the score:

... For more than a week I have been trying to write long letters to you. Never before has it been so difficult to find the right words to express what I wish to say to you! But finally I have to do it... The themes are marvellous and magnificent, but their working-out seems

---

421 See *ABB*, 396f. and *G-A* IV/2, 560f. for this letter, dated Munich, 30 September 1887. The original is in the Schalk collection in the *ÖNB*.

422 See *ABB*, 396 and *G-A* IV/2, 562 for Levi's letter to Schalk, dated Munich, 14 October 1887; the original is in the Schalk collection in the *ÖNB*

dubious and, in my opinion, the instrumentation is impossible.

Levi had reasonable doubts about the possible reaction of the orchestra and the public:

> ...What do your Viennese friends say, then? I cannot imagine that I have suddenly lost all my capacity to understand your music.

He advised Bruckner to make some changes and reassured him of his continuing support and devotion:

> ... Do not lose heart, take up your work once more, confer with your friends, with Schalk; perhaps a lot can be achieved through revision... Be good to me! Regard me as a fool, it does not matter to me; but don't think that my feelings towards you have changed or will ever change.
> In true devotion...[423]

Schalk confirmed Levi's suspicions a few days later. Bruckner had been devastated by Levi's critical reaction, but Schalk was confident that he would soon recover from the disappointment:

> ... Naturally your news has hit Professor Bruckner very hard. He is still miserable and inconsolable. It was to be expected, and yet it happened in the mildest form, thus protecting him from even more

---

[423] The original of Levi's letter to Bruckner, dated Munich, 7 October 1887, is in the Munich *Staatsbibliothek*. There is a reference to this letter in Robert Münster, 'Aus Anton Bruckners Münchner Freundes und Bekanntenkreis 1863-1886' in *BSL 1994* (Linz, 1997) and Benjamin Korstvedt discusses and quotes from it in his *Anton Bruckner: Symphony no. 8* (Cambridge, 2000), 18. It will be published complete for the first time in the forthcoming second volume of *HSABB*. My thanks to Dr. Andrea Harrandt for making the text available.

bitter disappointments. I hope that he will soon calm down and undertake a revision of the work, the first movement of which has been begun in accordance with your advice. It would certainly be better for him not to work at present, as he is upset, in despair, and no longer able to believe in himself. Meanwhile his colossal natural strength, both physical and moral, will soon help him to recover.[424]

Schalk's prediction was fulfilled sooner than expected. Two days after Schalk's letter to Levi, Bruckner was able to inform the latter personally that he would soon be engaged fully in revising the symphony and would carry out the task to the best of his ability. He estimated that this revision would take about a year to complete and looked forward to future rehearsals of the symphony, perhaps during the summer vacation of 1888 when Princess Amalie might be in Munich. It would also be expedient if Levi's projected performance of the Fourth was postponed until March 1888, 'because the Princess is usually in Munich during Lent' and 'Gutmann will not have finished printing before the New Year'.[425]

When Bruckner sent Levi the score of the Fourth four months later he was by then sufficiently far removed from the traumatic events of September / October 1887 to admit that Levi's reaction to the first version of the Eighth had been perfectly justifiable:

> ... I have certainly every reason to be ashamed - at least this time - on account of the Eighth. What a fool I have been! It now looks quite

---

424 Schalk's letter to Levi is dated Vienna, 18 October 1887. It was published for the first time in the *Vorlagenbericht* of Robert Haas's edition of the Fourth Symphony, *Anton Bruckner Sämtliche Werke* IV/1 (Vienna/ Leipzig: Musikwissenschaftlicher Verlag, 1936). It was also printed in Alfred Orel, ed., *Bruckner Brevier: Briefe, Dokumente, Berichte* (Vienna 1953), 240f. The original is in the *ÖNB*.

425 Bruckner's letter to Levi is dated Vienna, 20 October 1887. See *GrBLS*, 339f. for full text and *G-A* IV/2, 563 for extract; the location of the original is unknown.

different.[426]

Pre-publication work on the Fourth Symphony and further revision of the Third Symphony prevented Bruckner from devoting much time to a thorough revision of the Eighth until March 1889. Writing to Betty von Mayfeld in January 1888, he echoed what he had already said to Levi, predicting that the revision work would not be completed for some time 'as many alterations have to be made and I have too little time to work'.[427]

Towards the end of what had proved to be a difficult year for Bruckner he received the sad news from Hamburg that Eduard Marxsen had died.[428] Difficulties with the Eighth Symphony, slow progress with the revision of the Fourth, and now the loss of a good friend - not the most auspicious end to his 20th year in Vienna! On the other hand, Linz - the town that he had left with mixed feelings in 1868 - commemorated the 25th anniversary of the laying of the foundation stone of the new cathedral with a performance of his *Te Deum* on 29 September. Bruckner participated in the event as an organist and was given a reception afterwards in the *Stadt Frankfurt* hotel by members of the *Frohsinn* choir. Because of *Hofkapelle* duties Bruckner was not able to spend any time at St. Florian during the Christmas period, but he was able to visit his young friend Oddo Loidol in Kremsmünster.

---

426 See *GrBLS*, 340f. for the full text and *G-A* IV/2, 563 and 589 for extracts from this letter, dated Vienna, 27 February 1888; the original is in private possession.

427 See *ABB*, 220 and extract in *G-A* IV/2, 564 for this letter, dated Vienna, 30 January 1888; the original is in private possession.

428 See *ABB*, 363 for a letter from Schweitzer, dated Altona, 19 November 1887; the location of the original is unknown.

CHAPTER 6

Bruckner in Vienna: The Final Years (1888-1896)

1888 was not a particularly productive year for Bruckner in one respect - there are no original compositions from this year - but his letters and the Schalk correspondence provide glimpses of a considerable amount of revision work undertaken on three symphonies, the Third in particular. There were also several performances of his works outside Austria, the Seventh conducted by Karl Muck in Prague on 15 January and Wilhelm Bayerlein in Nuremberg on 23 January, the Fourth conducted by Anton Seidl in New York on 4 April, and the Te Deum conducted by Otto Kitzler in Brno on 13 April.[1] The review of the New York performance in the *Musical Courier* was complimentary to both Bruckner and the symphony. The reviewer had some reservations about the heavy orchestration at times, which tended to obscure the melodic material, and the undue prominence given to the brass. The performance left something to be desired and the hall was hardly big enough for the work to achieve its maximum effect. But there was no question about the originality of the symphony and Bruckner's thematic inventiveness, and the

---

1 The Nuremberg performance of the Seventh was reviewed in the evening edition of the *Korrespondent von und für Deutschland* 44 (24 January 1888), 1f., in the *Nürnberger Anzeiger* 25 (25 January 1888), 2, and the *Fränkische Kurier* (25 January 1888); for the texts of these reviews, see Franz Scheder, 'Bruckner-Aufführungen in Nürnberg' in *BJ 1989/90* (Linz 1992), 253ff. There was a report of Kitzler's performance of the Te Deum in the *Neue Zeitschrift für Musik* 84, 202; for the text, see Othmar Wessely, 'Bruckner-Berichterstattung in der Neuen Zeitschrift für Musik' in *BSL 1991* (Linz 1994), 139.

conductor was to be congratulated on his boldness in introducing the work to a public more used to standard fare.[2]

The indefatigable Joseph Schalk also played his arrangement of the Fourth at a so-called 'Ladies' Evening' of the *Wagner Society* in Vienna on 19 January and he and Ferdinand Löwe played a piano-duet arrangement of the first and third movements of the same symphony at a concert arranged by the Linz branch of the society on 9 April.

Although Levi had very generously provided an advance of 1000 florins the previous year so that the Fourth could be printed, it was not published (by Gutmann) until September 1889. Before its eventual publication Bruckner made several alterations, some no doubt the result of his experiencing a performance of the work in a special Bruckner concert organized by the *Wagner Society* and played by the Vienna Philharmonic under Hans Richter on 22 January. On 18 January, Bruckner wrote to Richter's wife, Marie, inviting her to the performance and mentioning in a postscript that, in compliance with her husband's wishes, he had made 'significant changes' to it.[3] In a preview of the concert in the *Wiener Tagblatt* on 20 January, Wilhelm Frey had no hesitation in describing Bruckner as 'the most important of all living organists and incontestably one of the most significant composers since Beethoven in the realm of absolute music' and in recommending that such an outstanding musical figure should have at least one of his works performed by the

---

2 This review of the New York performance (signed 'J.H.') appeared in the *Musical Courier* on 14 April; see *G-A* IV/2, 591-94 for a German translation.

3 See *OBB*, 217-18 for the text of this letter. Orel surmises that its recipient was Mrs. Speidel, the wife of the critic, Ludwig Speidel, but Andrea Harrandt has identified her as Marie Richter, the conductor's wife; the original of the letter is in the *Stadt- und Landesbibliothek*, Vienna. See also Rudolf Stephan, 'Bruckners Romantische Sinfonie' in *Anton Bruckner. Studien zu Werk und Wirkung. Festschrift Walter Wiora* (Tutzing 1988), 176.

Vienna Philharmonic each year.[4] As the concert, which also included a performance of Bruckner's *Te Deum*, was not part of the regular Philharmonic series, it was not widely reported. There were reviews in *Die Presse* and the *Wiener Abendpost*, however. In the former, the reviewer considered that the reception of the composer and his works by an enthusiastic audience went some way towards recompensing him for the years of envy and neglect he had been forced to endure, while, in the latter, Hans Paumgartner described the free rein that Bruckner had given to his imagination 'in the magic wood of Romanticism' and said that the symphony represented 'true nature, not a botanical garden with scientific descriptions of plants'.[5] On the same day as the review in *Die Presse*, 30 January, Bruckner wrote letters of appreciation to the Philharmonic and Hans Richter,[6] and to Betty v. Mayfeld. In the latter he mentioned that Princess Stephanie had congratulated him after the concert, and he also gave a progress report on other works:

> ... The 8th Symphony will not be finished for a long time as I have considerable alterations to make and too little time to work... During March the same 4th Symphony is to be performed in Munich. The 7th Symphony had huge successes in London, Boston and Prague...[7]

---

4 See *G-A* IV/2, 585f.

5 See *G-A* IV/2, 587 for the first review which appeared in *Die Presse* on 30 January and Norbert Tschulik, op.cit., 176 for the second review which appeared in the *Wiener Abendpost* on 6 February. Theodor Helm also reviewed the concert in the *Deutsche Zeitung* on 27 January - see Ingrid Fuchs, 'Bruckner und die österreichische Presse' in *BSL 1991* (Linz, 1994), 92, footnote 51. Helm also mentioned a performance of Bruckner's Seventh Symphony in Nuremberg conducted by Wilhelm Bayerlein on 23 January.

6 Bruckner described the performances as 'matchless'. See *ABB*, 220; the original is in the Vienna Philharmonic archives.

7 See *ABB*, 220; the original is privately owned.

Bruckner's letter to Betty v. Mayfeld was in response to an encouraging letter which she sent him on 27 January. Although she had not been able to attend the performance, news of its success had obviously reached her, and she sent her apologies for not being there to experience his 'new triumph'.

> ... At long last our compatriots are beginning to understand your music and the critics are becoming aware of your genius! What a miracle and illumination from above! I am full of pride that I have always recognized you and am sufficiently musical to understand your music and have a feeling for it. Three cheers for you, and may our Beethoven of today continue composing for a long time, so that your music will resound not only in Austria but throughout the world![8]

Between the Vienna and the projected Munich performances of the Fourth Symphony Bruckner carried out further revision work on the score. He informed Levi of these changes when he wrote to him at the end of February. Levi had mentioned 14 March as the date of performance, had invited Bruckner to stay with him in Munich and had asked him to send the score and parts of the symphony by the end of the month.[9] In sending the score to Levi Bruckner pointed out that it had been 'newly scored and tightened up'. He continued:

> I will never forget the success in Vienna. Since then I have taken the initiative and made some further changes. As they have been inserted in the score only, please take care! The pages and

---

8 The letter is dated Linz, 27 January 1888; the original is owned by the *Musikwissenschaftlicher Verlag*, Vienna who have made it available to the *IBG*. It will be printed for the first time in *HSABB* 2. My thanks to Dr. Andrea Harrandt for making the text available.

9 See *ABB*, 319f. for Levi's letter to Bruckner, dated Munich, 14 February 1888; the original is in St. Florian.

instruments which are new are shown in the enclosed sheets of paper...
N.B. The alterations can be seen in the score in any case. It is the only score I possess. The best reviews are also enclosed. Gutmann will send the orchestral parts...

Bruckner also thanked Levi for his invitation to stay with him, but declined, saying that he was not intending to come alone. Presumably he was hoping that one of his friends from Steyr, Carl Almeroth, would join him.[10]

Ferdinand Löwe made his own manuscript score of the Fourth; on 9 May 1887 Joseph Schalk informed his brother Franz that Löwe, with Bruckner's permission, had begun to rescore the work.[11] The differences between Bruckner's autograph score and the first edition, published by Gutmann in September 1889, can be explained largely by reference to Löwe's score which was discovered in 1939. Löwe not only re-scored parts of the work but also altered dynamics and agogic accents and changed the structure of the Scherzo and the Finale; for instance, the reprise of the first section of the latter, amounting to 48 bars, is omitted. Bruckner looked through Löwe's manuscript at least three times. The last date entered by Bruckner is 18 February 1888, almost a month after the Vienna performance and ten days before Bruckner's letter to Levi. Robert Haas has the following to say about the differences between the autograph and the first edition in the editorial report of his own edition of the Fourth in the first *Gesamtausgabe* (1936):

... the Scherzo, which ends smoothly as a *da capo* section in the autograph, comes to a sudden end in its first appearance in the first

---

10 See *GrBLS*, 340f. and *G-A* IV/2, 563 and 589 for this letter, dated Vienna, 27 February 1888; the original is privately owned. Which score did Bruckner send to Levi? See *SchABCT*, 550, note to entry for 27.2.88, for a possible explanation.

11 The original of this letter is in the *ÖNB*, F18 Schalk 158/8/4.

edition with a large *diminuendo* plunge before the coda; there is a new short transition to the Trio, and the *da capo* is then shortened by 65 bars and the coda by 2 bars. In the Finale a cut of 48 bars was made, eliminating the beginning of the reprise; instead the second subject (12 bars) appears at the beginning of the reprise in a new key relationship; in addition there are two instances of phrase extensions (one by two bars).

The Munich performance did not materialize because Levi took ill. Bruckner sent his condolences to Levi 'not so much on account of the postponement of the programme as on account of your damaged health'. He was unsure about Levi's suggestion that the concert could be given in the autumn, because Princess Amalie was never in Munich at that time of year. He complained that he was finding teaching and composing more of a burden. Hellmesberger had been asked for some financial support in 1887 but had refused it. Bruckner asked Levi to convey this information to Princess Amalie, and continued:

...(Last hope the 8th Symphony in Munich.) Would it not be conceivable to arrange an extra concert (as in Vienna) at a time when you have completely recovered?[12]

The copy of the score which Seidl used for his performance of the Fourth in New York in April 1888 contains other revisions. In the foreword to the '2. revidierte Ausgabe' (Vienna, 1953), Nowak mentions that this copy, unknown to Bruckner scholars until the mid-20th century and located in the Music Collection of the University of Columbia in New York, includes Bruckner's alterations - not only those of the copyist in the Cod. 19.476 score in the *ÖNB*, but also a number of others which were not subsequently added to the autograph. He argues, therefore, that the

---

12 See *GrBLS*, 341f. and *G-A* IV/2, 590 for this letter, dated Vienna, 9 March 1888; the original is in the Taut Collection, University Library, Leipzig.

New York score - the only one to contain these alterations - is 'the only model for the final, definitive format in which Bruckner wanted his 4th Symphony to be printed and made available to the public'. It contains, for instance, abridgements in the Andante, several additions to the instrumentation and, in the Finale, a change in time-signature from 4/4 to Tempo primo already at letter at U (and not a letter V) - all written by Bruckner himself. It also contains alterations made by others, including the re-composition of one or two small sections in the Finale. At the front of this New York manuscript there is a single sheet, written by Bruckner himself, bearing the dedication to the Lord Chamberlain, Prince Constantin Hohenlohe-Schillingsfürst. Nowak's edition of 1953, then, is a compilation of the first three movements of the second version of the symphony (1878) and the 1880 Finale, but it incorporates Bruckner's alterations in the copy sent to Seidl.[13]

Bruckner's diary entries for 1888 also include references to revision work on the Fourth. On 13 March: '1. und 2. Satz zugleich gerade u. Gegen-bwg. u. ½ Tact später Finale einen Tact später ger. u. Gegenb.; on 22 July: 'NB Stimmen neu corrigiren Paar ungerade Takte. Schluss bei 4. Sinf. Gutmann. Überschreitungen - gut sehen - '; August: 'Die Verkleinerung im 1. Satze der 4. Sinfonie ausbessern'.

Although Bruckner gave his approval to the final printing in September 1889 it was by no means whole-hearted. After looking through the printer's copy he did not sign it with his name or even with his initials which he usually did. Nowak's interpretation of this is that Bruckner 'appreciated the helpful idealism of his deeply devoted disciples and accepted their advice, but denied them his confirmation' and that he did not append his signature because 'the original was to be valid "for later

---

13 For further information about Seidl and the New York score, see Leopold Nowak, 'Neues zu Anton Bruckners "Romantischer"' in *ÖMZ* 8 (1953), 161-64, repr. in *Über Anton Bruckner*, 24ff. 'J.H.' (James Huneker?) reviewed the New York performance in the *Musical Courier* on 14 April. A German translation of this review can be found in *G-A* IV/2, 591-94.

times"'.[14]   In the autograph score, on the title-page of the Finale, he made it abundantly clear (by adding his own signature) that the abridgements were to be indicated in both the full score and piano arrangement by the addition of the symbols 'Vi - de'.[15]

Bruckner's Easter vacation (possibly 28 March - 2 April) and part of his summer vacation were spent at St. Florian. A few weeks before his Easter visit to St. Florian, however, the *Kyrie* from his F minor Mass was performed at a *Wagnerverein* concert in Vienna. There was a brief report in the *Wiener Abendpost* on 1 March.[16]

On his return to Vienna after his Easter break Bruckner wrote to Josef Gruber concerning five early settings of *Tantum ergo* which he had just revised and which he wished Karl Aigner to copy for publication purposes:

> ... As soon as I returned to Vienna I revised these *4 Tantum Ergo*, which belong together, as well as another separate setting. Please convey my respects to Prof. Deubler and ask him if he could arrange for Mr. Aigner to copy the score for St. Florian. And then would you be good enough to make them ready for publication? Please make sure that the *4 Tantum Ergo* remain together.
> I was delighted by the great success enjoyed recently in New York by the Fourth Symphony, conducted by the famous conductor...[17]

---

14   Nowak, op.cit.

15   Bruckner's express instructions were not consistently followed in the first edition, however. Nevertheless, a possible cut in the Andante (i.e. between bars 139 and 193) was not made - in accordance with Bruckner's instructions: 'N.B. The large cut (at letter H) should only be made if absolutely necessary, as it has an extremely adverse effect on the work'.

16   See Norbert Tschulik, op.cit., 176.

17   See *ABB*, 221 for this letter, dated Vienna, 24 April 1888; the location of the original is unknown. The five *Tantum Ergo* settings, WAB 41 and 42, date from 1846. See *ABSW* XXI/1, 35-41 and 139-45 for further details, and *ABSW* XXI/2, 41-51 and 150-57 for modern editions of both original and revised versions. The revised versions were published for the first time by Groß of

Bruckner did not have necrophiliac tendencies and so it was not so much a morbid interest in the dead Wagner as a genuine affection for his memory which led him to make an annual pilgrimage to his grave when he visited Bayreuth every summer. The same is true of his high regard for Beethoven and Schubert. The remains of both these composers were exhumed in 1888, on 21 June and 23 September respectively, and moved to specially prepared graves in the *Zentralfriedhof*. Bruckner was present on both occasions and took a particularly keen interest in the removal of Beethoven's body from the Währinger cemetery.[18]

On 21 July, at the beginning of the summer vacation, Bruckner travelled to Bayreuth with members of the Vienna *Wagner-Verein* (including Eckstein and Hugo Wolf) who had hired a special train. He certainly saw Richter conducting a performance of *Die Meistersinger*, may have been present at a performance of *Parsifal*, conducted by Felix Mottl who was standing in for the indisposed Hermann Levi, and visited the graves of Liszt and Wagner. Apart from the period 12-18 August when he was on *Hofkapelle* duty, he spent the rest of his vacation at St. Florian, Steyr, Linz and Kremsmünster.[19] The organ recitals which he gave in St. Florian abbey on 15 and 28 August were reported in the two main Linz newspapers. Much of the time at St. Florian was spent revising the Third Symphony. During his visits to Steyr he enjoyed the company of his three friends, Karl Reder, Carl Almeroth and Isidor Dierkes. Reder, Almeroth and three others formed a kind of cartel which undertook to pay Bruckner an annual sum of 600 florins until such times as his

---

Innsbruck in 1893.

18 For further details, see Carl Hruby, *Meine Erinnerungen an Anton Bruckner* (Vienna, 1901), 20f.; Richard von Perger and Robert Hirschfeld, *Geschichte der k.k. Gesellschaft der Musikfreunde in Wien* (Vienna, 1912), 188 and 195; *G-A* IV/2, 595f.; Kurt Dieman, *Musik in Wien* (Vienna-Munich-Zurich, 1970), 179.

19 A letter from Bruckner to his *Hofkapelle* colleague, Pius Richter, indicates that he had made his customary arrangement for sharing of responsibilities over the summer period. The original of this letter, dated Vienna, 9 July 1888, is in the *Stadt- und Landesbibliothek*, Vienna.

568

financial position improved. This arrangement lasted for three years until the pension from the Emperor came into force. Bruckner for his part gave a special concert for his friends once a year at St. Florian.

Bruckner's desire to gain further international recognition led him to remind Arthur Nikisch in Leipzig of an earlier promise to perform the Seventh in Berlin. In his first letter he also mentioned that Gutmann had sent the Fourth to Leipzig for printing and that he was revising the Eighth. In his second he asked Nikisch to give him several weeks' prior notice of a possible performance so that the Vienna branch of the *Wagner-Verein* could contact the Berlin branch.[20] There were encouraging signs, however, of a growing reputation outside Vienna. Bruckner's old teacher, Otto Kitzler, directed a performance of his *Te Deum* in Brno on 13 April which was reported in the *Neue Zeitschrift für Musik*.[21] Two issues of the Parisian music journal *Le Guide Musical* (6 and 13 September) contained an article on Bruckner and his music, entitled 'Un Symphonist d'Avenir Antoine Bruckner', by Jan van Santen Kolff. The main thrust of the article was that, while his contemporary Brahms had been worshipped for nearly twenty years, Bruckner had been neglected and was only now becoming recognized.[22] Bruckner wrote to Santen Kolff to thank him, and compared his generosity with the harsh treatment meted out to him in Vienna by Hanslick and others.[23]

---

20   See Steffen Lieberwirth, 'Anton Bruckner und Leipzig. Einige neue Erkenntnisse und Ergänzungen' in *BJ 1989/90* (Linz, 1992), 285 for these two letters, dated Vienna, 20 June and 23 November respectively. The originals are privately owned.

21   The report appeared in the *Neue Zeitschrift für Musik* 84 (25 April 1888), 202. See Othmar Wessely, 'Bruckner Berichterstattung in der Neuen Zeitschrift für Musik' in *BSL 1991* (Linz, 1994)., 139.

22   See *G-A* IV/2, 606f. for a German précis of this article.

23   The addressee of this letter, dated Vienna, 23 November 1888, is given as Dr. W.L. van Meurs, a Dutch librarian and admirer of Bruckner's music, in *G-A* IV/2, 612 and Cornelis van Zwol,

On 2 October Bruckner was an honorary guest of the *Gesellschaft der Musikfreunde* at the celebrations of the centenary of Simon Sechter's birth. Sechter's nephew, Moritz, was one of his favourite companions and a member of the small circle of friends (which included Löwe, Schalk, Markus, Vockner, Oberleithner and Lorenz) with whom he would often dine at the 'Zur Kugel' or the 'Gause' or the 'Riedhof' restaurants in the evenings, the restaurant being chosen according to the current quality of the Pilsner beer on offer!

As in 1887 Deubler conducted Bruckner's early *Requiem* (without *Offertorium* and *Benedictus*) in early November at St. Florian. His *Ave Maria*, WAB 6, was performed three times in the latter part of the year, first at the beginning of October by the Wels branch of the *Wagnerverein*, then on 8 November in Vienna at a *Wagnerverein* concert conducted by Josef Schalk, finally in Vienna again on 10 December as part of a *Singverein* concert.[24]

Bruckner spent his Christmas vacation at Kremsmünster. The attraction may very well have been a young lady he met there during the Summer vacation, Mathilde Feßl. Another young lady from Linz, Martha Rauscher, also made an impression on him during the summer. There are two of his letters to her extant. He requests and then acknowledges receipt of her photograph, mentions that he has been ill and is feeling

---

'Bruckner-Rezeption in den Niederlanden und im anglo-amerikanischen Raum' in *BSL 1991* (Linz, 1994), 149; the location of the original is unknown.

24 The *Wagnerverein* concert also included performances of another Bruckner motet, *Locus iste*, and some Wolf songs (sung by Ellen Forster). It was reviewed by Laurencin d'Armond in the *Neue Zeitschrift für Musik* 84 (5 December 1888), 530f; see Othmar Wessely, op.cit., *(BSL 1991)*, 139. One of the reviewers of the *Singakademie* concert, writing in *Vaterland* on 30 December 1888, pointed to many similarities between Bruckner's *Ave Maria* and Palestrina's motet, *Tu es Petrus*, which was also sung at the concert; see *G-A* IV/2, 617ff. for this review. Laurencin d'Armond reviewed this concert in the *Neue Zeitschrift für Musik* 85 (27 March 1889), 150f.; see Othmar Wessely, op.cit., 139.

'rather desperate' because of the work he has to do.[25]

Owing to pre-publication work on the Fourth Symphony and further revision of the Third Symphony, Bruckner was not able to devote much time to a thorough revision of the Eighth until March 1889. In his letter to Betty von Mayfeld at the end of January 1888 he intimated that it would take some time to finish it as 'considerable alterations' had to be made and he had too little time to work. In his letter to Santen Kolff in November he wrote that, although the Eighth was finished, cuts were being made here and there and some changes in the orchestration were also necessary.[26]

Why did Bruckner undertake the revision of Symphony no. 3? It is possible that, after Levi's initial unfavourable reaction to the Eighth, he felt that he would be able to make an earlier work more successful by 'correcting' parts of it. It could also be argued that he did not have the will and energy to embark immediately on a new work. But the course of events showed that 'the revision work was characterized more by insecurity and sudden changes of mind than by single-minded purposefulness. (Contrary to the opinion of a substantial part of the Bruckner literature, however, this cannot be cited as evidence of the inferior quality or irrelevance of this 1888/89 version)'.[27] Bruckner's memory was not entirely accurate when he wrote to Wolzogen in January 1889:

> I am well again, and have been working since last June on the 3rd Symphony in D minor which I have thoroughly improved...[28]

---

25 See *GrBB*, 78f. and *G-A* IV/2, 620f. for these two letters, dated Vienna, 5 and 23 November 1888 respectively; the originals of Martha's letters to Bruckner and his replies are privately owned.

26 See footnotes 8 and 23.

27 *LBSAB*, 133.

28 From Bruckner's letter to Hans von Wolzogen, dated Vienna, 1 January 1889. See *ABB*, 223; the location of the original is unknown.

In fact, Bruckner began with the revision of the Finale which seemed to him to require the most radical change. The earliest date which appears in the autograph is 5 March 1888 in bar 314. He completed his revision of this movement on 29 May, but later undertook a second revision of the Finale between 19 July and 30 September. Although he made use of pages from the first edition to insert corrections in the other movements, for the Finale he used a copy made by Franz Schalk which already contained three substantial cuts and new transitions composed by Schalk himself.[29] It appears that Bruckner had already discussed the new shape of the Finale with Schalk and the latter had prepared a version to which Bruckner now added the finishing touches.[30] Bruckner allowed two of Schalk's cuts to stand but rejected the third (bars 465-586 of the 1877 version) and replaced it with new material (bars 393-440 in the new version). The bridge passage preceding it, almost certainly Franz Schalk's work, remained unchanged.

The Schalk brothers' correspondence from June to the end of the year reveals that, while they agreed in principle with Bruckner's revision work (the cuts in particular), they found the painstaking attention to detail excessive and superfluous. All in all it would appear that Bruckner was not unduly influenced by the Schalks and frequently resisted their objections and rejected their advice. On 10 June Joseph informed Franz about progress in the revision work on the Finale and Bruckner's obsessive attention to detail which had effectively prevented him from starting work on the other movements.[31] At the end of June / beginning of July, Gustav Mahler, who had been largely responsible for the four-hand transcription of the second version, visited

---

29 Mus. Hs. 6081 in the *ÖNB*.

30 Bruckner refers to this movement in a letter to Schalk, dated Vienna, 23 February 1888. See *FSBB*, 72; the original is in the *ÖNB*.

31 See an extract from this letter in *LBSAB*, 134; the original is in the *ÖNB*, F18 Schalk 158/9/7.

Bruckner as he was passing through Vienna. He advised Bruckner to reject the entire revision plan and to draw on the already existing version for the new edition. Henry-Louis de la Grange refers to this visit, but is certainly wrong in suggesting 1884 as the date:

> On June 30, he [Mahler] passed through Vienna on his way to Perchtoldsdorf, where, like the year before, he and Fritz Lohr spent a week of relaxing music sessions and refreshing walking tours. No doubt this was when Mahler, on a visit to Bruckner, persuaded him to give up his idea of revising his Third Symphony. The editor Rättig had in fact persuaded Bruckner to rewrite his work, since none of the many conductors to whom he had sent the score would agree to play it. Bruckner had started work on the revision, and about fifty pages were already engraved. Mahler was firmly opposed to the idea, and the old master asked the editor to destroy the new pages, since an 'orchestral professional' had convinced him that revision was unnecessary.[32]

Joseph Schalk saw his position as Bruckner's 'assistant' threatened by Mahler's intervention (passages in letters of a later date reveal that Mahler for his part had very little sympathy for the Schalk brothers), and he wrote to Franz suggesting that publication be delayed until such times as he (Franz) would be in Vienna and able to exert some influence on the composer.[33] Joseph wrote to Franz again a week later, suggesting that it would be better to 'let sleeping dogs lie' in case Bruckner discovered that he (Joseph) had personally vetoed the reprinting of the old score.

---

32 Henry-Louis de la Grange, *Mahler* vol. 1 (1974), 115. De la Grange bases this on information provided by Auer in his *Anton Bruckner* (Leipzig: Musikwissenschaftlicher Verlag, 1941), 323. Although Auer does not give the exact date of the alleged visit, he places it between two other incidents dated 5 April and 28 May 1884.

33 See *LBSAB*, 134f. for and extract from this letter, dated Vienna, 13 July 1888; the original is in the *ÖNB*, F18 Schalk 158/9/9.

Löwe had already told Bruckner what he and the Schalks thought of Mahler's advice.[34]

Bruckner spent many hours of his vacation at St. Florian preparing the Third for the second edition. Karl Aigner and some of the choirboys were drafted in to help. Ferdinand Edlinger, later an organ student at the Conservatory and a schoolteacher, recalled meeting Bruckner outside the music room of the abbey one day:

> Bruckner... asked me if I could play the piano. When I replied modestly that I could certainly play 'a little', he led me to the piano and showed me the two upper staves of a page of full score. We sat down and played a few bars in piano duet. Suddenly he leapt up, clapped his hands with great joy and said to me, his eyes shining with happiness, 'Yes, that is fine. Hanslick can write what he wants'.[35]

An older student, Franz Wiesner, also reported:

> As we were senior students in the high school and already had a basic grounding in harmony - indeed quite a few of us, for instance Aigner, currently music teacher in the abbey, and Müller, director of music at Linz Cathedral, had a more thorough understanding of it - we came into close contact with the master as he was composing. If he had completed one part of a symphony movement, or had to make a choice between two alternatives, he called one of us, usually Aigner. We then played the string parts, for instance, and Bruckner played the other parts as he wished them to be heard. Now and then he asked , 'Which do you prefer?'[36]

---

34 See *LBSAB*, 135 for an extract from this letter, dated Vienna, 20 July 1888; the original is in the *ÖNB*, F18 Schalk 158/9/10. In his reply to Joseph's earlier letter, Franz said that he would write to Bruckner about the symphony - hence Joseph's advice.

35 *G-A* II/1, 302. Edlinger also reported that Bruckner seldom played the organ in services in later years. However, he was often asked to play a postlude - see *G-A* II/1, 304f.

36 *G-A* II/1, 302.

When Bruckner was in a good mood and wanted to have a break from composing, he would often play through movements of his symphonies to the choirboys, indicating instrumental entries etc. Aigner did not have an easy time. He had to check for parallel fifths and octaves and pay attention to the periodic structure and other details. Almeroth, his friend from Steyr, relates how he took infinite care over scoring and choosing the correct instrumental distribution of the notes of a chord, for instance, and playing the same chord several times until he had found what he felt was the correct choice of instruments.[37]

Joseph's decision to leave things as they were proved a wise one. Before leaving St. Florian for Kremsmünster on 9 September, Bruckner began revising the first movement. He completed his revision of this movement on 2 December. Joseph Schalk referred to his work on this movement when he wrote to his brother in October that Bruckner was well but 'sweating away pointlessly'.[38] The following month Franz wrote to Joseph expressing his concern that Bruckner should 'overcome his suicidal whims'.[39] Ten days later Joseph was able to tell Franz that Bruckner would very much like his opinion about the alterations he was making in both the Third and Eighth Symphonies:

> ... I am to say to you that, in the Finale, a large number of bars are being omitted between the G major passage and your favourite passage, as he calls it. I doubt if that is of any help. But he has to be allowed to hope; the main thing is to keep him in a good mood. At

---

37 G-A II/1, 303.

38 See *LBSAB*, 137 for an extract from this letter, dated Vienna, 5 October 1888; the original is in the *ÖNB*, F18 Schalk 158/9/17. Joseph's observation is corroborated by Bruckner's own words, in a letter to the music dealer Karl Tendler in Graz on the same day: 'I have no time at all to give concerts, and hardly any time even to compose...'; the location of the original is unknown.

39 See *LBSAB*, 137 for and extract from this letter, dated Reichenberg, 16 November 1888; the original is in the *ÖNB*, F18 Schalk 158/9/22.

any rate, write him a proper letter...[40]

On 18 December, Franz Schalk wrote two letters, one to his brother Joseph, the other - a 'proper letter' to Bruckner. In the former, he expressed his concern that Bruckner might feel neglected as a result of Joseph's enthusiasm for Wolf's music.[41] In the latter, he recalled with great pleasure his studies with the composer and regretted that he was no longer in Vienna to witness his work at first hand and give him his personal support. He sent his best wishes for the New Year and hoped that Bruckner would have the necessary energy to complete his Ninth Symphony.[42]

Bruckner began 1889 by sending his best wishes for the New Year to Hans von Wolzogen. The Third Symphony had been 'thoroughly improved', he wrote, but he was still experiencing the same opposition from supporters of the 'Brahms cult' and Hans Richter was too frightened of Hanslick's possible reaction to programme one of his symphonies![43] On 2 January, Joseph wrote to Franz about the New Year's eve celebrations in which he, Löwe, Hirsch, Wolf and Bruckner had participated.

---

40   See LBSAB, 137 for an extract from this letter, dated Vienna, 26 November 1888; the original is in the ÖNB, F18 Schalk 158/9/24.

41   See LBSAB, 119f. for an extract from this letter; the original is in the ÖNB, F18 Schalk 158/9/43.

42   See ABB, 365.

43   See earlier and footnote 28.

44   See LBSAB, 137f. for an extract from this letter; the original is in the ÖNB, F18 Schalk 158/10/11. Friction among the membership of the Wagner-Verein and Bruckner's peevishness about the growing popularity of Hugo Wolf are alluded to in an exchange of letters between Joseph and Franz at the end of January and beginning of February. See LBSAB, 120ff. for extracts from these letters, dated Vienna, 28 January and Reichenberg, 9 September 1889 respectively; the originals are in the ÖNB, F18 Schalk 158/10/13 and 158/10/14.

Bruckner had been very delighted and touched by Franz's letter.[44]

Bruckner had been associated with the *Akademischer Gesangverein* for many years. The conductor was no longer his old friend, Rudolf Weinwurm, but Hermann Grädener who was a keen Brahmsian. Nevertheless, Bruckner was elected an honorary member of the society on 22 January. He attended a committee meeting on 12 February to offer his thanks and wrote a letter which was read out at the next choir rehearsal.[45]

Hans Richter may or may not have been too unsure of critical response to programme one of Bruckner's symphonies in a *Gesellschaft* concert. But he was certainly prepared to conduct the Philharmonic in a concert organized by the *Wagner-Verein* on Sunday 24 February. In addition both Schalk and Löwe were active in promoting Bruckner's works in piano performances given at weekly meetings of the *Wagner-Verein* during February.

The Philharmonic concert, held in the large *Musikverein* hall, included the 'March of the Three Kings' from Liszt's *Christus,* the Venusberg music from Wagner's *Tannhäuser* and the second Vienna performance of Bruckner's Symphony no. 7. Bruckner, as usual, wrote a letter of appreciation to the Philharmonic after the concert and thanked the *Wagner-Verein* for its support.[46] Because of the 'private' nature of the performance (as was the case with the performance of the Fourth in January 1888), many of the leading critics were absent. Those who attended, however, were impressed. Writing in the *Deutsche Zeitung,* Theodor Helm

---

45 See Elisabeth Hilscher, 'Bruckner als Gelehrter - Bruckner als Geehrter' in *BSL* 1988 (Linz, 1992), 122.

46 The letters to the Vienna Philharmonic and the *Wagner-Verein* are both dated Vienna, 1 March 1889. See *ABB*, 224 for the former; the original is in the Vienna Philharmonic archives. The original of the latter is in the *Wiener Stadt- und Landesbibliothek*.

described the performance as a 'great artistic event' attended by people who were genuinely interested in the composer and his work. Accordingly it made a much greater impact that it had done three years previously at its first performance.[47] Writing in the *Fremdenblatt*, Ludwig Speidel was honest enough to confess that, although he was not fully able to understand the symphony and had very little time for Bruckner's young supporters, the work had great originality, particularly in the slow movement.[48] Alfred Gillhofer's review in *Das Vaterland* is very pro-Bruckner, adopting the familiar argument that the composer has had to struggle against difficult odds to gain a hearing. His works can be compared only with the finest, and they display a contrapuntal mastery and assured handling of orchestral polyphony. His inventive powers are such that the motivic material in one of his symphonies would furnish any other composer with enough ideas for ten works.[49]

Finally, in his review in the *Deutsches Volksblatt*, August Göllerich argued for the formation of a 'Bruckner Society' which would provide the composer with the financial security necessary for him to devote all his time and energy to composition.[50]

A week after the performance Joseph Schalk informed his brother Franz of the success of the concert. In his reply Franz expressed his pleasure and his hope that it would lead to a greater understanding of Bruckner's music.[51]

---

47 See *G-A* IV/2, 628f. for an extract from this review, dated 2 March 1889.

48 See *G-A* IV/2, 629f. for an extract from this review, dated 7 March 1889.

49 See *G-A* IV/2, 630-33 for an lengthy extract from this review, dated 3 March 1889.

50 See *G-A* IV/2, 633f. for extract from this review, dated 7 March 1889.

51 See *LBSAB*, 138f. for extracts from these letters, dated Vienna, 3 March 1889 and Reichenberg, 6 March 1889 respectively; the originals are in the *ÖNB*, F18 Schalk 158/10/17 and 158/10/18. Leibnitz describes it erroneously as a concert in which the piano four-hand arrangement was played.

Bruckner's relationship with Kremsmünster was strengthened in March when some of his manuscripts were sent there at the request of his friend, Oddo Loidol, who wrote to him on behalf of a fellow-priest, Father Hugo, who was beginning a manuscript collection. Loidol asked Bruckner if he could pass on any autographs or sketches which he no longer needed or to which he attached no particular importance.[52]

As Bruckner was fairly close to his sister Rosalie in Vöcklabruck, the death of his niece Johanna must have come as a great shock to him. Writing to Rosalie on 14 March, Bruckner sent his condolences and mentioned that a Mass had been read for her at the *Schottenstift* the day before. He also enclosed twenty florins to help towards funeral expenses.[53]

Apart from the Seventh Symphony in February, very few Bruckner works were performed in Vienna during the course of 1889. On 14 March Bruckner attended a performance of his String Quintet by the Hellmesberger Quartet in the small *Musikvereinsaal*. On Maundy Thursday (18 April), Joseph Schalk conducted a choir from the *Wagner-Verein* in a sacred concert in the *Minoritenkirche*. The programme ranged from some unaccompanied Palestrina motets to some Wolf songs and included Bruckner's *Locus iste* and *Ave Maria*. In his review of the concert, Hans Paumgartner stressed that it was not only vociferous support from his young friends that ensured success for Bruckner. He was above 'party politics' and everyone who

---

52 See *G-A* IV/2, 669 for this letter, dated Kremsmünster, 11 March 1889; the location of the original is unknown. According to a letter sent by Father Georg Huemer, music director at Kremsmünster abbey, to Franz Schaumann on 4 December 1896, Bruckner sent a parcel of sketches to the abbey on 12 April; the location of the original of the accompanying letter is unknown. For further information, see Altman Kellner, *Musikgeschichte des Stiftes Kremsmünster* (Cassel / Basel, 1956), 762f.

53 See *ABB*, 224 for this letter; the original is in the possession of the Hueber family, Vöcklabruck.

listened to these two motets was genuinely moved.[54] At a church celebration in Hamburg on 24 May and again during its anniversary celebrations in the *Am Hof* church on 26 October the *Ambrosius-Verein* of Vienna conducted by Julius Böhm sang Bruckner's *Locus iste*. On 6 October the *Church Music Society* of the *Votivkirche* conducted by Theobald Kretschmann sang two of Bruckner's graduals for mixed choir at a sacred music concert in the Ehrbar Hall. The reviewer for *Das Vaterland* commented on the ability of both Liszt and Bruckner to combine the old style with modern harmonic developments.[55]

Outside Vienna, performances of Bruckner's works during the year were few and far between. On Sunday 24 March the Graz *Singverein* performed the motet *Tota pulchra es*, WAB 46 and there were short reviews in both the *Grazer Tagespost* and the *Grazer Morgenpost*.[56] At the beginning of December, Karl Muck conducted the second Prague performance of the Symphony no. 7.[57]

Calendar entries indicate that Bruckner probably had *Hofkapelle* duties on 13, 14, 20, 21, 27 and 28 July and 11, 14 and 15 August during his summer break. It is not clear whether he arranged for another organist like Pius Richter to act as his substitute on some of these occasions. What is certain is that some days at the end of July and beginning of August were spent at Bayreuth and the rest of his holiday was divided between St. Florian and Steyr. As in the previous year (and *Hofkapelle*

---

54   See *G-A* IV/2, 670 for an extract from this review.

55   See *G-A* IV/2, 671 for an extract from this review.

56   Karl Savenau was the reviewer in the *Tagespost* (26 March) and '-ch' was the reviewer in the *Morgenpost* (27 March). For further details, see Ingrid Schubert, 'Bruckner, Wagner und die Neudeutschen in Graz' in *BSL 1984* (Linz, 1986), 37f.

57   Muck alluded to this performance and his earlier performances of the symphony in Graz and Prague when he wrote to Bruckner from Berlin on 26 December 1893, asking for information which could be used as pre-performance (6 January 1894) publicity material. See *ABB*, 333f.; the original is in St. Florian.

duties permitting) he may have taken advantage of the travelling arrangements organized by the *Wagnerverein* to travel to Bayreuth on a special train which left Vienna on Saturday 20 July. One of Bruckner's travelling companions was the young Joseph Venantius v. Wöss, who later edited several of his works for Universal Edition. The three operas which they attended were *Parsifal* (two performances), *Tristan und Isolde* and *Die Meistersinger*. Wöss tells of an occasion when he and a few others accompanied Bruckner below the theatre stage right to the foundations. Bruckner triumphantly secured a loose piece of brick from the foundations and said that he would use it as a paperweight in his apartment in Vienna![58]

Bruckner's young friend, August Göllerich, was also in Bayreuth and made use of the opportunity to introduce the Eighth Symphony to the violinist and composer, Alexander Ritter, and Richard Strauss. According to Göllerich, he and Strauss played the piano-duet version of the Adagio movement. Strauss was clearly much impressed, but did not have such a high opinion of the first movement.[59]

After his return from Bayreuth, Bruckner asked Göllerich if he could remember what was at the top of the two municipal towers (weathercock, cross, lightning conductor?) and the Catholic church (weathercock but no cross?).[60] Redlich makes some pertinent comments about this fixation - a kind of numeromania - which was clearly related to his obsession with prayer repetition as noted in his diaries:

> ... In moments of a more than usually troubled mental and spiritual condition (as, for instance, in the years 1887-9), the obsession with repetition and focussing morbid attention on the number and character of inanimate ornamental objects refused to be canalized into the

---

58 See *G-A* IV/2, 673-76 for this account.

59 See *G-A* IV/2, 676.

60 See *ABB*, 225 for this letter, dated Vienna, 12 August 1889; there is an English translation in H.F. Redlich, *Bruckner and Mahler* (London: Dent, 1955), 31. The location of the original is unknown.

purely musical or religious sphere alone.[61]

It is possible that this numeromania was accentuated by his intensive work on the Third and, particularly, the Eighth Symphonies during the year. Revision work on the Third was completed in March.[62] The printing took a long time, perhaps because Bruckner was not absolutely convinced about the rightness of revision. Eberle did not receive the printer's copy until 17 August and the publication of the score was not announced until November 1890. The printing costs were covered by Emperor Franz Josef.

No sooner had Bruckner completed revision work on the Third than he turned his attention once again to the Eighth. The Adagio was revised between 4 March and 8 May. Work on the Finale was completed on 31 July, the Scherzo was revised during August and September, and the opening movement was 'newly restored' between November 1889 and the end of January 1890, further work being undertaken until 10 March when he declared the movement 'completely finished'.[63] When revising the symphony Bruckner wrote out new copies of the first three movements but used the original manuscript of the Finale, amending it by erasing some passages, pasting over other passages and altering the order of pages.[64]

---

61 Redlich, op.cit., 31.

62 Although there is diary entry for 11 February which indicates completion - 'Am 11. Febr. 1889 Sinf. in D moll Nr. 3 ganz fertig' - Bruckner scrutinized the slow movement between 17 and 27 February and the Scherzo on 3 and 4 March.

63 One of Bruckner's diary-notebooks from this period, however, has the following entry under the slightly later date of 14 March: 'letzte auswendige Wiederholung v. I. Satze der 8 Sinf.' / 'final repetition by memory of the 1st movement of the 8th Symphony'.

64 The *ÖNB* shelf numbers of the autograph full scores of the individual movements in the first version are Mus. Hs. 6083 (first movement), Mus. Hs. 6084 (Scherzo), Mus. Hs. 19.480 vol. 3 (Adagio) and Mus. Hs. vol. 4 (Finale). The first and second movements in the second version are

We know, from various anecdotes of friends and pupils, that Bruckner often became so totally absorbed in his work that he would disregard visitors to his flat, even those who had appointments. No amount of knocking would arouse him from his labours. One such incident was later recalled by Emil Seling, a private pupil of Bruckner's during the 1889-90 period:

> ...'Today I will show you why I left you standing at the door recently. Come here and sit down'. And when I had taken my place beside his Bösendorfer piano, he played to me for almost half an hour the passages in the Eighth Symphony which he had just altered - the symphony which he had written four years earlier and was now thoroughly revising for the purpose of its first performance in Vienna. He drew my attention particularly to the fact that he felt he could not do without the harp in the Adagio, although he had banned this instrument from all his other symphonies because he thought it was too theatrical. He also repeated the passage which he called 'the death watch', making the remark that the 'dear Lord' had inspired him to write it...[65]

While working on this second version of the symphony, Bruckner sent the completed manuscripts to the movements to a professional copyist, Leopold Hofmeyer, in Steyr so that a fair copy of the entire work would be available. In a letter accompanying the Trio, Bruckner made a light-hearted reference to 'der Micherl', the Scherzo:

> ... How is Michael doing? I am now sending you his companion, the Trio, and enclose 10 florins as advance payment until such time as

---

Mus. Hs. 19.480 vols. 1 and 2. The third movement was privately owned by Lili Schalk when Nowak edited the second version for the *Gesamtausgabe* (*ABSW* VIII/2, 1955). The existence of a complete separate copy of the original version (Mus. Hs. 6001 in the *ÖNB*) enabled Nowak to prepare an authentic first edition of this version as *ABSW* VIII/1 in 1972.

65 See *G-A* IV/2, 693ff.

you send me a bill...[66]

Bruckner also referred to Hans Richter's great interest in the First Symphony in this letter. He wanted Bruckner to have it copied for future performance. Writing to Franz Schalk at about this time, Joseph Schalk also mentioned plans for a performance of the symphony.[67] Bruckner did not begin serious work on it, however, until after the Eighth was completed, and the concert in which it was performed did not take place until December 1891, more than two years later.

Joseph Schalk's letters to his brother in the second half of the year suggest some kind of temporary breakdown in his relationship with Bruckner. No reason is given, so we can only speculate that it was either connected with the revision of the Third Symphony or with Schalk's advocacy of Wolf (at Bruckner's expense?) Nor is it likely that Bruckner would have been caught up in the in-fighting among members of the *Akademischer Wagner-Verein* during 1889 which resulted in some leaving the society for political and anti-Semitic reasons and founding a breakaway *Richard Wagner-Verein* the following year.[68] A rift between Schalk and Bruckner is first

---

66 See *ABB*, 226 and *G-A* IV/2, 678f. for the text of this letter, dated Vienna, 11 November 1889; the original is in Wels and is privately owned.

67 See *LBSAB*, 144f. for an extract from this letter, dated Vienna, 30 October 1889; the original is in the *ÖNB*, F18 Schalk 158/10/40. Richter was evidently much taken with the work when Löwe played it through to him on the piano.

68 On 19 April the *Deutsches Volksblatt* included an article by August Göllerich in which the author recommended that the *Akademischer Gesangverein* introduce more choruses of a national German nature into their repertoire. See Elisabeth Hilscher, 'Bruckner als Gelehrter - Bruckner als Geehrter' in *BSL 1988* (Linz, 1992), 122. In this article (pp. 121-22), Hilscher also refers to Rudolf Weinwurm's earlier resignation from the Society in October 1887 because he was disturbed by the increasing anti-Semitic tendencies; his resignation was reported in the *Wiener Sonn- und Montagszeitung*, 7 November 1887, 4. See also Margaret Notley, 'Bruckner and Viennese Wagnerism' in *Bruckner Studies* (Cambridge: CUP, 1997), 54-71; Andrea Harrandt, 'Students and

suggested in a letter to Franz which Joseph wrote during his working holiday in Gmunden.[69] Franz's immediate response was that his brother was over-reacting.[70] On 25 September, Joseph sent a visiting card to Bruckner saying that he would be happy to carry out corrections in the Third Symphony without making any unnecessary changes in the autograph.[71] Towards the end of the year Joseph was able to report an improvement in his relationship with Bruckner.[72] In the meantime Bruckner's relationship with Franz appears to have remained as cordial as ever. On 1 October he sent name-day greetings to Franz and hoped that he would soon make a full recovery from his illness.[73]

In the autumn Wilhelm Floderer, choirmaster of the *Sängerbund* choir in Linz, informed Bruckner that Karl Kerschbaum had written a new text to replace Wallmann's original text for the male-voice piece *Sängerbund*, WAB 82, composed in 1882. In his reply Bruckner expressed his gratitude that one of his pieces was

---

Friends as "Prophets" and "Promoters" - The reception of Bruckner's works in the Wiener Akademische Wagner-Verein' in *Perspectives on Anton Bruckner* (Aldershot:Ashgate, 2001), 327-37.

69 See *FSBB*, 55ff. and *LBSAB*, 140ff. for this letter, dated Gmunden, 1 August 1889; the original is in the *ÖNB*, F18 Schalk 158/10/25.

70 See *LBSAB*, 142 for an extract from this letter, dated Reichenberg, 2 August 1889; the original is in the *ÖNB*, F18 Schalk 158/10/26.

71 This card, the original of which is in the *ÖNB*, F18 Schalk 146c, was one of the 'exhibits' in a special exhibition to mark the anniversary of Bruckner's birth in 1974; see Franz Grasberger, ed., *Anton Bruckner zum 150. Geburtstag. Eine Ausstellung im Prunksaal der Österreichischen Nationalbibliothek* (Vienna, 1974), 105.

72 See *LBSAB*, 146 for an extract from this letter, dated Vienna, 9 December 1889; the original is in the *ÖNB*, F18 Schalk 158/10/45.

73 See *FSBB*, 72. No precise dates of the illness are known and the Schalk correspondence does not provide any clues. The original of the letter is in the *ÖNB*, F18 Schalk 54/12.

being sung.[74]

There is an intriguing diary entry for 25 October - 'Okt. mit Brahms b. Igel im Freien'. This alludes to a meeting of the two composers in the *Zum roten Igel* inn arranged by friends. There was an Indian summer that year and the weather was warm enough for the composers and their respective entourages to have their evening meal in the open air. Both August Stradal and Friedrich Klose record several meetings of this composers at this particular inn. Evidently the conversation rarely went any deeper than the commonplace. There was a respect for but no particular understanding of each other's compositions.[75]

We do not know what prompted Bruckner to apply for the vacant position of music director at the *Burgtheater* in Vienna towards the end of the year. However, the duties were not particularly onerous - the provision of some music at the beginning and between the acts of theatrical performances - and perhaps Bruckner thought that the salary on offer would be sufficient for him to give up some of his teaching commitments and enable him to devote more time to composition. Was there also the question of prestige and the belief that the tenure of a position such as this would carry some weight in Viennese musical circles? After Bruckner had made a formal application to Dr. August Förster, the director of the Burgtheater, Förster

---

74 See *ABB*, 225f. and *GrBB*, 30 for this letter, dated Vienna, 11 October 1889; the location of the original is unknown.

75 See *G-A* IV/2, 687-92 for further information, including Decsey's and Stradal's reports of the meeting. See also Stephen Johnson, *Bruckner Remembered*, 151ff. which includes Max von Oberleithner's second-hand report. Oberleithner (1868-1935) was a music student of Otto Kitzler in Brno before coming to Vienna to study law at the University. He attended some of Bruckner's University lectures and then became one of his private pupils from the autumn of 1889 to 1894. He also played a prominent part in the revisions of some of Bruckner's works. An extract from Oberleithner's *Meine Erinnerungen an Anton Bruckner* (Regensburg: Bosse, 1933) is printed in *G-A* IV/2, 690ff.

wrote to Hermann Levi to ask for a reference. He was obviously sympathetic to Bruckner and wanted to do his best for him but did not know much about him and was certainly surprised that a man of Bruckner's age should wish to apply. In his reply Levi provided a warm appreciation of Bruckner's skill. He considered Bruckner's Seventh Symphony to be the most significant symphonic work to have been written for decades and was unable to explain why the composer had not achieved the breakthrough he deserved.[76] As Förster died shortly after the exchange of letters we do not know if any additional steps were taken. There is certainly no further correspondence in the *Burgtheater* archives, and Bruckner was not appointed to the post.

During the final months of the year, Dr. Arthur Seidl from Munich was in Vienna to give a lecture on 'Kunstlehre der Wagner'schen Meistersinger' at a meeting of the *Wagner-Verein*. He availed himself of the opportunity to attend one of Bruckner's University lectures while he was in Vienna and was somewhat embarrassed when the composer, on learning that Seidl was present, spent about half of the lecture carrying on a two-way conversation with him about Wagner, Nikisch, his appreciation of Levi and other matters![77]

The Schalk correspondence at the beginning of 1890 is concerned *inter alia* with Joseph's improved relationship with Bruckner, Bruckner's work on the revision of

---

76 See *GrBLS*, 358f. and *G-A* IV/2, 680f. for Förster's letter to Levi, dated Vienna, 14 December 1889; the original is in the *ÖNB*. For Levi's reply, dated Munich, 15 December 1889, see *G-A* IV/2, 681-83; the location of the original is unknown. Further details can be found in Ferdinand Scherber, 'Eine unbekannte Episode aus Anton Bruckners Leben' in *Signale für die musikalische Welt*, Berlin, 30 April 1913.

77 See *G-A* IV/2, 684f. for an extract from Seidl's obituary notice of Bruckner in the Dresdener Deutsche Wacht.

the Eighth and Joseph's plans to carry out his own revision of the F minor Mass.[78] Bruckner wrote to thank his reliable copyist, Leopold Hofmeyer, for the excellence of his most recent copying work , enclosed five florins, and warned him that he would soon be 'pestering' him again![79]

As Bruckner was putting the finishing touches to his revision of the Eighth he was shocked to learn of his brother Ignaz's 'misfortune', a bout of food poisoning from which he had made a miraculous recovery. He wrote to him with some concern and enclosed a gift of ten florins.[80]

Joseph's desire to revise the F minor Mass no doubt stemmed from his plans to perform the *Kyrie* and *Gloria* movements in a *Wagner-Verein* concert in March (with piano and brass rather than full orchestral accompaniment). When he wrote to Franz towards the end of February he mentioned not only the forthcoming performance of these two movements and a rehearsal of the *Gloria* attended by a delighted Bruckner, but also Levi's recent visit to Vienna during which Löwe had played through Bruckner's First Symphony. Joseph was keen for Franz to undertake some 'discreet' revision of the work himself.[81] Levi was clearly impressed with Bruckner's symphony and Löwe's playing. He wrote to the composer, saying that

---

78 See *LBSAB*, 147f. for extracts from Joseph's letters to Franz, dated Vienna, 2 January, 18 January and 31 January 1890, and Franz's letter to Joseph, dated Graz, 25 January 1890; the originals are in the *ÖNB*, F18 Schalk 158/11/10 and 12-14.

79 See *ABB*, 234 and *GrBB*, 48 for Bruckner's letter to Hofmeyer, dated Vienna, 2 February 1890; the original is owned privately. Hofmeyer had presumably completed his copy of the Trio which Bruckner had sent him on 11 November 1889; see pages 582-83.

80 See *ABB*, 227f. for Bruckner's letter to Ignaz, dated Vienna, 3 February 1890; the original is lost.

81 See *LBSAB*, 148f. for this letter, dated Vienna, 22 February 1890; the original is in the *ÖNB*, F18 Schalk 158/11/17.

it 'must be printed and performed' but pleading with him not to alter it too much.[82] On 6 March Joseph wrote to Franz and enclosed his own copy of the Adagio of the First which he hoped his brother would revise. He was also able to tell Franz of the successful performance of the two movements from the F minor Mass the day before.[83] Löwe played a solo piano arrangement of the Adagio and Scherzo from the Third Symphony at the same concert.[84]

Both partisan Bruckner supporters and non-partisan music lovers were increasingly concerned at the comparative infrequency of performances of his symphonies. Articles in *Das Vaterland* on 27 March and 15 April highlighted this; indeed the writer of the second article made the assertion that Bruckner had been forced to make alterations in his symphonies in order to guarantee performance.[85] Writing to Theodor Helm at the end of March, Bruckner went so far as to blame himself. He had 'taken the 1ˢᵗ Symphony from them' (the Vienna Philharmonic), the Third Symphony had not yet appeared in print (although Schalk had assured him three months earlier that it would be ready in good time), and Richter was not aware that

82   See *ABB*, 328 for this letter. It is undated but was written in Vienna the day before Levi returned to Munich; the original is lost.

83   See *LBSAB*, 149f. for this letter; the original is in the *ÖNB*, F18 Schalk 158/11/18.

84   Löwe was commended for 'achieving the best possible results in making the polyphony clear' by the reviewer of the *Musikalische Rundschau*, 10 March 1890. The concert as a whole was reviewed by Emil v. Hartmann in the *Neue Wiener Musik-Zeitung* 1 (1889-90), 131f. Hartmann compared Bruckner favourably with Brahms. See Gerold W. Gruber, 'Brahms und Bruckner in der zeitgenössischen Wiener Musikkritik' in *BSL 1983* (Linz, 1985), 209 and 217.

85   See *G-A* IV/3, 11f. and extract from the articles in *ABDS*, 40f. See also Franz Grasberger, 'Das Bruckner-Bild der Zeitung "Das Vaterland" in den Jahren 1870-1900' in *Festschrift Hans Schneider zum 60. Geburtstag* (Munich, 1981), 124f.

the Sixth had already been copied.[86] Nevertheless, he hoped to secure interest in the Eighth by dedicating it to Emperor Franz Josef and requested the latter's permission to print the dedicatory notice on the title-page of the score.[87] Bruckner received a reply in the affirmative,[88] a gesture which prompted the music critic of *Das Vaterland* to assert that a certain critic [Hanslick is obviously intended] would no longer be able to hinder performances of Bruckner's works.[89] The next step was to find a publisher for the symphony. On 28 April Bruckner wrote to Hermann Levi and asked for his help.[90]

Outside Austria Bruckner was receiving growing recognition. In America, Bernhard Ziehn, one of the music critics of the *Musical Courier*, took the opportunity, in a review of a piano recital given by Hans von Bülow in Chicago (and with reference to Bülow's edition of Beethoven's piano works), to take him to task for his conservative, pro-Brahms and anti-Wagner stance, and his failure to recognize the true stature of a composer like Bruckner.[91] There was a performance of the Seventh in Hamburg on 27 April and at the end of month Joseph Schalk accompanied Bruckner to Pressburg (Bratislava) to attend another performance of the same work. Joseph wrote to Franz to tell him about the visit and hoped that his brother would

---

86 See *ABB*, 228 (and extract in *G-A* IV/3, 10f.) for this letter, dated Vienna, 30 March 1890; the original is lost.

87 His letter to the Emperor via the Lord Chamberlain's office was probably written at the end of March or beginning of April; see *ABB*, 229 and *G-A* IV/3, 46f. where a draft of the letter is printed. The original is lost.

88 See *G-A* IV/3, 47 for this letter, dated Vienna, 16 April 1890; the original is in St. Florian.

89 See *G-A* IV/3, footnote 1 for an extract from this article (20 April 1890).

90 See *GrBLS*, 342; also extract in *G-A* IV/3, 48f. where the date is given as 23 April. The original is owned privately.

91 See *G-A* IV/3, 50ff. for extracts from this review, dated 20 April 1890.

come to Vienna at the beginning of June and bring with him the revisions of the *Gloria* of the F minor Mass and the Adagio of the First Symphony.[92]

The performance of Bruckner's Seventh Symphony in Pressburg (Bratislava) was given by the orchestra of the Pressburg *Kirchenmusik-Verein* conducted by Josef Thiard-Laforest who had been conductor of the Linz *Musikverein* from 1878 to 1881 and had made the composer's acquaintance during that time. On 14 March Bruckner wrote to Laforest to remind him that if he did not have any Wagner tubas available, he would have to use horns (as in the Leipzig performance). A fortnight later, on 28 March, Bruckner advised his friend to hire the Wagner tuba players from the Vienna *Hofoper* orchestra. In the event, Laforest adopted the same compromise as Nikisch in Leipzig and used bass flugelhorns instead of Wagner tubas.[93] The orchestra had about 50-55 players. On the day of the concert the *Pressburger Zeitung* published a long article about Bruckner and his Seventh Symphony. The symphony formed the second part of the concert which began with Berlioz's *Benvenuto Cellini* overture and continued with one of Thiard-Laforest's own works, a cantata for soprano and orchestra. On 28 April, the day after the concert, there was a glowing review of the symphony in the *Pressburger Zeitung*. A week later, Bruckner wrote to Laforest and enclosed the score of his D minor Mass which he asked his friend to have copied with a view to a possible performance in Bratislava. Later in the year he was made an honorary member of the Pressburg *Kirchenmusikverein*. He wrote a letter of warm appreciation to the Society on 27 January

---

92 See *LBSAB*, 151f. for an extract from this letter, dated Vienna, 1 May 1890; the original is in the *ÖNB*, F18 Schalk 158/11/22. In a letter to Franz, dated Vienna, 5 May 1890, Bruckner also mentioned work on the First Symphony; see *FSBB*, 72; the original of this letter is in the *ÖNB*.

93 This is confirmed by Franz Schmidt who, as a sixteen-year-old youth, attended the Bratislava performance. The flugelhornists were brought from a wind band in Kittsee.

1891.[94]

Declining health (his doctors diagnosed 'chronic laryngitis' and 'hypertension') forced Bruckner to request a year's leave absence from his Conservatory duties (16 hours per week). On 12 July his request was granted. Zellner, the secretary-general of the *Gesellschaft der Musikfreunde*, informed Bruckner separately that he would have to continue paying his contributions to the pension fund during his absence. However, Bruckner had been assured by a consortium of friends and supporters that he would receive an annual income of 1000 florins to compensate for this loss of salary.[95] Bruckner was still expected to undertake his organ duties at the *Hofkapelle*,

---

94 See Gabriel Dusinsky, 'Anton Bruckner und die Aufführung seiner Siebenten Symphonie 1890 in Pressburg (Bratislava)' in *BJ 1981* (Linz, 1982), 153 for further details of the Bratislava performance. Both the article in the *Pressburger Zeitung* 127, no. 115 (27 April 1890) and Bruckner's letter of thanks to the *Kirchenmusikverein* are reprinted in Dusinsky's article (the former in facsimile), 154ff. Bruckner's three letters to Thiard-Laforest (14 March, 28 March and 7 May 1890) were first published in the *Pressburger Zeitung* 134, no. 77, *Morgenblatt* (18 March 1897); the originals are lost. The original of Bruckner's letter to the *Musikverein* can be located in the Bratislava town archive. In the letter to his brother Franz written on 1 May 1890 (see earlier, footnote 92), Joseph Schalk remarked that Bruckner was in good spirits in spite of the shortcomings of the performance.

95   See *G-A* IV/3, 54-58 for details of the people involved and their contributions. See also Bruckner's letter later in the year (December) to one of his patrons, Prince Johann Liechtenstein, in which he sought assurance that his personal contribution of 300 florins would continue on an annual basis; this letter is printed in *G-A* IV/3, 56f., footnote: the original is in the *Stiftung Fürst Liechtenstein* in Vienna. Also in the *Stiftung Fürst Liechtenstein* are a letter, dated 17 July 1890, in which Vinzenz Fürstenberg gives the prince details of the sum of money which the consortium hopes to raise and asks him if he would be willing to make a contribution, details of the decision made by the prince on 30 July 1890 to make a contribution of 300 florins, and confirmation of this decision on 2 August; see *SchABCT*, 602ff. On 1 October Bruckner received a letter from the *Credit-Anstalt* bank in Vienna advising him that the sum of 1025 florins had been credited to his account. See *ABA* 66/3, 101; the original is in St. Florian. Writing to Hermann Levi on 2 October

however, and these duties kept him in Vienna until the end of July.[96]

Two letters written during the earlier part of the summer provide an amusing glimpse of Bruckner's keen eye for feminine beauty. He had evidently been embarrassed about information received in letters from Josef Gruber and a priest in St. Florian concerning an 'affair of the heart' with a young lady in Steyr and he asked Franz Bayer to throw some light on the matter. He also made further enquiries in a letter to Leopold Hofmeyer.[97]

On 31 July Bruckner played the organ at the wedding of Archduchess Marie Valerie, the Emperor's daughter, and Archduke Franz Salvator. His improvisation combined the 'Hallelujah' chorus from Handel's *Messiah* and the *Kaiserlied*. He received a fee of 100 ducats and was invited to stay at the imperial residence for a few days. He also gave an organ concert in the parish church on the morning of 2 August.[98] His travelling companion was Joseph Schalk who was amazed that Bruckner still possessed an impressive pedal technique.[99]

---

he informed him of his year's leave from the Conservatory and the promise of financial help from his friends. See *GrBLS*, 343f. and *G-A* IV/3, 70; the original of this letter is owned privately.

96 See *ABB* 231f. and *ABDS* 1, 22 for a letter to his *Hofkapelle* colleague, Pius Richter; the original is in the *ÖNB*.

97 See *G-A* IV/3 for Gruber's letter, dated St. Florian, 2 May 1890; *ABB*, 230f. and *G-A* IV/3, 67f. for Bruckner's letters to Bayer and Hofmeyer, dated Vienna, 21 June and 4 July respectively. The originals of the first two are lost; the original of the third is privately owned.

98 See *G-A* IV/3, 58-62 for details; these include a reminiscence of one of the singers in the church choir and an extract from a report of the wedding in the *Ischler Wochenblatt* 31 (3 August) which contains a review of Bruckner's organ playing. There is a sketch in the *ÖNB* of the original themes for improvisation (first and second themes from the Finale of Symphony no. 1) which Bruckner submitted to the Lord Chamberlain for approval but which were turned down as 'unsuitable'. See *ABA* 81/7, 109; a facsimile was published in *Die Musik* xvi (September 1924).

99 It seems that Bruckner gave an extra concert for some of his friends, including Schalk, Löwe and Nikisch. See *LBSAB*, 152 for a reference to Joseph's letter to Franz, dated Vienna, 14 August

Bruckner spent some time with his sister in Vöcklabruck either shortly before travelling to Ischl or immediately afterwards, and two diary entries for August mention the names of two young ladies in that town, Kamilla Wismar (Wiesmair) and Hedwig Fürthner, who had attracted his attention.[100] He also visited an old friend in Goisern, Franz Perfahl, who had been a teaching assistant in Ansfelden in the late 1830s and had taught young Bruckner violin and theory before he became a choirboy at St. Florian. Goisern was one of Bruckner's favourite holiday places during the 70s and 80s and he was usually asked to play the organ in both the Catholic and Evangelical churches there. As he was on sick leave from Conservatory duties, he was able to spend a longer period of time than usual at Steyr - from 14 August to the end of September. During that time he visited a former 'flame', Josefine Lang who, as Mrs. Weinböck, managed a large guest house in Neufelden.[101]

1890; the original is in the *ÖNB*, F18 Schalk 158/11/25.

100 Two letters from Poldi Horky, an assistant in a flower shop at the Sudbahnhof in Vienna, the first dated 4 October 1890, the second undated (but, judging from its contents, written shortly after the first) also indicate another short-lived friendship; the second in particular testifies to Bruckner's gentlemanly conduct. See *G-A* IV/3, 113f.; the originals of the correspondence are lost.

101 See *G-A* III/1, 354 and 609. Bruckner was accompanied by his friend Karl Waldeck from Linz. He improvised on the organ of Neufelden parish church on 16 September and, on the same day, received a signed photograph of Josefine's daughter, Caroline; this photograph is now in the library of the *Bruckner Konservatorium* in Linz. On 21 April 1891, Bruckner wrote to both Josefine and Caroline. He enclosed a photograph in his letter to Josefine and said that he looked forward to receiving her photograph in return; he described Caroline as his 'lieber Erzatz' - the 'dear substitute' for her mother - and, in his letter to her, recalled the happy time he had spent at Neufelden. In her reply (on 24 April), Caroline promised Bruckner that her mother would have her photograph taken and then send a copy to him. See *ABA*, 79 for the first and second letters, *ABB*, 244 for the second. There is a facsimile of the second in *ABA*, 41; the originals of both are in the *Oberösterreichisches Landesmuseum*. See *G-A* III/1, 612 for a reference to Caroline's letter; the original is in the *Oberösterreichisches Landesmuseum*, Linz.

It is significant that Bruckner missed St. Florian out of his holiday itinerary. He had been invited by Deubler to stay there but felt uneasy about taking up the invitation because it had not come from the abbot.[102] While in Steyr he played the organ at the parish church on at least two occasions. On 26 September, for instance, he improvised on themes from his *Te Deum* and First Symphony at a special thanksgiving service (for the reconstruction of the church tower which had been badly damaged by a fire in 1876). On 27 September he was present at the unveiling of a Schubert plaque at the house where Schubert stayed with his friend Johann Vogl on two occasions in 1825 and 1827. A festival concert held on the same day began with a performance of Bruckner's *Sängerbund*. His sojourn in Steyr was a 'working holiday', however - he worked on the revision of his First Symphony.

On his return to Vienna he was no doubt pleased to learn that Richter had decided to include the revised version of the Third Symphony in the concert programme for the coming Vienna Philharmonic season. On 2 October he drafted a letter to Leopold Zellner, secretary of the *Gesellschaft der Musikfreunde*, informing him that he wished to continue giving Harmony lessons, but not organ lessons, at the Conservatory in the event of a complete recovery.[103]

Finding a publisher for the revised Eighth Symphony was proving to be a difficult task. Hermann Levi did his best to help Bruckner and was even prepared to give some financial aid but there appeared to be no interest among the leading

---

102 See *ABB*, 232 for Bruckner's letter to Deubler, dated Steyr, 18 August 1890; there are extracts in *G-A* II/1, 307 and *G-A* IV/3, 66. The original is in St. Florian.

103 This draft is in his diary, *Fromme's Österreichischer Professoren- und Lehrer-Kalender 1890-91*. See *G-A* IV/3, 73 and *ABA* 83/4, 111; the diary is in the *ÖNB*. See also the references to J.E.Habert's correspondence with Ernst Klinger and Bernhard Deubler concerning dissatisfaction with Bruckner's method of organ teaching at the Conservatory in *G-A* IV/3, 78f. and the report of Hermann Häbock, one of his last organ students at the Conservatory, about Bruckner's lack of enthusiasm for organ teaching at this time in *G-A* IV/3, 115f.

publishers.

Although Levi was not well enough to give the first performance of the symphony himself, he recommended Felix Weingartner in Mannheim as a suitable replacement and suggested that the parts be written out as soon as possible. The performance could take place in November or December and publishers like Schott and Heckel could be invited to attend.[104] Although he hoped that Levi would still be able to conduct the work in Munich at a future date, Bruckner took his friend's advice and contacted Weingartner at the beginning of October.[105] He asked the young conductor if he would consider giving the first performance of the work and mentioned that Nikisch in Leipzig in Leipzig was also interested in performing it.[106] He wrote again to Weingartner on 11 October to inform him that he had just sent the score of the symphony to Munich where Levi would arrange to have the parts copied.[107]

At the end of October Bruckner's long-term financial position was made more secure. Largely at the instigation of Bishop Franz Maria Doppelbauer who spoke very warmly of the composer's contribution to the musical life of the region, a

---

104 See *ABB*, 320f. for Levi's letter to Bruckner, dated Munich, 20 September 1890; the original is in St. Florian

105 See *GrBLS*, 343f. (where it is incorrectly dated) and Walter Beck, *Anton Bruckner. Ein Lebensbild mit neuen Dokumenten* (Dornach, 1995), 63 for Bruckner's reply to Levi's letter, dated Vienna, 2 October 1890; the original is lost.

106 See *ABB*, 233 and *GrBB*, 129 for Bruckner's letter to Weingartner, dated Vienna, 2 October 1890. The originals of this and other letters from Bruckner to Weingartner can be found in the *Gesellschaft der Musikfreunde* library. Felix von Weingartner (1863-1942) studied in Graz and Leipzig before taking up conducting posts in Königsberg, Danzig, Hamburg and Mannheim. He later held posts in Berlin and Vienna, including directorship of the Court Opera (1908-11).

107 See *ABB*, 233 and *GrBB*, 129 for Bruckner's second letter to Weingartner. Viktor Christ was responsible for copying the score.

decision was made by the Upper Austrian Parliament to grant him an annuity of 400 florins. Bruckner received official notification on 11 November.[108]

In December Bruckner's Fourth Symphony was performed in Munich, the revised version of his Third was given its first performance in Vienna and Joseph Schalk made plans to give a concert in Graz, conducting the Styrian *Musikverein* orchestra in performances of Bruckner's Fourth and some of Hugo Wolf's orchestral songs. Writing to his brother Franz at the beginning of the month, he mentioned Bruckner's improved financial situation but was particularly concerned to solicit Franz's help and advice:

> ... The matter is settled and I am to conduct the concert on the 21st. I have been negotiating with Dr. Zwiedineck, the concert director, whom you will probably know and have written to him that you will oblige by conducting the preliminary rehearsals. First of all I must find out how many days' leave I can get from the Conservatory. I will probably come on the 16th, certainly not any earlier. Please put my mind at rest as soon as possible by letting me know if you can hold a number of rehearsals beforehand. The parts should be obtained from Gutmann immediately. Löwe tells me that it is possible the parts have not yet been printed. In that case, get hold of the handwritten ones. However, to a large extent these do not correspond with the new score. And so you will have some trouble. Anyway, will you arrange things so that we can manage three rehearsals? Come to an understanding with Dr. Zwiedineck immediately. There are a few of Wolf's orchestral songs as well, and these too will not be very easy. I cannot tell you how much I am looking forward to seeing you again. You will not be able to use the score of the IVth which I sent you; it is the first, mistake-ridden edition. The second edition, in which Bruckner and Löwe have made alterations, is the authentic one, and so you must obtain it. Everything will be in order when you receive the printed parts.
>
> I have also written to Dr. Zwiedineck to ask him if he would oblige by lending parts to the weaker, amateur members of the orchestra so that they can practise them at home. I am very concerned

---

108 Payments were to be made monthly, commencing 1 November. See *G-A* IV/3, 75-78; the original of this letter is in St. Florian.

about the strings. Nevertheless under no circumstances do I want to give up the Romantic symphony. Who knows whether I will have another opportunity in my life to conduct an orchestra...[109]

A week later he sent another letter to Franz. He was concerned about discrepancies between the written parts and the revised score of the Fourth and was certain that Franz Fischer in Munich, to whom he had written for the parts, had experienced the same difficulties. And, to make matters worse, Bruckner was not being particularly helpful![110] Franz conducted some preliminary rehearsals for his brother. The proved so difficult and unrewarding that he advised Joseph to postpone the concert. The main problem was that the majority of the string players were amateurs who did not have sufficient time to practise between rehearsals - 'it would be a great shame if the performance were to founder because of over-hasty preparation'.[111]

The performance of the Fourth in Munich, conducted by Franz Fischer, was successful but both Levi and Fischer mentioned problems with the written parts and difficulties in rehearsal as a result of discrepancies between the parts and the score (thus confirming Joseph Schalk's fears). The day after the performance both Fischer and Levi wrote to the composer:

> Your 4th Symphony (Romantic) had a sensational success at its performance in the Music Academy yesterday - I congratulate you wholeheartedly! The orchestra played excellently and, as for my own

---

109 See *LBSAB*, 153f. for this letter from Joseph Schalk to his brother, dated Vienna, 1 December 1890; the original is in the *ÖNB*, F18 Schalk 158/11/27.

110 See *LBSAB*, 154 for an extract from this letter, dated Vienna, 8 December 1890; the original is in the *ÖNB*, F18 Schalk 158/11/29.

111 See *LBSAB*, 155 for an extract from Franz's letter to his brother, dated Graz, 13 December 1890; the original is in the *ÖNB*, F18 Schalk 158/11/30.

humble part, I can only say that I did all I could to perform the work as well as possible. Unfortunately the musical material supplied by your publisher was so mistake-ridden that I had to correct mistakes even during the final rehearsal; consequently the rehearsals were painful affairs. Nevertheless, we did not allow our spirits to sag and we had a huge success which brought us great pleasure.

With cordial greetings from my dear colleague Levi who was unable to attend the performance because of illness...[112]

In his letter to Bruckner, Hermann Levi regretted that he had not been able to attend the performances of both the Symphony and the String Quintet because he had been confined to his house with laryngitis. Friends of his had reported, however, that Fischer's performance of the performance was extremely successful and the orchestra played most beautifully - all this in spite of one wasted rehearsal caused by mistakes in the parts which a copyist had to correct:

I would rather remain silent about Gutmann's behaviour. It is a scandal that the parts have not yet been copied and that the written ones are not even correct! He had sent only the string parts here - although I have been dealing with him for a good year! And if another town now wants to perform the symphony, parts are still going to be unavailable!![113]

Bruckner was delighted with a letter from an unexpected source, the German writer Paul Heyse, who told him that he had 'taken Munich by storm' and thanked

---

112   See *ABB*, 323 for Fischer's letter to Bruckner, dated Munich, 11 December 1890; the original is privately owned.   Also performed at this concert were Wagner's 'Faust' overture, Bruch's 'Frithjof' scene, and Brahms's 'Haydn' variations. Franz Fischer (1849-1918) was court music director in Mannheim (1877-79) and Munich (1879-1912). He conducted *Parsifal* at Bayreuth in the years 1882-84 and 1899.

113   See *ABB*, 321f. for Levi's letter to Bruckner, dated Munich, 11 December 1890; the original is in St. Florian.

him for making such an unforgettable experience possible. He hoped that the acclaim which he had received would to some extent make up for the many years of non-recognition he had been forced to endure.[114]

In his reply Bruckner thanked him for such an enthusiastic letter which he would certainly treasure. He also provided some programmatic details of the work and added that it was not his intention to combine all the main themes of the symphony in the Finale - that only happened in the Eighth:

> ... In the 4th Symphony (Romantic), what is suggested in the 1st movement is the horn which announces daybreak from the town hall. Then everything comes to life. In the second subject group, the theme is the 'zizipe' song of the titmouse. 2nd movement: song, prayer, serenade. 3rd: hunt, and the Trio like a hurdy gurdy playing during the midday meal-break in the woods. I am very annoyed that the critic of the 'Neueste Nachrichten' has such a low opinion of the Finale and even considers it to be a failure, and I wish that I had not read the report which has cast a shadow over my happiness. I will never trust this man again. The general opinion here is that the Finale is the best and most outstanding movement. It was by no means my intention to bring all the themes together. That happens only in the Finale of the 8th Symphony...[115]

114 See *ABB*, 308f. for Heyse's undated letter to Bruckner, Munich, December 1890. There is a facsimile of this letter between pp. 144 and 145 in *ABB*; the original is in St. Florian.

115 See *GrBLS*, 344-45 (where the addressee is given wrongly as Levi), Peter Raabe, *Wege zu Bruckner*, 190ff. and Constantin Floros, *Brahms und Bruckner. Studien zur musikalischen Exegetik* (Wiesbaden, 1980), 173 and 210, for this letter, dated Vienna, 22 December 1890; the original has been lost. The critic of the Munich *Neueste Nachrichten* was Heinrich Porges who, in spite of Bruckner's disappointment, appears to have been otherwise very favourably disposed towards the work - according to a letter from Franz Strauss to Richard Strauss on 13 December; see Franz Grasberger, ed., *'Der Strom der Töne trug mich fort'. Die Welt um Richard Strauss in Briefen* (Tutzing, 1967), which is cited in *SchABCT*, 615. Paul Heyse (1830-1914) lived and worked in Munich. He was also friendly with Brahms and Kalbeck. An article about his letter to Bruckner appeared in the *Illustriertes WienerExtrablatt* on Saturday 20 December 1890.

In spite of what appeared to be a cooling of relations with St. Florian earlier in the year, Bruckner wrote to Josef Gruber on 1 December to ask if any of his friends there would be coming to the performance of his Third Symphony in Vienna on 21 December.[116] Thanks to the generosity of the Emperor who contributed 1600 florins towards the printing costs, the second edition of the symphony had just been published.[117]

The concert on Sunday 21 December (the fourth in the *Gesellschaft* subscription series for the year) was conducted by Richter and included performances of Beethoven's 'Leonora' overture no. 2 and Grädener's Violin Concerto. The critical reception of Bruckner's symphony was again predictably divided between the pro- and anti-Wagner factions. In the *Neue freie Presse*, Hanslick praised the Scherzo movement for its unusual (for Bruckner) formal consistency but was extremely critical of the outer movements in which he detected the same faults which marred Bruckner's other compositions, viz. the co-existence of 'interesting, bold and original details' with 'empty, dry, often brutal passages'. He also rather drily observed the enthusiasm of students in the gallery and standing places who were still applauding vociferously long after the hall had been emptied and the lights turned out![118]

---

116   See *G-A* II/1, 307f.; the original of this letter is in the *Wiener Stadt- und Landesbibliothek*.

117   The recent publication of the second edition of the symphony was reported in the *Fremdenblatt* (1 November) and the *Neue Freie Presse* (3 November).

118   Review dated 24 December 1890 [but dated 23 December 1890 in some of the Bruckner literature]. See Hanslick, *Aus dem Tagebuche eines Musikers* (Berlin, 1892), 306. See also *G-A* IV/3, 86-90, Manfred Wagner, 'Bruckner in Wien' in *ABDS* 2 (Linz, 1980), 59, and Thomas Röder, *III Symphonie D-Moll Revisionbericht* (Vienna, 1997), 417. That Hanslick bore no personal feelings of animosity towards Bruckner is revealed by the fact that, shortly after this review, he sent the composer a signed photograph of himself with the dedication 'to my esteemed friend'. Bruckner mentioned this gesture in a letter to August Göllerich at the beginning of 1891 in which he also made reference to the highly successful performance of the symphony and the enthusiastic response

Writing in the *Wiener Montags-Revue*, Max Kalbeck also drew attention to the noisy enthusiasm of Bruckner's young supporters. As far as the symphony itself was concerned he could detect no significant difference between it and Bruckner's later works. The composer's veneration for Beethoven and Wagner was obvious - 'if one stands the Allegro of Beethoven's last symphony on its head, the beginning and end of Bruckner's first movement fall out'. There were some original ideas in the 'sultry atmosphere of this oppressive music' but they were short-lived, and it was to be regretted that such a richly talented composer 'could not find the necessary harmonious balance between desiring something on the one hand and being able to accomplish it on the other'.[119]

In his review of the performance in the *Wiener Tagblatt*, Richard Heuberger described the work as one of extreme contrasts. It was difficult to fathom how the individual parts of a Bruckner symphony belonged together:

> ... A section which apparently depicts the religious pomp of a Corpus Christi procession and in which one imagines seeing the gilded vestments of the priests is followed by a gently gambolling dance-like idea (for instance, the extremely pretty F sharp major motive in the final movement) which would make a fine piece of ballet music. Bruckner has used his fine instinct to discover a connection between the church and the theatre and to illustrate this musically - no rule book in the world can deny this ... All in all we can say that Bruckner's symphony awakens more interest than pleasure; one admires its magnificent sound rather than becoming engrossed in its thematic structure...[120]

---

of the audience. See *ABB*, 235f. for this letter to Göllerich, dated Vienna, 1 January 1891; the original is in the *Oberösterreichisches Landesmuseum*.

119 See *G-A* IV/3, 90ff. and Röder, op.cit., 422-23 for this review, dated 5 January 1891.

120 See *G-A* IV/3, 92ff. and Röder, op.cit., 414 for this review, dated 22 December 1890.

In a long article in the *Deutsche Zeitung* Theodor Helm provided a history of the work from its inception and compared the disastrous first performance in 1877 (when Bruckner conducted) with the enthusiastic reception given it thirteen years later under Richter's direction. Although there were a few reminiscences of Wagner, the symphony seemed to be more a 'spiritual child' of Beethoven. However, Bruckner had developed and given new shape to the Beethovenian stimuli to such an extent and had introduced so many original ideas that the first movement of his Third was 'one of the most inspired and most powerful to have been written in our century'. It possessed an impressive organic unity. As far as 'melodic invention' was concerned, the Adagio was one of the most beautiful slow movements since Beethoven. In the Scherzo Helm imagined he could see a medieval joust with the knights displaying their skills encouraged by beautiful ladies. The Trio, on the other hand, evoked the world of Upper Austria with a peasant couple dancing the Ländler. Bruckner, a child of the people, was well able to depict a scene from German folk-life. The thematic structure of this movement was masterly. Although a unified whole, it was full of delightful surprises - of orchestration and polyphonic writing, to name but two. Helm confessed that he was not able fully to understand the Finale - the most controversial movement. He felt that the polka-like secondary theme, although undeniably charming, did not have sufficient symphonic weight. Nevertheless there was much to admire in the movement, not least the impressive recall of the main first movement theme towards the end. Helm also mentioned the two different four-hand piano arrangements of the symphony - by Mahler [and Krzyzanowski] and, more recently, by Löwe and Schalk - both published by Th. Rättig.[121] In a separate review,

---

121 Helm's complete review, which appeared in the *Deutsche Zeitung* on 23 December 1890, is reprinted in *ABDS* 2, 60-63; see also Röder, op.cit., 415f. On 30 December Bruckner wrote to Helm to thank him for his excellent article and sent him a New Year's gift (a bottle of Klosterneuburg wine). See *ABB*, 228f.; the original of this letter has been lost. It seems that Bruckner visited Helm at his home in Landstraße Hauptstraße 51 shortly before the performance of the symphony in order

which appeared in the Leipzig *Musikalisches Wochenblatt* in January 1891, Helm confessed that he had misunderstood the symphony when it was first performed in 1877. Since then he had played through the four-hand piano arrangement with friends on several occasions and had 'seen the light'. Nevertheless he still considered that the Finale was more dramatic than symphonic, and that there were too many undisguised Wagnerian reminiscences.[122]

The reviewer for the *Neues Wiener Tagblatt* found the first movement too long-drawn-out and 'more a fantasia than a strongly unified symphonic movement' although it concealed an 'extraordinary fund of motives'. Both the Adagio and the Scherzo were much more tightly organized, while the Finale referred 'once again to the great theme from Beethoven's Ninth, the starting-point for Bruckner's work'.[123]

Robert Hirschfeld, the reviewer for *Die Presse*, was more concerned about the behaviour of Bruckner's supporters, specifically their noisy applause at the end of each movement, and considered this counter-productive and damaging to the composer's cause. The symphony was well able - in spite of some structural weaknesses - to 'hold its own' as a work of art. The last thing Bruckner needed was to be a pawn in the hands of a political/polemical faction.[124] The review of the

---

to go through the score of the work with him. Helm's daughter Mathilde recorded her impressions of Bruckner in her diary - see *G-A* IV/3, 105f. for extract.

122 See *G-A* IV/3, 95f. and Röder, op.cit., 424 for extracts from this review, which appeared in the *Musikalisches Wochenblatt* 22 (22 January 1891), 47f. See also Röder, op.cit., 420f. for an extract from Helm's *Wiener Musikbrief* which appeared in the *Pester Lloyd* on 31 December 1890.

123 See *ABDS* 2, 64 for a reference to this review, which appeared in the *Neues Wiener Tagblatt* on 23 December 1890.

124 Review dated 24 December 1890. See *ABDS* 2, 66 and both *G-A* IV/3, 98-101 and Röder, op.cit., 418 for longer extracts. Hirschfeld also wrote an article on the Third Symphony in the *Neue Wiener Musik-Zeitung* 2 (1 February 1891), 85-88.

performance in the *Ostdeutsche Rundschau*, however, is a good illustration of this. It is written from a nationalistic, pro-German and anti-Semitic standpoint, argues that Bruckner is an absolute musician par excellence and pours scorn on Hanslick and Heuberger for regarding Brahms as the ideal composer of absolute music and Bruckner as a composer who draws inspiration from extra-musical programmes.[125]

Hans Paumgartner also devoted some space to criticism of the rivalry between the pro- and anti-Bruckner factions in his review of the performance in the *Wiener Abendpost* on 24 December. After his favourable comments on the structure of the Fourth Symphony (on 6 February 1888), it is surprising to find Paumgartner criticising the lack of structural consistency and the rhapsodic nature of the Third; on the other hand he is full of praise for the 'passionate warmth of his musical language, the majestic greatness of his themes' and adds that the composer 'has the greatest things to say to us, and a drop of Beethovenian oil continually trickles down on to his head'; once again the distinctive orchestral character of the themes is praised.[126]

Bruckner was pleased to gain the support of Göllerich's successor as music critic of the *Deutsches Volksblatt*, a young man called Hans Puchstein. A meeting between Puchstein and Bruckner had been arranged for 24 December, but Bruckner wrote to Puchstein on the 23rd, regretting that he would not be able to keep the appointment and asking for another date. Bruckner had heard that Helm had been critical of Richter, and he asked Puchstein not to do the same, reminding him that

---

125 Review dated 11 January 1891. A copy of the complete review, written by Josef Stolzing, a prominent member of the breakaway *Neue Richard Wagner-Verein*, can be found in *ABDS*, 64f.; there are also extracts in *G-A* IV/3, 96f. and Röder, op.cit., 423. The review by 'n' in *Das Vaterland*, 22 December 1890, was less strident but emphasized the vociferous public appreciation of Bruckner, 'our great national composer', demonstrated at the concert; see Röder, op.cit., 415.

126 See Norbert Tschulik, 'Anton Bruckner in der Wiener Zeitung' in *BJ 1981* (Linz, 1982), 171-79, and Röder, op.cit., 419.

'we are aware of the situation'.[127] In an article on Bruckner in the *Deutsches Volksblatt* on 27 December, Puchstein said comparatively little about the performance of the Third, but concentrated instead on discussing the present critical reception of Bruckner in Vienna and stressing the need for more regular performances of the composer's works. He described him as the true successor of Beethoven and Wagner.[128]

Two other important reviews appeared in the *Fremdenblatt* and the *Deutsche Kunst- und Musik-Zeitung*. In the former, Ludwig Speidel described Bruckner as the only contemporary composer able to sustain the long musical paragraphs of a slow movement like the Adagio. On the other hand, he did not know how to harness the wealth of musical invention which flowed from his pen; there was sufficient material to satisfy the needs of half a dozen less well-endowed composers![129] In the latter, the reviewer recalled the first performance of the symphony in 1877, described some of the changes Bruckner had introduced since then, in particular the closing section of the final movement, but concluded that there were no essential differences between the two versions as regards 'the musical ideas or the structure of the individual movements' as even the large cut in the Finale was 'hinted at in the earlier score'. In any case, one cannot 'approach a Bruckner symphony with expectations of musical logic' as the composer tends to 'lose the thread' of musical continuity and to indulge in 'fantasy rather than composition'.[130]

---

127 See *ABB*, 235; the original of this letter is privately owned.

128 See *G-A* IV/3, 101f. and Röder, op.cit., 419f. for extracts from this article.

129 See Röder, op.cit., 421 for an extract from this review, dated 1 January 1891. Writing in the *Illustrirtes Wiener Extrablatt*, 23 December 1890, Josef Königstein made the same point but was much harsher in his overall evaluation of the work, which he described as 'fragmented and piecemeal throughout'; see Röder, op.cit., 416.

130 See Röder, op.cit., 422 for an extract from this review, signed by 'D' and dated 1 January 1891.

Reports of the performance appeared in other Austrian and German newspapers,[131] but perhaps the most interesting reaction came from the Finnish composer, Jean Sibelius, who was in Vienna at the time and was present at the concert. In a letter to his fiancée, Aino Järnefelt, he described Bruckner as the 'greatest living composer' whose symphony had made 'a great impression' on him. Admittedly it had its share of mistakes and miscalculations, the structure was 'mad' and it was quite 'un-Mozartian'; nevertheless, although the composer was 'an old man', there was something fresh and youthful about it. The impression Bruckner's Third made on the young Sibelius is certainly reflected in the orchestral textures of some of his early works, the *Kullervo* symphony in particular.[132]

Bruckner was extremely pleased with the performance and sent his customary letter of thanks to Richter and the Philharmonic on the day after the concert.[133] At the end of the year he wrote to Wolzogen in Bayreuth to give details of the concert and the favourable reception of the symphony. He had been able to weep with Hugo Wolf and Joseph Schalk - but one very important person had been missing, the dedicatee of the symphony![134]

Joseph Schalk wrote to Franz to give him the good news of the 'colossal success' of the performance. He added that he was very fearful of the projected performance of the Fourth in Graz, particularly when even the brilliant musicians of the Vienna Philharmonic were not able to overcome all the technical difficulties of the Third.

---

131   See Röder, op.cit., 425ff. for extracts from reviews in other papers, including the *Neue Zeitschrift für Musik* (Leipzig)

132   See E. Tawastsjerna, *Sibelius* vol. 1, 77f. Sibelius's letter to his fiancée is dated 21 December 1890.

133   See *ABB*, 227 and *GrBB*, 140 for this letter, dated Vienna, 22 December 1890; the original is in the Vienna Philharmonic archives.

134   See *GRBLS*, 357f. for this letter, dated Vienna, 31 December 1890; a facsimile of the letter, the original of which is privately owned, can be found in the 'Illustrierte Teil' of *GrBLS*, 102ff.

The amateur musicians especially would have to practise their parts diligently. The last thing he wanted was a mediocre performance, especially as a number of people would be travelling from Vienna to Graz to be at the performance.[135]

Coincidentally, the first printed version of the Third was performed in Linz on the same evening as the premiere of the new version in Vienna. It took place in the *Redoutensaal* and was played by the *Musikverein* orchestra conducted by Adalbert Schreyer. According to the review in the *Linzer Zeitung*, the original intention was to perform the work in its recently printed new version, but, as the older printed parts had been used for rehearsal purposes, there had not been enough time to make the necessary changes.[136]

Those orchestral performances of the Third Symphony helped to raise the composer's profile both inside and outside Austria. At the same time, piano arrangements of his works continued to be performed at meetings of the *Wiener Akademische Wagner-Verein* and the newly constituted *Richard Wagner-Verein*. On 8 October two movements from the Seventh Symphony were played at a meeting of the latter, and on 28 December Joseph Schalk directed a performance of the *Credo* from the F minor Mass (with Ferdinand Foll as pianist, and the solo violin part played by August Duesberg) at a meeting of the former.

Although Bruckner's compositional activities during the year were largely taken up with revision of earlier works and ongoing work on the Ninth, he found time to write a short male-voice chorus with solo tenor part, *Träumen und Wachen* WAB 87. It was composed on 15 December 1890 and dedicated to Dr. Wilhelm Ritter von Hartel, rector of Vienna University and later a government minister. In spite of

---

135 See *LBSAB*, 156f. for this letter, dated Vienna, 23 December 1890; the original is in the ÖNB, F18 Schalk 158/11/32.

136 See an extract from the review of this concert (*Linzer Zeitung*, 23 December 1890) in Röder, op.cit., 425f.

Bruckner's very 'shaky' conducting at its first performance a month later, the choir had been well rehearsed by the composer and was well received.[137]

The five works which underwent revision of some kind or other during 1890 were the Mass in F minor and the First, Third, Fourth and Eighth Symphonies. In some cases Bruckner was directly involved, in others only indirectly.

In a letter to his brother Franz on 18 January, Joseph Schalk mentioned that Bruckner had almost completed revision work on the Eighth and that he (Joseph) was rehearsing the *Kyrie* and *Gloria* of the F minor Mass with the *Wagner-Verein* choir.[138] Franz was planning to undertake a revision of the Mass, and when Joseph wrote to him again about a fortnight later, he asked if he could have the revised material in time for the final rehearsals at the end of February which Bruckner was going to attend.[139] But Franz did not have time to proceed with the revision at this point. In fact, during the summer of 1890, Joseph decided that he would take it upon himself to proceed with the revision. In the meantime, he informed Franz about the rehearsals of the *Kyrie* and *Gloria* movements which had met with Bruckner's approval. He hoped that the enthusiasm which he had succeeded in engendering in the singers would remain until the performance on 5 March. He regretted not having an orchestra at his disposal, however - 'then it would really go like a bomb'.[140] The

---

137 A sketch of the work, formerly owned by Löwe and now in the *ÖNB*, contains the note 'Entwurf 15/12 90 3/4 11 bis 1/2 Uhr' and a later addition: '4 Febr. 92'. Hartel lived in the same apartment block (Hessgasse 7) as Bruckner for many years; see *G-A* IV/3, 129f. footnote 2 for his portrayal of Bruckner's personality. The chorus was published by Rättig (T.R.223) in 1891, and by Adolf Robitschek Musikverlag, Vienna, in 1954. See Karl Lorenz's and Leopold von Schroeder's accounts of the first performance (part of the University celebrations to mark the centenary of Grillparzer's birth on 15 January 1891; Bruckner conducted the *Akademischer Gesangverein*) in *G-A* IV/3, 131ff.

138 See earlier reference to this letter, page 587, footnote 78.

139 See earlier reference to this letter, page 587, footnote 78.

140 See earlier reference to this letter, page 587, footnote 81.

'private' performance of the two movements in which the choir was accompanied by piano and brass was not to everyone's taste. Some people left during the performance. Nevertheless, Joseph was all the more keen to conduct it in a church with full orchestra. The most important thing was that Bruckner was delighted.[141]

In August Joseph wrote to Franz to tell him about his visit to Bad Ischl in the company of Bruckner and asked him to look at the *Credo* of the Mass with a view to revising it.[142] He had attempted to revise the *Kyrie* himself but had not got very far because of his lack of orchestral experience. It would be far better if Franz could do the whole thing. As soon as Franz returned the *Credo*, he would send him his attempt at scoring the *Kyrie* to look at.[143]

In his letter to Franz on 22 February Joseph mentioned Hermann Levi's recent visit to Vienna during which Ferdinand Löwe had played through Bruckner's First Symphony. It appears that, although Bruckner intended to revise it thoroughly, neither Schalk nor Levi felt that the symphony required a major revision. Indeed Levi wrote to Bruckner to express his admiration for the work, saying that it must be printed and performed, but begging him not to alter it too much.[144] Joseph mentioned that he had taken the opportunity of copying out the Adagio quickly before the 'threatened revision'. He was keen, however, that his brother rather than Bruckner should undertake a 'discreet' revision of the symphony.[145]

Bruckner was not to be dissuaded, however, and he began his own revision of the Symphony in March. Joseph continued with his own independent revision plans and sent the Adagio to his brother:

---

141   See earlier reference to this letter, page 588, footnote 83.

142   He had already asked his brother to look at the *Gloria* in May. See page 590, footnote 92.

143   See earlier reference to this letter, page 592, footnote 99.

144   See earlier reference to this letter, page 588, footnote 82.

145   See earlier reference to this letter, page 587, footnote 81.

... The small notes in pencil are Löwe's suggestions. I would be delighted if you could find the time the undertake the revision yourself. I am convinced that you will certainly steer clear of the too modern, so to speak comical, treatment of the orchestra and will proceed as reverently as possible. At all events there are passages which urgently require revision...[146]

On 1 May Joseph recalled his time in Pressburg with Bruckner. He hoped that Franz would be able to come to Vienna at the beginning of June and bring with him the revised *Gloria* of the F minor Mass as well as the Adagio of the First Symphony. A few days later, Bruckner wrote to Franz and referred to his own revision work on the First. 'The little besom has to be swept up', he said. He was obviously unaware of Joseph's plans - or perhaps chose to ignore them?[147] Reference has already been made to Bruckner's letter to Theodor Helm at the end of March in which he sought to divert blame from the Vienna Philharmonic to himself (and, by implication, those assisting him?) for the recent lack of performance of his works. After all, he had 'taken the "impudent little rascal" [reference to the First Symphony] away from them', the revised version of the Third Symphony had not yet been published (in spite of Joseph Schalk's assurance three months earlier that it would be ready in good time), and Richter was not aware that the Sixth Symphony had been copied.[148]

In his preface to the edition of the third version of the Third Symphony in the *Gesamtausgabe*, Leopold Nowak mentions differences between the second edition of 1890 and the printer's copy (Mus. Hs. 6081) upon which it was based, attributing them to the 'master's pupils who edited the work'. Nowak also specifies some of the differences between the second and third versions as regards dynamics, orchestration,

---

146 See earlier reference to this letter, page 588, footnote 83.

147 See earlier reference to these letters, page 590, footnote 92.

148 See earlier reference to this letter, page 589, footnote 86.

and the cuts in the slow movement and Finale.[149]

Finally, revision work on the Eighth was completed early in the year, a dedicatee was sought and found, and some progress was made in the attempts to find a publisher. The first movement of the symphony was 'newly restored' between November 1889 and the end of January 1890. On 18 January Joseph Schalk reported to his brother that Bruckner 'will be finished with the Eighth in a few days' time and is very enthusiastic about his work'.[150] At the end of the month, when Joseph wrote again to his brother, specifically about a revision of the F minor Mass, he added:

> ... Bruckner finished the new revision of the VIIIth the day before yesterday. The first movement now ends *pianissimo* as we all wished it would. He would undoubtedly be extremely pleased if you could use this opportunity to write to him...[151]

Further work on the first movement was undertaken until 10 March when he declared that it was 'completely finished', and a diary entry for 15 March reads '14.3.90 letzte auswendige Wiederholung v. I. Satze der 8. Sinf.'.[152]

As soon as he had received confirmation from the Lord Chamberlain that the Emperor would accept the dedication of the symphony, Bruckner wrote to Hermann Levi and asked him to lend his personal support to the efforts of the *Wagner-Verein* in Vienna to persuade Schott in Mainz to publish the work. Bruckner's unhappy experiences with the quality of Gutmann's work, the printing of the Fourth Symphony in particular, almost certainly persuaded him to look elsewhere for a

149 *Anton Bruckner Gesamtausgabe* III/3 (Vienna, 1959).

150 See earlier reference to this letter, page 587, footnote 78.

151 See earlier reference to this letter, page 587, footnote 78.

152 '14.3.90 final play-through by memory of the 1st movement of the 8th symphony'.

publisher:

> Vienna is ruled out, as I have already given away three symphonies
> and the Quintet for nothing at all. N.B. I received 50 florins for the
> Te Deum... The publishing firm that offers the most will get it. If no
> one offers anything, the foreign firm which can print it the most
> cheaply will get it. Perhaps the dedication to the Emperor will help
> a little...[153]

Bruckner's correspondence with Levi and Weingartner in the autumn includes references to some of the alterations he had made to the Eighth. On 2 October, for instance, he contacted Levi to inform him that he had written to Weingartner, and added in a postscript:

> The Finale has been greatly shortened. On account of its length I
> have recommended to Mr. Weingartner that he make cuts...[154]

The illness which had already forced Levi to give up his conducting duties temporarily also prevented him from replying immediately to Bruckner. When he eventually wrote in December, there was very little fresh information he could provide. Weingartner had not been in touch, but the orchestral parts were now being written out in Mannheim as the only competent copyist in Munich had been too busy to take on further work. Levi regretted that his recent illness after more than fifteen years of almost non-stop activity would more or less debar him from conducting in the immediate future, a task which he would have undertaken gladly under normal circumstances. Indeed, ill-health had even prevented him from attending recent

---

153 See earlier reference to this letter, page 589, footnote 90.

154 See earlier reference to this letter, page 595, footnote 105.

Munich performances of the Fourth Symphony and the Quintet.[155]

At the end of the year *Hofkapelle* duties kept Bruckner in Vienna during the Christmas period and prevented him from making his seasonal visits to Steyr and St. Florian. An entry in his diary: '26. Dez. 890. H.H. "So schön hat noch Keiner gespielt wie Bruckner heut in der Hofkapelle." (!)' indicates that Hellmesberger, the court music director, had been very complimentary about his playing at High Mass.[156]

Bruckner's financial position, invariably a source of concern to the composer, was in a healthy state at the beginning of 1891 - so much so that Viktor Boller, one of the organizers of the special pension fund for Bruckner, was able to inform Prince Fürstenberg , who had just promised a gift of 500 florins, that no more payments would be necessary in the immediate future.[157] Although Prince Liechtenstein's annual contributions of 300 florins were only temporary and were made on the condition that they would cease as soon as Bruckner's future security was secured, the composer requested that they continue until his death.[158]

---

155   See earlier reference to this letter, page 598, footnote 113.

156   Entry in *Fromme's österreichischer Professoren- und Lehrer-Kalender für das Studienjahr 1889/90*; the original is in the *ÖNB*.

157   See *G-A* IV/3, 125 for Boller's letter to Fürstenberg, dated 4 January 1891. See also *G-A* IV/3, 125, footnote for details of contributions; between 1 October 1890 and 20 May 1891 these amounted to nearly 4000 florins! Bruckner himself travelled from St. Florian to Ennsegg at the beginning of April to thank Fürstenberg personally. See *ABB*, 241 for Bruckner's letters to Fürstenberg, dated 31 March and 1 April; the original of the first is privately owned and the original of the second is in the *ÖNB*. On his return to Vienna from St. Florian, Bruckner wrote a third letter to Fürstenberg, dated 15 April, in which he thanked him for his gift of 500 florins and provided him with news of a forthcoming performance of the *Te Deum* at the Berlin Music Festival on 31 May. See *ABB*, 244 and *G-A* IV/3, 148 and footnote; the original of this letter is in the *ÖNB*.

158   See letter to Bruckner from the Liechtenstein court chancellor, dated 12 January 1891, and an undated letter from M. von Kempelen to the court chancellor (with a receipt date of 20 February 1891); Bruckner's request was granted; the originals are in the *Stiftung Fürst Liechtenstein*,

Bruckner now had sufficient financial backing to enable him to retire from his teaching position at the Conservatory. On 15 January he received two letters from the *Gesellschaft der Musikfreunde*, the first an official letter from the administration (one of the signatories being Hellmesberger) accepting his resignation and thanking him for his 22 years' invaluable service to the institution, the second from the Conservatory's pension association informing him that his pension would be 440 florins per annum payable in quarterly instalments of 110 florins.[159] On the same day the administration of the *Gesellschaft* gave official recognition to Bruckner's contribution to the musical life of Vienna by electing him an honorary member.[160]

Bruckner's friend, the music critic Gustav Schönaich, an admirer of both Bruckner and Brahms and one of the very few writers on music in Vienna who refused to adopt a partisan stance, wrote to the composer on 15 January to ask if it would be possible for Karl Frank, music director of the Nuremberg town theatre, to borrow the orchestral material of the Third Symphony for a performance of the work [on 27 March]. He also took the opportunity of thanking Bruckner for the 'unforgettable' and 'overwhelming' experience of the recent Vienna performance and for creating a work of such great spiritual richness.[161]

Vienna; see also *SchABCT*, 625f. and 632.

159   The texts of both letters can be found in *G-A* IV/3, 126ff.; the originals are in St. Florian.

160   Hans Richter was also elected an honorary member. Bruckner wrote a letter of thanks to the *Gesellschaft* on 18 February. See *ABA*, 111; the original is in the *Gesellschaft* library.

161   See *ABB*, 357f. and Andrea Harrandt, 'Gustav Schönaich - ein "Herold der Bruckner'schen Kunst"' in *BSL 1991* (Linz, 1994), 70. Schönaich wrote again to Bruckner to congratulate him on being elected an honorary member of the *Gesellschaft der Musikfreunde;* he also promised to make sure that the matter of a pension from the *Hofkapelle* was discussed in the *Gesellschaft der Musikfreunde*. See *ABB*, 358f. and Harrandt, loc.cit., 71 (where the letter is dated 1892). The originals of these two letters have been lost.

A repeat performance of the Third Symphony, organized by the *Wagner-Verein*, took place in the large *Musikverein* hall on Sunday 25 January at 12.30. Joseph Schalk wrote to his brother in advance, inviting him to come and adding that Bruckner would be overjoyed to see him. But Franz was unable to come because of difficulties at work. Joseph sympathised with him in his next letter and mentioned that Bruckner had written to him. Joseph was still looking forward to conducting Bruckner's Fourth in Graz, describing it as 'the greatest musical event in my life up to now'.[162]

The day after the repeat performance of the Third Bruckner wrote to Hermann Levi and expressed his delight at the enthusiasm of both the public and Hans Richter who evidently promised to perform the work at a forthcoming London concert.[163] On 27 January Bruckner also informed Felix Weingartner about the successful repeat performance of the Third. He was more concerned at this point, however, about the planned first performance of the revised version of the Eighth and asked Weingartner if there had been any rehearsals of the work, reiterating his request that the cuts in the Finale be observed.[164] This letter, with its performance directions and programmatic references, is of primary importance in any discussion of the two versions of the Eighth:

... How is the Eighth going? Have you held any rehearsals yet? How

---

162 See *LBSAB*, 157f. for extracts from these two letters, dated Vienna, 12 and 15 January 1891; the originals are in the *ÖNB*, F18 Schalk 158/12/4 and 158/12/5

163 See *GrBLS*, 346 for Bruckner's letter to Levi, dated Vienna, 26 January 1891; the original has been lost.

164 According to Hugo Wolf, Bruckner was furious about the apparent unnecessary delays in performing the Eighth. In a letter to Oscar Grohé in Mannheim(14 January, 1891), Wolf said that he done his best to reassure Bruckner that Weingartner was acting from the best of motives; see *SchABCT*, 626.

does it sound? Please strictly observe the cuts in the Finale as indicated; otherwise it would be far too long, and is valid only for later times, and for a circle of friends and connoisseurs. You may alter the tempi as you wish (and as you need for purposes of clarity). Please tell me what I owe you for the copying expenses.

Do you have a sympathetic critic in Mannheim? Will Schott come from Mainz? Is there any hope of having it printed? The symphony is dedicated to the Emperor, and I would prefer the good Emperor not to have to pay the publication costs for this work at least. Hans Richter has already been pestering me about the symphony.

To repeat, please tell me how the Eighth sounds.

In the first movement, the passage for trumpets and horns based on the rhythm of the theme is the pronouncement of death which gets gradually louder during its sporadic appearances and is finally very prominent; at the end - resignation. Scherzo: main theme - called 'German Michael'; the fellow wants to go to sleep in the second section but, in his reverie, cannot find his little song; finally it is inverted plaintively. Finale: at that time our Emperor was visited by the Tsar in Olmütz [sic]; hence strings: ride of the Cossacks; brass: military music; trumpets: fanfares as their Majesties meet. All the themes at the end; (humorous) there is great pomp when German Michael returns from his travels, just as when the king appears in the second act of *Tannhäuser*. There is also the death march and then (brass) transfiguration in the Finale...[165]

Although Bruckner was invited to attend the Graz performance of the Fourth

---

165 See *ABB*, 237f. and *GrBB*, 129ff. for this letter, dated Vienna, 27 January 1891; the original is in the *Gesellschaft der Musikfreunde* library. Auer's transcription of the letter, however, contains two mistakes - 'endlich klagend kehrt er selber um' (referring to 'German Michael' turning himself round) instead of 'endlich klagend kehrt es selbes um' (referring to an inversion of the musical material) - which distorts the meaning of the programme of the Scherzo movement. The 'meeting of the Emperors', to which Bruckner alludes, was the meeting of Emperor Franz Josef, Tsar Alexander III and Kaiser Wilhelm I of Germany at Skierniewice in September 1884. For fuller discussion, see Constantin Floros, 'Die Fassungen der Achten Symphonie von Anton Bruckner' in *BSL 1980* (Linz, 1981), 6, footnote 7, Floros, *Brahms und Bruckner. Studien zur musikalischen Exegetik* (Wiesbaden, 1980), 191f. and 227f. (facsimile of the original), and Benjamin Korstvedt, *Bruckner Symphony no. 8* (Cambridge, 2000), 24 and 51f.

conducted by Joseph Schalk on 1 February, he had to decline because of ill health and the additional complication of a fall on the ice which caused him to limp badly and forced him to cancel some *Hofkapelle* duties.[166] The orchestral concert was preceded by a concert of the Graz *Wagner-Verein* on 30 January; Joseph Schalk played his solo piano arrangement of the first and second movements from the Fourth Symphony and the Adagio from the String Quintet was also performed.[167] There was high praise for Schalk's conducting of the symphony on 1 February in the *Grazer Volksblatt*, and the possibility of his assuming the vacant position of musical director of the Steiermark *Musikverein* was mooted - but this did not materialize.[168]

In another letter to Puchstein, Bruckner mentioned the 'brilliant' repeat performance of the Third in Vienna and the acclaimed performance of the Fourth in Graz.[169]

On 11 February, von Wolzogen wrote to Bruckner and congratulated him on the successful performances of his works in Vienna and Munich. His main purpose in writing, however, was to ascertain that the details of an anecdote about Bruckner's dedication of the original version of the Third to Wagner were correct. He was intending to include this anecdote in a new edition of his *Erinnerungen an Richard*

---

166 See *FSBB*, 72f. (complete) and *LBSAB*, 158 (extract) for Bruckner's letter to Franz Schalk, dated Vienna, 31 January, 189; the original is in the *ÖNB*, F18 Schalk 54/17.

167 This concert was reviewed (probably by Theodor Helm) in the morning edition of the *Grazer Tagespost* (1 February 1891); see Ingrid Schubert, 'Bruckner, Wagner und die Neudeutschen in Graz' in *BSL 1984* (Linz, 1986), 38 and 58.

168 See *LBSAB*, 158f. for the review in the *Grazer Volksblatt* (6 February 1891). There was also a review by Theodor Helm in the morning edition of the *Grazer Tagespost* (3 February 1891) and an article on the Fourth Symphony by 'Dr. G.' in the *Grazer Morgenpost* (4 February 1891); see Schubert, loc.cit., 38 and 58. A performance of Bruckner's *Germanenzug* by the *Grazer Männergesangverein* on 1 March 1891was also reviewed in the *Grazer Morgenpost* and *Grazer Tagespost*; see Schubert, loc.cit., 37f. and 58.

169 See *ABB*, 238f. for this letter, dated Vienna, 5 February 1891; the original has been lost.

Wagner.[170] In his reply Bruckner provided an account of his friendship with Wagner, the dedication of the Third, and his final visit to the ailing master.[171] A few days later Bruckner also received a letter from Theodor Helm. Helm mentioned the Graz performance of the Fourth, Hirschfeld's analysis of the Third in the *Neue Wiener Musik-Zeitung* and the Vienna Philharmonic's performance of the Third the previous December, but he also congratulated Bruckner on a more recent successful performance of the Third in Prague and informed him of a projected performance of the same work in Warnsdorf.[172] Bruckner alluded to this Prague performance in a visiting card to Helm, but he provided his friend with more information about current activity in a letter written the previous day. He mentioned that Richter was going to perform the Third in London, he had completed his revision of the First Symphony and had re-commenced work on the Ninth.[173] He had already conveyed similar information to Hermann Levi a few days earlier:

---

170 See *ABB*, 382f. for this letter which was sent from Bayreuth; the original is in St. Florian.

171 See *ABB*, 166ff. for the text of this undated letter. Auer suggests a much earlier date - 1884 - but its content, in particular the reference to stomach problems in a postscript, points to February 1891 as the proper date. We know that Bruckner was unwell with stomach trouble at the time; see *ABB*, 240 for his letter to his brother Ignaz, dated Vienna, 19 February 1891, in which he encloses 10 florins and thanks his brother for sending him some meat but asks him not to send any more until the autumn because of his stomach problems. See in particular Franz Scheder, 'Zur Datierung von Bruckners Brief an Wolzogen (Auer nr. 137)' in *BJ 1984/85/86* (Linz, 1988), 65ff. The originals of Bruckner's letters to Wolzogen and Ignaz Bruckner have been lost.

172 See *ABB*, 297f. for Helm's letter to Bruckner, dated Vienna, 17 February 1891: the original has been lost. The Prague performance of the Third took place on 14 February and was conducted by Karl Muck. The review in the *Prager Tagblatt* (16 February) criticized the lack of cohesion in places but was otherwise complimentary; see Röder, op.cit., 428.

173 See *ABB*, 239f. for the letter and card, dated Vienna, 18 and 19 February respectively; the originals have been lost.

... I have only three pages of performance directions to complete, then I will turn my attention to the Ninth (D minor); I have already written down most of its themes...[174]

Bruckner's hopes of a first performance of the Eighth in Germany were short-lived. Levi had written to Weingartner to ask for a performance date and to suggest that he send the bill for the cost of copying to him and not to Bruckner. Levi included this information in a letter to Bruckner written on 7 February.[175] In his reply to Levi, Weingartner was able to provide him with two important pieces of information: the performance of the Eighth had been scheduled for 26 March, and neither Levi nor Bruckner would have to incur the expense of copying the parts, as a consortium in Mannheim had provided the sum of 300 marks for this purpose.[176] Bruckner was unaware of these developments when he wrote to Levi on 10 February. On 6 March Joseph Schalk informed his brother of the projected performance of the Eighth in Mannheim as well as Bruckner's hard work on the Ninth - encouraged by Hugo Wolf who visited him frequently.[177] Eventually, on 20 March, Weingartner wrote to Bruckner with the information that a performance of the Eighth had been put back from Thursday 26 March to Thursday 2 April; he asked the composer's permission to alter the instrumentation at some points as the Mannheim orchestra

---

174 See *GrBLS*, 346f. for this letter, dated Vienna, 10 February 1891; the original is privately owned. Bruckner's work on the Ninth at the time is corroborated by an account of a visit to Bruckner at the beginning of March by J.L. Nicodé, a conductor and composer from Dresden one of whose works was being performed in Vienna by the *Männergesangverein*. According to Nicodé, Bruckner's work-desk was covered with manuscript paper, most of it belonging to the Ninth. Bruckner played extracts from the work to Nicodé and his wife, and Nicodé recalls the composer saying that, in the event of the fourth movement not being completed, the *Te Deum* should be substituted. See *G-A* IV/3, 144-47.

175 See *ABB*, 323f. for Levi's letter to Bruckner; the original is in St. Florian.

176 See *G-A* IV/3, 143 for an extract from this letter, dated Mannheim, 8 February 1891.

177 See *LBSAB*, 160f.; the original is in the *ÖNB*, F18 Schalk 158/12/9.

did not have as many string players as the Vienna Philharmonic and he feared that the wind instruments would dominate the strings:

> ...Yesterday I held the first orchestral rehearsal of your Eighth Symphony. Strings only at first, then wind. The sound effect will be a powerful one.
> You obviously had the large Viennese string section in mind when you scored the work. As the large number of wind players in our orchestra here frequently has an overpowering effect on the relatively small string section, I would ask your permission to remove the woodwind and horn doublings in a few passages. You may rest assured that I will make these reductions, which, of course, are only necessary when small string sections are involved, in an artistic manner and perhaps in such a way that you will not even be aware of them.
> I should be very grateful if you would be so kind as to send me a few biographical details about yourself which I can use for an introductory article in the local newspapers.
> As we are having a performance of the St. Matthew Passion on the 27th (Good Friday), I have had to postpone the VII. Academy Concert until the 2nd of April (Thursday) which... will have no effect on the attendance, as these Academy Concerts are completely sold out from the beginning of the season.[178]

Eager to have his work performed, Bruckner willingly gave his consent and made further reference to the cuts in the Finale:

> ... As I have been suffering from throat and stomach problems for a long time, I have been advised to spend some time in the country; and so I find myself now at St. Florian abbey in Upper Austria, 1 hour 30 minutes' journey from my birthplace, Ansfelden (1824). I undertook my more extensive studies with Prof. Sechter in Vienna from 1855 to 1861; I then studied composition until 1863.
> By all means make the necessary changes for your orchestra, but please do not alter the full score; and also leave the orchestral parts

---

178   See *ABB*, 368f. for this letter; the original is in St. Florian.

unchanged when preparing them for print - that is one of my most ardent requests.

If Schott was willing to publish the work, the purpose would then be fulfilled and I would be extremely happy. It is a great comfort to me that a highly gifted man like yourself should take so much trouble to help me and my work to gain recognition!

Please observe the cuts in the Finale, as the movement would be too long otherwise and would have a most detrimental effect.[179]

Bruckner also provided August Göllerich with news about the planned first performance, appending in a footnote to a letter '2. April in Mannheim 8. Sinf'.[180] During his vacation at St. Florian Bruckner was invited by Bishop Doppelbauer to play the organ at Linz Cathedral during the Easter Sunday service which included a performance of Haydn's 'Nelson' Mass. He had an audience with the bishop after the service and lunched with his friends at the *Kanone* restaurant.[181] There were also two another performances of the Third Symphony during this period. The first was conducted by Karl Frank in the Nuremberg Town Theatre on 27 March[182]; the second was conducted by Joseph F. Hummel as part of the "II. Vereins- und

179 See *ABB*, 241 (where date is given erroneously as 17 March) and *GrBB*, 131f. for this letter, dated St. Florian, 27 March 1891; the original is in the *Gesellschaft der Musikfreunde* library, Vienna.

180 See *ABB*, 242 for this letter, dated St. Florian, 27 March 1891; the original is in the *Gesellschaft der Musikfreunde* library, Vienna.

181 See *ABB*, 242 and *GrBB*, 127 for a letter to his old friend Karl Waldeck, dated St. Florian, 27 March 1891, in which Bruckner mentioned that he hoped to see him while he was in Linz; the original of this letter has been lost. See also *G-A* II/1, 309, *G-A* III/1, 613 and *G-A* IV/3, 148.

182 See Franz Scheder, 'Frühe Bruckner-Aufführungen in Nürnberg' in *BJ 1989/90* (Linz, 1992), 246f. for extracts from reviews of the performance, including those in the *Nürnberger Stadtzeitung* (31 March 1891), the *Fränkische Kurier* (31 March 1891) and the *Nürnberger Anzeiger* (1 April 1891); see also Röder, op.cit., 429.

Abonnement-Concert der Internationalen Stiftung Mozarteum' in Salzburg.[183]

At this point in time all was set fair for a performance of the Eighth in Mannheim. And then came the disappointing news that Weingartner would not be able to conduct the work as he had been promoted to a new post as musical director of the court opera and royal orchestral concerts in Berlin. In any case the tuba players would certainly have required more rehearsals:

> ...You have no idea how truly sorry I am that I can no longer perform your symphony. The call to Berlin came so suddenly and my change of position was so unexpected that I could not even complete the series of subscription concerts here but had to leave the final one to my successor. I am driven very hard at the theatre at present. I have to conduct almost every second day, and that leaves me little time to prepare for concerts. Only a large number of rehearsals can do full justice to a work like yours, and I would no longer be able to hold them. There was also another factor, viz. that the brass players whom we engaged from the military band, which supplies us with our reinforcements, to play the tubas had never even blown the instruments. I had already held three special rehearsals of your symphony with the four tuba players without being able to achieve a reasonable sound. In my despair I contacted you by telegram, but you had left Vienna, as I discovered from your letter which arrived from St. Florian the next day. I console myself with the knowledge that your work perhaps would not have achieved the desired effect with our small string section (we have only eight first violins) and that this will be better realized elsewhere. Rest assured, dear Bruckner, that I am a sincere admirer of your musical gifts and will perform one of your works in Berlin as soon as possible. Do not be angry with me. Not I, but circumstances beyond my control have prevented a

---

183 See Gerhard Walterskirchen, 'Bruckner in Salzburg - Bruckner-Erstaufführungen in Salzburg' in *IBG Mitteilungsblatt* 16 (1979), 17 for extracts from reviews of the concert in the *Salzburger Zeitung* (10 April 1891) and the *Salzburges Volksblatt*; see also Röder, op.cit., 429f. On 10 April Bruckner sent a card to Helm to inform him of the 'sensational success' of the Salzburg performance; see *ABB*, 240; the original has been lost

performance of your symphony here.[184]

At first Bruckner was not entirely convinced by Weingartner's explanation and, in a letter to Levi, expressed his suspicion that the symphony had 'not pleased Mr. Weingartner or sounded bad'. He was also concerned about the costs incurred in copying the parts. Should he send Levi the appropriate amount?[185] Levi confirmed that Weingartner had been called to Berlin; as far as payment was concerned, he (Levi) would now foot the bill!:

> ... I was most disappointed to learn that your 8th Symphony is not to be performed in Mannheim. Weingartner assured me repeatedly that it would be performed on 26 March, and I had already arranged to have leave for that day. It seems that Weingartner has lost his bearings somewhat as a result of his call to Berlin and has not been able to acquire the necessary composure and concentration - which is understandable, of course. It can all be put down again to your old enemy - misfortune!! As far as the copying costs are concerned, please leave this in my hands. I had already asked Weingartner earlier to send me the bill, but he replied as follows on 8 February:
> > 'Neither Bruckner nor you needs to pay for the copying costs, because a consortium here has put 300 marks at my disposal specially for this concert'.
> Now I will send the money immediately to Mannheim. Weingartner wrote to me that Richter will perform the 8th in London. Is that true?[186]

---

184 See *ABB*, 369f. for this letter, dated Mannheim, 9 April 1891; the original is in St. Florian.

185 See *GrBLS*, 347f. for Bruckner's letter to Levi, dated Vienna, 18 April 1891; the original was formerly in the *Staatsbibliothek*, Berlin, but has been lost. Bruckner had received a copy of the bill and, on telegraphing Mannheim, was informed that payment should be made to Schuster, the leader of the Mannheim orchestra.

186 See *ABB*, 324f. for this letter, dated Munich, 19 April 1891; the original is in St. Florian. It seems that the performances of both Hugo Wolf's *Christnacht* and Bruckner's Eighth had already been put back another week before (?) Weingartner's call to Berlin. In the event, Wolf's piece was

In replying to Levi, Bruckner made it clear that he (Levi) would still be the ideal conductor of the symphony and, to a certain extent, he was relieved that 'the small orchestra with the military tubas' in Mannheim had not been able to perform it.[187]

There were two performances of Bruckner's *Te Deum* outside Austria in the first half of the year, the first in Christiania (Oslo), Norway, the second in Berlin as part of the 28th *Composers' Convention*. The Norwegian performance was given on 21 February by the *Musikforeningen* under the direction of Iver Holter and was widely reported in the Norwegian newspapers.[188]

At the beginning of May, Bruckner was contacted by Otto Leßmann, editor of the Berlin *Allgemeine Musikzeitung*, and asked to send a photograph for a preview of the performance of the *Te Deum* at the end of the month; Bruckner sent an immediate reply.[189] On 11 May, he wrote to Göllerich, describing him as his 'chosen, authorized biographer', and adding that he looked forward to seeing him in Berlin

---

performed at a concert on 9 April and Bruckner's symphony was replaced (?) by Liszt's *Faust* symphony. It was Bruckner's Third, not his Eighth, which was mooted for performance in London.

187 See *GrBLS*, 352 (where it is incorrectly dated 22 April 1892), and Walter Beck, *Anton Bruckner. Ein Lebensbild mit neuen Dokumenten* (Dornach, 1995), 65; there is a facsimile of the first page of the letter in Beck, 64; the original is owned privately.

188 For further information and extracts from the reviews in the *Aftenposten, Dagbladet, Morgenposten, Morgenbladet* and *Norske Intelligenssedler* (22 - 24 February), see Bo Marschner, 'Aufführungen größerer Werke von Anton Bruckner in den nordischen Ländern 1891-1991. Teil 1: Norwegen' in *IBG Mitteilungsblatt* 37 (1991), 30, and '100 Jahre Bruckner-Rezeption in den nordischen Ländern' in *BSL 1991* (Linz, 1994), 185 and 199.

189 Leßmann's letter to Bruckner, dated Berlin, 3 May 1891, is mentioned in *G-A* IV/3, 156; Bruckner's reply, dated Vienna, 5 May 1891, is cited in Renate Grasberger, 'Bruckner-Bibliographie', *ABDS* 4 (Graz, 1985), 17; the original of the first has been lost, the original of the second is in the *Bibliothek des Stadtrates*, Munich.

at the end of the month.[190]   Ten days later he wrote to Dr. Richard Sternfeld, president of the Philharmonic Choir in Berlin, to acknowledge receipt of his letter and to enquire about the location and time of the *Te Deum* rehearsal.[191] On the same day, Siegfried Ochs, the conductor of the Berlin Philharmonic Choir, wrote to Bruckner to invite him to both the last choral rehearsal and final full choral and orchestral rehearsal of the work.[192] Bruckner was accompanied to Berlin by his pupil, Max von Oberleithner, and stayed at the *Kaiserhof* hotel.[193] He received a very enthusiastic welcome, was well-looked after by friends and, to cap all, the performance on 31 May was a great success, von Bülow (not known for his love of Bruckner!) was extremely complimentary, and there were promises of further German performances of his symphonies and the *Te Deum* in the future.[194] Bruckner was clearly delighted

---

190   See *ABB*, 245; the original is owned privately.   Bruckner's words are 'berufener, authorisierter Biograf'.

191   See *ABB*, 246 and *GrBB*, 119 for Bruckner's letter, dated Vienna, 21 May 1891; the original is privately owned. Sternfeld's letter to Bruckner has been lost. Dr. Richard Sternfeld (1858-1926) was a history teacher, music journalist and prominent Wagnerian.

192   See *ABB*, 340f. for Ochs's letter to Bruckner, dated Berlin, 21 May 1891; the original is in the *ÖNB*. Siegfried Ochs (1858-1929) was a prominent choir director. He founded his own choir in 1882 and this became the Philharmonic Choir in 1887.

193   Bruckner had received an invitation to stay with Weingartner, but had declined; see *G-A* IV/3, 156.

194   See *G-A* IV/3, 150f. for Ochs's reminiscence of the final rehearsal (29 May), and 156ff. for Oberleithner's reminiscences of the visit; see also Stephen Johnson's translation in his *Bruckner Remembered*, 62ff. A repeat performance of the *Te Deum* was planned for later in the year; there is no firm evidence that an extra performance took place at the beginning of June.

195   On 12 June Bruckner wrote to both Hermann Levi and Theodor Helm and mentioned the performance and the possibility of other performances of his works in Berlin, Dresden and Stuttgart the following winter. He asked Helm to provide a report in the *Deutsche Zeitung*. See *GrBLS*, 348f.

and did not fail to mention his Berlin success in letters written at this time.[195] In his first letter to Helm he reported that all the Berlin newspaper reviews of the performance were favourable, particularly those of Leßmann and Tappert. Leßmann, in his review, noted that there was greater appreciation of Bruckner 'on the slow-moving Spree than on the quickly-flowing Danube' and described the triumphant performance as 'probably the most impressive and remarkable event in the entire festival'.[196] In the *Kleines Journal* Tappert described the three main ingredients in the *Te Deum* as 'Gregorian chant, Beethoven's symphonic language and Wagner's dramatically intensified expression' and reported that the difficulties of the work had been magnificently surmounted in the performance.[197] Wilhelm Blanck, reviewing the performance for the *Berliner Fremdenblatt*, remarked that the style of the work was

---

for the letter to Levi, *ABB*, 246f. and *GrBB*, 39f. for the letter to Helm. The original of the former is privately owned and that of the latter is in the *Wiener Stadt- und Landesbibliothek*. On 15 June Bruckner thanked Helm for his support and promised to send him a gift of wine - see *ABB*, 248f. and *GrBB*, 41f.; the original has been lost. Also on 15 June he sent name-day greetings to his landlord, Dr. Oelzelt von Newin, and referred to the Berlin success; see *ABB*, 248; the original is in the *Gesellschaft der Musikfreunde* library. On 14 June Bruckner wrote to Bernhard Deubler in St. Florian, expressing concern about the health of his brother and requesting medical attention for him. The Berlin experience had been 'quite indescribable', he said, and there were to be further perfomances of his works later in the year; see *ABB*, 247 and *GrBB*, 25; the original is in St. Florian.

196 See *G-A* IV/3, 154 for an extract from this review in the *Musikalisches Wochenblatt* (28 June); Leßmann also provided an earlier review (12 June) for his own *Allgemeine Musik-Zeitung;* there is a reference to it in Mathias Hansen, 'Anton Bruckner in Norddeutschland', *BSL 1991* (Linz, 1994), 109. Bruckner's *Te Deum* was part of a three-hour programme on 31 May. D'Albert and Weingartner also conducted works by Bach, Bruch, Dvorák, d'Albert, Cornelius, MacDowell and Draeseke.

197 See *G-A* IV/3, 155 for an extract from Tappert's review of 2 June 1891.

fundamentally different from that of the extracts from a Mass by Max Bruch which opened the concert. The overwhelming elemental power of the choral unison passages was particularly memorable.[198]

While in Berlin Bruckner befriended a young parlour-maid at the hotel called Ida Buhz. There was probably never any serious intention on Bruckner's part of becoming engaged to the girl, but, always a stickler for convention, he introduced himself formally to Ida's parents. Bruckner received ten letters from Ida, all of a factual, conversational nature and expressing concern for his health and well-being, between his first and second (1894) visits to Berlin. None of his letters of reply has been found.[199]

Bruckner and Oberleithner returned to Vienna by way of Dresden and attended a performance of the play *Die Welt, in der man sich langweilt*, in which one of Bruckner's favourite actresses, Clara Salbach, had a leading role. Ernst von Schuch, music director of the Court Opera, also arranged for them to attend two Wagner operas, *Das Rheingold* and *Die Walküre*. According to Oberleithner, Bruckner was tired and overwrought., some of his nervous problems returned, and it was not until

---

198   See *G-A* IV/3, 155f. for this review, and 153 for an extract from the review in the Berlin *Börsen-Courier*, both dated 2 June 1891.

199   On 16 October 1891, for instance, Ida wrote to Bruckner to say how delighted she was that the photograph of herself which she had sent him had brought him pleasure; see *G-A* IV/3, 160f. for further information, including an extract from this letter. On 20 December Bruckner mentioned Ida in a letter to Karl Waldeck and said that she 'wants to have me at any price'. A year later (26 November 1892), Josef Leitenmayr, a friend in Kremsmünster, wrote to Bruckner about another girl who had attracted his attention and asked about his 'Berlin girl' (no doubt, tongue in cheek) -was it true that 'Dr. Bruckner will be getting married'? The originals of Ida's letters are not available; the original of Bruckner's letter to Waldeck is also not available but the original of Leitenmayr's letter to Bruckner can be found in St. Florian. Also see Max von Oberleithner's reminiscences and Stephen Johnson, op.cit., 64ff. for Bruckner's friendship with Ida and his relationships with women in general.

they were on their way back to Vienna that normality began to return![200]

Nevertheless, there was no doubt that Bruckner's *Te Deum* had made a significant impression in Berlin. On 15 June, Siegfried Ochs wrote to send greetings from a number of his Berlin admirers who wished to receive a signed photograph. More important from Bruckner's point of view, however, was the information that a Berlin publishing house, Raabe and Plothow, had expressed interest in publishing the Eighth Symphony. An 'up front' payment of 1200 florins would be required. Ochs said that he would be prepared to supervise the printing and asked Bruckner to send the full score and piano score of the work.[201] In his reply Bruckner said that he would accept Raabe and Flotow's offer, and sent his best wishes to his Berlin friends. He thanked Ochs once again for his inspired direction and hoped that he and von Bülow would perform some of his symphonies in the future.[202]

Compared with the various problems Bruckner experienced in having his symphonies published, negotiations with the Innsbruck firm, Johann Groß, concerning the publication of the D minor Mass and several early short sacred pieces (5 settings of *Tantum ergo*, a setting of the *Pange lingua* and the 1856 setting of *Ave Maria*) were extremely uncomplicated thanks to the help of the industrialist Theodor Hämmerle, an admirer of the composer and son-in-law of Simon Reiß who owned the firm. A contract was signed at the end of June and Bruckner entrusted Oberleithner with the responsibility of preparing the scores and checking the

---

200 See Oberleithner's reminiscence, as printed in *G-A* IV/3, 158ff, and Stephen Johnson, op.cit., 67f.

201 See *ABB*, 341f.; the original is in St. Florian

202 See *ABB*, 249f. for Bruckner's letter, dated Vienna, 26 June 1891. On 31 July Joseph Schalk wrote to Oberleithner re corrections to the Eighth Symphony which he felt were necessary to 'save' the work; see *ABA*, 105, and original in the *ÖNB*, F32 Oberleithner 168. A few days later, on 5 August, Schalk wrote to Oberleithner again about the corrections and advised him to 'chase up' the publishers; see *ABA*, 33 (facsimile), 105 (text) and original in the *ÖNB*, F32 Oberleithner.

proofs.[203]

Also at the end of June (Monday 29th) concert-goers in London heard the first British performance of the Third Symphony. It was the last item in a concert conducted by Hans Richter in the St. James's Hall and was preceded by Haydn's Symphony no. 101 in D and some excerpts from Wagner's operas (one of Elisabeth's arias from *Tannhäuser*, the *Vorspiel* and *Liebestod* from *Tristan und Isolde*, and Senta's ballad from *Der fliegende Holländer*). In a review of the symphony in *The Guardian*, the author recalled Richter's performance of the Seventh in London in 1887, describing that symphony as 'little more than a sonorous medley of Wagnerian reminiscences'. Discussing the Third, he avoided any mention of Wagnerian influence, but compared it unfavourably with Beethoven and took both Richter and the Viennese to task for a lack of critical judgment:

> ...Herr Bruckner, with all his learning - or, perhaps, because of all his learning - has not escaped perpetrating one of the naïvest 'cribs' on record. He starts away in D minor, and with one of the most characteristic themes from the Choral Symphony of Beethoven also in the same key. The theme is diluted, but it is unmistakable and it is brought back in the finale. Other Beethovenish reminiscences abound. For the rest the symphony is, to use a favourite word of the author of the analytical programmes, extremely 'strepitous'. Herr Bruckner here has the advantage of Beethoven; he has a bigger band, and he makes all possible use of it. The work is not dull; it is a strange mixture of learning and frivolity, like a professor masquerading as a pierrot. But it is one of the most remarkable examples of which we are aware of the giant's robe in music. The Viennese must be strangely forgetful of their greatest composer. As for Dr. Richter, we can only explain the anomaly on the supposition that the immense amount of music he has produced has tended to

---

203 See *G-A* IV/3, 164-68, Nowak's preface to *ABSW* XVI and *ABSW* XXI, *Revisionbericht*. The full score and piano score (arr. Ferdinand Löwe) of the Mass appeared in print in the spring of 1892. The shorter pieces were published in 1893.

blunt his critical faculties...[204]

For some time Bruckner had cherished the ambition of securing an honorary doctorate and had written to several foreign universities without success. Now at last some of his friends sensed that the time was right to obtain testimonials from prominent musicians with a view to putting his name forward in Vienna. Indeed Bruckner himself sent a telegram to Hermann Levi to ask him for a testimonial; but Levi, in his reply, suggested that it would be better and more diplomatic if one of his friends or colleagues approached him.[205] After a formal approach had been made, Levi sent a testimonial to Professor Simon Reinisch, Dean of the Faculty of Philosophy at the University, warmly supporting Bruckner's application and describing him as 'the most important symphonist of the post-Beethoven period'.[206] Hanslick declined to give his support, but Hellmesberger provided a very positive testimonial in which he said that it was:

... a real pleasure to have the opportunity of expressing his conviction

---

204   From review in *The Guardian* (8 July 1891), signed 'C.L.G.' See Röder, op.cit., 430f.

205   See *GrBLS*, 349 for Bruckner's telegram, dated Vienna, 17 June 1891; the original is in the *Gesellschaft der Musikfreunde* library. See *ABB*, 325f. for Levi's reply, which is dated Munich, 16 June 1891 (obviously a mistake as it refers to the telegram and must have been written after its receipt); the original is in St. Florian.

206   See *GrBLS*, 349ff. for Levi's testimonial, dated Bayreuth, 24 June 1891. It was drafted the day before, however, and Felix Mottl suggested some changes. See *ABA*, 4 (facsimile of original in the *ÖNB*) and 95 (text of draft). See also Franz Grasberger, *Anton Bruckner zwischen Wagnis und Sicherheit. Ausstellung im Rahmen des Internationalen Brucknerfestes* (Linz, 1977), 98 for the text of the corrected form; the original is in the *Österreichisches Staatsarchiv*. Bruckner wrote to Levi on 23 October to inform him that the Emperor had confirmed his honorary doctorate and to thank him again for the part he had played in providing a reference. He also recommended Franz Schalk for a vacant post in Munich. See *GrBLS*, 351; the original is in the *Gesellschaft der Musikfreunde* library.

as a musician that Bruckner is one of the most important, if not the most important, contemporary composer of the symphony whose works in this category as well as in the realms of church music and chamber music bear the stamp of originality and of technical mastery.[207]

At a professorial meeting on 4 July, Bruckner's name was officially proposed by Professor Josef Stefan, Professor of Physics. The proposal was accepted and confirmed by Senate on 10 July, and the Ministry for Education and Culture was officially informed on 11 July. Imperial sanction was given on 29 September and the Senate was informed of the Emperor's approval on 2 October.[208] On 19 October Bruckner asked a member of the college of Professors if he could ensure that the certificate of his honorary doctorate included a reference to him as a 'symphonist'.[209]

During his summer vacation Bruckner visited Bayreuth and attended performances of Parsifal, Tannhäuser (the Bayreuth premiere of the Paris version was on 22 July) and, possibly, Tristan. He spent most of August in Steyr where he worked on his Ninth Symphony and played the organ at some services in the parish church.[210] He

---

207 See G-A IV/3, 179f. for Hellmesberger's testimonial, dated Vienna, 18 June 1891. On 31 October, Bruckner was a guest at a special ceremony to mark Hellmesberger's completion of forty years' service at the Conservatory.

208 See Robert Lach, Die Bruckner-Akten des Wiener Universitäts-Archives (Vienna, 1926), 54ff., G-A IV/3, 183-86, Schwanzara, op.cit., 72, and ABA,111; the originals of these documents can be found in Vienna University library and the Österreichisches Staatsarchiv.

209 See ABA, 95 and IGB Mitteilungsblatt 15 (Vienna, June 1979), 34. There is a facsimile in Renate Grasberger et al. eds., '"Symphoniker... mein Lebensberuf". Die Entfaltung des Schöpferischen bei Anton Bruckner' in Ausstellung des Anton Bruckner Institutes Linz Schwäbisches Hall 1990, 11; the original is in private possession. The addressee, who was asked to contact Professor Julius Hann, the new Dean of the Faculty, may have been Professor Reinisch, Hann's predecessor.

210 On 8 August, he wrote from Steyr to Weingartner to thank him for his congratulations (no doubt about his successful application for a doctorate) and to urge him to perform some of his works

was at St. Florian from 27 to 31 August,[211] stayed with his sister at Vöcklabruck for a few days and then spent a short time (5-7 September) at the home of the Reischl family in Altheim, Upper Austria. Minna, the daughter of the house, attracted his attention, but the eventual outcome was predictable![212] Bruckner returned to Steyr via Linz on 9 September and stayed there until 18 September, playing the organ in the parish church and in the neighbouring Benedictine monastery at Admont and

---

in Berlin. See *ABB*, 250 and *GrBB*, 132f.; the original is in the *Gesellschaft der Musikfreunde* library.

211 See *G-A* IV/3, 177 for a reference to a letter Bruckner sent from St. Florian to his *Hofkapelle* colleague, Pius Richter, on 30 August. He thanked Richter for standing in for him and said that he would be back in Vienna by 19 September; the original of this letter is in the *Wiener Stadt- und Landesbibliothek*.

212 For further details of his stay at Altheim, see *G-A* III/1, 614. On 16 September Minna wrote to Bruckner, regretting that she could not accept his 'most flattering proposal' and stressing that he should not 'entertain any future hopes'; but she wrote to him again at the beginning of October, enclosing her photograph; this photograph is now in the library of the *Bruckner-Konservatorium* in Linz. Bruckner replied, enclosing a photograph, on 23 October. On 7 November, the day of Bruckner's 'graduation', she wrote another letter, thanking him for his photograph and renewing her request for a 'Tantum ergo' which he had promised to compose for her. The original of Minna's first letter is in St. Florian, and the original of Bruckner's letter is privately owned; the originals of Minna's other letters have been lost. Correspondence with Waldeck in November and December suggests that he hoped his friend would act as a go-between. Waldeck had strong reservations, however; although, 'as an old acquaintance and friend', he held Bruckner in the highest esteem, he felt that he could not do anything on Bruckner's behalf 'because of the age difference - in a case such as this the decisive factor is the affection of the bride which should eliminate all other considerations' (from letter to Bruckner, dated 11 November 1891; the original is in St. Florian). Bruckner and Minna kept in touch for a few years, however. On 12 October 1893 she wrote to the composer that, although there was not yet a certain 'Yes', she hoped to get her parents' agreement eventually!; see *G-A* III/1, 615; the original has been lost..

befriending Franz Bayer, the new organist and choir director at Steyr.[213]

At the end of October Göllerich maintained wider German interest in Bruckner's music when he conducted a performance of the Fourth Symphony in Nuremberg.[214] Bruckner was delighted with the success and, in his letter of thanks to Göllerich, asked him to enlighten Porges in Munich who had written to him in 1890 about the Finale of the work, viz. it was not his intention to combine all the themes as he had done in the Finale of the Eighth Symphony.[215]

On 7 November Bruckner and a small circle of invited friends gathered in the senate hall of the University for the official degree ceremony. Professor Adolf Exner, the rector of the University, and Professor Josef Stefan, the Dean of the Faculty of Philosophy, both spoke of his signal contribution to the teaching and composition of music. Bruckner for his part said that he would have been able to provide a more eloquent response if an organ had been available![216] Nevertheless, Bruckner did provide an eloquent response - the dedication of the revised version of his First Symphony to the University. On 14 November, Professor Exner wrote to Bruckner

213 See *G-A* IV/3, 172-77; also Renate Grasberger and Erich W. Partsch, 'Bruckner - skizziert', *ABDS* 8 (Vienna, 1991), 47f. for an anecdote about the excursion to Admont. Writing to his brother Franz on 21 September, Joseph Schalk mentioned that Bruckner had just returned to Vienna from his summer vacation; see *LBSAB*, 163f. and F18 Schalk 158/12/23 for the original in the *ÖNB*.

214 The concert, which took place on 28 October, also included performances of Liszt's symphonic poem *Mazeppa* and E-flat Piano Concerto. It was thoroughly previewed and reviewed in the local press. There were also reports in other papers, including the *Musikalische Rundschau* (10 November), the *Ostdeutsche Rundschau* (10 November)and the *Neue Zeitschrift für Musik* 87 (25 November). See Franz Scheder, 'Frühe Bruckner-Aufführungen in Nürnberg' in *BJ 1989/90* (Linz, 1992), 237-44.

215 See *ABB*, 251 for this letter, dated Vienna, 31 October 1891; the original has been lost.

216 See *G-A* IV/3, 186-89; also *G-A* IV/3, 189-92 and Carl Almeroth, *Wie die Bruckner-Büste entstand* (Vienna: Engel, 1899; repr. Vienna, 1979) for details of Bruckner's sittings for the sculptor Viktor Tilgner at this time. See also *ABDS* 7 (Graz, 1990), 157f.

to thank him on behalf of the University for this dedication.[217]

Bruckner almost certainly received several congratulatory letters. Although some of these, and his replies, have been lost, several are extant.[218] More telegrams and good wishes were sent on and before Friday 11 December when the *Akademischer Gesangverein* organized a special celebration of Bruckner's achievement in the *Sophiensaal*. An estimated 3000 friends, students and colleagues attended to pay tribute to the composer, music by Wagner, Weber and Bruckner himself (his choral piece, *Germanenzug*) was performed, and several speeches were made. Bruckner was particularly moved by Professor Exner's speech which ended with the memorable sentence - 'I bow before the former assistant teacher in Windhaag'. He must have felt that the years of struggle and tribulation were now at an end and his achievements as a musician were at long last being given due recognition.[219]

---

217 See Robert Lach, op.cit., 59 and *G-A* IV/3 for the text of what is probably the draft of this letter, and *ABA*, 112 for what is probably the text of the fair copy; the original of the former is in the Vienna University library and that of the latter is in the *ÖNB*.

218 These include (a) a letter to Karl Waldeck (Vienna, 20 November 1891; see Franz Gräflinger, *Liebes und Heiteres um Anton Bruckner*, Vienna 1948; the original has been lost); (b) a letter to the *Frohsinn* choral society (Vienna, 20 November 1891; see *ABB*, 252; the original is in the *Singakademie* archives); (c) a letter to the Vienna Philharmonic (Vienna, 25 November 1891; see *GrBB*, 140f.; the original is in the Vienna Philharmonic archives); (d) a visiting card to Otto Kitzler (Vienna, November [no date given]; see *ABB*, 254 and *GrBB*, 54f.; the original has been lost).

219 See *G-A* IV/3, 196-201, which includes an extract from the Annual Report of the *Akademischer Gesangverein*; see also Schwanzara, op.cit., 76-79, Elisabeth Maier, 'Anton Bruckners Arbeitswelt' in *ABDS* 2 (Graz, 1980), 201ff., and Elisabeth Hilscher, 'Bruckner als Gelehrter - Bruckner als Geehrter' in *BSL 1988* (Linz, 1992), 123f. Bruckner's own copy of the programme is in the *ÖNB*, and the Annual Report of the *Akademischer Gesangverein* can be found in the Vienna University library. In *G-A* IV/3 Auer makes specific mention of the fact that Göllerich was not asked to give a speech, no doubt because of his strong nationalistic and anti-Semitic views and his tendency to make controversial statements. He was present at the celebration, however. Bruckner wrote to him on 5 December, mentioning forthcoming performances of his works in

One of Bruckner's friends who was presumably absent was Hans von Wolzogen who wrote to the composer regretting that he would not be able to attend forthcoming performances of his works in Vienna. He enclosed a little book - *Erinnerungen an Richard Wagner* - in which Bruckner was mentioned.[220]

The performances alluded to by Wolzogen were that of the revised version of the First Symphony by the Philharmonic conducted by Richter on 13 December and the *Te Deum* by the Philharmonic orchestra and chorus conducted by Wilhelm Gericke a week later, on 20 December. There was also a performance of the *Te Deum* in Amsterdam at the beginning of the month.[221]

The presence of almost 70 different dates in the autograph between 12 March 1890 and 18 April 1891 testifies to Bruckner's intensive revision on the First Symphony.[222] It is more than likely that Bruckner was present at rehearsals of the work and even took an active part in them.[223] After the concert, which also included

---

Vienna and looking forward to a possible reunion with his friend - see *ABB*, 252f.; the original of this letter is privately owned.

220 See *ABB*, 383f. for this letter, dated Bayreuth, 9 December 1891; the original is in St. Florian. The book was essentially a printed version of some lectures Wolzogen had given in different places, including Vienna, and also contained a reference to Bruckner's relationship with Wagner. See also earlier, page 618, footnotes 170 and 171.

221 The performance in Amsterdam, on 3 December was given by the *Excelsior* choral society and the Concertgebouw Orchestra conducted by Henri Viotta. See Nico Steffen, 'Die Bruckner-Tradition des Königlichen Concertgebouw-Orchesters - Teil 1' in *IBG Mitteilungsblatt* 39 (December 1992), 9 for further details, including an extract from the review of the concert in the *Algemeen Handelsblad* (6 December).

222 The important dates in the autograph (Mus.Hs. 19.473 in the *ÖNB*) are Finale, 12 March - 29 June 1890, Scherzo and Trio, 5 July - 17 August (in Steyr); Adagio, 18 August (also in Steyr) - 24 October; first movement, 25 November 1890 - 18 April 1891.

223 There is an entry by Bruckner himself - 'nach Belieben des P.T.H. Hofkapellmeisters' ('in accordance with the court music director's wishes') - at letter K in the Finale in an accurate copy of the autograph score in the Vienna Philharmonic Orchestra library (IV/24); other pencilled entries

works by Beethoven and Spohr, Bruckner wrote his customary letter of thanks to conductor and orchestra.[224]

There was the usual wide range of reactions in the press reviews. Writing in the *Deutsche Zeitung*, Theodor Helm, who had been given the opportunity of getting to know the work prior to its performance, spoke of its historical interest, viz. the fact that its original version was written at a time when Bruckner had very little knowledge of Wagner. The first movement exhibited a rich variety of ideas often combined in ingenious polyphonic combinations; their motivic inter-connection would only become clear after several hearings. While many composers would have been content to write just one of the melodies in the slow movement, Bruckner presented us with two equally delightful themes. This rich seam of melodic invention combined with exceptional instrumental awareness resulted in a movement of great originality - 'no Adagio of greater depth and significance has been written since Beethoven'. The rhythmically vital Scherzo and *Ländler*-like Trio movement was a worthy successor to the 'Lustiges Zusammensein der Landleute' movement in Beethoven's *Pastoral* symphony. In the finale, Bruckner made exhaustive use of a trill figure reminiscent of a similar figure in the third variation of Beethoven's String Quartet in C sharp minor op. 131, a work which he almost certainly did not know in 1865. As in the first movement there were also some

---

in this score are probably by Hans Richter. See Gunter Brosche's foreword to the edition of the Vienna version of the symphony - *ABSW* 1/2 (Vienna, 1980) - in which he refers to two earlier editions of this version, viz. the 1893 Doblinger edition of the score and parts (as well as a piano score arranged by Ferdinand Löwe) which should be treated with caution as it often differs from Bruckner's autograph and the copy used for engraving cannot be identified, and Robert Haas's much more accurate (but not always entirely reliable) 1935 score as part of the earlier Complete Edition.

224 See *ABB*, 253 and *GrBB*, 141 for this letter, dated Vienna, 16 December 1891; the original is in the Vienna Philharmonic archives.

'Wagnerisms'.[225]

In his review for *Die Presse*, Dr. Robert Hirschfeld remarked that the Vienna Philharmonic should have chosen a work already known to the public - the Third, Fourth or Seventh Symphonies - as a way of celebrating Bruckner's doctorate. It would have been better to reserve the First for a *Wagner-Verein* concert. It was a work from Bruckner's *Sturm und Drang* period. While many characteristic features of the later Bruckner symphonies were present in the work there was not the same organic unity and, particularly in the outer movements, too many subsidiary contrapuntal ideas got in the way of the main themes.[226]

Max Kalbeck described the symphony as 'all fantasy and hardly any reality. How beautifully it begins and how horribly it ends...' and conceived a rather bizarre programme for it. The only movement which gave him any pleasure was the Scherzo which was reminiscent of a Breughel painting in its earthiness.[227] In his equally scathing review in the *Illustriertes Wiener Extra-Blatt*, Josef Königstein wrote that the symphony demonstrated 'the composer's characteristic helplessness

---

225 Helm also points out that Bruckner heard *Tristan und Isolde* for the first time in Munich in June 1865, just a month after the completion date of the first movement of the symphony in its original version - 'Linz, 14 Mai 1865'. See *G-A* IV/3, 206-10 for the text of Helm's review (17 December 1891). Helm also provided a review for the *Musikalisches Wochenblatt* 23 (1892), 4f. and 16f.

226 See Rudolf Louis, *Anton Bruckner* (Munich: Müller, 1918), 325ff. for this review, dated 24 December 1891; there is an extract in *G-A* IV/3, 210f. There was a solo piano performance of the second and fourth movements of the symphony at a *Wagner-Verein* concert on 30 December. Ferdinand Löwe was described as a 'peerless interpreter of Bruckner's music' who played the two movements 'from memory with thrilling effect'. My thanks to Dr. Andrea Harrandt for providing this information.

227 See Louis, op. cit., 324f. and *G-A* IV/3, 211ff. for this review which appeared in the *Wiener Montags-Revue*, 21 December 1891.

in constructing his large-scale works'. It lacked organic unity. Its best movement, the Scherzo, showed 'reasonable flow and reasonable harmonic logic' in its first half.[228]

Richard Heuberger had several reservations about the work - the last movement did not provide a satisfactory end to the symphony, and, in spite of many original and inventive ideas, the first movement contained a lot of monotonous patches - but found its orchestration brilliant and sonorous, albeit often too ornate and sumptuous. Bruckner had never been able to transfer the frugality of his private life to his organ playing and orchestral scoring![229] Felix von Wartenegg, the music critic for the *Neue Zeitschrift für Musik*, also found the Scherzo the most approachable movement. Because of their disjointedness, lack of proper thematic development and usually too noisy orchestration, the other movements would probably bring pleasure only to Bruckner's friends and admirers.[230]

Finally, Hans Paumgartner described the symphony as an 'interesting work' with a particularly successful Scherzo; the slow movement and Finale, however, had structural deficiencies and Bruckner tended to wander away from the straight path of formal consistency.[231]

One of Bruckner's friends, Gustav Schönaich, was eloquent in his appreciation of the work. Writing to Bruckner 'almost a week' after the performance, he said that it had greatly impressed him. He called it 'a doctorate for eternity ... a new

---

228 See Louis, op.cit., 323f. for this review, dated 14 December 1891.

229 See Louis, op.cit., 328f. and *G-A* IV/3, 213f. for Heuberger's review which appeared in the *Neue Musik-Zeitung* 13/1 (1892), 3.

230 See Louis, op.cit., 329 and Othmar Wessely, 'Bruckner-Berichterstattung in der Neuen Zeitschrift für Musik' in *BSL 1991* (Linz, 1994), 141f. for this review in the *Neue Zeitschrift für Musik* 88 (6 April 1892), 163.

231 This review appeared in the *Wiener Abendpost* on 18 December 1891. See Norbert Tschulik, 'Anton Bruckner in der Wiener Zeitung' in *BJ 1981* (Linz, 1982), 171f.

mountain... and the gates of hellish criticism will never prevail against it'.[232]

Both Hirschfeld and Paumgartner were more positive in their reviews of the *Te Deum* which was performed a week after the First Symphony. Hirschfeld felt that the obvious constraint of words prevented Bruckner from allowing his musical ideas to ramble. The work was clearly inspired by deeply-held religious convictions and its full effect may have been realised in the wider spaces of a church building.[233]

There is nothing to suggest that Bruckner spent his Christmas vacation away from Vienna. Perhaps he was too exhausted to visit St. Florian or Steyr. 1891 had been a successful and fulfilling year. 1892 was to bring the first performance of the revised version of the Eighth and the composition of three choral pieces, the motet *Vexilla Regis* WAB 51, the secular choral piece *Das deutsche Lied* WAB 63 and the setting of *Psalm 150* WAB 38 for choir and orchestra.

At the end of 1891 Richard Heuberger, a member of the committee planning the *Music and Theatre Exhibition* in Vienna in 1892, asked Bruckner if he would be prepared to compose a hymn or cantata for mixed choir and orchestra to be performed at the opening concert. Bruckner, unaware of the fact that Brahms had also been approached but had declined, wrote to Heuberger on 2 January 1892 to say that he would be willing to fulfil this request. Heuberger then suggested either Psalm 98 or Psalm 150 as a possible text.[234]

---

232 See *ABB*, 359f. and Andrea Harrandt, 'Gustav Schönaich - ein "Herold der Bruckner'schen Kunst"' in *BSL 1991* (Linz, 1994), 70 for this undated letter; the original is in the *ÖNB*.

233 Hirschfeld's review of the work followed his review of the First Symphony in *Die Presse*, 24 December 1891; see Louis, op.cit., 327f. Paumgartner's review appeared in the *Wiener Abendpost*, 23 December 1891; see Tschulik, op.cit., 177. In a review of the 1891 Vienna concert season in the *Neue Zeitschrift für Musik* 88 (1892), 139, Felix von Wartenegg referred to the 'very small audience' at the concert on 20 December; see Othmar Wessely, loc. cit., 141.

234 See *G-A* IV/3, 230f. and Franz Grasberger, foreword to the score in the Complete Edition, *ABSW* XX/6 (Vienna, 1964) for references to Heuberger's original letter to Bruckner (23 December

The score of the D minor Mass was now in print and Siegfried Ochs, who had just received a copy, wrote to Bruckner with immense enthusiasm. He hoped to be able to perform the *Te Deum* the following season and the Mass at a later date.[235] Bruckner was delighted with Ochs's interest in the two works and informed him of the recent successful performance of the *Te Deum* in Vienna. He described Ochs as his 'second artistic father' [Levi was his first] and recommended his First Symphony and other symphonies for future performance. The First Symphony was his 'most difficult and best'. Although it was 'difficult to understand after one hearing', it made a 'considerable impression'.[236]

The first new composition of the year was the motet *Vexilla Regis*. It is Bruckner's last smaller sacred work and was written between 4 and 9 February, possibly in response to a request from Deubler in St. Florian for a hymn for the Good Friday liturgy, but more probably from an 'inner urge'.[237] On 7 March he enclosed the motet with a letter to Deubler:

> ... I have composed it following the dictates of a pure heart. May it find grace! My request would be that Mr. Aigner rehearses it very

---

1891) and Bruckner's reply; the original of Heuberger's letter to Bruckner is in St. Florian, but the location of the original of Bruckner's reply is unknown.

235 See *ABB*, 342f. for Ochs's letter to Bruckner, dated Berlin, 20 January 1892; the original is in St. Florian.

236 See *ABB*, 255f. and *GrBB*, 96f. for Bruckner's letter, dated Vienna, 3 February 1892; the location of the original is unknown.

237 See *ABSW* XXI/1 (Vienna, 1984), 186 and full critical report in *ABSW* XXI/2, 148-58. The autograph score (Mus. Hs. 24.262) and sketches (dated 4 February 1892; Mus. Hs. 28.228) are located in the *ÖNB*. The motet was first published in 1892 by Weinberger Verlag in an *Album der Wiener Meister* specially produced for the *Music and Theatre Exhibition*. For a modern edition, see *ABSW* XXI/1, 159-64.

slowly and thoroughly with the boys!...[238]

The first performance of the motet was in St. Florian abbey on Good Friday (15 April). Bruckner was unable to attend because of swollen feet. He wrote to Deubler on 14 June to thank him for the performance and to apologize for his absence.[239]

On 7 March Bruckner informed Heuberger that he had decided to set *Psalm 150* 'on account of its particular majesty' and on 31 March he said that he would prefer to think in terms of the closing concert of the Exhibition for the performance of the work because he would not have it ready in time for the opening:

> ... So far as I can judge at the moment, it will be impossible for me to have the 150th Psalm ready for the opening in spite of the capacity for work which I - an old man - still possess (the closing ceremony would be a better proposition). But the problems of rehearsal!!![240]

Composition of the psalm was also mentioned in letters to Theodor Helm and Oddo Loidol.[241]

---

238 See *ABB*, 257; the original is in St. Florian.

239 See *ABB*, 259 for this letter, and *G-A* IV/3, 219f. for further discussion; the location of the original of the letter is unknown. Timothy Jackson subjects the work to detailed harmonic and rhythmical analysis in his article 'Bruckner's Metrical Numbers' in *19th-Century Music* xiv/2 (1990), 114-27; there is a facsimile of the first of two pages of sketches on page 118.

240 See *G-A* IV/3, 231 for extracts from both letters which were first printed in their entirety in the *Neues Wiener Tagblatt*, 13 March 1936; the location of the originals in unknown.

241 He also told Helm that the writer of a recent article in the Berlin *Börsen-Courier* (on 17 March) had recommended the performance of his Fourth Symphony in the city; see *ABB*, 256f. and *GrBB*, 42f. for Bruckner's letter to Helm, dated Vienna, 26 March 1892; the location of the original is unknown. Bruckner was writing to Loidol in Kremsmünster to say how delighted he was to receive an invitation from the abbot to spend the Whit holiday period at the abbey. Unfortunately work on the Psalm might prevent him from taking up the offer - in which case he hoped that the

In 1877-78 Gustav Mahler was largely responsible for a four-hand arrangement of the second version of Bruckner's Third Symphony. Now, fifteen years later, in his capacity as music director in Hamburg, he arranged for Bruckner's *Te Deum* to be performed in the Good Friday concert there. He was obviously taking a risk, as Hamburg was a Brahms stronghold and a previous attempt by Julius Bernuth to schedule the work in a *Singakademie* programme had been unsuccessful. One of Bruckner's pupils, William Sichal, rehearsed the choir and his obvious enthusiasm for the work and Mahler's excellent conducting on the day of the concert guaranteed a success. The day after the performance Mahler wrote to Bruckner to say that the work had been received with tumultuous applause and he had made a definite 'breakthrough' in the city. He would send some newspaper reviews in due course.[242] Wilhelm Zinne wrote to Bruckner two days later, describing Mahler as a 'true admirer of your works'. He enclosed some newspaper reviews and mentioned Hermann Kretzschmar's hostility and von Bülow's lack of understanding.[243]

---

invitation could be postponed until the summer vacation; see *ABB*, 257f. and *GrBB*, 68f. for Bruckner's letter to Loidol, dated Vienna, 26 April, 1892. In fact, on 1 June, Bruckner wrote again to Loidol, complaining about the heat and saying that swelling of his feet, particularly the right one, prevented him from playing the organ and getting about much. He would not be able to travel to Kremsmünster for the Whit period; see *ABB*, 258 and *GrBB*, 69; the originals of the letters to Loidol are in Kremsmünster abbey.

242 See *ABB*, 329f. for this letter, dated Hamburg, 16 April 1892; there is a facsimile in Auer, *Bruckner* (Zurich/Leipig/Vienna, 1923), supplement; the original is in St. Florian abbey.

243 See *ABB*, 387ff. for Zinne's letter, dated Hamburg, 18 April 1892; the location of the original is unknown.. Later in the year (in July), on the way to Italy for a holiday, Zinne and his wife visited Bruckner, and the two men met on another occasion during the Exhibition. See *G-A* IV/3, 246-56 for Zinne's recollection of the visit, his description of Bruckner's apartment, Bruckner's playing to him of extracts from his works, the Eighth and Ninth Symphonies in particular, etc. On 6 August, Zinne wrote to Bruckner to send him holiday greetings from Naples; see *ABB*, 391f. ; the location of the original is unknown.   Hermann Kretzschmar's hostility is not surprising in view of his

Reviewing the *Te Deum* in the *Hamburger Korrespondent*, Josef Sittard detected the same characteristics which were hallmarks of the symphonies, namely the sudden juxtaposition of 'often completely heterogeneous episodes which are harmonically self-sufficient', the 'sharply delineated subdivision in periodic structure', and the 'rich harmonic language'. Although a master of instrumentation, Bruckner only used thick colours where they were necessary.[244] In the *Hamburger Tageblatt*, Louis Bödecker wrote that the work deserved to be ranked alongside Berlioz's *Te Deum* and Liszt's *Graner Festmesse*. From beginning to end its expressive power was overwhelming.[245] Emil Krause's review in the *Fremdenblatt* 'damned with faint praises' - an attitude which, according to Zinne, was not surprising in view of his negative opinion of the Seventh Symphony.[246]

The *Te Deum*, with its combination of religious fervour, choral splendour and striking orchestral colours, was fast becoming Bruckner's most 'exportable' work. Another performance - in the USA at the end of May - had an enormous choir of about 800 singers and attracted a huge crowd of almost 7000.[247]

In the meantime plans for a performance of the Eighth in Vienna were making slow progress. At the end of January Joseph Schalk wrote to Franz in somewhat pessimistic terms about this projected performance and foresaw more 'bitter

---

negative criticism of Bruckner's Seventh in his *Führer durch den Konzertsaal*. On the other hand, von Bülow's alleged 'lack of understanding' is more surprising in view of his positive attitude towards the work after the Berlin performance in May 1891.

244   See *G-A* IV/3, 224ff. for this review, dated 16 April 1892.

245   See *G-A* IV/3, 226f. for this review, dated 17 April 1892.

246   See *G-A* IV/3, 227f. for this review, dated (no doubt erroneously) 15 April 1892.

247   The performance took place in Cincinatti on 26 May and was conducted by Theodor Thomas. In his letter to Loidol (26 April; see above, footnote 241), Bruckner mentioned both the Hamburg and forthcoming 'St. Louis' performances of the *Te Deum*; it is more than likely that he was confusing St. Louis with Cincinatti.

experiences' for the composer.[248] The appearance of the symphony in print - published by the Berlin firm, Robert Lienau (represented by Robert Haslinger in Vienna) - in March, however, meant that a major obstacle had been removed.[249] Bruckner referred to the symphony in a letter to Helm at the end of March; he pointed out that the 'deutscher Michel' of the Scherzo was 'certainly not a joke - the Austrian/German character is intended...'[250] By the time he wrote to Loidol a month later he knew that the Eighth would be performed in Vienna during the following concert season.[251]

After its highly successful Bruckner evening in December 1891, the *Akademischer Gesangverein* was probably confident that the composer would respond positively to a request for a choral piece to be composed specially for the *Deutschakademisches Sängerfest* in Salzburg at the beginning of June 1892. Bruckner duly obliged with *Das deutsche Lied* for male voices, four horns, three trumpets, 3 trombones and tuba. The words were provided by Erich Fels (Professor Aurelius Polzer) of Graz, and, according to the date on the autograph, the piece was composed on 29 April.[252] Seventeen choirs took part in the festival and Bruckner's work was given its first performance by three massed choirs (including the *Wiener Akademische Gesangverein*) in the *Aula academica*, Salzburg on Pentecost Sunday, 5 June. As in *Sängerbund*, written for the *Oberösterreichisch-Salzburgischer Sängerfest*

---

248   See *LBSAB*, 166 for an extract from this letter, dated Vienna, 29 January 1892; the original is in the *ÖNB*, F18 Schalk 158/13/4.

249   Emperor Franz Josef also arranged for 1500 florins to be given towards the printing. The work was published both in full score and in a piano-duet arrangement made by Joseph Schalk.

250   From Bruckner's letter to Helm, dated Vienna, 26 March 1892; see footnote 241.

251   He provided this information in his letter, dated Vienna, 26 April 1892; see footnote 241.

252   The autograph is in the *ÖNB*, Mus. Hs. 3187, and the sketches are in the *Gesellschaft der Musikfreunde* library.

in Wels ten years earlier, Bruckner quoted deliberately from Kalliwoda's well-known male-voice chorus, *Das deutsche Lied.*[253]

The International Music and Theatre Exhibition in Vienna opened on Saturday 7 May. The *Akademischer Wagner-Verein* was responsible for several of the concerts. On the evening of 15 June, an Exhibition Orchestra specially assembled by Hermann Grädener gave a performance of Bruckner's Fourth Symphony. The conductor was Joseph Schalk.[254] Hans Puchstein provided a comprehensive review in the *Deutsches Volksblatt* and was extremely critical of Hanslick's failure to recognize Bruckner's stature. Schalk's conducting also received warm praise.[255]

253 Bruckner was present when this choral piece was performed again in Vienna on 2 July. For further information, see *G-A* IV/3, 235f.; Theodor Helm, 'Anton Bruckner als Männerchor-Componist' in *Festblätter zum 6. deutschen Sängerbundesfest in Graz 1902/* no. 3, 86; and Andrea Harrandt, 'Bruckner und das bürgerliche Musiziergut seiner Jugendzeit' in *BSL* 1987 (Linz, 1989), 97f. Harrandt provides short extracts from three reviews of the piece - in the *Ostdeutsche Rundschau* (10 July 1892 and 10 June 1899) and the *Jahrbuch des Wiener akademischen Gesang-Vereins* 1891/92, 53. See also Elisabeth Hilscher, 'Bruckner als Gelehrter - Bruckner als Geehrter' in *BSL 1988* (Linx, 1992), 120f. for the reviews of the work in the *Deutsches Volksblatt* (8 June and 7 July 1892)and *Ostdeutsche Rundschau* (12 June 1892). *Das deutsche Lied* WAB 63, edited by Viktor Keldorfer, was first published in 1911 by Universal Edition (U.E. 3300). The *Akademischer Gesang -Verein* also performed Bruckner's *Germanenzug* during the Festival. It was reviewed by Josef Stolzing in the *Ostdeutsche Rundschau* (5 June 1892).

254 On 28 May Joseph wrote to Franz and referred to this concert which included music by Wagner and Liszt as well as Wolf's *Das Fest auf Solhaug* for chorus and orchestra. The original date was Sunday 12 June but it was put back three days. See *LBSAB*, 167 for an extract from this letter; the original is in the *ÖNB*, F18 Schalk 158/13/8. See also Bruckner's letter to Deubler (14 June; footnote 239) in which he mentioned the performance of the symphony the following evening and added that his Third Symphony and perhaps also his Seventh would be performed later.

255 See *G-A* IV/3, 237-42 for this review, dated 29 June 1892; there is also an extract in *LBSAB*, 168. Bruckner had written to Puchstein earlier in the year, mentioning that Speidel had confused his Second Symphony, first performed in 1873, with his First. See *ABB*, 254f. for this letter, dated

The *Wiener Männergesangverein* conducted by Eduard Kremser performed *Germanenzug* on 20 June and Ferdinand Löwe made his debut as a Bruckner conductor when he conducted the Exhibition Orchestra in a performance of the Third Symphony on 9 July.[256]

Siegfried Ochs made further contact with Bruckner in June.[257] He said that he was willing to conduct the *Te Deum* during the Composers' Convention in Vienna later in the year. He then alluded to plans for performing other Bruckner works in Berlin as well as his intention of broaching the subject of the Eighth once again with Weingartner:

> ... Next winter I intend to perform your Mass or give a repeat performance of the Te Deum here. We want to perform Berlioz's Requiem and, as it lasts only three quarters of an hour [sic!], a second work would fit in very well. Weingartner is coming to see me tomorrow evening and I will use the opportunity to broach the subject of the Eighth Symphony. Richter is conducting three concerts here, however. Could he not bring one of your symphonies?
>
> I only wish that I had the opportunity; then I would perform them one after the other. I now possess the scores of the E major, E flat major, D minor and Eighth Symphonies. How blind the conductors of our symphony concerts are to allow such magnificent works to escape their attention! But rest assured that I am doing what I can to prevail upon others to perform your works when, unfortunately, I am not in a position to be able to conduct them myself.[258]

Vienna, 3 January 1892; the original is owned privately. The performance of the Fourth was also reviewed in other papers, including the *Musikalisches Wochenblatt* (Theodor Helm) and *Vaterland*.

256   See Erich Schenk, 'Ferdinand Löwe' in *IBG Mitteilungsblatt* 26 (October 1985), 5-11; also *LBSAB*, 167f.

257   Hugo Wolf wrote to Ochs after the performance of the Fourth and described it as 'nothing less than a cannibalistic success'.

258   See *ABB*, 343ff. for the full text of this letter, dated Berlin, 18 June 1892; the original is in St. Florian

Bruckner still clung to the hope that Levi would be able to conduct the Eighth Symphony in Munich, however.[259] But this was not to be.

During the summer Bruckner increased his future financial security by entering into a contract with the Viennese publisher, Josef Eberle, which gave the latter the exclusive right to print the First, Second, Fifth and Sixth Symphonies, the E minor and F minor Masses, Psalm 150, some male voice compositions, and any works that Bruckner would compose in the future. Bruckner was guaranteed a percentage of receipts as well as an annual payment of 300 florins, commencing 1893.[260]

Also during his summer vacation Bruckner visited Bayreuth for the last time. He travelled on the special train chartered by the *Wagner-Verein* and was warmly greeted on his arrival. Unfortunately, because he was surrounded by so many well-wishers, he temporarily lost contact with his porter and discovered that he did not have his suitcase when he arrived at his hotel. Much to his relief the honest porter had taken it to the local police-station where he was able to retrieve it.[261] After returning to Vienna,[262] he spent a few days with his pupil Cyrill Hynais in Klosterneuburg and then a short time at Steyr before going to Carlsbad for the

---

259 This is made clear in his letter to Levi, dated Vienna, 24 July 1892, in which he also mentions his ill health, the completion of Psalm 150 etc. See *GrBLS*, 353. The original is in the *Gesellschaft der Musikfreunde* library, Vienna, and there is a facsimile in **Plate 5**.

260 This contract was signed by both parties on 14 July 1892. See *G-A* IV/3, 259-62 for details of the contract; there is a copy of this contract in the private possession of the Hueber family in Vöcklabruck.

261 The whole episode is recounted in *G-A* IV/3, 262ff.

262 See *G-A* IV/3, 246-52 for Wilhelm Zinne's reminiscences of time spent in Vienna with Bruckner in late July.

648

cure.[263]

Bruckner was rather annoyed that the *Allgemeiner deutsche Musikverein*, which had moved its Composers' Convention from Munich to Vienna for 1892, was considering a performance of his Psalm 150 and not one of his symphonies. In a letter to Adolf Koch von Langentreu, vice-president of the *Gesellschaft der Musikfreunde*, he pointed out that the Psalm was already earmarked for the closing concert of the *Music and Theatre Exhibition* and expressed his surprise that, in Vienna of all places, one of his symphonies had not been selected for performance. After all, Levi had been prepared to perform either the Seventh or Eighth Symphony in Munich.[264] Bruckner learned on 1 August that only a quarter of an hour was being allotted to each composer in the Convention concerts and that Brahms and Goldmark, for example, were only having short overtures played. Writing to Hynais from Steyr on 11 August he asked him to negotiate with Gutmann about his fee (for providing a piano/vocal score of the Psalm), to find out whether Gericke or Richter was

263 On 27 July Bruckner wrote from Vienna to his brother Ignaz in St. Florian, sending him name-day wishes and enclosing a gift of ten florins. He mentioned that he had to go to Carlsbad to take the cure; the original of this letter is in the *Gesellschaft der Musikfreunde* library. It was during this period that Bruckner wrote to the Lord Chamberlain's office requesting retirement from *Hofkapelle* duties on the grounds of ill-health, and enclosing a medical report (dated 11 July 1892) signed by three doctors, which gave details of his medical condition; see *ABDS* 1, 116-19, and Manfred Wagner, *Bruckner* (Mainz, 1983), 206f.

264 Letter dated Vienna, 27 July 1892. Bruckner also mentioned that he was about to leave for Steyr; from there he would go to Carlsbad. See *ABB*, 259f. and *GrBB*, 33f for this letter, which was first printed in the *Neue Zeitschrift für Musik* 84 (1917); the location of the original is unknown. Bruckner also informed Albert Gutmann on the same day (27 July) that Bronsart von Schellendorf, the president of the *Allgemeiner deutsche Musikverein*, would prefer a performance of the shorter Psalm instead of the longer Seventh Symphony; a facsimile of this letter can be found in Albert Gutmann, *Aus dem Wiener Musikleben. Künstlererinnerungen* (Vienna, 1914); the original of this letter is owned privately.

conducting the work at the closing concert of the Exhibition, and to give him the dates of the final three rehearsals so that he could attend them if necessary. The performance of the work at the Composers' Convention could be regarded as a sort of dress rehearsal for the Exhibition concert.[265]

While he was in Steyr Bruckner also wrote with some concern to his friend Oddo Loidol who had been ill. He mentioned his own illness and the need to take a cure, adding that he had finished composing Psalm 150.[266] He wrote to *Frohsinn* in Linz, probably in response to a request from the choral society, and said that he had written *Das deutsche Lied* for the *Wiener Akademische Gesangverein* for performance at the Salzburg Choir Festival.[267] During his time in Steyr he took the opportunity of visiting Kronstorf to search for the manuscripts of the sacred works he had written while a student teacher there. Unfortunately, because the schoolmaster was not at home, he had to leave empty-handed! His poor health probably prevented him from taking up Johann Burgstaller's invitation to play the organ in Linz.[268] When he sent name-day greetings to Deubler in St. Florian on 18 August, he wrote:

---

265 Bruckner was making the point that the Composers' Convention was actually part of the *Music and Theatre Exhibition*. See *ABB*, 261f.; the original is in the *ÖNB*.

266 See *ABB*, 260 and *GrBB*, 70 for this letter, dated Steyr, 2 August 1892; the original is in Kremsmünster

267 See *ABB*, 261 for this letter, dated Steyr, 2 August 1892. Later in the year Bruckner sent the score of this choral piece to *Frohsinn*; see *ABB* , 265 for the accompanying letter, dated Vienna, 18 October. The originals of both letters are in the *Singakademie* archives in Linz.

268 See *G-A* IV/3, 267. Franz Bayer accompanied him on his visit to Kronstorf. Burgstaller had asked him to play at a special Pontifical Mass.

... I am in Steyr with swollen feet and am not able to play the organ; I need the Carlsbad cure. I have to return to Vienna for the German Music Festival in September. According to letters from Weimar, they want to perform my newest composition, Psalm 150.[269]

On the same day he informed Hynais that the first rehearsal of his Psalm 150 would be in Vienna on 5 September. He asked him to use a piano score or, if one was not yet available, to play from the full score at the rehearsal.[270]

Once again there was some romantic interest of an innocent nature during the summer months, the first episode concerning a Hungarian waitress called Aurelia Stolzar whom he had met at the *Music and Theatre Exhibition* in Vienna in July. He sent her his photograph, received a letter of thanks from her with photograph enclosed on 17 August, and wrote to her again from Steyr on 23 August.[271] The second episode, concerning Anna Rogl, a young lady he met during a brief sojourn in St. Florian in August or September, is described in some detail in Göllerich-Auer. He wrote to Anna from Steyr on 1 October, enclosing a photograph and suggesting a meeting at Amstetten on 5 October.[272] On 19 September Bruckner also received

---

269   See *ABB*, 262; the original is in the *ÖNB*.

270   See *ABB*, 263 for Bruckner's letter to Hynais, dated Steyr, 18 August 1892; the original is in St. Florian.

271   See Walter Beck, op. cit., 73 for this letter and a facsimile of the dedication and photograph; the original of the photograph is in the Beck Collection, Munich. See *ABA*, 80 for Aurelia's letter to Bruckner; the original of her photograph is in the library of the *Bruckner-Konservatorium*, Linz. Thje original of Bruckner's second letter to Aurelia Stolzar is in the *ÖNB*.

272   See *G-A* II/1, 311ff. for further information, and *ABB*, 264 for Bruckner's letter; the original is in the *Oberösterreichisches Landesmuseum*, Linz. The meeting took place at the home of Baron Lederer where Anna Rogl was a chambermaid.

another letter from Ida Buhz in Berlin.[273]

Bruckner stayed in Upper Austria until the beginning of October. The Composers' Convention was cancelled because of exaggerated rumours of a cholera outbreak, and it was felt that it would not be suitable to conclude the *Music and Theatre Exhibition*, which had run into severe financial problems, with a work like Psalm 150. He spent the period 19-25 September in Kremsmünster where he visited the indisposed Oddo Loidol and continued work on his Ninth Symphony.[274]

While he was on holiday at Adalbert von Goldschmidt's villa in Grundlsee during the summer, Franz Schalk informed Joseph for the first time about his revision of Bruckner's Fifth Symphony the first performance of which he wanted to give in Graz:

> ... My work on the Vth progresses very slowly but I am moving forwards. I have now arrived at the final bars of the first movement. I had enormous difficulty with the development section. Löwe will find little to please him there, as my chief concern was to retain all the subsidiary contrapuntal motives as far as possible... Goldschmidt goes to Carlsbad next week. From then on I hope to take gigantic strides forward and even bring my work to its conclusion during the

273 See *G-A* IV/3, 270ff. for extracts from this letter and another letter, dated Berlin, 17 November 1892. In both letters, Ida expresses concern for Bruckner's health and interest in performances of his works; the location of the originals is unknown.

274 See *G-A* IV/3, 268f. for Loidol's record of Bruckner's stay. On 18 October, Bruckner wrote to Loidol from Vienna, and enclosed two pieces which he had promised to send to the Kremsmünster *Gymnasium* pupils, viz. the plainchant harmonization *Iam lucis* WAB 18 (1868) and his 'favourite "Tantum ergo"', the *Pange lingua* WAB 33 (1868; publ. 1885). See *ABB*, 264f. and *GrBB*, 71ff.; the original is in Kremsmünster abbey. On 26 November the organist at Kremsmünster abbey, Josef Leitenmayr, provided Bruckner with some information about a young lady who had attracted his attention during his stay; see *G-A* IV/3, 270 and footnote 199.

holidays...[275]

On 23 September Franz asked Joseph to enquire whether the publisher Eberle would cover the cost of printing the new parts for the Fifth. As far as his own involvement with the symphony was concerned, he had done a lot of preparatory work on the Finale 'in his head' without writing it down as yet. Nevertheless, he hoped that everything would be finished in time for a performance either in November or March.[276] A month later Joseph wrote to Franz to report that Bruckner was well and was hoping to hear from him about the performance of the Fifth. He himself (i.e. Joseph) was continuing his revision work on the orchestration of the F minor Mass which he was finding difficult because of lack of experience. There was no question of any crisis of conscience concerning these unauthorized tinkerings with Bruckner's original intentions. Both Joseph and Franz had an idealistic view of their efforts, seeing them as acts of friendship.[277] On 9 December Franz asked Joseph to send him [the first] three movements of the Fifth,[278] and Joseph replied that he would send them 'as soon as you wish'.[279]

Bruckner resumed his University teaching at the beginning of October but his long period of service at the *Hofkapelle* came to an end. His resignation on grounds of

---

275 See *LBSAB*, 168 for this extract from Franz Schalk's letter to Joseph, dated Grundlsee, 14 August 1892; the original is in the *ÖNB*, F18 Schalk 158/13/9.

276 See *LBSAB*, 168f.; the original is in the *ÖNB*, F18 Schalk 158/13/11. Nowak dates this letter 25 November 1892 in the *Revisionsbericht* of his edition of Symphony no. 5 (Vienna, 1985), 69.

277 See *LBSAB*, 169 for an extract from Joseph's letter to Franz, dated Vienna, 25 October 1892; the original is in the *ÖNB*, F18 Schalk 158/13/13

278 Mentioned by Nowak in Symphony no. 5 *Revisionsbericht*, 70.

279 See *LBSAB*, 169f. and Nowak, op.cit., 70 for this letter, dated Vienna, 11 December 1892; the original is in the *ÖNB*, F18 Schalk 158/13/15.

ill-health was accepted in October and Hellmesberger wrote a formal letter to Bruckner to advise him of the decision.[280]

Towards the end of the year there were performances of Bruckner's Third Symphony in Amsterdam and The Hague,[281] and two important Bruckner premieres in Vienna - Psalm 150 in the first of the season's *Gesellschaft* concerts conducted by Wilhelm Gericke on 13 November, and the revised version of Symphony no. 8 in a Philharmonic concert conducted by Hans Richter on 18 December. The first edition of the Second Symphony, supervised by Cyrill Hynais, was also published at around the same time as Psalm 150.[282]

Dates in the autograph score of the Psalm indicate that Bruckner completed it on 29 June but made subsequent corrections on 7 and 11 July. It was published by Doblinger in November 1892.[283] A gap of nearly thirty years separates Psalm 150

---

280 Letter dated Vienna, 28 October 1892. See *G-A* IV/3, 273 and fuller details of the relevant documentation in *ABDS* 1, 120-24, including (1) Hellmesberger's letter to the Lord Chamberlain's office, dated 21 October, in which he recommends that Bruckner's resignation be accepted, 'all the more so as the artistic quality of his organ playing has been less than acceptable for several years'; (2) the draft of the letter from the Lord Chamberlain's office to the *Hofkapelle*, dated 24 October; (3) the draft of Hellmesberger's letter to Bruckner. The formality of the draft of the latter is very surprising. There are no expressions of gratitude for Bruckner's long period of service. Perhaps these were added in the fair copy?

281 The performances were given on 13 October in Amsterdam and 21 December in The Hague by the Concertgebouw Orchestra conducted by Willem Kes and Richard Hol respectively. See Cornelis van Zwol, 'Holland: ein Brucknerland seit 1885' in *BJ 1980* (Linz, 1981), 137; Nico Steffen (*IBG Mitteilungsblatt* 39), 9f.; Thomas Röder, op.cit., 432.

282 The copy made by Tenschert was used for the engraving. The symphony was published by Doblinger (full score, D. 1769; parts, D. 1770; piano score, arr. J. Schalk, D. 1806).

283 The autograph is in the *ÖNB*, Mus. Hs. 19.484. The plate number of the full score is D. 1859, and Cyrill Hynais was responsible for editing the piano score (D. 1780). Editions of the work since then include those by Universal Edition (U.E. 2906; 1910), Wiener Philharmonischer Verlag

from Bruckner's previous psalm setting. It is his last sacred composition for chorus and orchestra and embodies the fruits of a lifelong struggle for perfection, all 'ad maiorem Dei gloriam'. Together with the *Te Deum*, with which it has many features in common, it bears eloquent testimony to the composer's religious inspiration and displays a monumental, almost primitive strength of expression. Unfortunately, it was not well received at its first performance. Apparently there were too few rehearsals of what is by no means an easy work for singers in particular, and its placing in the programme - after a Schubert overture and before Liszt's Piano Concerto in E flat - militated against a favourable reception. Writing in *Die Presse*, Robert Hirschfeld accepted that the work had the richness of sound one would expect from a Bruckner composition. Unfortunately, however, the composer had not taken the limitations of the human voice into account, with the result that there were some impossible choral passages.[284] Hans Paumgartner was if anything more critical. It was one thing for Beethoven to stretch his voices to the limit in the Finale of the Ninth - this was the natural 'outflow and outward expression of the artist's vast inner life'. It was quite another for Bruckner to attempt the same thing - in his case it was merely 'unsingable and ugly'.[285] Hanslick had very little to say in his review in the *Neue Freie Presse*, but he criticised the Psalm's 'nasty chromatic progressions'.[286] Max Kalbeck thought that Bruckner had interpreted the Psalm to

---

(W.Ph.V. 205; 1924), Eulenburg (E.E. 4599; ed. Redlich, 1960) and Musikwissenschaftlicher Verlag (*ABSW* XX/6; ed. Grasberger, 1964).

284 See Louis, op.cit., 330f. for this review, dated 19 November 1892; there is also a brief extract in *G-A* IV/3, 275.

285 See Louis, op.cit., 329f. and *G-A* IV/3, 275f. for this review, dated 18 November 1892, in the *Wiener Abendpost*.

286 Hanslick's article, which appeared in the *Neue Freie Presse* on 17 November 1892, is mentioned briefly in *G-A* IV/3, 276; there is an extract from it in Norbert Tschulik, *Anton Bruckner im Spiegel seiner Zeit* (Vienna, 1955), 50f.

mean 'Praise the Lord in all keys and make Him a sacrifice of a dozen choristers, a solo soprano and a first violinist. A change of fundamental meaning, albeit an enharmonic one!...'[287]

The reviews in the Ostdeutsche Rundschau, Wiener Extrablatt and Vaterland, on the other hand, were much more positive and complimentary.[288] Theodor Helm and Hans Puchstein showed the greatest understanding of the work. Helm felt that the choir and orchestra had not done justice to it. In some places Gericke had adopted far too fast a tempo with the result that the vocal ensemble became blurred; in other places he had allowed the orchestra to drown the voices.[289] Puchstein also noted that the performance of what was admittedly a very difficult work had not been totally convincing, and yet there was no doubt that Gericke had devoted a considerable amount of time to rehearsing it.[290]

Joseph Schalk's performance of his solo piano arrangement of the first movement from the Eighth Symphony during an 'internal evening' of the Wagner-Verein on 22 November was described by one reviewer as a 'commendable preparation' for the forthcoming orchestral performance of 'this most remarkable work'.[291] Other reviewers were more critical, however. One remarked that difficult works of this

---

287 See Louis, op. cit., 331f. and G-A IV/3, 276 (brief mention) for this review, dated 21 November 1892, in the Wiener Montags-Revue.

288 Josef Stolzing's article in the Ostdeutsche Rundschau (20 November 1892) is mentioned in Ingrid Fuchs, 'Bruckner und die österreichische Presse (Deutsch-nationale Blätter)' in BSL 1991 (Linz, 1994), 91. The Extrapost review (14 November 1892) is quoted and the Vaterland review is briefly mentioned in G-A IV/3, 277.

289 See G-A IV/3, 277ff. for Theodor Helm's review, dated 18 November 1892, in the Deutsche Zeitung.

290 See G-A IV/3, 279ff. for Hans Puchstein's review, dated 25 November 1892, in the Deutsches Volksblatt.

291 From review in the Deutsche Zeitung (by Theodor Helm?), dated 24 November 1892.

nature demanded 'a four-hand performance at the very least' and even then were of interest only to those who already knew them. For those who were not acquainted with the work, a piano performance was of very little practical use'.[292] Another made the point that, even in the hands of accomplished pianists who were able to produce an orchestral sound on the piano, there was something 'extremely incomplete' about the piano arrangements of the 'most recent orchestral works written by German composers'.[293] Joseph Schalk and others continued to give piano (two-hand and four-hand) performances of Bruckner's works, but comments of this nature suggest that they were no longer fulfilling their original purpose - or were no longer necessary now that orchestral performances of the symphonies were becoming more frequent.

The orchestral performance of the Eighth on 18 December was undoubtedly one of Bruckner's greatest triumphs in Vienna. Brahms, Johann Strauss, Hugo Wolf and Siegfried Wagner were but four of the important musical figures who attended. Emperor Franz Josef was not able to come but he was represented by Crown Princess Stephanie and Archduchess Valerie. Bruckner had an unusual reward for Hans Richter - 48 hot doughnuts! - and wrote his customary letter to the Philharmonic to thank the players and the conductor for their 'masterly performance'.[294] Apart from Hanslick who made the usual comments about the 'transference of Wagner's dramatic style to the symphony', hoped that this 'nightmarish, confused music' was not to be the music of the future, and took Joseph Schalk to task for his over-elaborate

---

292 From review in the *Deutsches Volksblatt* (by Hans Puchstein?), dated 7 December 1892.

293 From review in the *Ostdeutsche Rundschau* (by Josef Stolzing?), dated 18 December 1892.

294 See *ABB*, 266 and *GrBB*, 141f. for this letter, dated Vienna, 21 December 1892; see also Otto Schneider, 'Anton Bruckners Briefe an die Wiener Philharmoniker' in *ÖMZ* 29 (1974), 188. There is a facsimile of the letter in Wilhelm Jerger, *Briefe an die Wiener Philharmoniker* (Vienna, 1942), 44; the original is located in the Vienna Philharmonic archives. For further information about the performance and its aftermath, see *G-A* IV/3, 283-86.

programmatic account of the work in the printed programme,[295] and, to a lesser extent, Heuberger and Kalbeck, the critical reviews of the performance were extremely favourable.[296] Heuberger considered that it did not have the same melodic freshness as Symphonies 1, 3, 4 or 7 and yet there were many passages of great inventiveness in the first three movements, the slow movement in particular - 'one of the most beautiful that Bruckner has written up to now'. On the other hand, there was lack of coherence and inspiration in the Finale, although the orchestration here and in the other movements was extremely rich and colourful.[297] Max Kalbeck admitted that it was by far the best of the composer's works that had been performed thus far, surpassing the earlier works in 'clarity of layout, succinctness of expression, precision of detail and logic of ideas'. Nevertheless, it was by no means a model symphony - many cuts could profitably have been made, particularly in the prolix Finale. But he would gladly listen to the first three movements again, if only to experience the 'magnificent orchestral sound'.[298]

In his review of the work in the *Österreichisches Volkszeitung*, Balduin Bricht described it as 'the pinnacle of contemporary music', while the reviewer in *Das Vaterland* referred to Bruckner's symphonic output in general as representing a new

---

295　This programme is reprinted in *G-A* IV/3, 288ff. and *LBSAB*, 170ff.; the original is in the ÖNB, F18 Schalk 415/2. In his letter to Franz on 11 December Joseph mentioned the forthcoming performance of the Eighth; see earlier and footnote 279. Hanslick's article in the *Neue Freie Presse* (23 December 1892) is reprinted in *G-A* IV/3, 290-94.

296　See, however, Felix Wartenegg's review in the *Neue Zeitschrift für Musik* 89 (26 July 1893), 324, which has nothing good to say about the work, except for the Scherzo. This review is reprinted in Wessely, *BSL 1991*, 143; there is also an extract in Louis, op.cit., 336.

297　See *G-A* IV/3, 294ff. for Heuberger's review, dated 19 December 1892, in the *Wiener Tagblatt*.

298　See *G-A* IV/3, 297-300 for Kalbeck's review, dated 19 December 1892, in the *Wiener Montags-Revue*.

phase in the development of the symphony.[299] The indisposed Paumgartner was unable to attend the performance but his stand-in was well-disposed towards the composer.[300] In *Die Presse*, Robert Hirschfeld prefaced his favourable review of the work with a lengthy discussion of the contemporary state of music criticism. Like most of the other reviewers, he found the Finale to be the weakest movement of the four. In compensation, however, there was the wonderful conclusion of the first movement, the 'unspeakably beautiful' slow movement, and the orchestration throughout. But Hirschfeld was, if anything, even more severe than Hanslick in his criticism of the programmatic description of the symphony.[301] Bruckner was particularly pleased with Theodor Helm's review in the *Deutsche Zeitung* but, in writing to him, was at pains to point out that all four main themes of the symphony were combined in the Finale at letter Zz in the score, a detail which he thought that Helm had overlooked.[302] In his reply, Helm thanked Bruckner for the 'mighty impression created by your sublime Eighth Symphony' and added that he was aware that 'not only the main themes of the three earlier movements but also that of the last movement was combined in the magnificent Finale', apologizing that he had not

---

299 See *G-A* IV/3, 301 for short extracts from the reviews in these two journals, both dated 21 December 1892.

300 See Tschulik, op.cit., 177f. for this review, dated 30 December 1892.

301 See Louis, op. cit., 332-36 for this review, dated 23 December 1892.

302 See Manfred Wagner, 'Zur Rezeptionsgeschichte von Anton Bruckner Achter Symphonie' in *BJ 1991/92/93* (Linz, 1995), 115 for this review, dated 28 December 1892, in the *Deutsche Zeitung*; see also Renate Grasberger et al., 'Bruckner-Rezeption' in *ABIL-Informationen* 4 (Linz, 1991), 5 for a reference to Helm's earlier review, dated 21 December 1892, in the *Pester Lloyd*, and *SchABCT* for a reference to Helm's review in the Leipzig *Musikalisches Wochenblatt* (29 December 1892). Bruckner's letter to Helm, dated Vienna, 3 January 1893, is printed in *ABB*, 267; the original is in the *Gesellschaft der Musikfreunde* library.

made this clear in his review.[303] In a letter to Levi in January 1893 Bruckner mentioned a report of the Philharmonic players that they 'had never experienced such jubilation in any of their previous concerts as they had with the Eighth Symphony'. Evidently Hans Richter had called him the symphonist and was continually whistling motives from the work. 'Whence this change?', asked Bruckner, and added 'Woe is me if Hanslick hears of it'.[304]

Apart from the critical reviews of the first performance of the symphony,[305] we are fortunate to have two eye-witness accounts, those of Amand Loidol and Hugo Wolf. Writing to his brother Oddo in Kremsmünster the day after the performance, Amand provided details of the occasion - the work lasted from 12.30 until 2.00, the large hall was completely full, Crown Princess Stephanie was in the royal box, Wagner's son Siegfried was in the audience, Bruckner received a wreath after each movement (the first evidently paid for by the Emperor) - and of the performance:

> ... in the grandest style: 10 double basses etc., also two harps which participated in a particularly lively fashion in the 2nd and 3rd movements. The highlight is the Adagio. It begins in D flat major, then G flat, A flat, and ends in C major!...

---

303   See *ABB*, 298-301 for this letter, dated Vienna, 5 January 1893; the location of the original is unknown.

304   See *GrBLS*, 354 for complete text of this letter, dated Vienna, 14 January 1893, and *G-A* IV/1, 262, *G-A* IV/3, 288 and 311 for extracts; the location of the original is unknown.

305   See Renate Grasberger, *ABIL-Informationen*, 5, Ingrid Fuchs, *BSL 1991*, 91, Manfred Wagner, *BJ 1991/92/93*, 111 and 115, and *SchABCT*, 700 for references to and quotes from reviews or articles by Camillo Horn in the *Deutsches Volksblatt* no. 1425 (20 December 1892)[see also footnote 306], Wilhelm Frey in the *Neues Wiener Tagblatt* (20 December 1892), Josef Stolzing in the *Ostdeutsche Rundschau* (25 December 1892), Hans Puchstein in the *Deutsches Volksblatt* [?] (28 December 1892), Eusebius Mandyczewski in the *Deutsche Kunst- und Musikzeitung* 20 (1 January 1893), 3; and Max Graf in the *Musikalische Rundschau* (1 January 1893).

In a second letter, Amand enclosed a friendly review of the work by Camillo Horn in the *Deutsches Volksblatt*, and mentioned the generally favourable reception of the symphony as well as the fine conducting and orchestral playing.[306]

Hugo Wolf enthused about the symphony in two letters to Emil Kauffmann. In the first he described the highly successful reception of the work:

> ... This symphony is the creation of a giant and surpasses all the composer's other symphonies in spiritual dimension, fecundity and greatness. The success was almost unparalleled in spite of the mischievous Cassandra-like predictions even among Bruckner's own supporters. It was a total victory of light over darkness, and a storm of applause broke forth with elemental power at the end of each movement. In short, it was a triumph which would not have disgraced a Roman emperor. What feelings Brahms must have had as he witnessed the work and its electrifying effect from his seat in the director's box! I would not like to have been in his shoes for all the tea in China.[307]

In his second letter, Wolf had more pertinent things to say about the structure of the work:

> ... Your enthusiasm for Bruckner's Eighth fills me with great joy. I share your view entirely concerning the profoundly moving Adagio. In fact, nothing similar can be placed alongside it; certainly not, as far as content is concerned. On the other hand, it is not entirely successful structurally, probably on account of its excessive breadth and scope. In this respect Bruckner is inferior to Beethoven. However, the first movement in its highly energetic, concise version

---

306   For texts of both letters, dated Vienna , 19 December and 28 December respectively, see *GrBLS*, 252-56; the location of the originals is unknown.

307   The date of this letter is given incorrectly as 25 December in *G-A* IV/3, 286f., but correctly as 23 December by Nowak in his foreword to the 1955 edition of the second version of the symphony (*ABSW* VIII/2); the original is privately owned.

is quite unique and perhaps the most accomplished of its kind. The effect of this movement is simply overwhelming, negating all attempts at criticism.

Sadly the composer has been ill with an incurable complaint for a long time now and under the best circumstances has only a few years to live. It is to be hoped that he will complete his Ninth and thus, like another Titan, complete the victory procession of his imperishable creations.[308]

Early in the New Year, one of Bruckner's admirers, Louis Nicodé, who had already conducted a performance of the Seventh Symphony in Dresden, wrote to him about the possibility of a Dresden performance of the Eighth and about the availability of score and parts. In his reply Bruckner pointed out that the symphony was now available in print:

> ... My Eighth is published in Berlin by Lienau and Schlesinger (their representative here in Vienna is Haslinger). I am not able to do any more. Under no circumstances would I want to pester the Philharmonic who, together with Richter and the public, are very enthusiastic about the work.[309]

Nicodé eventually conducted the third performance of the Eighth in Dresden exactly three years after its Viennese premiere - on 18 December 1895.[310] It was nearly ten years before the symphony was heard in Vienna again, in a performance conducted by Ferdinand Löwe on 3 March 1902. Two months earlier, on 13 January

---

308 See E. Hellmer, ed., *Hugo Wolf. Briefe an Emil Kauffmann* (Berlin, 1903), 87ff. for the text of this letter, dated Vienna, 10 March 1893; there is also an extract in *G-A* IV/3, 287.

309 See *ABB*, 334f. for Nicodé's letter (undated) to Bruckner from Dresden, and *ABB*, 268 for Bruckner's reply, dated Vienna, 9 January 1893; the location of the originals is unknown.

310 The second performance was in Olmütz, conducted by Vladimir Labler, on 22 October 1893.

1902, Weingartner in Berlin belatedly fulfilled his promise to conduct the work.[311] Although he was in poor health Bruckner was able to spend Christmas at St. Florian. It was from St. Florian that he sent New Year greetings to Otto Kitzler. Kitzler had written to Bruckner to invite him to conduct his Fourth Symphony and give an organ recital in Brno but he had to decline because of the state of his health and because he would have to expend a lot of nervous energy in performing one of his own works.[312]

Bruckner's Christmas vacation brought him only temporary respite from his deteriorating health. Shortly after returning to Vienna, he wrote to Oddo Loidol and expressed the hope that he would soon recover from his illness.[313] He himself was far from well, however, and he continued to suffer from oedema, cardiac insufficiency and breathlessness. His condition worsened so much during January that he consulted one of the leading Viennese medics of the time, Professor Leopold Schrötter von Kristelli. According to Schrötter's assistant, Dr. Alexander von Weismayr, who had already met Bruckner in Steyr and whose father was an old friend of the composer, Bruckner was confined to bed and put on a strict milk diet for a fortnight. There was a marked improvement in his condition and he was able to get

---

311 Before this, Weingartner conducted performances of the Fourth in Berlin (1895, 1897) and Munich (1900), and the Fifth also in Berlin (1900) and Munich (1900). Later in 1902, Weingartner conducted Bruckner's Sixth Symphony in Berlin. He gave five performances of the Seventh in October and November 1904 (Munich, Frankfurt, Berlin, Stuttgart and Nuremberg).

312 See *ABB*, 266 and *GrBB*, 55 for Bruckner's letter to Kitzler, dated St. Florian, 27 December 1892; the original is in the *Oberösterreichisches Landesmuseum*, Linz.

313 See *ABB*, 267 and *GrBB*, 72 for Bruckner's letter to Loidol ,dated Vienna, 4 January 1893; the location of the original is unknown. Loidol, unfortunately, did not recover and died on 31 January. Bruckner sent condolences to the abbot and the rest of the Kremsmünster community on 1 February; illness prevented him from attending the funeral. See Altman Kellner, op.cit., 759 for Bruckner's letter to Father Sebastian Mayr, dated Vienna 1 February 1893; the original is in Kremsmünster.

up at the end of this period. From this time onwards, however, Dr. Weismayr made regular house calls.[314]

During his illness Hermann Levi wrote to him, apologizing for his long silence but giving him the good news that he hoped to perform one of his symphonies, either the Third or the Seventh in February, and another - the Seventh - during the Composers' Convention in May.[315] In his reply Bruckner recommended to Levi that he use the 1890 edition of the Third which was 'incomparably better' than the first edition for which he no longer had any time. He also took the opportunity of informing Levi of the very successful performance of the Eighth in Vienna and of his own rather frail condition.[316] Levi conducted the Third at an *Akademie-Konzert* in Munich on 3 February and wrote to Bruckner that, although the public reception was not particularly enthusiastic, the orchestral players were delighted with the work.[317] The composer replied immediately, thanking both Levi and the orchestra and mentioning

---

314 See *G-A* IV/3, 304ff. for Professor Schrötter's and Dr. Weismayr's diagnosis of his condition. See also *G-A* IV/3, 307 for an extract from Hans Richter's letter to Bruckner's sister, Rosalie Hueber, dated Vienna, 22 February 1893. Rosalie was so concerned about her brother's health that she had written to Richter. He was able to reassure her that 'thanks to his strong constitution and the skill of the doctors', Bruckner was now out of danger and on the road to recovery.

315 See *ABB*, 326f. for this letter, dated Munich, 12 January 1893; the original is in St. Florian.

316 See earlier and footnote 304 for this letter from Bruckner, dated Vienna, 14 January 1893; the location of the original is unknown.

317 See *ABB*, 327 for this letter, dated Munich, 6 February 1893; the original is in St. Florian. This concert was reviewed in the *Münchner Allgemeine Zeitung* (evening edition, 4 February 1893) and the *Münchner Neueste Nachrichten* (5 February 1893). Levi also conducted the Berlin Philharmonic in a performance of the same work on 16 October 1893. This concert was reviewed in the *Neue Preußische Zeitung* 488 (17 October 1893), 2, the *Vossische Zeitung* (evening edition, 17 October 1893), the *National-Zeitung* (morning edition, 18 October 1893) and the *Neue Berliner Musik-Zeitung* (19 October 1893). See Röder, op.cit., 433-36 for extracts from the reviews of both concerts. Levi conducted the Adagio from the Seventh in Munich on 27 May.

that he was now feeling much better.[318]

During his illness Bruckner felt isolated. This was no doubt because his doctor had instructed Kathi, his housekeeper, not to allow any visitors. When Bruckner complained to Levi on 14 January that 'even Schalk and Löwe have forsaken me' and to Göllerich on 10 March that 'no one wants to come or, at most, very infrequently. The Wagner Society is everything to them! Even Oberleithner is there all the time...', he was perhaps unaware of his doctor's orders.[319] But he received a very sympathetic letter from Ida Buhz in Berlin. She wished she could be with him to look after him and she looked forward to seeing him again soon and hearing some of his music.[320]

Although Bruckner was well enough to attend a performance of his male-voice piece *Tafellied* WAB 86 by the *Akademischer Gesangverein* on 11 March,[321] he was not prepared to venture any further than Vienna so soon after his illness. He made this clear in a letter to Otto Kitzler who was probably still clinging on to the hope that Bruckner would be able to play the organ, even although he had already ruled out

---

318 See *GrBLS*, 355 and Walter Beck, op.cit., 76 for this letter, dated Vienna, 8 February 1893. There is a facsimile of the first page of the letter in Beck, op.cit., 75. The original is in the Beck collection, Munich.

319 See *ABB*, 268f. and *G-A* IV/3 (extract) for Bruckner's letter to Göllerich; the original is privately owned.

320 See *G-A* IV/3, 313 for extracts from both this letter, dated Berlin, 15 March 1893, and another letter written two months later - dated Berlin, 6 May 1893; the location of the originals is unknown.

321 The performance was conducted by Raoul Mader, with whom Bruckner had some disagreement about the proper tempo of the piece. See *G-A* I, 237ff. and *G-A* IV/3, 314 for further details, including extracts from Theodor Helm's review in the *Deutsche Zeitung* and Puchstein's (?) in the *Deutsches Volksblatt*.

conducting his Fourth Symphony in Brno in an earlier letter.[322]

In his letter to Göllerich Bruckner complained that, although he had heard a few months previously from friends that Joseph Schalk was going to perform his F minor Mass, Schalk himself had only told him about it 'a few days ago'. Six years earlier, Schalk had also left it rather later to inform Bruckner of his intention of giving a performance (with Franz Zottmann) of his four-hand piano arrangement of the Fifth Symphony. On this occasion, there were some unpleasant scenes at the final rehearsals with Bruckner attended. In spite of his self-doubts, Joseph completed his revision of the orchestration of the Mass, but sent his work to Franz for correction. Franz made several corrections at the beginning but less and less from that point onwards, and Joseph was concerned that his brother may not have taken so much care with his supervision as he had hoped.[323] The performance, under the auspices of the *Wagner-Verein*, too place in the large *Musikverein* hall on 23 March. Schalk conducted the Eduard Strauss Orchestra and the *Wagner-Verein* choir supplemented by members of the *Akademischer Gesangverein*. Bruckner was delighted with the performance and it is reported that Brahms, who was present, visibly joined in the applause. Theodor Helm wrote that, as 'an apostolically inspired singer for the Lord', Bruckner had achieved 'a triumph no less brilliant than the one secured as a bold, mighty symphonist in the fourth Philharmonic Concert on

---

322 See *GrBL*, 28, *GrBB*, 55f. and *ABB*, 269f. for Bruckner's letter, dated Vienna, 14 March 1893; the original is in the *Oberösterreichisches Landesmuseum*, Linz. See also earlier and footnote 312. Kitzler conducted the Fourth in Brno on 21 April and informed Bruckner of the acclaimed performance in a letter to the composer, dated Brno, 22 April 1893. See *ABB*, 311f.; the original is in St. Florian.

323 See *LBSAB*, 176 for Joseph's letter to Franz, dated Vienna, 1 March 1893; the original is in the *ÖNB*, F18 Schalk 158/14/10.

18 December'.[324] In his review for the *Fremdenblatt*, Ludwig Speidel pointed out that the Mass text had acted as a restraining influence on the composer with the result that there was a well-judged balance between the old and the new. Of the many fine passages in the work the most successful were those depicting the Passion and the Last Judgment in the *Credo* where the composer's inventive powers were at their greatest.[325]

In reporting to his brother, Joseph Schalk mentioned Hans Richter's complimentary reference to his conducting and Bruckner's seemingly unbearable behaviour at the final rehearsals.[326] This was almost certainly due to two factors - Bruckner's ill-health and the reservations he must have had about Schalk's re-scoring of the work.

Bruckner spent Easter partly at St. Florian and partly at Steyr. He stayed at St. Florian until Easter Saturday, and heard his motet, *Vexilla regis*, for the first time on Good Friday. On Easter Sunday (2 April) his D minor Mass was performed at Steyr Parish Church. Franz Bayer, the choir director, took no less than 26 rehearsals in preparing the work and augmented the church choir with singers from the local

---

324   See *G-A* IV/3, 315ff. and *LBSAB*, 176f. for extracts from Helm's review, dated 24 March 1893, in the *Deutsche Zeitung*. Helm followed this up with another review on 28 March; see extract in *G-A* IV/3, 317.

325   See *G-A* IV/3, 318ff. for this review, dated 23 April. See also Louis, op.cit., 336f. and Othmar Wessely, *BSL 1991*, 143f. for Felix Wartenegg's equally complimentary review in the *Neue Zeitschrift für Musik* 89 (27 September 1893), 400. Other reviewers of the performance included Max Graf in the *Musikalische Rundschau* 8/7, 58f., Luigi von Kunits in the *Österreichische Musik- und Theaterzeitung* 5 (1892/93) 13/14, 4, Camillo Horn in the *Deutsches Volksblatt* (25 September), and Richard Heuberger in the *Deutsche Kunst- und Musikzeitung* 20 (1 April 1893), 82.

326   See *LBSAB*, 177f. for Joseph's letter, dated Vienna, 15 April 1893; the original is in the *ÖNB*, F18 Schalk 158/14/12.

choral society.[327] Bruckner was well enough to play the organ and improvised on themes from the Mass during the service; he also played excerpts from his Eighth Symphony at an evening celebration in his honour.[328] There were reports of the performance in the Steyr and Linz newspapers and, when Bruckner wrote to Franz Bayer on 22 April recalling the excellent performance of the Mass, he mentioned his annoyance at the comparison made between his use of organ points and Brahms's use of a similar device in the *German Requiem* in a review in the *Steyrer Zeitung* on 6 April; he insisted that 'counterpoint was nothing more than a means to an end'.[329] Nevertheless, he was particularly pleased to be elected an honorary member of the Steyr *Musikverein*, as the honour had been granted him by a 'native town'.[330]

On Good Friday (31 March), two days before the Steyr performance of the D minor Mass, Gustav Mahler performed the same work (and the *Te Deum*) in the Hamburg city theatre. Wilhelm Zinne, who had visited Bruckner in 1892, wrote to the composer on 26 March to tell him of Mahler's decision to perform these two

---

327 When he wrote to the Steyr parish priest, Johann Aichinger, to thank him for his invitation to spend the Easter weekend at Steyr, Bruckner registered his astonishment that Bayer had been able to prepare a performance of the Mass. See *ABB* 270f. and *G-A* II/1, 319 (extract) for this letter, dated St. Florian, 31 March 1893; the original is in the *Gesellschaft der Musikfreunde*, Vienna. Bruckner also invited Therese Petcher, a friend of his deceased sister Nani, to the performance of the Mass. See *ABB*, 270 for this letter, dated 31 March 1893; the location of the original is unknown.

328 See *G-A* II/1, 318f. and *G-A* IV/3, 320ff. for further information.

329 See *ABB*, 271f. and *GrBB*, 9. A facsimile of the original, which is in the *ÖNB*, can be found in *GrBLS*m between pages 58 and 59; see also H.F. Redlich, *Bruckner and Mahler*, 63.

330 Bruckner was officially notified of the honour on 24 April; the original of the letter from the Steyr *Musikverein* is in the possession of the Hueber family in Vöcklabruck. For Bruckner's letter of thanks, dated Vienna 27 April 1893, see *G-A* IV/3, 323 (where it is incorrectly dated 24 April) and Erich W. Partsch, *IBG Mitteilungsblatt* 35 (1990), 10; the location of the original is unknown, but it was printed in the *Festschrift Gesellschaft der Musikfreunde in Steyr 1838-1963*.

works in preference to the Eighth Symphony which he had also considered.[331] Bruckner made sure that Helm was kept up to date with news of recent performances of his works outside Vienna, including Bayer's performance of the D minor Mass in Steyr, Mahler's performances of the Mass and the *Te Deum* in Hamburg, and performances of the Fourth in Brno and Troppau.[332]

There was a recurrence of Bruckner's illness in the middle of April and he had to go on a strict milk diet once again. On 4 May he wrote to Viktor Christ, one of his pupils, asking him to convey his thanks to Christ's sister who had sent him some flowers and his father who had evidently sent him good wishes.[333] He was certainly heartened by the news of successful performances of his works in Düsseldorf, Dresden and Leipzig in May and June.[334] The fact that his brother Ignaz sent him

---

331 See *ABB*, 392ff. and *G-A* IV/3, 323f. (extract) for Zinne's letter; the location of the original is unknown. See also *G-A* IV/3, 324ff. for a review of the Mass in the *Hamburgische Korrespondent* which is critical of the lack of structural unity.

332 See *ABB*, 271, *GrBB*, 44 and *G-A* IV/3, 322 (extract) for Bruckner's letter to Theodor Helm, dated Vienna, 22 April 1893; the original is in the *Wiener Stadt- und Landesbibliothek*. The Troppau performance of the Fourth, conducted by Friedrich Keitel who had visited Bruckner in Vienna and had been given some practical advice, was on 19 April.

333 In this visiting card Bruckner told Christ that he had been ill again 'for three weeks'. See *ABB*, 272 and *G-A* IV/3, 329f.; the location of the original is unknown.

334 The *Te Deum* was performed at the *Lower Rhenish Music Festival* in Düsseldorf on 21 May, Psalm 150 made such an impression in Dresden that it was performed twice, and the Seventh was performed for the second time in Leipzig on 6 June - see Lieberwirth, *ABDS* 6, 68-75 for further details, including reviews in the *Leipziger Zeitung* (7 June) and *Leipziger Neueste Nachrichten* (8 June). Writing to Vinzenz Fink in Linz on 1 July, Bruckner recommended the Psalm for performance and mentioned the two recent Dresden performances. See *ABB*, 274 and extract in *G-A* IV/3, 338; the location of the original is unknown. A fortnight earlier, in a letter to Bernhard Deubler, in which he sent condolences on the death of Deubler's father, he mentioned some recent performances of his works and said that Richter intended to perform the *Te Deum* with 4000 (!)

some of his favourite meat from St. Florian in May probably indicates that he had recovered from his recent setback.[335] And he was certainly well enough to enjoy a visit on 27 May from Dr. Wilhelm Schmid, a professor of Philology at Tübingen University who had become a great admirer of his music after being introduced to it by Hugo Wolf.[336]

During this time Bruckner was working on his choral and orchestral piece, *Helgoland* WAB 71, commissioned by Eduard Kremser and the Vienna *Männergesangverein* for their 50th anniversary, and Franz Schalk was making slow progress in his revision of Bruckner's Fifth Symphony. When he wrote to Joseph on 11 April, he complained of a nervous condition resulting from the pressure of work, and said that he would not be able to devote any more time to the Finale of the symphony until the summer break.[337] Joseph encouraged him to press forward with the work:

> ... Bruckner talks about the score of the Vth. Not surprisingly he has become distrustful because no performance has taken place...[338]

During the summer months Joseph took a five-week cold water cure for his asthma at a spa near Graz but did not visit his brother who spent his holiday again at the

---

singers. See *ABB*, 273 for this letter, dated Vienna, 14 June 1893; the original is in St. Florian.

335   See *ABB*, 273 and *GrBB*, 16 for Bruckner's letter to Ignaz, dated Vienna 25 May 1893, in which he enclosed seven florins to pay for the meat. He also complained about the 'terrible heat' in Vienna. The location of the original is unknown.

336   See Wilhelm Schmid, 'Erinnerungen an Anton Bruckner' in *Neue Musik-Zeitung* 23 (1902), 168ff.; also *G-A* IV/3, 334-38

337   See *LBSAB*, 178f.; the original of Franz's letter is in the *ÖNB*, 158/14/11.

338   See *LBSAB*, 179 for this letter, dated Vienna, 17 May 1893; the original of Joseph's letter is in the *ÖNB*, F18 Schalk 158/14/15.

Goldschmidt villa in Grundlsee. Before leaving for Graz, Joseph wrote to Franz to find out how his work on the Fifth was progressing. Franz replied from Grundlsee that he had started from scratch again with his revision of the Finale and would soon finish it.[339] On 27 July Franz was able to inform Joseph that he had just got to know the Finale thoroughly for the first time.[340]

Dates on the autograph of *Helgoland* and references to it in his letters give us some indication of Bruckner's progress on the work from April to August. The sketches were completed on 27 April, the choral parts on 24 May, the string parts on 18 June, the woodwind parts on 7 July, the brass parts on 23 July; the work was completed by 7 August while Bruckner was still in Vienna, but he continued to add 'finishing touches' until the end of the month.[341] On 14 August he invited Eduard Kremser, the conductor of the *Männergesangverein*, to visit him the following day or the day after to discuss the work. As Cyrill Hynais had taken on the task of copying the full score and preparing a piano reduction, he was also asked to come.[342]

A fortnight later Bruckner wrote from Steyr to Hynais, mentioned some corrections he had made in the work and asked him to prepare a second score for Kremser and make sure that the final corrections were also inserted in the score already

---

339 See Nowak, *ABSW* V *Revisionsbericht* for reference to these two letters, dated Vienna 6 July and Grundlsee 21 July respectively.

340 See *LBSAB*, 179 for an extract from Franz's letter written from Grundlsee; the original is in the *ÖNB*, F18 Schalk 158/14/22.

341 The autograph full score (Mus. Hs. 19.485) and the majority of the sketches (Mus. Hs. 6038 and 29.304) are in the *ÖNB*. In a letter to Viktor Christ, dated Vienna, 18 July 1893, he mentioned that a recurrence of his illness had prevented him from completing the work so far. See *ABB*, 274 and extract in *G-A* IV/3, 339 (where it is dated 8 July); the location of the original is unknown.

342 See *GrBB*, 64f. for Bruckner's letter to Kremser; the location of the original is unknown.

prepared.[343] Exactly a month later Bruckner asked Hynais for confirmation that the corrections had been inserted in the score. He was also keen to know how the work sounded and was concerned that the tempi should not be too quick. He was surprised that Kremser had not written to him and asked Hynais to ensure that the work was given sufficient rehearsal time and all necessary corrections were put at Kremser's disposal.[344] Bruckner obviously heard that the work had been well rehearsed because he mentioned this specifically when he wrote to Kremser at the beginning of October, asking him the date of the final rehearsal which he would attend if his health permitted.[345] Bruckner was elected an honorary member of the *Männergesangverein* on 22 September,[346] and *Helgoland* was given its first performance in the *Winter-Reitschule* of the *Hofburg* during the Society's 50th anniversary concert on 8 October. The words, by August Silberstein, narrate the story of the imminent invasion of the island of Heligoland by a Roman fleet and the miraculous intervention of a wild storm which throws the Roman ships on the rocks and saves the islanders. As with many male - voice choruses of this period, there are strong German nationalist overtones in the text. Bruckner's setting has that 'primitive' grandeur reminiscent of parts of the *Te Deum* and Psalm 150, and the harmonic gestures and orchestral colour of the Seventh and Eighth Symphonies are frequently

---

343   See *G-A* IV/3, 331 and 341 for extracts from this letter, dated Steyr, 28 August 1893; the location of the original is unknown.

344   See *G-A* IV/3, 341f. for this letter, dated Steyr, 28 September 1893; the location of the original is unknown. Bruckner also referred to another bout of illness which had incapacitated him for almost two weeks.

345   See *GrBB*, 66 and *G-A* IV/3, 342 (extract) for this letter, dated Steyr, 2 October 1893; the location of the original is unknown.

346   Bruckner wrote to the *Männergesangverein* on 14 October, thanking them for this honour. See *ABA*, 111 for text and 43 for facsimile of end of letter; the original is in the archives of the *Wiener Männergesangverein*.

recalled.[347]

Bruckner, who had remained in Steyr until the beginning of October,[348] attended the performance of *Helgoland* and was warmly applauded. The newspaper reviews were mixed, the most frequent criticism being that, while the orchestral depiction of the tempestuous elements was successful, the voices were over-stretched.[349]

At the beginning of September, while he was in Steyr, he received a letter from Gertrud Bollé-Hellmund (a pseudonym for Elisabeth [?] Bollé), an admirer of his

---

347 See *G-A* IV/3, 330-34 for a discussion of the music. For an evaluation of the 'appropriateness' of Bruckner's setting, viz. the combination of traditional and novel stylistic features, see Johannes-Leopold Mayer, 'Die Zweilichtigkeit des Erfolges Anton Bruckners "Helgoland" im historischen Umfeld des Wiener Männerchorwesens' in *BJ 1980* (Linz, 1980), 21-26; for a discussion of the symphonic aspect of the piece, see Wolfgang Grandjean, 'Anton Bruckners "Helgoland" und das Symphonische' in *Die Musikforschung* 48 (1995), 349-68; and for comments on the specifically 'German qualities' of the work, see Alexander L. Ringer, '*Germanenzug* bis *Helgoland*: Zu Bruckners Deutschtum'* in Albrecht Riethmüller, ed., *Bruckner-Probleme. Beiheft zum Archiv für Musikwissenschaft* 45 (Stuttgart, 1999), 25-34. *Helgoland* was dedicated to the *Wiener Männergesangverein* - 'Dem Wiener-Männer-Gesang-Verein zur Feier seines 50jährigen Bestandes gewidmet'. It was first published by Doblinger, Vienna (Hynais's piano arrangement and the choral parts in 1893, the full score [D.2334] and the orchestral parts in 1899). There is a modern edition in *ABSW* XXII/2 (Vienna, 1987), 214-76, and this edition contains the dynamic and agogic marks added by Kremser with Bruckner's approval.

348 He did not feel well enough to spend any time in St. Florian during the summer months. On 7 August he wrote to Franz Bayer in Steyr and mentioned the 'up and down' state of his health. He probably left Vienna for Steyr around 16 August (after his meeting with Kremser). See *ABB*, 274f. for Bruckner's letter; the original is in the *Stadtpfarre*, Steyr..

349 The concert, which was attended by Emperor Franz Josef, included choral works by Max Bruch, Herbeck, Kremser, Schubert, Schumann and Wagner. Extracts from reviews in *Vaterland* (9 October), *Fremdenblatt* (9 October), by Hanslick in the *Neue Freie Presse* (11 October 1893),and Robert Hirschfeld in *Die Presse* (12 October 1893) can be found in Louis, op.cit., 337, *G-A* IV/3, 355ff., and Johannes-Leopold Mayer, loc.cit., 22.

music, offering to provide him with an opera libretto of a religious nature which, she was sure, would be suitable.[350] In his reply, Bruckner said that the libretto should be 'à la Lohengrin, Romantic, religious, mysterious and, above all, free from all impurities'. He also mentioned his ongoing work on the Ninth which, because of his present ill-health, would probably take him another two years to complete.[351] A fortnight later Franz Bayer wrote, on Bruckner's behalf, to Gertrud Bollé to inform her that, owing to ill-health, the composer would be unable to give serious consideration to an opera project at the present time.[352]

In the meantime Franz Schalk was continuing work on his version of the Fifth. Leibnitz comments that the whole episode of the Graz performance of this symphony, which can be reconstructed from the Schalk correspondence, is quite astonishing, almost unbelievable:

> ... In brief Joseph and Franz Schalk deceived Bruckner quite deliberately, ostensibly with the best of intentions and with a good conscience. They led him to believe that his own version was to be performed in Graz and did not inform him of the revisions being

---

350 See *G-A* IV/3, 342ff. for this undated (?) letter written from Berlin; the location of the original is unknown. The libretto was 'Astra', based on Richard Voß's *Toteninsel*.

351 See *ABB*, 276 and *GrBB*, 12f. for this letter, dated Steyr, 5 September 1893; the location of the original is unknown. Bruckner also alluded to the uncertain state of his health when he wrote to Philipp Wolfrum at the end of August, regretting that he would not be able to travel to Heidelberg in December for a performance of his Third Symphony. See Walter Beck, op. cit., 76 (and Scheder's comments in *SchABCT*, 716) for this letter, dated Steyr, 29 August 1893; the original is in the Beck Collection, Munich. See also Röder, op.cit., 436f. for a review of the December concert in the *Heidelberger Zeitung* (14 December 1893).

352 See *GrBB*, 13 for an extract from this letter, dated Steyr, 21 September 1893; the location of the original is unknown. Bruckner had no idea at this juncture that Bollé-Hellmund was none other than the woman he had met on several occasions in Vienna about six years before. See Bollé's account in *G-A* IV/3, 346-52.

made. On the other hand they wanted him to be present at the performance. The primary intention was one which had already been in evidence in Joseph's performance of the F minor Mass. Bruckner was to be presented with a 'fait accompli' and was to be persuaded through hearing it and through success with the public that the improvements made sense. The Bruckner literature had remained unaware of the brothers' behaviour hitherto, because Lili Schalk suppressed the crucial passages of the correspondence in her book and, furthermore, attempted by means of misinformation to eliminate every appearance of 'suspicion' of her dead husband...[353]

The unexpurgated letters tell a different story, however. On 23 September, Franz wrote to Bruckner requesting the parts of the Fifth so that he could begin rehearsals of the work.[354] In his *Revisionsbericht* of the symphony, Nowak has this comment to make:

> ... It cannot be ascertained which parts are being referred to here. Schalk could only make use of parts which tallied with his revision of the Fifth.[355]

The explanation, however, is that after Bruckner had given the parts to Joseph and asked him to send them on to Franz, Joseph held on to the parts and asked Franz to write to Bruckner confirming receipt so that the composer would be under the impression that they had arrived safely in Graz.[356] The problem now was to have the parts copied from the revised score. The brothers hoped that Oberleithner would be able to help. In an undated letter from Franz to Joseph, 13 February 1894 is given

---

353 *LBSAB*, 179f.

354 See *ABB*, 366 for the text of this letter; the location of the original is unknown.

355 Nowak, op.cit., 70.

356 See *LBSAB*, 180f. for Joseph's letter to Franz, dated Vienna, 4 December 1893; the original is in the *ÖNB*, F18 Schalk 158/14/25.

as the projected date of the performance of the symphony.[357]

The decline in his health forced Bruckner to give serious consideration to his last will and testament. He completed it on 10 November and his signature was witnessed by Ferdinand Löwe, Cyrill Hynais and Dr. Theodor Reisch; the latter was appointed as executor. A month earlier his brother Ignaz wrote to him from St. Florian concerning the wish he had expressed to be buried in the abbey; the abbot would be prepared to grant this wish if he mentioned it specifically in his will.[358] And so Bruckner made his wishes clear, namely that he should be buried underneath the great organ and financial provision should be made for four Masses to be said during the year, one on his birthday, one on his name-day, one on the anniversary of the day of his death, and one for his parents, brothers and sisters. His estate was to be divided equally between his brother Ignaz and his sister Rosalie. They were to have equal shares in the proceeds from the sale of his music which, he hoped, would be much greater after his death than during his lifetime when they had yielded very little. The original manuscripts of his works - 'the symphonies of which there are eight so far, and the Ninth will soon be completed, God willing, the three great Masses, the Quintet, the Te Deum, Psalm 150 and the choral work Helgoland' - were to be given to the Imperial Court Library. Permission was to be given to the publishers Jos. Eberle to borrow these manuscripts for a specified time for printing purposes. 400 florins was to be given to his housekeeper, Katharina Kachelmayr, in recognition of her faithful service over many years. In the event of her still being his housekeeper at the time of his death, this legacy was to be increased by 300 florins to

---

357 See *FSBB*, 61 and *LBSAB*, 181 for this undated letter. Nowak (*Revisionsbericht*, 70) suggests Autumn 1893 as the date. The original is in the *ÖNB*, F18 Schalk 158/14/3.

358 See *G-A* II/1, 319f. for an extract from Ignaz's letter, dated St. Florian, 9 October 1893; the original is in St. Florian.

700 florins.[359]

At the beginning of November Bruckner received the good news that Ochs and Weingartner were planning performances of some of his works in Berlin early in 1894. Siegfried Ochs invited him to come to Berlin. In his reply Bruckner suggested to Ochs that the *Te Deum* and Seventh Symphony be performed. As far as his own attendance was concerned, he would have to follow his doctor's advice - he had only recently recovered from another bout of illness.[360] As a result of an improvement in his health during December his doctor gave him the 'all clear' for a visit to Berlin in January but suggested that he spend Christmas in Vienna rather than over-exerting himself by travelling to St. Florian. In fact his young friend, Josef Kluger, arranged for him to spend Christmas at Klosterneuburg,[361] but he was certainly back in Vienna to attend a performance of his Quintet on 28 December.

There was no doubt that the concerts in Berlin were going ahead. Unfortunately, Weingartner, who was to perform the Seventh on 6 January, had taken ill, but Karl

359 See *ABB*, 276ff., *GrBB*, 148-51 and *G-A* IV/3, 359ff. for the complete text of the will; there is a facsimile of the original, which is located in the Vienna *Stadt- und Landesbibliothek*, in Rolf Keller, 'Die letztwilligen Verfügungen Anton Bruckners', *BJ 1982/83* (Linz, 1984), 111f.

360 See *ABB*, 275, *GrBB*, 133 (where recipient is given erroneously as Weingartner) and *G-A* IV/3, 362 for Bruckner's letter to Ochs, dated Vienna, 8 November 1893; the original is in the *Gesellschaft der Musikfreunde* library.

361 On 30 December, Bruckner wrote from Vienna to Deubler in St. Florian to say that he had spent Christmas at St. Florian and that he was about to set off for Berlin to attend performances of his Seventh Symphony, *Te Deum* and Quintet. See *ABB*, 279f. for this letter; the original is in. St. Florian. He also informed his sister Rosalie of his improvement in health, imminent departure for Berlin, and the forthcoming performances of some of his works in Vienna and elsewhere, when he wrote to her from Vienna on 23 December. See *ABB*, 279 and *G-A* IV/3, 363f.; the location of the original is unknown. There is also an undated letter to Franz Bayer in Steyr, obviously written at this time, in which Bruckner mentions the Berlin performances and a performance of his Second Symphony in Vienna on 14 January [1894]. See *ABB*, 289f.; the location of the original is unknown.

Muck stepped into the breach. In the second of two letters he sent to Bruckner during the Christmas period, he asked the composer to supply him with information about the composition and performance of the Seventh, together with a thematic analysis of the work.[362]

In spite of the frequent recurrences of ill-health during 1893, which made it difficult or well-nigh impossible for Bruckner to devote sustained periods of attention to his Ninth, he forged ahead with work on the symphony. During his ten-year involvement with the Ninth, Bruckner discarded and replaced a considerable amount of preliminary work on all movements of the symphony. This is particularly true of the Trio section of the Scherzo. Whereas there is only one version of the latter extant, there are three quite different versions of the Trio, the first and second of which have parts for solo viola. During 1893 and 1894 Bruckner worked on the Adagio, completed the scores of the first movement and the Scherzo, and produced the second (in F sharp major) and third versions of the Trio.[363]

---

362 See *ABB*, 333f. and *G-A* IV/3, 365f. for these two letters, dated Berlin, 23 and 26 December respectively; the originals are in St. Florian. Muck also reminded Bruckner that he had conducted the symphony three times before, once in Graz in March 1886 and twice in Prague in January 1888 and December 1889.

363 The majority of the source material is located in the *ÖNB*, but important sketches can also be found in other libraries, including the *Wiener Stadt- und Landesbibliothek* and the *Biblioteka Jagiellonska* in Cracow. Key dates are: 21 September 1887 (completion of first draft score of the first movement), 4 January 1889 (sketch of first Scherzo), February 1891 (references to work on the Ninth in letters to Levi and Helm), end April 1891 (date at beginning of the score of the first movement; Mus. Hs. 19.481 in *ÖNB*), 14 October 1892 (date at end of the score of the first movement), 2 January 1893 (date in sketch of the Adagio), 27 February 1893 (date at the end of the score of the Scherzo, including Trio no. 2), 28 February 1893 (date on a sketch of the Adagio), 23 December 1893 (completion of score of the first movement), 15 February 1894 (date at the end of the Scherzo, including the third, definitive version of the Trio), March - September 1894 (various dates in sketches of the Adagio), 31 October 1894 (first date at end of score of the Adagio), 30

November 1894 (last date at end of score of the Adagio). See later for details of Bruckner's work on the Finale of the symphony from May until his death in October 1896. For further details of the first three movements of the Ninth in particular, see: Ferdinand Löwe, ed., *Anton Bruckner: IX Symphonie D moll* (Vienna: Doblinger, 1903) [the first edition of the symphony, including full score: D.2895, four-hand piano arrangement by Löwe and Schalk: D.2910, and Löwe's two-hand piano arrangement: D.3115); Karl Grunsky, *Anton Bruckner. 9. Symphonie in d-Moll. Erläutert* (Leipzig: Seeman, 1903); Max Auer, 'Anton Bruckners IX. Symphonie in der Originalfassung' in *Zeitschrift für Musik* 99 (1932), 861-64; Alfred Orel, *Anton Bruckner: IX Symphonie D moll (Originalfassung)*, vol. IX of *Sämtliche Werke. Kritische Gesamtausgabe* (Vienna, 1934); idem, 'Zur Enstehung von Bruckners 9. Symphonie' in *Bruckner-Blätter* 6/1-2, 2-7; Max Auer, 'Die IX. Symphonie in der Originalfassung' in *Bruckner-Blätter* 6/3 (1934), 40ff.; Louis Biancolli, 'Bruckner's Ninth Symphony' in *Chord and Discord* 2/4 (1946), 36-40; Robert Simpson, 'The Ninth Symphony of Anton Bruckner' in *Chord and Discord* 2/6 (1950), 115ff.; Leopold Nowak, ed., *IX. Symphonie in D moll. Originalfassung. 2. Revidierte Ausgabe*, ABSW IX (Vienna: Musikwissenschaftlicher Verlag, 1951), Charles L. Eble, 'The Ninth Symphony of Bruckner' in *Chord and Discord* 2/7 (1954), 19f.; Harold Truscott, 'The "Ninth" in Perspective' in *The Monthly Musical Record* 88 (1958), 223-28; Leopold Nowak, 'Symphonie Nr. 9 in d-Moll' in *Musikblätter der Wiener Philharmoniker* 15 (1960/61), 133-47; Hans F. Redlich, foreword to Eulenburg score of Symphony no. 9 (E.E. 6437), ed. Hans-Hubert Schönzeler (Autumn 1963); Michael Adensamer, 'Bruckners Einfluss auf die Moderne (mit Beispielen aus dem Adagio der 9. Symphonie)' in *BJ 1980* (Linz, 1980), 27-31; Constantin Floros, 'Zur Deutung der Symphonik Bruckners. Das Adagio der Neunten Symphonie' in *BJ 1982* (Linz, 1982), 89-96; Robert Schollum, 'Umkreisungen. Anmerkungen zum Beginn des Adagio der Neunten Symphonie Bruckners' in *BJ 1982* (Linz, 1982), 97-102; Mariana Sontag, *The Compositional Process of Anton Bruckner: A study of the sketches and drafts for the first movement of the IX. Symphony* (doctoral thesis, University of Chicago, Illinois, 1987); Hans-Hubert Schönzeler, *Zu Bruckners IX. Symphonie: die Krakauer Skizzen* (Vienna: Musikwissenschaftlicher Verlag, 1987); Peter Gülke, 'Bruckner von seiner Neunten Sinfonie aus gesehen' in *Brahms-Bruckner. Zwei Studien* (Bärenreiter: Kassel-Basel, 1989); Franz Scheder, 'Zur Datierung zweier Autographen Anton Bruckners: 1. Skizzenblätter zur Neunten Symphonie 2. Bruckners Brief vom 31. Oktober 1894' in *BJ 1987/88* (Linz, 1990), 63ff.; Benjamin Gunnar Cohrs, 'Zahlenphänomene in Bruckners Symphonik. Neues zu den Strukturen der Fünften und Neunten Symphonie' in *BJ 1989/90* (Linz, 1992), 35-75; Mariana Sontag, 'A New Perspective on Anton Bruckner's Composition of the Ninth Symphony' in *BJ 1989/90* (Linz, 1992), 77-114; John A. Phillips, 'Die Arbeitsweise Bruckners in seinen letzten Jahren' in *BSL 1992* (Linz, 1995), 153-78; Benjamin Gunnar Cohrs, 'Der Mikrofilm der Krakauer Bruckner-Skizzen in der Österreichischen Nationalbibliothek' in *BJ 1994/95/96* (Linz, 1997), 191ff.; idem, 'Die Problematik

Before leaving for Berlin Bruckner sent visiting cards to Karl Aigner and Göllerich and his wife.[364] Joseph Schalk informed Franz that there was a slight improvement in Bruckner's medical condition and he was being tended by a nurse who had been recommended by Professor Schrötter; Ignaz Bruckner, 'a poor copy of the original' had also spent some time with his brother.[365]

On the evening of 3 January, Bruckner, in the company of Prince Karadjordjevic and Hugo Wolf travelled overnight from Vienna to Berlin. The two composers intended to be present at performances of their works, namely Bruckner's Seventh Symphony, *Te Deum* and String Quintet and Wolf's *Elfenlied* (for solo soprano, women's chorus and orchestra), the choral version of Mörike's *Der Feuerreiter*, an elaboration of the song for voice and piano written originally in 1888, and the orchestral versions of two other solo songs - Margit's song from the music to Ibsen's *Fest auf Solhaug*, and Goethe's *Anakreons Grab*.

Bruckner attended the final rehearsal of his symphony on the morning of Saturday 6 January. In the evening concert it shared the programme with works by Mendelssohn (*Fair Melusine* overture), Haydn and Mozart. There were reviews in

---

von Fassung und Bearbeitung bei Anton Bruckner, erläutert anhand der drei Trios zum Scherzo der Neunten Symphonie' in *BSL 1996* (Linz, 1998), 65-84; idem, ed., *IX. Symphonie D-Moll Scherzo und Trio. Älteres Trio mit Viola Solo, ABSW [zu Band IX/2]* (Vienna: Musikwissenschaftliches Verlag, 1998).

364 In his card to Aigner, dated 1 January 1894, he asked him to send him a bill (for copying?). See Beck, op.cit., 770; the original is in the Beck Collection in Munich. He sent New Year's greetings to Göllerich and his wife and mentioned his impending trip to Berlin. See *ABB*, 254 for this undated card; there is a facsimile in Schneider Musikantiquariat, Catalogue 236 (Tutzing, 1979), 10; the location of the original is unknown..

365 See *LBSAB*, 181 for an extract from this letter, dated Vienna, 2 January 1894; the original is in the *ÖNB*, F18 Schalk 158/15/16.

several papers, including the Berlin *Börsen-Courier*, the *Vossische Zeitung*, the *Neue Preußische Zeitung* and the *Allgemeine Musik-Zeitung*. The reviewer for the *Börsen-Courier* remarked that the main weakness of the symphony was the lack of sufficient organic connection between the different themes and motives, but this was more than compensated for by 'the ravishingly beautiful themes, the burning, holy fervour which glows through all the movements and the marvellous instrumentation'. The reviewer went on to say that the public reception of the work was 'very friendly on the whole, albeit by no means commensurate with the significance of the work - which, of course, is normally the case'.[366]

On 7 January both Bruckner and Wolf attended the final rehearsal of their choral pieces by the Philharmonic Choir, and, on the evening of the same day, Bruckner is reported to have celebrated his 'engagement' to Ida Buhz with her family.[367] Ida had accompanied Bruckner to the performance of the Seventh the previous evening and she was also with him when his *Te Deum* was performed on 8 January. Two of Wolf's pieces - *Elfenlied* and *Der Feuerreiter* - were particularly well received, as was Bruckner's piece which was performed in the second half of the concert.[368]

---

366   See *G-A* IV/3, 367ff. for this review, dated 7 January 1894 and signed 'O. E.' in the *Boursen-Courier*.

367   As Bruckner attended a performance of Wagner's *Fliegende Holländer* on the evening of the 7th, however, it is more likely that this 'celebration' took place the following day. Indeed Ochs, in his *Geschehenes, Gesehenes* (Leipzig, 1922), 318f. recalls that it was in the afternoon and reports that his wife went to the *Kaiserhof* hotel, where Bruckner was staying, in an attempt to have this 'engagement' cancelled!

368   See *G-A* IV/3, 370f. for the review of the concert in the *Boursen-Courier* (9 January 1894). See also Ernst Decsey, *Hugo Wolf* (Berlin, 1921), 99 for a reference to Wilhelm Tappert's review of the concert in the *Kleines Journal*. Reports of the Berlin performances of the Seventh Symphony and *Te Deum* also appeared in French papers - *Le Monde artiste* (21 January 1894), *Ménestrel* (21 January 1894) and *Guide musical* (21 January 1894); see Josef Burg, 'Der Komponist Anton Bruckner im Spiegelbild der französischen Musikpresse seiner Zeit' in *BJ 1987/88* (Linz, 1990), 105

Ochs later recalled Bruckner's delighted reaction to the rehearsal and performance of the *Te Deum*. Evidently he gave a 20-mark coin to Ochs after the rehearsal and, when the no doubt somewhat embarrassed conductor refused to take it, suggested that he pass it on to the timpanist for his outstanding contribution, in particular his drum roll on the note B near the beginning of the work, an addition made by Ochs and approved by the composer.[369] Bruckner also sent a telegram to his friend Theodor Helm in Vienna to reassure him of the successful performances of his two works.[370]

Hugo Wolf provided detailed information about the visit to Berlin in three letters to Melanie Köchert. In the first he referred to the performance of Bruckner's Seventh conducted by Muck:

> ... The performance of Bruckner's Symphony no. 7 was a masterly achievement by Muck. The first two movements did not make much of an impression. It wasn't until after the Scherzo and the Finale that Bruckner was applauded. He also appeared on the podium at the end. Bruckner is very happy with his success.

---

for German translations of extracts from these reports.

369 See Ochs, op.cit., 321f., *G-A* IV/3, 371f., and Günter Brosche, 'Anton Bruckner und Hugo Wolf' in O. Wessely, ed., *Bruckner-Studien* (Vienna, 1975), 183. Bruckner made further reference to this when he wrote to Ochs on 14 April. See *ABB*, 282 and *GrBB*, 99; the original of this letter is not extant. On 15 April Ochs wrote to Bruckner in support of a request by Mrs. Sommerfeld for a photograph of the composer and a few bars of music [from the *Te Deum*] for inclusion in the journal *Über Land und Meer*. See *ABB*, 345 for the text of this letter; the original is in St. Florian. On 18 April Bruckner wrote to an 'unbekannte Dame' (according to Gräflinger in *GrBB*, 122), presumably Mrs. Sommerfeld., enclosing the 'requested' items. The original of this letter is owned privately.

370 The original of this telegram, dated Berlin, 9 January 1894, is in the *ÖNB*. Later in January (on Tuesday 23) Theodor Helm and his son visited Bruckner in his apartment. He talked to them about the Adagio of his Seventh Symphony and also played an extract from the Adagio of his Ninth. See Ernst Decsey, *Bruckner. Versuch eines Lebens* (Stuttgart, 1922), 223.

In the next letter Wolf compared the reception given to the performance of his vocal works with the more enthusiastic reception accorded to Bruckner's works. Although he by no means begrudged Bruckner his success he was not particularly pleased to be playing 'second violin' to Bruckner's 'first violin' and he recalled the words from the Old Testament that Saul slew 1,000 but David slew 10,000. Wolf stayed on in Germany and visited Mannheim, Stuttgart and Tübingen before returning to Vienna. In his third letter he makes reference to another of Bruckner's rash proposals of marriage.[371]

Wolf is alluding here to Bruckner's 'engagement' to Ida Buhz, of course. In spite of this, another lady, Margarethe Boucher, attracted his attention while he stayed in Berlin. On his return to Vienna he sent a photograph of himself and she reciprocated by sending him her photograph on 30 January.[372] Although there was obviously no future in his 'relationship' with Ida Buhz, it is evident that she was genuinely fond of him. Her letter to him on 13 February, recalling the Berlin performances of his works, makes that clear.[373] But the fact that she was a Protestant and not prepared to convert to Catholicism was an insurmountable stumbling-block for Brucker, and so marriage was out of the question.[374]

There was a performance of Bruckner's String Quintet on 10 January, played by

---

371 These three letters, dated 8, 9 and 17 January respectively, can be found in Grasberger, ed., *Hugo Wolf. Briefe an Melanie Köchert*, 77ff.

372 See *G-A* IV/3, 373f. for references to this brief correspondence, including another letter from Margarethe Boucher, dated 20 February 1894, in which she mentioned that Bruckner had not acknowledged receipt of her photograph; the location of the originals of these letters is unknown.

373 See *G-A* IV/3, 377f. for extracts from this letter; the original is in St. Florian.

374 Her last recorded letter to Bruckner is dated Berlin, 21 July 1894. See *G-A* IV/3, 415 for extracts ; the original is in St. Florian. In September Anita Muck wrote to her husband to inform him that she had tried unsuccessfully to contact Ida. See extract from this letter, dated Wiesbaden, 20 September 1894, in *G-A* IV/3, 415; the original is not extant.

the Waldemar Meyer Quartet with Adalbert Gülzow taking the 2nd viola part, at a concert arranged by the Berlin *Wagner-Verein*. Bruckner returned to Vienna shortly afterwards and may not have been present at the second performance of his *Te Deum* on 11 January. Ochs, who was unwell, was able neither to conduct nor to accompany Bruckner to the station for his return journey.[375] Bruckner, whose own delicate health had withstood a week of exciting events, did not feel well enough, however, to accept an invitation to attend a performance of his *Te Deum* in Mainz on 17 January.[376]

Gertrud Bollé contacted Franz Bayer in Steyr, enclosed some reviews, and informed him of the favourable critical and public reaction to Bruckner's works in Berlin. Unable to meet Bruckner after the performance of the *Te Deum*, she tried to contact him at his hotel, but her letter arrived there after Bruckner had left and was forwarded to him in Vienna. Her main concern was that he should now know her by her real name and not her 'masculine pseudonym'.[377]

A performance of Bruckner's Second Symphony, conducted by Hans Richter, had been scheduled for the Philharmonic concert on 14 January but the composer asked

---

375 In a letter written to Ochs on his return to Vienna, Bruckner thanked the conductor and his excellent choir for the performance of the *Te Deum*; this letter is owned privately. In his reply, Ochs mentioned that he had been ill since the day of the composer's departure; he hoped, however, to rehearse the F minor Mass for a possible performance the following season. See *ABB*, 346f. for this letter, dated Berlin, 23 February and Frankfurt 27 February 1894; the original is in St. Florian.

376 When he was in Berlin, Bruckner received this invitation from Dr. Ludwig Strecker. The Mainz performance was conducted by Fritz Volbach.

377 See *G-A* IV/3, 378-81 for Bollé's letter to Bayer, dated Berlin, 15 January 1894; the location of the original is unknown. See *ABB*, 296f. for Bollé's letter to Bruckner, dated Berlin, 16 January 1894; the location of the original is unknown.

684

for it to be postponed until later in the year.[378] The Berlin performances in January and the first French performance of a Bruckner symphony in Paris on 18 March must have encouraged the composer and convinced him that his reputation as a symphonist was no longer confined to German-speaking countries. Charles Lamoureux, who conducted the Third Symphony, had been introduced to Bruckner's music by his pupil, Ludwig Oblat, who reported the success of the performance in the Viennese journal, *Musikalische Rundschau*. In a letter to Oblat, Bruckner asked him to thank Lamoureux and suggested other works for the conductor's consideration, giving details of those works which had been printed.[379]

Bruckner's doctor gave him permission to spend Holy Week and Easter at St. Florian; this was to be his last visit to the abbey. He played the organ at some services, including High Mass on Easter Sunday (25 March), improvising on original themes and the fugal theme from Psalm 150. Johann Hayböck, a teacher in St. Florian, recalled a meeting with Bruckner, his brother Ignaz, and Karl Aigner on Maundy Thursday when Bruckner once again mentioned his desire to be buried underneath the organ in the abbey or, if permission was not forthcoming, in Steyr or Vienna.[380] On 14 April Bruckner supplied a testimonial for Aigner, testifying to his

---

378   When Bruckner wrote to Siegfried Ochs again on 10 March, he recalled the Berlin performance of the *Te Deum* with gratitude, and mentioned the postponement of the performance of the Second Symphony as well as a recent visit from Hermann Levi. See *ABB*, 280f. and *GrBB*, 97f.; the original is not extant.

379   See *ABB*, 281 for Bruckner's letter to Oblat, dated Vienna, 13 April 1894; the original is not extant. See also Josef Burg, *BJ 1987/88*, 101f. for further information including a facsimile of two pages of the programme, and 103f. for extracts from reviews of the symphony in *Art Musical* (22 March), *Ménestrel* (25 March) and *Monde artiste illustré* (25 March).

380   See *G-A* II/1, 321ff. and *G-A* IV/3, 384.

abilities as a violinist, organist, pianist and music teacher.[381]

The Schalk correspondence during the first four months of the year is largely taken up with the preparation for and the eventual performance of Bruckner's Fifth in Graz. Joseph succeeded in obtaining Oberleithner's financial help for the copying of the parts of the symphony. However, Franz was encountering various difficulties in rehearsing the symphony. The first movement was proving particularly intractable. Moreover, rehearsals for the forthcoming performance of *Tristan* were consuming a lot of his time and energy.[382] On 10 February Franz reported that the performance of the symphony would have to be delayed. He himself was exhausted with the effort put into *Tristan* and was seeing the doctor regularly as a result of his nervous condition which was not improving. He asked how Bruckner was and if it was possible that he would come to Graz. He also asked if Joseph had taken care of the payment to the copyist, and requested one or two printed articles about Bruckner which he could arrange to have reproduced in Graz if necessary.[383]

Joseph was incensed about the postponement of the concert and asked his brother if he had considered what effect an unsuccessful performance would have on Bruckner.[384] Until the middle of March there were still doubts about the performance of the work. Joseph was annoyed that Oberleithner had wasted his money paying for the copying of parts which might not now be needed, and it looked as if Bruckner's original score would be used for the first edition (Bruckner was asking for it as

---

381 This is the date given by Elisabeth Maier in 'Bruckneriana in Vöcklabruck', *Studien zur Musikwissenschaft* 42 (Tutzing, 1993), 297, footnote 27. The testimonial is printed in *G-A* II/1, 262f. where it is given the date 4 April; the original is owned by the Hueber family in Vöcklabruck.

382 This is the gist of an undated letter, quoted in *FSBB*, 62 and *LBSAB*, 181f.; the original is in the *ÖNB*, F18 Schalk 158/15/5.

383 See *LBSAB*, 182 for an extract from this letter; the original is in the *ÖNB*, F18 Schalk 158/15/17.

384 See *LBSAB*, 182f. for an extract from this letter, dated Vienna, 18 February 1894; the original is in the *ÖNB*, F18 Schalk 158/15/18.

Eberle wanted to start printing).[385]

In spite of various difficulties, the Fifth went through several sectional and full rehearsals and was performed in Graz on 9 April. An announcement in the morning edition of the *Grazer Tagblatt* of 8 April provided the erroneous information that Bruckner would be coming to Graz to attend the performance.[386] The symphony came second in the programme, after Beethoven's overture *The Consecration of the House*.[387] Bruckner was unaware of the several changes Franz had made. All that he knew was that twelve extra wind instruments were to be added to the orchestra for the repeat of the chorale at the end of the Finale. Franz had asked for his permission to do this and Bruckner had readily granted it. In its revised version, the Finale was shortened by 122 bars. Besides two smaller cuts (bars 13-14, 622-25), the development was reduced by 30 bars (bars 324-353) and the reprise of the main and subsidiary themes was deleted (bars 374-459). As a result the clearly recognizable sonata form in Bruckner's original version loses its symmetry. The development does not have the breathing-space of the extended second theme-group but proceeds directly to the final climactic process which culminates in the triumphant return of the wind chorale. This interference in the structure is all the more remarkable as Bruckner suggested his own substantial abridgement for practical use, albeit at a different point in the movement, viz. bars 270-373 (letters L-Q), resulting in the omission of a large part of the fugal development.[388]

---

385 See *LBSAB*, 183f. for an extract from Joseph's letter to Franz, dated Vienna, 20 March 1894; the original is in the *ÖNB*, F18 Schalk 158/15/19.

386 See Nowak, Symphony no. 5 *Revisionsbericht*, 71.

387 The second half of the concert consisted of Liszt's Piano Concerto in E flat and the Prelude to Wagner's *Die Meistersinger*. There is a copy of the concert programme in the *Oberösterreichisches Landesmuseum*, Linz. See also *LBSAB*, 184.

388 In his analysis of the work, Göllerich mentions the added brass instruments in the Finale but there is not enough detail for the reader to determine whether he is referring to the original version

In the event the performance was a great success and Franz informed Bruckner of this in a letter written on 10 April.[389] The critical reaction was also favourable. Writing in the *Grazer Volksblatt*, Carl Seydler pointed to the obvious stylistic similarities between Wagner and Bruckner but made a distinction between Wagner the 'dramatist' and Bruckner the 'lyricist'.[390] Franz Petrich, reviewing the concert for the *Grazer Tagespost*, had nothing but praise for the conductor and the orchestra and drew particular attention to the work's 'energetic rhythms, impressive abundance of ideas... outstanding melodic beauties, incomparable polyphony, bold harmony, surprising modulations, excellent organ points, overpowering climaxes, immense contrapuntal technique, humour, deep feeling and a dazzling display of instrumental colours'.[391] Julius Schuch, the *Grazer Tagblatt* reviewer, recalled Joseph Schalk's performance of the Fourth in Graz. In the Fifth, as in the Fourth, Bruckner displayed his deep admiration for Wagner - but without compromising his own individuality. The work could be likened to the 'musical diary of an inspired artist who provides interesting glimpses of his different moods...'[392]

On returning to Vienna after being present at the performance, Joseph wrote a letter of gratitude to Franz, informing him that Bruckner, who was still confined to bed, had been very excited to hear of the successful performance and would soon be writing to him. Bruckner's wish was that Franz would conduct the Vienna

---

or Schalk's revised version; see *G-A* IV/3, 395-411.

389   See *ABB*, 366f. and Nowak, *ABSW* V *Revisionsbericht*, 71f.; the original is in St. Florian.

390   This review appeared in the *Grazer Volksblatt* 81 (11 April 1894). See Nowak, *ABSW* V *Revisionsbericht*, 77f. for complete review and *G-A* IV/3, 389f. for extract.

391   See *G-A* IV/3, 390-94 and *LBSAB*, 185ff. for this review in the *Grazer Tagespost* (10 April 1894). See also Ingrid Schubert, *BSL 1984*, 58.

392   See Nowak, *ABSW* V *Revisionsbericht*, 76f. for this review in the *Grazer Tagblatt* 97 (10 April 1894). There was also a review by a 'Dr. G.' in the *Grazer Morgenpost* on 11 April.

Philharmonic in a performance of the Fifth the following autumn. Joseph asked Franz to return the score of the symphony and several copies of the Graz reviews.[393]

This request to return the full score as well as the piano reduction of the symphony was repeated in another letter to Franz on 16 April.[394] In the meantime, on 12 April, Bruckner wrote a letter of thanks to Franz from his sick-bed and mentioned the possibility of his conducting the work in Vienna; he had already recommended this to the *Wagner-Verein*.[395] Joseph mentioned the 'receipt of scores' - obviously a reference to those he had requested - when he wrote to Franz a month later.[396] During the second part of the year Joseph worked on a piano arrangement of the revised symphony, using the score which Franz had sent him. On 6 August he wrote to his brother that, as well as recovering from illness, he had made a 'completely new arrangement of the first movement of the Fifth'.[397] On 27 September, however, Franz wrote to Joseph advising him not, under any circumstances, to have the score of the Fifth published for performance purposes.[398] As Leibnitz points out, Bruckner would have been confronted with the reality of which he was unaware - namely that Franz had altered the score of the work in many places - if a performance of the symphony in Vienna had materialized

---

393 See *LBSAB*, 188ff. and Nowak, *ABSW* V *Revisionsbericht*, 72 for this letter, dated Vienna, 11 April 1894; the original is in the *ÖNB*, F18 Schalk 158/15/20.

394 See Nowak, *ABSW* V *Revisionsbericht*, 73; the original is in the *ÖNB*.

395 See *FSBB*, 73, *LBSAB*, 190f. and Nowak, *ABSW* V *Revisionsbericht*, 73; the original is in the *Bergbau- und Heimatmuseum Reichenau an der Rax*.

396 See *LBSAB*, 191f. and Nowak, *ABSW* V *Revisionsbericht*, 73 for this letter, dated Vienna, 24 May 1894; the original is in the *ÖNB*, F18 Schalk 158/15/22.

397 See Nowak, *ABSW* V *Revisionsbericht*, 73 for a reference to this letter; the original is in the *ÖNB*, F18 Schalk 158/15/27.

398 See Nowak, *ABSW* V *Revisionsbericht*, 73 for a reference to this letter; the original is in the *ÖNB*.

during his lifetime.[399]

The recurrence of illness confined Bruckner indoors until the middle of May when he was able to attend Mass on Whit Monday (14 May).[400] Earlier in May there were performances of his *Germanenzug* and the first movement of the Fourth Symphony in Troppau. During the summer, Bruckner spent two months in Steyr (26 July - 30 September). A fortnight before his vacation, however, he received the pleasing news from Franz Posche, the mayor of Linz, that he had been granted honorary citizenship of the town. He was sent a certificate prepared by Professor Leitner and signed by Posche and two members of the town council, Franz Schober and Rudolf Prohaska.[401]

As Bruckner was not able to visit St. Florian he sent his brother Ignaz greetings on his name-day, enclosed ten florins, and said that Kathi, his housekeeper, would send on some clothes that he could no longer use. He also asked his brother to pass on his good wishes to Karl Aigner and Josef Gruber.[402] Is there a suspicion of envy or even of 'sour grapes' in Ignaz's birthday greetings to his brother at the beginning of September; or perhaps no more than an acknowledgment of the inevitable? Ignaz wrote that the only reason that he (Ignaz) was treated with any consideration at St.

---

399   See *LBSAB*, 191. The parts used for the Graz performance and Franz Schalk's copy of the score (engraver's copy for the first edition) have been lost   The first edition was published by Doblinger in 1896 (full score: D. 2080; Joseph Schalk's four-hand piano arrangement: D. 2062). For further details, see Nowak, *ABSW* V *Revisionsbericht*.

400   He was accompanied by Anton Meißner. See the latter's account in *G-A* IV/3, 411f.

401   There was a report of the honour in the *Linzer Tagespost* 158 (13 July 1894). See *G-A* IV/3, 412f. for Poche's letter to Bruckner and for details of the diploma; the original of the letter is not extant. Andrea Harrandt suggests that the original of the certificate is probably in St. Florian.

402   See *ABB*, 282f. for this undated letter, sent from Steyr to reach Ignaz on his name-day (31July); the original is in St. Florian. Bruckner also mentioned that his doctor would be coming to Steyr.

690

Florian was because of the reputation of his famous brother![403]

Bruckner celebrated his 70ᵗʰ birthday on 4 September while he was in Steyr. He received more than 200 letters and telegrams from musical organizations (for instance, the *Akademischer Wagner-Verein*, the *Wiener Männergesangverein*, the *Singverein* of the *Gesellschaft der Musikfreunde*, *Frohsinn*, the *Linzer Sängerbund*, and Hans Richter and the Vienna Philharmonic) students and student organizations, old friends, former pupils, admirers and important dignitaries, including the Prince Bishop of Vienna, the mayor of Vienna, the governor of Upper Austria, and Princess Lobkowitz. There were also various tributes in newspapers and journals, a testimony to the high esteem in which Bruckner was now held.[404]

One of his oldest friends, Rudolf Weinwurm, described him as a 'modern Hercules of art conquering the world' and recalled the days when he belonged 'only to me and a few other friends'; now, however, he 'belonged to the world which would never

---

403 See *G-A* II/1, 324f. for an extract from Ignaz's letter, dated St. Florian, 3 September 1894; the original is in St. Florian.

404 These include Theodor Helm in the *Deutsche Zeitung* 8147 and 8148 , 3 and 4 September 1894; Ludwig Speidel in *Fremdenblatt* , 4 September 1894 (see Manfred Wagner, *Bruckner*, 213-17), Ludwig Hevesi in *Fremdenblatt*, 4 September 1894 (see *G-A* IV/3, 423-27 and Wagner, op.cit., 217ff.); Camillo Horn in *Deutsches Volksblatt* , 4 September 1894), Gustav Schönaich in the *Wiener Tagblatt*, 4 September 1894, articles in the evening edition of the *Neue Freie Presse* , *Die Presse*, *Linzer Volksblatt*, *Wiener Allgemeine Zeitung* (all 4 September 1894), *Wiener Zeitung*, 5 September 1894, *Neues Wiener Tagblatt*, 5 September 1894, *Neue Freie Presse* , 6 September 1894, *Linzer Tagespost* , 8 September 1894, Hans von Wörz in the *Wiener Sonn- und Montagszeitung*, 10 September 1894 (see extract in Louis, op. cit., 339) and Hans Paumgartner in the *WienerAbendpost*, 15 September 1894 (see extract in Tschulik, op.cit., 178); also *Schweizerische Musik-Zeitung* 34 (1894), 164, *Allgemeine Musik-Zeitung* 21 (1894), 468, *Neue Berliner Musikzeitung* 48 (1894), 399. On 11 September Bruckner inserted a small advert in the *Neue Freie Presse*, thanking all those who had sent him birthday wishes.

grow tired of esteeming and admiring him...'[405]   Of particular interest is a congratulatory letter sent by the *Wiener Tonkünstlerverein* which has several signatories, including Johannes Brahms, Ignaz Brüll and one or two other noted anti-Wagnerians. It highlights his great popularity with the Conservatory and University students and assures him that he can 'look back to a long life and think with satisfaction of the recognition and honours' he had received for his 'serious and lofty ambitions'.[406] It was fitting that a delegation from the Steyr town council, including the mayor, should visit Bruckner and present him with official greetings from the town which had almost become his second home during the summer months.[407]

Towards the end of his memorable stay in Steyr, Bruckner added a codicil to his will; financial provision of 4000 florins was to be made towards the upkeep of his grave and, in the event of his wish to be buried under the great organ of St. Florian not being fulfilled, he was to be buried in Steyr. However, assurances had already

---

405 See *ABB*, 377f. for this letter from Weinwurm, dated Vienna, 3 September 1894; the original is in St. Florian.

406 See *G-A* IV/3, 420f. for this letter, dated Vienna, October 1894; the original is in St. Florian. The original of Bruckner's reply to this letter, dated Vienna, 31 October 1894, is in the *Gesellschaft der Musikfreunde* library. See also *GrBLS*, 232f. for a letter from his sister Rosalie - the original is not extant; *ABB*, 367 for a letter from Franz Schalk, dated Graz, 3 September 1894 - the original is in St. Florian; *ABB*, 379 for belated greetings from Hugo Wolf, dated Traunkirchen, 15 September 1894 - there is a facsimile of the original, which is located in the *ÖNB*, in *ABB*, after p. 336; Günter Brosche, 'Anton Bruckner und Hugo Wolf' in O. Wessely, ed., *Bruckner-Studien* (Vienna, 1975), 180, for Bruckner's reply to this letter, dated Steyr, 23 September 1894 - there is a facsimile of this letter, which is privately owned, in Franz Grasberger, *Hugo Wolf. Persönlichkeit und Werk. Eine Ausstellung zum 100. Geburtstag* (Vienna, 1960), after page 76. Other hitherto unpublished greetings will appear in the forthcoming second volume of *Bruckner Briefe*, ed. Andrea Harrandt. My thanks to Dr. Harrandt for supplying this information.

407 See *G-A* IV/3, 416ff. Bruckner was also elected an honorary member of the Steyr *Liedertafel* and the Vienna *Schubertbund*.

been given that he could be buried at St. Florian. On 9 September Johann Aichinger, the parish priest, had written to Johann Breselmayr, master of the novices and dean at St. Florian, conveying Bruckner's wishes that he be laid to rest beneath the great organ, and Breselmayr's letter of reply contained a postscriptum in which Ferdinand Moser, the provost of the abbey, reassured him that Bruckner's wish would be fulfilled. Bruckner obviously needed a lot of convincing![408]

On 26 September Bruckner wrote to his housekeeper to inform her of his impending return to Vienna.[409] Clearly he had not deemed it necessary to follow his doctor's advice to return to Vienna earlier if the weather did not improve.[410]

The events leading up to the performance of Bruckner's F minor Mass at a *Gesellschaft* concert on 4 November again illustrate the thin dividing-line between well-intentioned 'meddling' and dishonest distortion on the part of Bruckner's friends. Oberleithner, who was preparing the proof copy of the work with Joseph Schalk, hoped to include certain of his own revisions in the printed version. Both of them had already collaborated in the printing of the Eighth and certain 'corrections' had been made which had not been noticed by Bruckner. In the case of the F minor Mass, however, there was an altercation between Bruckner, Schalk and Oberleithner, as Joseph made clear when he wrote to Franz on 24 May:

> ... The cause of it was a sudden outbreak of anger on Bruckner's part
> that something could have been altered without his knowledge in the

---

408   See *G-A* IV/3, 427-30 and Rolf Keller, *BJ 1982/83*, 105f. for further details of the codicil, signed by Bruckner on 25 September and witnessed by Bayer and two others. See *ABA*, 117f. for extracts from Aichinger's letter to Breselmayr and the latter's reply, dated St. Florian, 11 September 1894; the originals are in St. Florian and the Vienna *Stadt- und Landesbibliothek* respectively.

409   See *ABA*, 100 for facsimile and 101 for transcription of this letter; the original is in the *ÖNB*.

410   See *G-A* IV/3, 430, footnote 1 for a reference to this letter from Professor Schrötter, dated Vienna, 11 September 1894; the original is in St. Florian.

F minor Mass which is now at the printing stage. With the greatest impetuousness he demanded back his score which is in Oberleithner's safe keeping at present. Fortunately the printed score has not yet been published and it can only be hoped that Bruckner will forget the whole matter in the meantime - otherwise there will be a terrible fuss. The agitation has made him ill again, and he won't allow any of us to visit him...[411]

In his reply a few days later Franz thanked his brother for his favourable comments on the Graz performance of the Fifth, alluded briefly to Joseph's problems with Bruckner and provided information about a new position in Prague he was to take up in the autumn of 1895.[412]

According to the Göllerich-Auer biography this was the final break between Bruckner and Joseph Schalk and Ferdinand Löwe, although there is a footnote to the effect that 'J. Schalk informed his brother of several visits', which suggests that some kind of contact was maintained.[413] This is corroborated by the Schalk correspondence which reveals that, after an interruption, relationships with Bruckner gradually returned to their former amicable level. There is no mention of Bruckner in Joseph's letters to Franz written during June and July 1894. On 1 August, however, Joseph reported that Bruckner was in Steyr and that he intended to travel there on 4 September to congratulate him on his 70th birthday. Whether he would also travel to Munich depended on recovery from illness and progress made in his piano arrangement of Bruckner's Fifth.[414]

We do not know if Joseph actually visited Bruckner in Steyr as he had planned

---

411 See *LBSAB*, 191f. for extracts from this letter; see also footnote 396.

412 See *FSBB*, 63f. and *LBSAB*, 192f. (extracts) for this letter, dated Graz, 27 May 1894; the original has been lost.

413 *G-A* IV/3, 527.

414 See *LBSAB*, 194 for an extract from this letter; the original is in the *ÖNB*, F18 Schalk 158/15/26.

to but, on 3 October, he mentioned his intention of visiting Bruckner, now back in Vienna, within the next few days.[415] Bruckner himself wrote to Joseph on 6 October (albeit with the formal greeting 'Hochverehrter H. Professor'), asking him if he would act as his representative in rehearsals of the F minor Mass and, before that, play through the work for Wilhelm Gericke, as he was too ill to leave his apartment.[416] With the regular fluctuations in Bruckner's health from the end of the year until his death, the composer presumably never got round to comparing the 1894 first edition of the Mass with his own original autograph and so a 'terrible fuss' was averted![417] Joseph, however, maintained contact with Bruckner and kept Franz regularly informed of his condition. He also repeatedly tried to get Franz to come to Vienna with the Prague Opera Orchestra to give a performance of Bruckner's Fifth Symphony - but without success.[418]

Bruckner was able to resume teaching duties at the University on 29 October,[419] and was well enough to attend both the final rehearsal (3 November) and performance (4 November) of his F minor Mass, as well as a performance of Mozart's *Requiem* in the *Hofkapelle* on 2 November.[420] He was accompanied by Karl Waldeck from

---

415   See *LBSAB*, 194 for a reference to this letter; the original is in the *ÖNB*, F18 Schalk 158/15/31.

416   See *LBSAB*, 195; the original is in the *ÖNB*, F18 Schalk 151/2/5/1.

417   The F minor Mass was published in 1894 by Doblinger (full score: D. 1866; piano score arr. Joseph Schalk: D. 1861).

418   Ferdinand Löwe and the Munich Kaim Orchestra had the distinction of giving the symphony its first performance in Vienna on 1 March 1898. During the 1898/99 concert season the first truly Viennese performance of the work was given by Gustav Mahler and the Vienna Philharmonic.

419   See *G-A* IV/3, 432-37 and Ernst Schwanzara, *Anton Bruckner Vorlesungen*, 94ff. for Theodor Altwirth's report (incomplete) of the lecture in the *Linzer Montagspost* on 5 November.

420   Hugo Wolf referred to the final rehearsal and performance of the Mass in a letter to Hugo Faißt.

Linz on all three occasions. Hanslick reviewed the performance of the Mass in the *Neue Freie Presse* on 13 November. The main points of his criticism were that the work belonged to the church and not to the concert hall, and the same weaknesses evident in the symphonies were also present in the Mass, viz. lack of musical logic and stylistic inconsistency - 'Albrechtsberger arm in arm with Wagner'.[421] At Bruckner's University lecture on 5 November he told his students that he was very pleased with the performance, although he felt that Gericke had taken the *Kyrie* and the first part of the *Gloria* too quickly. He also mentioned that Waldeck had been at the performance and explained how Waldeck had been responsible for a complete revision of the 'Et incarnatus est' section in the *Credo* over 25 years earlier. Bruckner was particularly pleased that Brahms had joined in the applause at the end of the performance; it is reported that Bruckner made a point of thanking him. His lecture on 12 November was his last. He referred to his work on the Ninth Symphony, saying that the first three movements were now complete, although he still had to put some finishing touches to the third. The *Te Deum* was to be used as the fourth movement if he was unable to complete the work before his death. Towards the end of November Bruckner's health deteriorated rapidly. Joseph Schalk was so concerned that he asked Franz to write to Bruckner immediately 'since the catastrophe could happen any day'.[422] But Bruckner was able to attend the postponed performance of his revised Second Symphony on 25 November in a Philharmonic concert conducted by Hans Richter. The audience reception was warm and Bruckner was cheered after each movement; but the reviews were mixed. Helm, writing in the *Deutsche Zeitung*, was complimentary, Heuberger, writing in the *Wiener Tagblatt*, less so. In his last large-scale review of a Bruckner

---

He had already mentioned in a letter to Melanie Köchert (mid-October?) that he intended to travel to Vienna on 20 October as he did not want to miss the performance of the Mass.

421 See *G-A* IV/3, 438-44 for Hanslick's review in the *Neue Freie Presse* 10857 (13 November).

422 See *LBSAB*, 195 for extracts from this letter, dated Vienna, 21 November 1894; the original is in the *ÖNB*, F18 Schalk 158/15/33.

work, Hans Paumgartner described the Second as the most genial of all the symphonies.[423]

Earlier in the year Bruckner's salary as a University lecturer was increased from 800 to 1200 florins.[424] Almost certainly some adjustment would have been made for the 1894-95 academic year after Bruckner's retirement on health grounds. At the end of November, however, he received a letter from the Lower Austrian Parliament informing him that he had been granted an honorarium of 600 florins for 1895 and a subsidy of 150 florins for 1894 'for composition purposes'.[425]

Bruckner was so ill at the beginning of December that he received the last rites on 9 December. But his health improved to such an extent that he was able to spend Christmas at Klosterneuburg and even play the organ at High Mass on 26 December. There was a relapse immediately afterwards, Bruckner contracted pleurisy, and his condition became so serious again that his brother Ignaz came from St. Florian to be with him and to assist his housekeeper. Ignaz stayed for six weeks until there was another improvement in Bruckner's condition.[426] In the meantime, a 'Bruckner

---

423 See *G-A* IV/3, 449ff. for extracts from Helm's review in the *Deutsche Zeitung* (30 November 1894) and Heuberger's in the *Wiener Tagblatt*, Andrea Harrandt, *BSL 1991*, 66ff. for reference to Schönaich's review in the *Extrapost* (26 November 1894), and Norbert Tschulik, *BJ 1981*, for reference to Paumgartner's review in the *Wiener Abendpost* (4 December 1894). Paumgartner also reviewed Ferdinand Löwe's performance of his solo piano arrangement of the first movement from Bruckner's Sixth Symphony at a *Wagner-Verein* concert on 29 November. On 18 December, both concerts were reviewed in the *Ostdeutsche Rundschau* 347; see Nowak, *ABSW* VI *Revisionsbericht* (Vienna, 1986), 62.

424 See Robert Lach, op.cit., 60ff. for texts of the internal University correspondence (19 and 24 February, 2 March) ratifying this.

425 See *ABA*, 102 for this letter, dated 28 November 1894. It is also mentioned in *G-A* IV/3, 447; the original is in the *ÖNB*.

426 On 1 January 1895 Ignaz wrote to Johann Nepomuk Hueber in Vöcklabruck that another improvement in Bruckner's condition had astonished his doctors. See Elisabeth Maier, *Studien zur*

celebration' which was arranged by the *Wagner-Verein* and was to include a performance of his Seventh Symphony conducted by Ferdinand Löwe was postponed indefinitely.

At the end of January 1895 Bruckner followed the advice of his doctor, Professor Schrötter, and wrote to the Lord Chamberlain to enquire if there were any suitable ground-floor or first-storey apartments to rent.[427] Prince Liechtenstein replied in the negative,[428] but Anton Meißner, Bruckner's secretary, learnt from one of his friends, a chaplain in Belvedere, that there was a house standing empty in the grounds of the palace and made a formal approach to Archduchess Marie Valerie.[429] By the middle of May this lodge - the 'Kustodenstöckl' - was placed at Bruckner's disposal on Emperor Franz Josef's recommendation. Bruckner moved to his new spacious home, with the help of Meißner and Kathi Kachelmayr, on 4 July.[430]

Musikwissenschaft 42, 290 for the text of this letter; the original is in the possession of the Hueber family in Vöcklabruck.

427 See *G-A* IV/3, 500f. for the text of this letter, dated Vienna, 28 January 1895; the original, which has Bruckner's signature but was written by an amanuensis (possibly Meißner?), is in the library of the *Stiftung Fürst Liechtenstein*, Vienna.

428 See *G-A*, 501f. for this letter, dated Vienna, 6 February 1895; the original is in the library of the *Stiftung Fürst Liechtenstein*, Vienna.

429 For the text of this letter, written on Bruckner's behalf by Meißner and dated Vienna, 19 February 1895, see Erich W. Partsch, 'Anton Meißner, der letzte "Sekretär" Bruckners' in *BJ 1984/85/86* (Linz, 1988), 59 and 60 (facsimile); the original of the letter is in the *Haus-, Hof- und Staatsarchiv*, Vienna.

430 Bruckner mentioned his imminent move to the Belvedere in a letter, dated Vienna, 19 June 1895, written to his sister Rosalie who had been ill. See *ABB*, 285 and extract in *G-A* IV/3, 513; the original is in the *Heimathaus*, Vöcklabruck. Auer reports that, at Bruckner's request, Meißner had to destroy quite a number of manuscript pages during the preparations for the move, for instance the scores of Psalm 146, Psalm 112 and Symphony no. 'O'. However, although the autograph score of Psalm 146 is incomplete, the autographs of Psalm 112 and the Symphony are available. There is

Another bout of severe ill-health in April and May prevented Bruckner from going to St. Florian at Easter and from attending the 50th anniversary celebrations of *Frohsinn* in Linz which culminated in the unveiling of a memorial plaque on Bruckner's birth house in Ansfelden on Sunday 12 May. *Frohsinn* sang several pieces, including Beethoven's *Ehre Gottes* and Floderer's *Bruckner-Hymne*, a setting of words by Karl Kerschbaum.[431] Ill health also prevented him from having a summer break in Steyr, but he wrote to his friend Franz Bayer on three occasions. On 26 June he asked him for some news from Steyr and mentioned his imminent move to a house in the Belvedere. On 9 July he told Bayer that it was unlikely that he would be able to travel for some time, and on 22 July, in a reply to a letter from Bayer, he said how shocked he was to hear of the illness of another Steyr friend, the parish priest Aichinger.[432]

Bruckner's former landlord, Dr. Oelzelt von Newin, wrote to him on two occasions. In the first, a card dated 2 July, he sent Bruckner good wishes for the

---

no doubt, however, that a substantial amount of sketch material was destroyed at the time.

431 See *G-A* IV/3, 509 for reference to a letter from *Frohsinn* to Bruckner, dated Linz, 8 April 1895, expressing disappointment that the composer would not be able to attend the unveiling ceremony, and enclosing a special brochure written for the occasion by Franz Brunner; and *ABA*, 119 for the good-wish telegram from *Frohsinn*, dated Ansfelden, 12 May 1895; the original of the former is in St. Florian , and the original of the latter is in the *ÖNB*.   Also see *GrBB*, 32 for Bruckner's letter of thanks to *Frohsinn*, dated Vienna, 19 May 1895. There is a facsimile of the original in Walter Abendroth, *Bruckner. Eine Bildbiographie* (Munich, 1958), 116; the original itself is in the *Stadtarchiv*, Linz.

432 See *ABB*, 285ff. for these three letters. The original of the first is in the *ÖNB*, the originals of the second and third are in the *Museum*, Steyr; there is a facsimile of the final two pages of the first letter in Gräflinger, *Anton Bruckner. Sein Leben und seine Werke* (Regensburg, 1921), after p. 128. See also Elisabeth Maier, *Studien zur Musikwissenschaft* 42 (1993), 292f. for the text of a letter from Bayer to Bruckner, dated 1 July 1895. Aichinger died later in the year, and Bruckner's *Requiem* was sung at his funeral service in Steyr on 4 December. See *ABB*, 289 for Bruckner's letter to Bayer, dated Vienna, 10 December 1895; the original is in the *ÖNB*.

move to the Belvedere, and in the second, a letter dated 11 July, he agreed to become, in effect, a member of the consortium which provided the composer with financial help.[433] Gertrud Bollé also persisted with her efforts to interest Bruckner in an opera subject and offered to send him a libretto if he wished to read it. Meißner replied on Bruckner's behalf, hinting that the composer would not undertake any fresh composition projects until he had finished the Ninth, but promising to read some excerpts to Bruckner if she sent the libretto. On 6 July, two days after Bruckner's move to the Belvedere, Meißner acknowledged receipt of the libretto of *Astra* and conveyed Bruckner's thanks but offered little hope of Bruckner being able to make use of it.[434]

Bruckner made a partial recovery at the end of the summer and even felt well enough to contemplate resuming his weekly University lectures, but his doctors advised against it. Given his physical frailty by now, a relapse in his condition was more than likely; and, in any case, it appears that applications were already being sought for a replacement.[435]

There were several performances of Bruckner works during the year. The Third

---

433 See *G-A* IV/3, 519 and 521 for reference to the former and extracts from the latter. Oelzelt von Newin had rented the apartment in the Hessgasse to Bruckner at very reasonable terms, and this new arrangement was no doubt meant to take the place of the old.

434 See *G-A* IV/3, 528-32 for Bollé's letter to Bruckner, dated Berlin, 5 May 1895, Meißner's first reply (date not known), and second reply; the originals are not extant. Also see earlier, pages 673 and 683, footnotes 350 and 377.

435 Earlier in the year, on 30 April, Bruckner wrote a letter to the Faculty of Philosophy at the University in support of Franz Ludwig Marschner's application for a University lectureship. At a faculty meeting on 15 May, Bruckner's letter was read out, but the general feeling was that his reference was not sufficiently detailed. See Theophil Antonicek, 'Anton Bruckner als akademischer Gutachter' in *BJ 1982/83* (Linz, 1984), 82ff which also includes facsimiles of Bruckner's original draft and the fair copy written by Meißner and signed by Bruckner; the originals of these documents are in the Vienna University library.

Symphony was conducted by Erich W. Degner in Graz on 10 February, the Fourth Symphony was conducted by Mahler in Hamburg on 18 February and by Weingartner in Berlin on 9 March, and Levi conducted one of the symphonies (possibly No. 2) in Munich..[436] There were also performances of the *Te Deum* in Warnsdorf, *Germanenzug* in Linz (17 March; *Frohsinn* conducted by Floderer) and Chicago (15 December), the String Quintet in Leipzig (Prill Quartet, 16 November),[437] Symphony no. 7 in Frankfurt (18 December; conducted by Ludwig Rottenberger),[438] Symphony no. 8 in Dresden (18 December, conducted by Louis Nicodé)[439] and two further performances of the Fourth in Linz (25 October,

---

436   See Ingrid Schubert, *BSL 1984*, 39 and 58 and Röder, *III. Symphonie Revisionbericht*, 439f. for reference to and extracts from Julius Schuch's review of the performance in the *Grazer Tagblatt* (11 February 1895) and the review by 'V.P.' in the *Grazer Morgenpost* (12 February 1895). Weingartner sent Bruckner a telegram on the day of the Berlin performance - 'the first three movements were applauded enthusiastically, the last made a deep impression...'; see *G-A* IV/3, 507, however, for Auer's comment that Weingartner had 'mutilated' the symphony by making cuts and that the Berlin reviews were, with a few exceptions, very unkind. Meißner wrote on Bruckner's behalf to thank him for the Berlin performance; see *ABB,* 283 for this letter (undated); the originals of the telegram and Bruckner's letter are not extant.

437   This was the first performance of the work in the city. It was given in the small hall of the Gewandhaus.   For further information and reviews of the performance in *Signale für die musikalische Welt, Musikalisches Wochenblatt, Leipziger Neueste Nachrichten* and the *Leipziger Zeitung*, see Steffen Lieberwirth, *ABDS* 6, 76-81. On 4 December, Bruckner sent greetings to Nikisch in Leipzig. See *ABB,* 288; the original is not extant.

438   See *G-A* IV/3, 539 for an extract from Engelbert Humperdinck's favourable review of the Frankfurt performance in the *Fremdenblatt* (20 December 1895) also Othmar Wessely, *BSL 1991,* 146 for another review of the performance, signed 'hs.', in the *Neue Zeitschrift für Musik* 92 (29 January 1896), 52.

439   See extracts from reviews by Karl Söhle (*Deutsche Wacht,* 20 December 1895) and Alphons Maurice (*Österreichische Musik- und Theater-Zeitung* 8/8-9, 11, 1 January 1896) in *G-A* IV/3, 537f. Nicodé invited Bruckner to attend the performance (which was planned originally for 27 November),

conducted by Adalbert Schreyer) and Dresden (15 November, conducted by Adolf Hagen).[440] Eighteen months after Franz Schalk's performance of the Fifth in Graz, another of Bruckner's pupils, Ferdinand Löwe, conducted the work in Budapest on 18 December. There is some discrepancy between Auer's report of a relatively successful performance and Joseph Schalk's less sanguine report to his brother of a revolt among the orchestral musicians being averted thanks to the intervention of some of the more level-headed members.[441]

At the beginning of May Archduchess Gisela of Bavaria informed Bruckner that she had recommended to her friend, the Princess of Monaco, that one of his symphonies be included in a series of classical concerts there; she suggested that Bruckner send one of his works. In his reply Bruckner thanked her and mentioned his fragile physical condition. At the end of July he wrote to her again to reassure her that, in compliance with her wish, he had instructed Gutmann to send the score and parts of the Seventh Symphony to Monaco; he was also able to tell her that, thanks to the kindness of her father, Emperor Franz Josef, he had just moved to a house in

---

but Bruckner had to decline because of his poor health. See *ABB*, 287f. for Bruckner's first reply, dated 30 August, 1895, and 291f. for Bruckner's belated letter of thanks to Nicodé, dated Vienna, 24 February 1896; the original of the former is in St. Florian, but the original of the latter is not extant.

440 On 4 December Bruckner sent Schreyer a reference in which he recommended him for a conducting position on the strength of several excellent performances of his works he had directed in Linz. See Othmar Wessely, 'Ein unbekanntes Bruckner-Dokument' in *Oberösterreichischer Kulturbericht* 20 (14 May 1948); the original is in the library of the *Oberösterreichisches Landesmuseum* in Linz. See *G-A* IV/3, 534ff. for Karl Söhle's appreciative review of the Dresden performance in the *Deutsche Wacht* (17 November)

441 See *G-A* IV/3, 540 for Auer's comments and *LBSAB*, 202f. for an extract from Joseph's letter, dated Vienna, 28 December 1895; the original is in the *ÖNB*, F18 Schalk 158/16/32. Six weeks earlier, on 13 November, Joseph informed Franz that Löwe had been invited to conduct a performance of the symphony in Budapest. See *LBSAB*, 202 for an extract from this letter; the original is in the *ÖNB*, F18 Schalk 158/16/27.

the grounds of the Belvedere.[442]

Work on the Ninth continued at an understandably slow pace. During the year Bruckner entrusted the autograph manuscripts of the symphony to Karl Muck.[443] The first references to the Finale occur in May. Writing to Franz on 13 May, Joseph said that Bruckner had made a remarkable recovery and was 'now intending to take up the Finale of the Ninth'.[444] A note in Bruckner's calendar on 24 May: '24. Mai 895. 1.mal Finale neue Scitze' and the date '8. Juni' on a page of these preliminary sketches clearly indicate the completion of a certain amount of work on the Finale before his move to the lodge in the Belvedere at the beginning of July. In mid-July an article in the Steyr newspaper, *Der Alpenbote*, reported on Bruckner's move to the Belvedere and referred to his completion of the first three movements of the Ninth and the existence of sketches for the fourth movement.[445] As we have seen, Meißner, in acknowledging receipt of an opera libretto for Bruckner, thanked Gertrud Bollé and confirmed that the composer was working slowly on the Ninth which he would want to complete, in any case, before even contemplating writing an

---

442   See *ABB*, 284 and 288 for Bruckner's two letters to the Archduchess, dated 10 May and 31 July 1895; the originals are not extant..

443   It is possible that Bruckner did this because he did not trust his friends. See *LBSAB*, 191ff. for a discussion of Bruckner's strained relationships with his younger Viennese colleagues at this time. Joseph Schalk's note in Bruckner's calendar on 4 October 1895: 'Die ersten 10 Bogen des ersten Satzes der neunten Symphonie zum Arrangement erhalten' suggests that he received some discarded sheets or part of Meißner's copy [Mus. Hs. 29.305 in the *ÖNB*] which includes some of Schalk's insertions.   See also John Phillips, 'Neue Erkenntnisse zum Finale der Neunten Symphonie' in *BJ 1989/90* (Linz, 1992), 130.

444   See *FSBB*, 64 and *LBSAB*, 199 for extracts from this letter; the original is in the *ÖNB*, F18 Schalk 158/16/10.

445   See John Phillips, *BJ 1989/90*, 131 for the text of this report in *Der Alpenbote* 56 (14 July 1895), 4.

opera.[446] The reminiscences of one of Bruckner's doctors, Dr. Richard Heller, who seems to have had some knowledge of music, can be regarded as being fairly reliable. Although Heller suggested to Bruckner that he write down the principal ideas of the last movement, the composer persisted in writing everything out ('the complete instrumental development') laboriously page by page. Progress was slow because Bruckner's hands trembled so much. There were inevitable blots and mistakes which had to be carefully erased and pasted over.[447] Bruckner adopted his usual practice of beginning with a particell or short-score sketch (sometimes no more than a single line), each bar numbered metrically within a periodic scheme. By the end of 1895 he had already begun writing the fugal section of the movement.

The Schalk brothers' correspondence during the final eighteen months of so of Bruckner's life contains reports of his failing health as well as references to the printing of the Fifth Symphony (based on Franz Schalk's revision) and to the E minor Mass. According to Joseph, the latter also needed some correction and he suggested that his brother peruse it. All this was done without or with very little reference to Bruckner. On 18 February Joseph wrote to his brother:

> ... Bruckner's infirmity goes on and on. There is no cure for it. He sits in his easy-chair each day from 4 to 6 and 8.30 to 11.30 and can now eat only milky foods because the swelling has started up again. As you can imagine, he is very depressed.[448]

In April 1895 the score of Symphony no. 5 was sent to Eberle for printing. There

---

446 See earlier, page 699 and footnote 434 (letter dated Vienna, 6 July 1895)

447 See G-A IV/3, 526ff. and Max Auer, 'Bruckners letzter behandelnder Arzt' in Karl Kobald, ed., In Memoriam Anton Bruckner. Festschrift zum 100 Geburtstage Anton Bruckners (Zurich-Vienna-Leipzig, 1924), 26f.

448 See FSBB, 64 and LBSAB, 198f. for extracts from this letter; the original is in the ÖNB, F18 Schalk 158/16/8.

is a reference to this in Bruckner's 1894/95 calendar - 'Eberle Part. 5. Sinf.' Also in the calendar are comments by Anton Meißner 'Die Partitur der V. Symphonie die jetzt zum Druck verwendet wird' (May) and 'Original-Partituren (im gesiegelten Paquet [!]... 5 Symphonie vollständig...' (July); there is also a reference here to other scores which were 'sealed' in preparation for the move to the Belvedere. Writing to Franz on 6 July, two days after Bruckner's move, Joseph mentioned that he had not yet received the proofs of the symphony from the printer.[449]

On 13 May Joseph was able to report to Franz that Bruckner's health had improved to such an extent that he was considering resuming work on the Finale of the Ninth.[450] Franz replied that he was very pleased to hear this news and added that he had always regarded Bruckner as his 'musical father' and tried as far as possible to be a 'good son'.[451]

Joseph's letter to Franz on 6 July was mainly concerned with the score of the E minor Mass which he regarded as being in 'great need of revision', a task which he hoped that Franz would be willing to take on.[452] Almost a week later Joseph wrote to Franz again to report that he had visited Bruckner who was still in fairly good health although very weak.[453]

Franz was willing to take on the task of revising the score of the Mass and was able to report to Joseph at the end of July that he had almost completed the *Credo*

---

449   See *LBSAB*, 199 for an extract from this letter; the original is in the *ÖNB*, F18 Schalk 158/16/14. See also Nowak, *Symphony no. 5 Revisionsbericht*, 73.

450   See earlier, p. 702 and footnote 444.

451   See *LBSAB*, 199 for an extract from this letter, dated Graz, 16 May 1895; the original is in the *ÖNB*, F18 Schalk 158/16/11.

452   See above and footnote 449.

453   See *FSBB*, 64 for an extract from this letter, dated Vienna, 12 July 1895; the original is in the *ÖNB*, Schalk collection.

movement.[454] In August Franz moved to Prague to take up the position of music director at the *Deutsches Landestheater*. Joseph was keen to know what his brother thought of the Mass as he was hoping to include it in the *Wagner-Verein* programme for the following season.[455] The date of the second proofs of the Fifth was stamped '27 August 1895' by Eberle. Two days later Joseph contacted Franz again and asked if he would be prepared to check these proofs.[456]

At the beginning of September Franz Schalk reassured Joseph that the E minor Mass was well worth performing; the *Sanctus* and *Benedictus* movements in particular would have a powerful effect on a wider audience. But there were some considerable difficulties in the vocal parts. As far as his new appointment was concerned, the first concert would be in October and he was still vacillating between Berlioz's *Harold in Italy* symphony and Bruckner's Fifth. He intended to telegram birthday greetings to Bruckner the following day.[457] On 19 September Joseph wrote again to Franz and asked him to send the corrected Mass as soon as possible so that parts could be prepared. As far as the Fifth was concerned, it was important that Franz take an hour of his time to proof-read the score and check the time- and tempo-markings in particular. Eberle's own proof reader had transferred all the markings from the piano score to the full score and he [Joseph] had deleted several of these but had retained others. If Franz wished to make any further changes he

---

454 See *LBSAB*, 199 for an extract from this letter, dated Graz, 31 July 1895; the original is in the *ÖNB*, F18 Schalk 158/16/16.

455 See *LBSAB*, 199f. for extracts from Joseph's letters to Franz, dated Vienna, 7 August and 24 August 1895; the originals are in the *ÖNB*, F18 Schalk 158/16/17 and 158/16/19.

456 See Nowak, *Symphony no. 5 Revisionsbericht*, 73 for a reference to this letter, dated Vienna, 29 August 1895; the original is in the *ÖNB*, Schalk collection.

457 See *LBSAB*, 200 for an extract from this letter, dated Prague, 2 September 1895; the original is in the *ÖNB*, F18 Schalk 158/16/21.

should use a blue pencil so that they could be identified easily.[458] In his next letter to Franz, Joseph asked him to return the proofs of the Fifth as soon as possible as Eberle required them. He also mooted the possibility of Franz and the Prague orchestra performing the symphony in Vienna - 'otherwise it will, unfortunately, fall into the hands of Richter'. Three days later, Joseph repeated his request for a speedy return of the proofs and enclosed a congratulations' card from Bruckner; he also mentioned that there was no improvement in Bruckner's health.[459] Writing again on 14 October, Joseph once more raised the possibility of a performance of the Fifth in Vienna, provided that Neumann, the chief conductor of the Prague orchestra, was willing to free his players for a couple of days for this purpose.[460] Franz replied that it would be impossible at present to bring the Prague orchestra to Vienna for a performance of the Fifth. Neumann was certainly sympathetic to the idea but they were experiencing difficulties in arranging even their own 'domestic' concerts in Prague! In any case extra forces would have to be found to provide a large enough orchestra to perform the symphony in Vienna. He was hoping to perform the symphony, however, at the second *Gesellschaft* concert in Prague.[461] In the meantime, however, Löwe had been invited by the Philharmonic in Pest to conduct a concert there on 18 December, and Löwe was hoping to include the Fifth in the programme. Joseph was certain that this would prompt Richter to programme the work in Vienna during the

---

458 See *LBSAB*, 200f. for an extract from this letter; the original is in the *ÖNB*, F18 Schalk 158/16/22.

459 See *LBSAB*, 201 and Nowak, *Symphony no. 5 Revisionsbericht*, 74 for extracts from these two letters, dated Vienna, 3 and 6 October 1895; the originals are in the *ÖNB*, F18 Schalk 158/16/23 and 158/16/24. The 'congratulations' were either for Franz's name-day or for his new appointment.

460 See *LBSAB*, 201 for an extract from this letter; the original is in the *ÖNB*, F18 Schalk 158/16/25.

461 See *LBSAB*, 210f. for an extract from this letter, dated Prague, 15 October 1895; the original is in the *ÖNB*, F18 Schalk 158/16/25a.

season.[462] Franz's suggestion that he and his brother collaborate in a joint Bruckner concert in Vienna met with Joseph's enthusiastic approval.[463] When Joseph wrote to Franz again at the end of the year to report *inter alia* on recent performances of Bruckner's works including the Fifth in Pest, he asked him not to forget to 'write a couple of lines to Bruckner in the New Year'.[464]

Bruckner spent Christmas in his house in the Belvedere. A man of routine, he would have faithfully maintained his daily religious devotions and, weather and health permitting, gone for daily walks in the park in the company of his housekeeper and Anton Meißner.[465] On 10 December he sent his customary Christmas and New Year greetings to his sister Rosalie in Vöcklabruck and his brother Ignaz in St. Florian, enclosing 10 florins in both letters as usual.[466] On the same day he wrote to Franz Bayer in Steyr and Ernst Lanninger in Hörsching. In his letter to Bayer he enclosed 25 florins, presumably his contribution to the expenses of Aichinger's funeral at which his Requiem was sung, and a reference in which he testified to Bayer's skills as a conductor and organist.[467] His letter to Lanninger, the parish priest of Hörsching, was probably in response to a request for information. He confirmed that his cousin,

---

462   See earlier, p. 701 and footnote 441 re Joseph's letter to Franz, Vienna, 13 November 1895.

463   See *LBSAB*, 202 for an extract from Joseph's letter to Franz, dated Vienna, 17 December 1895; the original is in the *ÖNB*, F18 Schalk 158/16/31.

464   See earlier, p. 701 and footnote 441 re Joseph's letter to Franz, Vienna, 28 December 1895.

465   See *G-A* IV/3, 513-17 and 523ff. for Meißner's and Heller's accounts.

466   See *ABB*, 290 for the text (almost identical) of both letters; the original of his letter to Rosalie is not extant, the original of his letter to Ignaz is in St. Florian.

467   See also earlier reference to this letter (page 698, footnote 432). The text of Bruckner's reference can be found in Carl H. Watzinger, 'Franz Bayer, ein Freund Anton Bruckners' in *Brucknerland. Mitteilungen des Brucknerbundes für Oberösterreich* 2/1975, 22. The original of this reference is in the *Kulturamt der Stadt Steyr*; there is a facsimile in Hans Hubert Schönzeler, *Bruckner* (Vienna, 1974), before p. 97.

J.B. Weiß, had given him his first organ lessons in the years 1835-37 and made a particular request that Weiß be remembered in Mass.[468]

A special 'Bruckner edition' of the *Österreichische Musik- und Theater-Zeitung* on 15 December must have brought the ailing composer particular pleasure. There were biographical contributions from Victor Boller, Theodor Helm and Victor Joss and articles on the Eighth Symphony by Helm and the F minor Mass by Brzetislav Lvovsky.[469] Bruckner was invited to attend the Christmas celebrations of the *Wiener Männergesangverein*, but we do not know if he was well enough to attend.

On 5 January 1896, however, he was able to attend a Philharmonic concert in which his Fourth Symphony was performed. Most of the reviews were positive, but Max Kalbeck, writing in the *Wiener Tagblatt*, described the work as a 'product of fantastic arbitrariness, effusiveness and egotism, an ecstatic revelry of unclear feelings, a flood of frenzied thoughts alternating with fixed ideas...'[470] Bruckner heard one of his own works for the last time at a *Gesellschaft* concert on 12 January which included works by Brahms, Herbeck as well as the *Te Deum*.[471] His last

---

468 See *ABB*, 291 for Bruckner's letter to Lanninger; the original is owned privately. An article, almost certainly by Lanninger, appeared in the *Linzer Volksblatt* 288 (14 December 1895). It concerned Bruckner's time in Hörsching and Johann Baptist Schiedermayr's high opinion of Weiß. The text can be found in Franz Zamazal, 'Zeitgenössische Notizen über Anton Bruckner, Ludwig Edlbacher und Georg Huemer', *BJ 1991/92/93* (Linz., 1995), 200.

469 Extracts from some of the articles can be found in Claudia C. Röthig, 'Studien zur Systematik des Schaffens von Anton Bruckner', *Göttinger musikwissenschaftliche Arbeiten* 9 (Göttingen/Kassel, 1978), 78f., 104 and 119.

470 See *G-A* IV/3, 549f. for extracts from this review, dated 8 January 1896. See also Theophil Antonicek, *BSL 1991*, 82ff. and Andrea Harrandt, *BSL 1991*, 68f. for extracts from Josef Scheu's review in the *Arbeiter-Zeitung* (10 January) and Gustav Schönaich's review in the *Neue musikalische Presse* (12 January).

471 The Vienna Philharmonic Orchestra and Chorus were conducted by Richard von Perger. Theodor Helm's review of the concert appeared in a supplement to the *Österreichische Musik- und*

public appearance was at a special Palm Sunday concert given by the Philharmonic and the *Wiener Männergesangverein* conducted by Hans Richter on 29 March.

As in 1895 there were several performances of his works inside and outside Austria during 1896. In Graz, Erich W. Degner repeated the success of 1895 (Third Symphony) with a performance of the First Symphony on 11 April.[472] There were four performances of the Second Symphony (in Innsbruck, conducted by Josef Pembaur; in Brno, conducted by Otto Kitzler, 25 March; in Prague, conducted by Felix Dorfner, March; in Heidelberg, conducted by Philipp Wolfrum, 25 November), one of the Third (conducted by Joseph F. Hummel at a *Mozarteum* concert in Salzburg, 16 December), four of the Fourth (in Linz, conducted by Adalbert Schreyer, 25 March; in Frankfurt, 30 October; in Munich, conducted by Franz Fischer, November; in Leipzig, conducted Hans Sitt, 9 November), seven of the Seventh (in Stuttgart, conducted by Alois Obrist, 16 February [Adagio only]; in Troppau, conducted by Ludwig Grande, June; in Berlin, conducted by Nikisch, 26 October [Adagio only]; in Dresden, conducted by Louis Nicodé, 28 October [Adagio only]; in Vienna, conducted by Hans Richter, 8 November; in Helsingfors, conducted by Robert Kajanus, 12 November; in Lucerne, conducted by Peter Fassbaender, 21 November [without the Adagio]), two performances of the String Quintet (both in Vienna - by the *Böhmisches Streichquartett*, 27 March,[473] and the *Duisburg Quartet*,

---

Theater-Zeitung 8 / 12-13, 10; see Gerold W. Gruber, *BSL 1983*, 214 for an extract. Hanslick devoted a single sentence to the *Te Deum* in his review in the *Neue Freie Presse* 11273 (17 January); see Theophil Antonicek, 'Wagner, Bruckner und die Wiener Musikwissenschaft' in *BSL 1984* (Linz, 1986), 72.

472 See Ingrid Schubert, *BSL 1984, 39* for references to a review in the *Grazer Extrablatt* (13 April), Friedrich von Hausegger's review in the *Grazer Tagblatt* (13 April) and Victor Prochaska's review in the *Grazer Morgenpost* (14 April).

473 According to Josef Suk, one of the members of the Quartet, he and Dvořák visited Bruckner and invited him to the performance (Brahms and Dvořák sextets were also included in the concert) -

23 November), two performances of the D minor Mass (in Steyr, conducted Franz Bayer, early April; in Graz, 22 December), a performance of two movements from the E minor Mass (the *Sanctus* and *Benedictus*, in a *Wagner-Verein* concert in Vienna, 19 March),[474] three performances of the Requiem (in Steyr, conducted Franz Bayer, 23 May; in St. Florian, conducted Bernhard Deubler, 16 October; in Vienna, conducted Julius Böhm, 2 November) and another Viennese performance of the *Te Deum* (given by the *Laibacher Musikverein*, conducted by Matej Hubard (23 March). Several of these performances as well as others of the smaller sacred and secular works were occasioned, of course, by Bruckner's death in October and were a memorial tribute to him. Nevertheless, the undeniable increase in the number of performances reflects the willingness of conductors and orchestras to take advantage of the fact that more of Bruckner's works were now available in print. During 1896, for instance, the full score, parts and Joseph Schalk's four-hand piano arrangement of the Fifth Symphony and the score and, possibly, the vocal parts of the E minor Mass were published for the first time.[475]

Bruckner was unable to take up Kitzler's offer to attend the performance of his Second Symphony in Brno on 25 March. On hearing of the success of the performance, however, Bruckner wrote to his former teacher, congratulating him

---

but he declined, because he was working on the Finale of the Ninth.

474 This is mentioned by Karl Pfannhauser in the second part of his article 'Zu Anton Bruckners Messe-Vertonungen', *IBG Mitteilungsblatt* 26 (October 1985), 18. We can assume that Joseph Schalk conducted these two movements with piano accompaniment (by Cyrill Hynais, whose piano score of the Mass was published by Doblinger in 1899?)

475 The forthcoming publication of the Fifth by Doblinger was advertised in Hofmeister's *Monthly Report of Music and Literature* in April 1896. The orchestral parts of the E minor Mass, also published by Doblinger, did not appear until 1899, however.

and mentioning that his health was deteriorating gradually.[476]

In April Franz Bayer not only conducted a performance of Bruckner's D minor Mass in Steyr but took the composer's place at a baptismal service. Bruckner had agreed to become a godparent to his cousin Eduard Zachhuber's young son Anton, but was not well enough to attend. Bruckner wrote to thank Bayer, enclosing five florins and sending his best wishes to young Anton and congratulations to Zachhuber.[477] On 10 May the *Steyrer Zeitung* reported a visit by Bayer to Bruckner at the latter's specific request. Although out of bed, Bruckner spent most of the time in his armchair. Bayer also provided the information that Bruckner had probably sketched the last movement of the Ninth Symphony in full but no longer held out any hope of his being able to 'fully elaborate' it.[478] Bruckner wrote to Bayer again at the end of May to thank his friend for performing his Requiem at the funeral service of Archduke Karl Ludwig on 23 May.[479]

By the middle of May visits of friends and well-wishers were now strictly limited on his doctor's advice.[480] His housekeeper, Kathi Kachelmayr, had been staying overnight for some time and she was now assisted by her daughter, Ludowika

---

476   See *ABB*, 312f. for Kitzler's invitation, dated Brno, 20 March 1896, and *GrBB*, 56f. for Bruckner's letter to Kitzler, dated Vienna, 27 March 1896; the original of Kizler's letter is in St. Florian, but the original of Bruckner's letter is not extant. Kitzler visited Bruckner during the last months of his life; see *G-A* IV/3, 566.

477   See *ABB*, 292f. for this letter, dated Vienna, 17 April 1896; the original is not extant.

478   *Steyrer Zeitung*, 'Lokalnachrichten' 38/3; also published in the *Linzer Volksblatt* (12 May 1896). See John Phillips, *BJ 1989/90*, 136 for reference to this article.

479   Mentioned in *G-A* IV/3, 557; no date given.

480   See footnote 473 for reference to a visit from Dvorák and Suk at the end of March. Grieg was also in Vienna at about the same time. He attended a concert of the *Männergesangverein* on 22 March and gave a recital on 24 March. See *G-A* IV/3, 555 for details of a short visit to Bruckner in the company of Julius Epstein.

Kutschera. Ignaz also came from St. Florian to spend some time with his brother. On 9 May Joseph Schalk wrote to his brother that he had visited Bruckner the previous day. Although terribly emaciated, Bruckner had enough spirit to send his best wishes to Franz.[481] In spite of his deteriorating physical condition Bruckner seems to have been genuinely pleased to see his visitors.[482]

At the beginning of July serious pneumonia took its toll on Bruckner. He was confined to bed and, on Ignaz's advice, took the last rites on the 17th. Again Bruckner rallied and began to show clear signs of improvement. On 30 July he sent his best wishes to Ignaz on his name-day. A fortnight later he wrote with some concern to Josef Gruber at St. Florian to ascertain why Ignaz, who was now back in St. Florian, had not replied to his letter and another two letters sent to him.[483]

There was a noticeable improvement in Bruckner's condition during August. He was able to spend longer periods out of bed and even to go for short walks. Dr. Heller was confident enough to go on holiday 'with an easy conscience'. But there was a relapse during September and by the end of the month he was in a critical condition. On the 24th Joseph reported to Franz that the composer was extremely ill and increasingly afflicted with religious mania. He dared not enter Bruckner's room because of the distressing effect it would have on him. He asked his brother to make sure that he performed the Fifth in Prague before Weingartner in Berlin and Richter

---

481 See *LBSAB*, 203 for a reference to this letter; the original is in the *ÖNB*, F18 Schalk 158/17/17.

482 See *G-A* IV/3, 567, note 1 for a list of friends who visited Bruckner during this period; *G-A* IV/3, 569 for Eckstein's account of a visit by Hugo Wolf; *G-A* IV/3, 564 and 570f. for extracts from Dr. Heller's letters to his wife (9 July - 14 August) in which the composer's ailing health is mentioned; and *G-A* IV/3, 569 for the 'certificate of health' which Heller prepared for Bruckner on 20 July as a means of reassuring him.

483 See *ABB*, 293f. for Bruckner's first letter to Ignaz and his letter to Gruber, dated Vienna, 11 August 1896; the original of the former is not extant, and the original of the latter is in the *ÖNB*.

in Vienna.[484]

Bruckner's last letter, a very brief 'farewell', was sent to his brother Ignaz and Karl Aigner in St. Florian.[485] His final diary entry of prayers, in *Fromme's Österreichischer Professoren- u. Lehrer-Kalender 1894/95*, was for 10 October, the day before his death.[486] On 11 October worked on the Finale of his Ninth during the morning and even planned to take a short walk in the afternoon, but he passed away peacefully at 3.00.[487] An obituary speech was given by the Mayor of Vienna at the beginning of a council meeting on Tuesday 13 October. The council resolved to pay the costs of the funeral cortege which took place the following day and was followed by a service at the *Karlskirche*.[488] Bruckner's wish to be buried underneath the great

484 See *FSBB*, 64ff. and *LBSAB*, 203f. for extracts from this letter; the original is in the *ÖNB*, F18 Schalk 158/17/25.

485 See *ABB*, 294 and *GrBB*, 16 for this letter, dated Vienna, 7 October 1896. There is a facsimile of this letter between pages 328 and 329 in *G-A* II/1 and a facsimile of part of the letter in *ABA*, 47; the original is in the *Dermota Collection*, Vienna.

486 There is a facsimile of Bruckner's prayer entries from 28 September to 10 October 1896 in *G-A* IV/4, after page 24.

487 See *G-A* IV/3, 574f. for an account of Bruckner's last day, drawn from the reminiscences of Anton Meißner and Kathi Kachelmayr.

488 See *G-A* IV/3, 579-93 for details of the many individuals and organizations at the funeral as well as the music sung and played which included an excerpt from Bruckner's *Germanenzug* (*Akademische Gesangverein* and a horn quartet from the Vienna Philharmonic, conducted by Josef Neubauer) and the Adagio from Bruckner's Seventh Symphony (arranged for brass by Löwe and played by the brass section of the Vienna Philharmonic, conducted by Hans Richter). See also Steffen Lieberwirth, *ABDS* 6, 82ff. for reports in the *Leipziger Neueste Nachrichten* and *Leipziger Tageblatt* (15 October), Manfred Wagner, *Bruckner*, 221 and *passim* for reports and references to reports in several newspapers, including the *Illustriertes Wiener Extrablatt, Reichspost, Linzer Tagespost, Linzer Volksblatt*, and Renate Grasberger, 'Bruckner-Bibliographie', *ABDS* 4 (Graz, 1985) for references to many other reports.

organ at St. Florian was fulfilled on 15 October. Ferdinand Moser, the provost of St. Florian, officiated at the service, Josef Gruber played the organ, the abbey choir, conducted by Deubler, sang Bruckner's *Libera me* WAB 22 and *Frohsinn* from Linz performed a choral piece by Mendelssohn.[489]

Obituary notices in Austrian and foreign papers testify to the high esteem in which the composer was held.[490] There are also letters written by friends which refer to Bruckner's death. Perhaps the most poignant is Wolf's letter to Hugo Faißt in which he relates how he stood at the door of the *Karlskirche* so that he could join the funeral procession but was turned away because he could not prove that he was a

---

489 See *G-A* II/1, 329-32 for the report in the *Linzer Volksblatt* (15 October) and Manfred Wagner, *Bruckner*, 225-28 for the report in the *Linzer Tagespost* (16 October).

490 Only a few can be mentioned here. They include the obituaries in *Die Presse* (Gustav Schönaich [?], 12 October), the *Deutsches Volksblatt* (Camillo Horn, 12 October; see Manfred Wagner, *Bruckner*, 324f.), *Neue Freie Presse* (Richard Heuberger,13 October; see Manfred Wagner, *Bruckner*, 313-16), *Leipziger Volkszeitung* ('H.M.', 13 October; see Lieberwirth, *ABDS* 6, 82f.), *Linzer Tagespost* (13 October; see Manfred Wagner, 'Die Nekrologe von 1896: rezeptionstiftend? - oder Wie Klischees von Anton Bruckner entstanden' in *Musik-Konzepte* 23/24 [Munich, 1982], 120ff.), *Wiener Allgemeine Zeitung* (Albert Kauders, 13 October; see Wagner, *Musik-Konzepte*, 134f.), *Deutsche Zeitung* (Theodor Helm, 13 October), *Wiener Zeitung* (Robert Hirschfeld, 13 October) and *Fremdenblatt* (Ludwig Speidel, 16 October; see Wagner, *Bruckner*, 319f. for extract). Theodor Helm also contributed a biographical article to the *Musikalisches Wochenblatt* on 17 December and Hirschfeld was responsible for subsequent Bruckner articles in both the *Wiener Zeitung* and the *Wiener Abendpost*, for instance a lengthy article in the latter on 21 November in which he assessed Bruckner's place in the history of music and said that his music represented a fusion of the 'strictly Classical, extravagantly Romantic and modern dramatic influences'. Joseph Schalk paid his own personal tribute in his Annual Report for the *Wagner-Verein*; see *G-A* IV/3, 601f. In his obituary notice in the *Musical Times* xxxvii / 645 (1 November 1896), 742, the writer alluded to Bruckner's lack of recognition in Britain, contrasting this with the situation in Austria and Germany where the composer's name was one 'around which some fierce, if bloodless, battles have been fought'.

member of the *Singverein*.[491]

A particularly fitting student memorial gathering in honour of Bruckner was held by the *Wiener Akademischer Gesangverein* on 28 October. Speeches in tribute to Bruckner were given by the president, Franz Schaumann, and the rector of the University, Professor Simon Reinisch.[492]

There is a gap in the Schalk brothers' correspondence in October, so we have no record of their initial reaction to his death. Joseph wrote to Franz on 8 November, mentioning the wreath he had bought on Franz's behalf, another wreath which Cosima Wagner had sent to St. Florian, and referring to the memorial concert given earlier that day by Hans Richter and the Philharmonic (a performance of Bruckner's Seventh), which had been acclaimed by all accounts but he had been unable to attend himself because of his 'continuing poor state of health'. Joseph was concerned that this was the only memorial concert which had been planned - neither the *Singverein* nor the *Wagner-Verein* was offering anything - and hoped that the old idea of Franz and the Prague orchestra performing the Fifth in Vienna could be revived - 'in January, if possible, as the Berlin Philharmonic is coming later'.[493]   But it was Ferdinand Löwe, who had already conducted the work in Budapest and Munich, who gave the first Viennese performance on the Fifth on 1 March 1898. Franz Schalk conducted the work in Prague during 1898 but did not perform it in Vienna until 28 November 1909.

---

491   This letter to Faißt is dated Vienna, 25 October 1896. In an earlier letter to Heinrich Potpeschnigg, dated Vienna, 12 October 1896, Wolf claims that people still have no conception of Bruckner's importance; see *ABA*, 99. The *Wiener Stadt- und Landesbibliothek* owns the originals of two letters sent to Theodor Helm, the first dated Dresden, 14 October 1896 (sent by Louis Nicodé), the second dated Vienna, 27 October (sent by Oskar Berggrün).

492   See *G-A* IV/3, 603ff. for an extract from the Annual Report of the *Akademischer Gesangverein*.

493   See *LBSAB*, 204 for an extract from this letter; the original is in the *ÖNB*, F18 Schalk 158/17/28.

Right up until a few hours before his death Bruckner worked slowly and fitfully on his Ninth Symphony. The amplification of particell material into full score seems to have happened fairly quickly. For his full score Bruckner used a *Bogen* or double sheet of 24-stave paper, numbering the right-hand corner of the top page and proceeding from one *Bogen* to the next rather than 'interleaving' them. Each page usually has four bars, and thus each *Bogen* sixteen bars. For the first few *Bogen* Bruckner himself ruled the pages into bars and listed the instruments in the left-hand margin. The preparation of later *Bogen* was carried out by someone else, probably Meißner.[494] The first 1896 date to appear in the material is '14 Jänner' on Mus. Hs. 6085 / 77r. There are no other dates until May which suggests that the obvious decline in Bruckner's health between January and May inevitably slowed down the creative process. There are three sketches, probably for the coda, which almost certainly date from the end of May. On one of them, a particell sketch of a 24-bar passage, three dates appear, '21. Donnerstag, 22. Freitag, 23. Samstag'; underneath, beside what is probably an earlier draft of the same passage, is the note 'Nacht von Don[nerstag] auf Fr[eitag]'. On the last date to be recorded in the manuscript material - 11 August - Bruckner was obviously well enough to draft some bars in the development section. By this point, however, he had certainly resigned himself to the fact that he would never complete the movement. To those who visited him a month or so before his death, for example Carl Almeroth and Adalbert von Goldschmidt, he invariably suggested that the *Te Deum* would form the best conclusion under the circumstances; and indeed there are indications in the score of possible 'entry points' for the *Te Deum*. It was not until a week after Bruckner's death that any attempt was made to bring some order into the somewhat chaotic state in which the manuscripts had been left. The fact that, according to Richard Heller, both the 'authorized and unauthorized had swooped down like vultures upon

---

494 Most of these *Bogen* are in the *ÖNB*, sign. nos. Mus. Hss. 6085, 6087 and 19.645.

their prey'[495] and had removed various manuscripts, including some *Bogen* from the Finale, made it well-nigh impossible for the executors of Bruckner's estate to make a proper inventory. According to a deposition made on 18 October and signed by Theodor Reisch, Ferdinand Löwe and Joseph Schalk, Schalk was given the task of sifting through the existing 75 double sheets of Finale sketches and putting them in order.[496]

---

495 Quoted by Auer, 'Anton Bruckners letzter behandelnder Arzt', 35.

496 See *G-A* IV/3, 608 for the text of this deposition. Ill health prevented Schalk from completing this task. It was not until 1934 that an attempt was made by Alfred Orel (see below) to publish some of the drafts and sketches of the Finale. As more sketches have come to light since then, other attempts have been made by Bruckner scholars, notably William Carragan (see below) and John Phillips (see below) to create performing versions of the movement. For further information, consult the following: Alfred Orel, 'Skizzen zum 4. Satz von Bruckners 9. Symphonie' in *Der Merker* 12 (1921), 411-19; idem, ed., *Entwürfe und Skizzen zur IX. Symphonie* (Vienna, 1934); Oskar Lang, 'Die Entwürfe zum Finale der IX. Symphonie Anton Bruckners' in *Allgemeine Musikzeitung* 61 (1934), 445ff.; H.F. Redlich, 'The Finale of Bruckner's Ninth Symphony' in *The Monthly Musical Record* 79 (1949), 143-49; Nicola Samale and Giuseppe Mazzuca (transl. Katherine S. Wolfthal), *Introduction to the Finale of Bruckner's Ninth Symphony* (Milan, 1986); William Carragan, foreword to his completion of the Finale of the Ninth [1983] (New York: Bruckner Archive, 1987); Hartmut Krones, 'Symposium zur "Fertigstellung" von Bruckners IX. Symphonie im Österreichischen Kulturinstitut in Rom' in *Österreichische Musikzeitschrift* 42 (1987), 521f.; Frank J. Plash, 'Zur Aufführung des rekonstruierten Finale von Bruckners Neunten Sinfonie' in *BJ 1984/85/86* (Linz, 1988), 154 [report of a performance of William Carragan's reconstruction from the sketches of the Finale of the Ninth in the Carnegie Hall, New York on 8 January 1984]; Cornelis van Zwol, 'Der Finalsatz der Neunten Symphonie Anton Bruckners. Ein Referat in Utrecht (15. November 1986). Ein Symposion in Rom (11. bis 12. Mai 1987)' in *BJ 1987/88* (Graz, 1990), 31-38 [a survey of various attempts at the reconstruction of the movement since the publication of the sketches by Alfred Orel in the first Complete Edition (1934), with particular reference to Carragan's and Samale / Mazzuca's]; idem, 'Die Vollendung bei Anton Bruckner - Der Finalsatz seiner IX. Symphonie, *Fragment or Completion*' in *Proceedings of the Mahler X Symposium Utrecht 1986* (Rotterdam, 1991), 193-205; John A. Phillips, 'Neue Erkenntnisse zum Finale der Neunten

In his will Bruckner made gifts of 4000 florins to St. Florian, 300 florins to Steyr Parish Church, and 700 florins to Kathi Kachelmayr. The original manuscripts of most of his works were entrusted to the Imperial Court Library, but some were given to institutions and individuals. The lack of a proper inventory meant that no distinction could be made between the 'authorized' and the 'unauthorized', an unfortunate situation which led to many problems later. The rest of his estate was divided between Ignaz Bruckner and Rosalie Hueber and her heirs. At the end of the year, Ignaz wrote to Rosalie concerning the division of the estate and said that she should hold on to some documents which were of no interest to either Linz or Vienna, because 'a time would probably come when they would be of some value', a prophetic comment and one which has inspired many, including the writer of this book, to investigate further.

———————————————

Symphonie Anton Bruckners' in *BJ 1989/90* (Vienna, 1992), 115-203; idem, 'Zum leidigen Thema "Finale der Neunten Symphonie Anton Bruckners' in *Österreichische Musikzeitschrift* 47/1 (1992), 22-25; Nicola Samale, John A. Phillips, Giuseppe Mazzuca (and with the assistance of Gunnar Cohrs), *Anton Bruckner IX. Symphonie D-Moll Finale. Rekonstruktion der Autograph-Partitur nach den erhaltenen Quellen. Aufführungsfassung. Studienpartitur* (Adelaide, 1992); John A. Phillips, ed., *IX. Symphonie D-Moll Finale. Faksimile-Ausgabe sämtlicher autographen Notenseiten, ABSW (zu Band IX/4)* (Vienna: Musikwissenschaftlicher Verlag, 1996); William Carragan, 'Structural Aspects of the Revision of Bruckner's Symphonic Finales' in *BSL 1996* (Linz, 1998), 177-88; William Carragan, Gunnar Cohrs, John A. Phillips, Herbert Vogg, Franz Zamazal, 'Round -table: "Zum Finale der Neunten Symphonie"', *BSL 1996* (Linz, 1998), 189-210; Benjamin Gunnar Cohrs, 'Anmerkungen zur Kritischen Neuausgabe der Neunten Symphonie Anton Bruckners' in *Mitteilungsblatt der IBG* 55 (December 2000), 18-20; John A. Phillips, 'The facts behind a "legend": the Ninth Symphony and the Te Deum' in *Perspectives on Anton Bruckner* (Aldershot: Ashgate, 2001), in preparation.

SELECT BIBLIOGRAPHY

N.B. Not all the authors of articles in the *Bruckner Jahrbuch*, the *Bruckner Symposion Linz* reports and *19th-century Music* cited in footnotes in the main text are included here.

Antonicek, Theophil. 'Anton Bruckner und die Wiener Hofmusikkapelle', in *Anton Bruckner. Dokumente und Studien* 1. Graz, 1979.

------------------------. ' "Sein Meister Anton Bruckner". Bruckner-Freunde und Bruckner-Schüler in den Akten des Unterrichtsministeriums', in *Bruckner-Symposion 1994 Bericht* (Linz, 1997), pp. 55-64.

Auer, Max, ed. *Anton Bruckner. Gesammelte Briefe. Neue Folge.* Regensburg, 1924.

------------. *Anton Bruckner als Kirchenmusiker.* Regensburg, 1927.

------------. *Anton Bruckner. Sein Leben und Werk.* Zurich / Leipzig / Vienna, 1947.

Banks, Paul. 'Vienna: Absolutism and Nostalgia', in Jim Samson, ed., *The Late Romantic Era* (London, 1991), pp. 74-98.

--------------. 'Fin-de-Siècle Vienna: Politics and Modernism', in *ibid.*, pp. 362-88.

Beck, Walter. *Anton Bruckner. Ein Lebensbild mit neuen Dokumenten.* Dornach, 1995.

Biba, Otto. 'Anton Bruckner und die Orgelbauerfamilie Mauracher', in Othmar Wessely, ed., *Bruckner-Studien* (Vienna, 1975), pp. 143-62.

------------. 'Bruckner-Neuerwerbungen des Archivs der Gesellschaft der Musikfreunde in Wien', in *Mitteilungsblatt der IBG* 17 (May 1980), pp. 20-24.

------------. 'Anton Bruckners Orgel im Alten Dom zu Linz restauriert', in *Singende Kirche* 28 (1981), 120-22.

------------. 'Die Orgel im Alten Dom zu Linz - ein Dokument zu Bruckners Orgelpraxis', in *BJ 1982/83* (Linz, 1984), pp. 75-79.

Boyer, John W. *Political Radicalism in Late Imperial Vienna.* Chicago and London, 1981.

Brosche, Günter. 'Die Wiener Fassung der Ersten Symphonie von Anton Bruckner', in *Österreichische Musikzeitschrift* 36 (1981), pp. 395-400.

--------------------. 'Neuerwerbungen der Musiksammlung der Österreichischen Nationalbibliothek 1984 und 1985', in *Österreichische Musikzeitschrift* 41 (1986), pp. 26-32.

720

----------------------. 'Quellen für künftige Forschungen. Neuerwerbungen 1991 der Musiksammlung der Österreichischen Nationalbibliothek', in *Studien zur Musikwissenschaft* 42 (Tutzing, 1993), pp. 419-31.

----------------------. 'Wichtige Neuerwerbungen der Musiksammlung der Österreichischen Nationalbibliothek 1993', in *Österreichische Musikzeitschrift* 49 (1994), p. 572f.

----------------------. 'Ideologische Einflüsse auf das Nachleben Anton Bruckners', in *Österreichische Musik - Musik in Österreich: Beiträge zur Musikgeschichte Mitteleuropas; Theophil Antonicek zum 60. Geburtstag* (Tutzing, 1958), pp. 451-61.

Brüstle, Christa. *Anton Bruckner und die Nachwelt. Zur Rezeptionsgeschichte des Komponisten in der ersten Hälfte des 20. Jahrhunderts.* Stuttgart, 1998.

Busch, Hermann. 'Anton Bruckners Tätigkeit als Orgelsachverständiger', in *Ars Organa* 39 (1971), pp. 1585-93.

Carragan, William. 'The early version of the Second Symphony', in Crawford Howie, Timothy Jackson and Paul Hawkshaw, eds., *Perspectives on Anton Bruckner* (Aldershot, 2001), in preparation.

Cohrs, Benjamin G. 'Zahlenphänomene in Bruckners Symphonik. Neues zu den Strukturen der Fünften und Neunten Symphonie', in *BJ 1989/90* (Linz, 1992), pp. 35-75.

----------------------. 'Der Mikrofilm der Krakauer Bruckner-Skizzen in der Musiksammlung der Österreichischen Nationalbibliothek', in *BJ 1994/95* (Linz, 1997), pp. 191-94.

----------------------, ed. *Anton Bruckner. IX Symphonie D-Moll, Scherzo und Trio: Entwürfe. Älteres Trio mit Viola-Solo (1893): Autograph Partitur (ABSW zu IX/2).* Vienna, 1998.

----------------------. 'Anmerkungen zur kritischen Neuausgabe der Neunten Symphonie Anton Bruckners', in *Mitteilungsblatt der IBG* 55 (December 2000), pp. 18-20.

Cooke, Deryck. 'Bruckner', in *The New Grove* 3 (London, 1980), pp. 352-71.

Crittenden, Camille. *Johann Strauss and Vienna: operetta and the politics of popular culture.* Cambridge, 2000.

Decsey, Ernst. *Bruckner. Versuch eines Lebens.* Stuttgart, 1922.

Doernberg, Erwin. *The Life and Symphonies of Anton Bruckner.* London, 1960.

Eckstein, Friedrich. *Erinnerungen an Anton Bruckner.* Vienna, 1923

Endler, Franz. *Vienna. A Guide to its Music and Musicians.* Portland, 1989.

Federhofer, Hellmut. 'Anton Bruckner im Briefwechsel von August Halm (1869-1929) - Heinrich Schenker (1868-1935)', in *Festschrift Walter Wiora "Anton Bruckner zu Werk und Wirkung"* (Tutzing, 1988), pp. 33-40.

Fifield, Christopher. *True Artist and True Friend. A Biography of Hans Richter.* Oxford, 1993.

Fischer, Hans Conrad. *Anton Bruckner. Sein Leben. Eine Dokumentation.* Salzburg, 1974.

Floros, Constantin. *Brahms und Bruckner. Studien zur musikalischen Exegetik.* Wiesbaden, 1980.

-----------------------. 'On unity between Bruckner's personality and production', in *Perspectives on Anton Bruckner* (Aldershot, 2001), in preparation.

Flotzinger, Rudolf. 'Bruckners Rolle in der Kulturgeschichte Österreichs', in Albrecht Riethmüller, ed., *Bruckner-Probleme: Internationales Kolloquium 7.-9. Oktober 1996 in Berlin. Beihefte zum Archiv für Musikwissenschaft* 15 (Stuttgart, 1999), pp. 9-24.

Frieberger, Rupert G. 'Die Bruckner-Orgel im alten Dom vom Linz', in *In Ehrfurcht vor den Manen eines Großen. Zum 75. Todestag Anton Bruckners* (Linz, 1971), pp. 41-52.

-------------------------. 'Die Bruckner-Orgel in der Ignatiuskirche in Linz - ein historisches Instrument', in *Singende Kirche* 18 (1971), pp. 151-54.

Fuchs, Ingrid. ' "Künstlerische Vater" und "Vormünder". Bruckner und die zeitgenössischen Dirigenten seiner Symphonien', in *Bruckner Symposion 1994 Bericht* (Linz, 1997), 65-86.

Gal, Hans. *Johannes Brahms.* London, 1963.

Gault, Dermot. 'For Later Times', in *Musical Times* 137 (1996), pp. 12-19.

Gilliam, Bryan. 'The Two Versions of Bruckner's Eighth Symphony', in *19th-Century Music* 16 (1992), pp. 59-69.

Glöggl, Franz X. *Erklärendes Handbuch des musikalischen Gottesdienstes.* Vienna, 1828.

Göllerich, August and Max Auer. *Anton Bruckner. Ein Lebens- und Schaffensbild.* 4 volumes in 9. Regensburg, 1922-37. Reprinted Regensburg, 1974, incl. supplementary volume containing corrections and additions.

Gräflinger, Franz. *Anton Bruckner. Bausteine zu seiner Lebensgeschichte.* Munich, 1911.

---------------------. *Anton Bruckner. Sein Leben und seine Werke.* Regensburg, 1921.

---------------------, ed. *Anton Bruckner. Gesammelte Briefe.* Regensburg, 1924.

---------------------. *Anton Bruckner. Leben und Schaffen. (Umgearbeitete Bausteine).* Berlin, 1927.

---------------------. *Liebes und Heiteres um Anton Bruckner.* Vienna, 1948

Grandjean, Wolfgang, ed. *Anton Bruckner. I. Symphonie c-Moll - 2. Satz Adagio (ursprüngliche Fassung), 3. Satz Scherzo (ältere Komposition)* (*ABSW zu I/1*). Vienna, 1995.

-------------------------. 'Anton Bruckners "Helgoland" und das Symphonische', in *Die Musikforschung* 48 (1995), pp. 349-68.

Grasberger, Franz, ed. *Bruckner-Studien.* Vienna, 1964.

722

----------------------. 'Anton Bruckners Auslandsreisen', in *Österreichische Musikzeitschrift* 24 (1969), pp. 630-35.

----------------------, ed. *Anton Bruckner zum 150. Geburtstag. Eine Ausstellung im Prunksaal der Österreichischen Nationalbibliothek.* Vienna, 1974.

----------------------, ed. *Anton Bruckner zwischen Wagis und Sicherheit. Ausstellung im Rahmen des Internationalen Brucknerfestes.* Linz, 1977.

----------------------. 'Das Bruckner-Bild der Zeitung "Das Vaterland" in den Jahren 1870-1900', in *Festschrift Hans Schneider zum 60. Geburtstag.* Munich, 1981.

Grasberger, Franz, Othmar Wessely et al., eds. *Anton Bruckner Dokumente und Studien (ABDS).* Graz and Vienna, from 1979.

---, *Bruckner Jahrbuch (BJ).* Linz and Vienna, from 1980.

---, *Bruckner Symposion Linz Bericht.(BSL).* Linz, from 1980.

Grasberger, Renate. *Werkverzeichnis Anton Bruckner (WAB)* Tutzing, 1977.

----------------------. *Bruckner-Bibliographie (ABDS 4).* Graz, 1985.

----------------------. *Bruckner-Ikonographie. Teil 1: 1854 bis 1924 (ABDS 7).* Graz, 1990.

Grasberger, Renate and Erich W. Partsch. *Bruckner-skizziert. Ein Porträt in ausgewählten Erinnerungen und Anekdoten (ABDS 8).* Vienna, 1991.

Grebe, Karl. *Anton Bruckner in Selbstzeugnissen und Bilddokumenten.* Hamburg, 1972.

Gruber, Gerold W. 'Brahms und Bruckner in der zeitgenössischen Wiener Musikkritik', in *BSL 1983* (Linz, 1985), pp. 201-18.

----------------------. 'Bruckner und die österreichische Presse (Offiziöse Blätter)', in *BSL 1991* (Linz, 1994), pp. 85f.

Grüninger, Fritz. *Anton Bruckner. Der metaphysische Kern seiner Persönlichkeit und seiner Werke.* Augsburg, 1930, 2/1949.

--------------------. *Der Meister von Sankt Florian. Wege zu Anton Bruckner.* Augsburg, 1950.

Gülke, Peter. *Brahms - Bruckner. Zwei Studien.* Kassel, 1989.

Haas, Robert. *Anton Bruckner.* Potsdam, 1934.

Haas, Robert and Alfred Orel, eds. *Anton Bruckner Sämtliche Werke, Kritische Gesamtausgabe*, im Auftrage der Generaldirektion der Österreichischen Nationalbibliothek und der Internationalen Bruckner-Gesellschaft. Vienna, Leipzig and Wiesbaden, 1930-53.

Hager, Leopold. *Die Bruckner-Orgel im Stifte St. Florian.* St. Florian, 1951.

Halm, August. *Die Symphonie Anton Bruckners.* Munich, 1923.

Hanslick, Eduard. *Geschichte des Concertwesens in Wien.* Vienna, 1869.

---------------------. *Die moderne Oper*, 9 vols. Berlin, 1875-1900.

Harrandt, Andrea et al., eds., *Mitteilungsblatt der Internationalen Bruckner-Gesellschaft*. Vienna, from 1974.

Harrandt, Andrea. 'Bruckner und das bürgerliche Musiziergut seiner Jugendzeit', in *BSL 1987* (Linz, 1989), pp. 93-103.

----------------------. 'Harmonielehreunterricht bei Bruckner - Zu zwei neuaufgefundenen Vorlesungsmitschriften', in *BSL 1988* (Linz, 1992), pp. 71-83.

----------------------. '"Ausgezeichneter Hofkapellmeister" - Anton Bruckner an Felix Mottl. Zu Neuerwerbungen der Österreichischen Nationalbibliothek', in *Studien zur Musikwissenschaft* 42 (Tutzing, 1993), pp. 335-50.

----------------------. 'Gustav Schönaich - ein "Herold der Bruckner'schen Kunst"', in *BSL 1991* (Linz, 1994), pp. 63-71.

---------------------- and Erich W. Partsch, 'Unbekannte Bruckner-Autographe entdeckt', in *Österreichische Musikzeitschrift* 49 (1994), p. 332.

----------------------. 'Ein unbekannter Brief zu Bruckners Wiener Umfeld', in *Mitteilungsblatt der Internationalen Bruckner-Gesellschaft* 44 (June 1995), pp. 26-28.

----------------------. 'Eine unveröffentlichte Vorlesungsmitschrift. Karl Heissenberger als Theorieschüler Bruckners an der Universität', in *BJ 1991/92/93* (Linz, 1995), pp. 155-89.

----------------------. '"Oberösterreichische Wald" und "heimatlicher Boden". Das Bruckner-Bild der Tagespresse', in *BSL 1993* (Linz 1996), pp. 39-46.

----------------------. '"... den ich als einzigen, wahren Freund erkenne..." Anton Bruckner und Rudolf Weinwurm', in *BSL 1994* (Linz, 1997), pp. 37-48.

----------------------. 'Bruckner and the Liedertafel Tradition: his Secular Music for Male Chorus', in *Choral Journal* xxxviii/5 (1996-97), pp. 15-21.

----------------------. 'Bruckner-Rezeption in Wiener Akademischen Wagner-Verein', in *BJ 1994/95/96* (Linz, 1997), pp. 223-34.

----------------------. 'Bruckner und die Chormusik seiner Zeit', in *Oberösterreichische Heimatblätter* 51/3-4 (1997), pp. 184-95.

---------------------- and Otto Schneider, eds. *Anton Bruckner Briefe 1852-1886* (*Anton Bruckner Sämtliche Werke* XXIV/1). Vienna, 1998.

----------------------. 'Die Briefe Anton Bruckners: Probleme der Quellenlage und der Edition', in Riethmüller, ed., *Bruckner-Probleme* (Stuttgart, 1999), pp. 35-46.

----------------------. 'Students and friends as "prophets" and "promoters": the reception of Bruckner's works in the *Wiener Akademische Wagner-Verein*', in *Perspectives on Anton Bruckner* (Aldershot, 2001), in preparation.

Harten, Uwe. 'Zu Anton Bruckners vorletztem Münchener Aufenthalt', in *Studien zur Musikwissenschaft* 42 (Tutzing, 1993), pp. 323-33.

----------------. 'Bruckner und die österreichische Presse (Liberale Blätter)', in *BSL 1991* (Linz, 1994), pp. 93-98.

724

\-\-\-\-\-\-\-\-\-\-\-\-\-\-\-\-, ed. *Anton Bruckner. Ein Handbuch*. Salzburg, 1996.

\-\-\-\-\-\-\-\-\-\-\-\-\-\-\-\-. 'Zu Bruckners Wiener "Leidenszeit"', in *BSL 1994* (Linz, 1997), pp. 13-18.

Hartmann, K.A. and W. Wahren. 'Briefe über Bruckner', in *Neue Zeitschrift für Musik* 126 (1965), pp. 272-76, 334-38 and 380-87.

Hawkshaw, Paul. 'The Date of Bruckner's "Nullified" Symphony in D Minor', in *19ᵗʰ-Century Music* 6 (1983), pp. 252-63.

\-. *The Manuscript Sources for Anton Bruckner's Linz Works: a Study of His Working Methods from 1856 to 1868*. Ann Arbor, 1984.

\-. 'From Zigeunerwald to Valhalla in Common Time. The Genesis of Anton Bruckner's Germanenzug', in *BJ 1987/88* (Linz, 1990), pp. 21-30.

\-. 'Weiteres über die Arbeitsweise Bruckners während seiner Linzer Jahre. Der Inhalt von Kremsmünster C 56.2', in *BSL 1992* (Linz, 1995), pp. 143-52.

\-. 'Das Kitzler-Studienbuch: ein unschätzbares Dokument zu Bruckners Arbeitsweise', in *BSL 1995* (Linz, 1997), pp. 95-109.

\-. 'An anatomy of change: Anton Bruckner's revisions to the Mass in F minor', in Timothy Jackson and Paul Hawkshaw, eds., *Bruckner Studies* (Cambridge, 1997), pp. 1-31.

\-. 'A Composer learns His Craft. Anton Bruckner's Lessons in Form and Orchestration, 1861-63', in *The Musical Quarterly* 82 (1998), pp. 336-61.

\-. 'Bruckners Psalmen', in Riethmüller, ed., *Bruckner-Probleme* (Stuttgart, 1999), pp. 71-84.

\-. 'Bruckner', in *The New Grove*, 2ⁿᵈ edition. London, 2001; in preparation

\-. 'A composer learns his craft: lessons in form and orchestration', in *Perspectives on Anton Bruckner* (Aldershot, 2001), in preparation.

Herbeck, Ludwig. *Johann Herbeck*. Vienna, 1885.

Hilscher, Elisabeth. 'Bruckner als Gelehrter - Bruckner als Geehrter', in *BSL 1988* (Linz, 1992), pp. 119-27.

\-. 'Genie versus Markt. Anton Bruckner und seine Verleger', in *BSL 1994* (Linz, 1997), pp. 139-50.

Hinrichsen, Hans-Joachim. '"Halb Genie, halb Trottel". Hans von Bülows Urteil über Anton Bruckner', in *Mitteilungsblatt der IBG* 55 (December 2000), pp. 21-24.

Hollnsteiner, Johannes. *Das Stift St. Florian und Anton Bruckner*. Leipzig, 1940.

Horn, Erwin. 'Eine Visitenkarte mit Bruckner-Noten', in *BJ 1991/92/93* (Linz, 1995), pp. 117-29.

\-\-\-\-\-\-\-\-\-\-\-\-\-\-\-\-. 'Zwischen Interpretation und Improvisation. Anton Bruckner als Organist', in *BSL 1995* (Linz, 1997), pp. 111-39.

--------------. 'Die Orgelstücke Bruckners', in *Bruckner-Vorträge, Bruckner-Tagung Wien 1999 Bericht* (Vienna, 2000), pp. 21-34.

Howie, Crawford. 'Traditional and Novel Elements in Bruckner's Sacred Music', in *The Musical Quarterly* 67 (1981), pp. 544-67.

--------------. 'Bruckner Scholarship in the Last Ten Years (1987-96)', in *Music and Letters* 77 (1996), pp. 542-54.

--------------, Timothy Jackson and Paul Hawkshaw, eds. *Perspectives on Anton Bruckner*. Aldershot, 2001.

--------------. 'Bruckner - the travelling virtuoso', in *Perspectives on Anton Bruckner* (Aldershot, 2001), in preparation.

Hruby, Karl. *Meine Erinnerungen an Anton Bruckner*. Vienna, 1901.

Jackson, Timothy and Paul Hawkshaw, eds. *Bruckner Studies*. Cambridge, 1997.

Jackson, Timothy. 'Bruckner's *Oktaven*: the problem of consecutives, doubling, and orchestral voice-leading', in *Perspectives on Anton Bruckner* (Aldershot, 2001), in preparation.

--------------. 'The Adagio of the Sixth Symphony and the Anticipatory Tonic Recapitulation in Bruckner, Brahms and Dvorák', in *Perspectives on Anton Bruckner* (Aldershot, 2001), in preparation.

--------------. 'Bruckner', in *The New Grove*, 2nd edition. London, 2001; in preparation.

Jerger, Wilhelm. *Briefe and die Wiener Philharmoniker*. Vienna, 1942.

--------------. '"Hochlöbliche, Hochverehrte philharmonische Gesellschaft!" Die Briefe Anton Bruckners an die Wiener Philharmoniker nebst einem unbekannten Brief an August Göllerich sen.', in *Oberösterreichische Heimatsblätter* 28 (1974), pp. 149-53.

Johnson, Stephen. *Bruckner Remembered*. London, 1998.

Kaiser, Fritz. 'Ludwig Grandes Erinnerungen an seinen Lehrer Anton Bruckner und die Bruckner-Aufführungen in Troppau', in *BSL 1994* (Linz, 1997), pp. 49-54.

Kantner, Leopold M. 'Die Frömmigkeit Anton Bruckners', in *Anton Bruckner in Wien. Eine kritische Studie zu seiner Persönlichkeit* (*ABDS* 2). Graz, 1980, pp. 229-78.

Keller, Rolf. 'Die letztwilligen Verfügungen Anton Bruckners', in *BJ 1982/83* (Linz, 1984), pp. 95-115.

--------------. 'Anton Bruckner und die Familie Albrecht', in *BJ 1984/85/86* (Linz, 1988), pp. 53-56.

--------------. 'Frühe Freunde Bruckners im deutschen Südwesten. Der Beginn der Bruckner-Pflege in Baden-Württemberg', in *BSL 1994* (Linz, 1997), pp. 151-60.

Kellner, Altman. *Musikgeschichte des Stiftes Kremsmünster*. Kassel/Basel, 1956.

--------------. 'Der Organist Bruckner', in *Bruckner-Studien* (Vienna, 1964), pp. 61-65.

Kerschbaum, Karl, ed. *Chronik der Liedertafel "Frohsinn" in Linz über den 50jährigen Bestand vom 17. März 1845 bis anfangs März 1895.* Linz, 1895.

Kitzler, Otto. *Musikalische Erinnerungen.* Brno, 1904.

Klose, Friedrich. *Meine Lehrjahre bei Bruckner. Erinnerungen und Betrachtungen.* Regensburg, 1927.

Kobald, Karl, ed. *In Memoriam Anton Bruckner.* Zurich-Vienna-Leipzig, 1924.

Kocher, L. *Die Tonkunst in der Kirche.* Stuttgart, 1823.

Korstvedt, Benjamin, M. *Anton Bruckner: Symphony No. 8* (Cambridge Music Handbook). Cambridge, 2000.

----------------------------. '"Harmonic daring" and symphonic design in the Sixth Symphony: an essay in historical musical analysis', in *Perspectives on Anton Bruckner* (Aldershot, 2001), in preparation.

Korte, Werner. *Bruckner und Brahms. Die spätromantische Lösung der autonomen Konzeption* (Tutzing, 1963).

Kosch, Franz. '"Der Beter Anton Bruckner". Nach seinen persönlichen Aufzeichnungen' in *Bruckner-Studien* (Vienna, 1964), pp. 67-73.

Kowar, Helmut. 'Vereine für die Neudeutschen in Wien', in *BSL 1984* (Linz, 1986), pp. 81-90.

Kurth, Ernst. *Bruckner.* Berlin, 1925.

Lach, Robert. *Die Bruckner-Akten des Wiener Universitäts-Archives.* Vienna-Prague-Leipzig, 1926.

Lang, Oskar. *Anton Bruckner. Wesen und Bedeutung.* Munich, 1924, 2/1943.

--------------. 'Anton Bruckner in zeitgenössischen Briefwechsel', in *Zeitschrift für Musik* 99 (October 1932), p. 880f.

Laßl, Josef. *Das kleine Brucknerbuch.* Salzburg, 1965.

Laux, Karl. *Anton Bruckner. Leben und Werk.* Leipzig, 1940.

Leibnitz, Thomas. *Die Brüder Schalk und Anton Bruckner.* Tutzing, 1988.

--------------------. '"Francisce" und der "Generalissimus". Die Brüder Schalk als Interpreten und Bearbeiter der Werke Bruckners', in *BSL 1994* (Linz, 1997), pp. 87-94.

--------------------. 'Anton Bruckner: "Deutscher" oder "Österreicher"? Deutungen, Vereinnahmungen, Hintergründe', in *Österreichische Musik - Musik in Österreich: Beiträge zur Musikgeschichte Mitteleuropas; Theophil Antonicek zum 60. Geburtstag* (Tutzing, 1998), pp. 463-76.

--------------------. 'Anton Bruckner and "German music": Josef Schalk and the establishment of Bruckner as a national composer', in *Perspectives on Anton Bruckner* (Aldershot, 2001), in preparation.

Leitner, Franz. *Anton Bruckner in Vöcklabruck.* Vöcklabruck, 1996.

Lepel, Felix von. *Zehn Briefe von Anton Bruckner.* Berlin, 1953.

Lieberwirth, Steffen. 'Bruckner-Aufführungen im Gewandhaus zu Leipzig', in *BJ 1984/85/86* (Linz, 1988), pp. 103-15.

----------------------. 'Anton Bruckner und Leipzig. Die Jahre 1884-1902' (*ABDS* 6). Graz, 1988.

----------------------. 'Die erste Organist eines Orgelkonzertes im Neuen Gewandhaus zu Leipzig - Anton Bruckner', in *BJ 1987/88* (Linz, 1990), pp. 87-92.

----------------------. 'Anton Bruckner und Leipzig. Einige neue Erkenntnisse und Ergänzungen', in *BJ 1989/90* (Linz, 1992), pp. 277-88.

Liebisch, Haymo. *Anton Bruckner. 1824 bis 1896 - einst und jetzt. Ein Bericht.* Steyr, 1996.

Litschauer, Walburga. 'Anton Bruckner als Organist in Wien', in *Anton Bruckner. V. Internationales Gewandhaus-Symposion Leipzig 1987. Kongreßbericht. Dokumente zur Gewandhausgeschichte* (Leipzig, 1988), pp. 70-73.

----------------------. 'Bruckner und die Wiener Kirchenmusiker', in *BSL 1985* (Linz, 1988), pp. 95-102.

----------------------. 'Bruckner und das romantische Klavierstück', in *BSL 1987* (Linz, 1989), pp. 105-10.

Litschel, H., ed. *Vom Ruf zum Nachruf. Künstlerschicksale in Österreich, Anton Bruckner. Landesausstellung Oberösterreich 1996 im Stift St. Florian.* Linz, 1996.

Loos, Helmut. 'Zu Bruckners Kirchenmusik', in Riethmüller, ed., *Bruckner-Probleme* (Stuttgart, 1999), pp. 64-70

Louis, Rudolf. *Anton Bruckner.* Munich, 1905.

Ludwig, V.O. *Anton Bruckners Klosterneuburger Fahrt.* Vienna, 1921.

Macartney, C.A. *The House of Austria.* Edinburgh, 1978.

Märker, Michael. 'Hat Bruckner das Adagio der Zweiten im "*Mendelssohnschen Stil mit Honigsüße*" komponiert? Über die Mendelssohn-Rezeption Anton Bruckners', in *BSL 1997* (Linz, 1999), 177-86.

Mahling, Christoph-Hellmut, ed. *Anton Bruckner. Studien zu Werk und Wirkung. Walter Wiora zum 30 Dezember 1986.* Tutzing, 1988.

----------------------. '"Der Zeiten Wandel zeigte sich". Zur Berichterstattung über Anton Bruckner in deutschen Musikzeitungen von 1871 bis zu Beginn des 20. Jahrhunderts', in *ibid.*, pp. 101-48.

Maier, Elisabeth. 'Anton Bruckners Arbeitswelt', in *Anton Bruckner in Wien* (*ABDS* 2). Graz, 1980, pp. 161-228.

----------------------. 'Anton Bruckners Weg in den Jahren 1843-1855', in *Anton Bruckner und Leopold Zenetti* (*ABDS* 3). Graz, 1980, pp. 11-16.

----------------------. 'Anton Bruckners Frühwerk - Einflüsse und Vorbilder', in *ibid.*, pp. 127-61.

----------------------. 'Anton Bruckners "Gesangs-Akademie". Zum biographischen Umfeld eines bisher unbekannten Dokumentes', in *BJ 1982/83* (Linz, 1984), pp. 89-94.

728

----------------------. 'Brahms und Bruckner. Ihr Ausbildungsgang', in *BSL 1983* (Linz, 1985), pp. 53-71.

----------------------. 'Neue Bruckneriana aus Privatbesitz', in *Mitteilungsblatt der IBG* 36 (June 1991), pp. 6-13

----------------------. 'Bruckners oberösterreichische Lehrer', in *BSL 1988* (Linz, 1992), pp. 35-49.

----------------------. 'Vom Talent zum Genie. Anton Bruckners Linzer Jahre', in *Mitteilungsblatt der IBG* 39 (December 1992), pp. 27-34.

----------------------. '"Es wird schon einmahl eine Zeit kommen, wo es einen Wert haben wird..." Bruckneriana in Vöcklabruck', in *Studien zur Musikwissenschaft* 42 (Tutzing, 1993), pp. 283-322.

----------------------. '"Kirchenmusik auf schiefen Bahnen". Zur Situation in Linz von 1850 bis 1900', in *BSL 1990* (Linz, 1993), pp. 109-117.

----------------------. *Anton Bruckner. Leben eines Künstlers.* Linz, 1996.

----------------------. 'A hidden personality: access to an "inner biography" of Anton Bruckner', in *Bruckner Studies* (Cambridge, 1997), pp. 32-53.

----------------------. ' "... er muß aber wenige oder gar keine Freunde haben..." Anton Bruckners persönliche Beziehungen', in *BSL 1994* (Linz, 1997), pp. 7-12.

----------------------. '"*Sechzigjährige Eiche*" und "*Musikalischer Ätna*", Anton Bruckners 60. Geburtstag', in *Österreichische Musik - Musik in Österreich: Beiträge zur Musikgeschichte Mitteleuropas; Theophil Antonicek zum 60. Geburtstag* (Tutzing, 1998), pp. 423-40.

----------------------. 'Zwischen den Zeilen - Versuch eines Persönlichkeitbildes Anton Bruckner', in *BSL 1998* (Linz, 2000), pp. 221-31.

Marschner, Bo. '100 Jahre Bruckner-Rezeption in den nordischen Ländern', in *BSL 1991* (Linz, 1994), pp. 185-200.

Marx, Eva. 'Bad Kreuzen - Spekulation und kein Ende', in *BSL 1992* (Linz, 1995), pp. 31-39.

Mayer, Johannes-Leopold. 'Musik als gesellschaftliches Ärgernis - oder: Anton Bruckner, der Anti-Bürger. Das Phänomen Bruckner als historisches Problem', in *ABDS* 2 (Graz, 1980), pp. 75-160.

McClatchie, Stephen. 'Hans Rott, Gustav Mahler and the "New Symphony": New Evidence for a Pressing Question', in *Music and Letters* 81/3 (August 2000), pp. 392-401.

McColl, Sandra. *Music Criticism in Vienna 1896-1897.* Oxford, 1996.

----------------------. 'Max Kalbeck and Gustav Mahler', in *19th-Century Music* 20 (1996), pp. 167-83.

----------------------. 'Karl Kraus and Musical Criticism. The Case of Max Kalbeck', in *The Musical Quarterly* 82 (1998), pp. 279-308.

Medici di Marignano, N., ed. Rosemary Hughes. *A Mozart Pilgrimage, being the Travel Diaries of Vincent and Mary Novello in the Year 1829.* London, 1955.

Meindl, Konrad. *Leben und Wirken des Bischofs Franz Josef Rudigier von Linz*, 2 vols. Linz, 1891/92.

Meran, Christoph and Elisabeth Maier. 'Anton Bruckner und Charles O'Hegerty. Zur Geschichte eines lange verschollenen Bruckner-Autographs', in *BJ 1994/95/96* (Linz, 1997), pp. 195-210.

Metzger, Heinz-Klaus and Rainer Riehn, eds. *Anton Bruckner (Musik-Konzepte 23/24)*. Munich, 1982.

Mitterschiffthaler, Gerald K. 'Die Beziehungen Anton Bruckners zum Stift Wilhering', in Othmar Wessely, ed., *Bruckner-Studien* (Vienna, 1975), pp. 113-41.

Münster, Robert. 'Aus Bruckners Münchner Freundes- und Bekanntenkreis 1863-1886', in *BSL 1994* (Linz, 1997), pp. 161-174.

Musil, Robert. *Der Mann ohne Eigenschaften*. Reinbeck bei Hamburg, 1978. English translation by Sophie Wilkins as *The Man without Qualities*. London, 1995, 2/1997.

Newlin, Dika. *Bruckner-Mahler-Schoenberg*. New York, 1947.

Notley, Margaret. 'Bruckner and Viennese Wagnerism', in *Bruckner Studies* (Cambridge, 1997), pp. 54-71.

Nowak, Leopold. *Te Deum laudamus. Gedanken zur Musik Anton Bruckners*. Vienna, 1947.

-------------------- et al., eds. *Anton Bruckner Sämtliche Werke. Kritische Gesamtausgabe, herausgegeben von der Generaldirektion der Österreichischen Nationalbibliothek und der Internationalen Bruckner-Gesellschaft*. Vienna, 1951-.

--------------------. *Anton Bruckner. Musik und Leben*. Vienna, 1964.

--------------------. *Anton Bruckner. Musik und Leben*. Linz, 1973.

--------------------. *Über Anton Bruckner. Gesammelte Aufsätze*. Vienna, 1985.

--------------------. 'Anton Bruckners Kirchenmusik', in *BSL 1985* (Linz, 1988), pp. 85-93

Oberleithner, Max von. *Meine Erinnerungen an Anton Bruckner*. Regensburg, 1933.

Oeser, Fritz. *Die Klangstruktur der Bruckner-Symphonie. Eine Studie zur Frage der Originalfassungen*. Leipzig, 1939.

--------------. *Anton Bruckner. 3. Symphonie in d-Moll. 2. Fassung von 1878. Einführung zur Studienpartitur*. Wiesbaden, 1950.

Orel, Alfred. *Unbekannte Frühwerke Anton Bruckners*. Vienna, 1921.

--------------. *Anton Bruckner. Das Werk - der Künstler - der Zeit*. Vienna, 1925.

--------------. 'Anton Bruckner. Entwürfe und Skizzen zur IX. Symphonie', *Anton Bruckner - Sämtliche Werke, 9. Band, Sonderdruck*. Vienna, 1934.

--------------. *Ein Harmonielehrekolleg bei Anton Bruckner*. Berlin-Vienna-Zurich, 1940.

Pachovsky, Angela. 'Bruckners weltliche Chöre', in *Bruckner-Vorträge, Bruckner-Tagung Wien 1999 Bericht* (Vienna, 2000), pp. 35-46.

Partsch, Erich, W. 'Anton Meißner, der letzte "Sekretär" Bruckners', in *BJ 1984/85/86* (Linz, 1988), pp. 57-62.

------------------------. 'Unbekannte Bruckner-Dokumente zum Revolutionsjahr 1848', in *Mitteilungsblatt der IBG* 44 (June 1995), pp. 19-25.

------------------------. 'Eugen Megyesi Schwartz. Bruckner-Schüler und Komponist', in *BJ 1991/92/93* (Linz, 1995), pp. 191-96.

------------------------. 'Die Bruckner Musikautographe im Welser Stadtarchiv', in *Mitteilungsblatt der IBG* 46 (June 1996), pp. 5-12.

------------------------, ed. *Katalog: Anton Bruckner in Steyr. Ausstellung im Stadtpfarrhof Steyr 1996.*

------------------------. '"Unser berühmter Landsmann". Zur Bruckner-Bericherstattung in der Steyrer Presse bis 1896', in *BJ 1994/95/96* (Linz, 1997), pp. 289-94.

------------------------. 'Ein Voralberger Fabrikant als Bruckner-Mäzen', in *Österreichische Musik - Musik in Österreich: Beiträge zur Musikgeschichte Mitteleuropas; Theophil Antonicek zum 60. Geburtstag* (Tutzing, 1998), pp. 385-94.

Palmer, Peter, Howie, Crawford and Cox, Raymond, eds. *The Bruckner Journal.* Nottingham, 1997-.

Pass, Walter. 'Studie über Bruckners ersten St. Florianer Aufenthalt', in *Bruckner-Studien* (Vienna, 1975), pp. 11-51.

Perger, Richard von, and Robert Hirschfeld. *Geschichte der k.k. Gesellschaft der Musikfreunde in Wien.* Vienna, 1912.

Phillips, John A. 'Neue Erkenntnisse zum Finale der Neunten Symphonie Anton Bruckners', in *BJ 1989/90* (Linz, 1992), pp. 115-203.

--------------------. 'Zum leidigen Thema "Finale der Neunten Symphonie Anton Bruckners"', in *Österreichische Musikzeitschrift* 47 (1992), pp. 22-25.

--------------------. 'Die Arbeitsweise Bruckners in seinen letzten Jahren', in *BSL 1992* (Linz, 1995), pp. 153-78.

--------------------, Nicola Samale, Giuseppe Mazzuca (and with the assistance of B.G.Cohrs), eds. *Anton Bruckner IX. Symphonie D-Moll Finale. Rekonstruktion der Autograph-Partitur nach den erhaltenen Quellen. Aufführungsfassung. Studienpartitur.* Adelaide, 1992.

--------------------, ed. *Anton Bruckner. IX. Symphonie D-Moll, Finale (unvollendet): Faksimile-Ausgabe sämtlicher autographen Notenseiten (ABSW zu IX/4).* Vienna, 1996.

--------------------. 'The facts behind a "legend": the Ninth Symphony and the Te Deum', in *Perspectives on Anton Bruckner* (Aldershot, 2001), in preparation.

Pleasants, Henry, ed. *Eduard Hanslick. Music Criticisms 1846-1899.* London, 1963.

------------------------. *The Music Criticism of Hugo Wolf.* London and New York, 1978.

Prosl, Robert M. *Die Hellmesberger. Hundert Jahre aus dem Leben einer Wiener Musikerfamilie.* Vienna, 1947.

Quoika, Rudolf. *Die Orgelwelt um Anton Bruckner. Blicke in die Orgelgeschichte Alt-Österreichs.* Ludwigsburg, 1966.

Redlich, Hans F. 'The Finale of Bruckner's Ninth Symphony', in *The Monthly Musical Record* 79 (1949), pp. 143-49.

---------------------. *Bruckner and Mahler.* London, 1955.

Rehberger, Karl. 'St. Florian und Anton Bruckner bis 1855. Einige neue Aspekte', in *BSL 1994* (Linz, 1997), pp. 31-36.

Reitterer, Hubert. Anton Bruckner und Alois Höfler. Zwei Universitätslehrer', in *BSL 1988* (Linz, 1992), pp. 129-36.

Riethmüller, Albrecht, ed. *Bruckner-Probleme: Internationales Kolloquium 7.-9. Oktober 1996 in Berlin. Beihefte zum Archiv für Musikwissenschaft 45.* Stuttgart, 1999.

Ringer, Alexander L. '*Germanenzug* bis *Helgoland*: Zu Bruckners Deutschtum', in *Bruckner-Probleme* (Stuttgart, 1999), pp. 25-34.

Röder, Thomas. 'Auf dem Weg zur Bruckner-Symphonie'. *Beihefte zum Archiv für Musikwissenschaft 26.* Stuttgart, 1987.

-------------------. 'Eigenes angewandtes Nachsinnen - Bruckners Selbststudium in Fragen der Metrik', in *BSL 1992* (Linz, 1995), pp. 107-22.

-------------------. *Anton Bruckner. III. Symphonie D-Moll Revisionsbericht* (*ABSW* zu III/1-3). Vienna, 1997.

-------------------. 'Die Dritte Symphonie - unfaßbar', in *BSL 1996* (Linz, 1998), pp. 65-84.

-------------------. 'Anton Bruckners Glaube', in *Bruckner-Probleme* (Stuttgart, 1999), pp. 50-63.

-------------------. 'Anton Bruckners Erste Symphonie', in *Bruckner-Vorträge, Bruckner-Tagung Wien 1999 Bericht* (Vienna, 2000), pp. 47-57.

-------------------. 'Master and disciple united: the 1889 Finale of the Third Symphony', in *Perspectives on Anton Bruckner* (Aldershot, 2001), in preparation.

Sachs, Jürgen. 'Entstehungs- und Aufführungsdaten der Messen, des Te Deum und der Symphonien Anton Bruckners', in *BJ 1989/90* (Linz, 1992), pp. 265-75.

Schalk, Lili. *Franz Schalk. Briefe und Betrachtungen.* Vienna/Leipzig, 1935.

Scheder, Franz. 'Zur Datierung einer Korrespondenzkarte Anton Bruckners', in *Mitteilungsblatt der IBG* 31 (1988), pp. 20-21.

-------------------. 'Zur Datierung von Bruckners Brief an Wolzogen (Auer Nr. 137)', in *BJ 1984/85/86* (Linz, 1988), pp. 65-67.

-------------------. 'Zur Datierung zweier Autographen Anton Bruckners', in *BJ 1987/88* (Linz, 1990), pp. 63-65.

732

——————————. 'Frühe Bruckner-Aufführungen in Nürnberg', in *BJ 1989/90* (Linz, 1992), pp. 235-64.

——————————. *Anton Bruckner Chronologie 1824-1896. Band I: Textband. Band II: Registerband.* Tutzing, 1996.

——————————. 'Zu Bruckners Aufenthalt in Dresden', in *Mitteilungsblatt der IBG* 48 (June 1997), pp. 25-27.

——————————. *Anton Bruckner Chronologie. Nachtrag 1996-1998. Addenda und Corrigenda.* Nuremberg, 1998.

——————————. *Anton Bruckner Chronologie. Die Jahre 1897-1999. Band I: Textband. Band II: Registerband.* Nuremberg, 1999.

Schenk, Erich and Gernot Gruber. '"Die ganzen Studien". Zu Josef Vockners Theorieunterricht bei Anton Bruckner', in *Bruckner-Studien* (Vienna, 1975), pp. 349-77.

Schenk, Erich. 'Franz Schalk (1863-1931)', in *Mitteilungsblatt der IBG* 19 (1981), pp. 5-19.

——————————. 'Ferdinand Löwe', in *Mitteilungsblatt der IBG* 26 (October 1985), pp. 5-11.

Schneider, Otto. 'Anton Bruckners Briefe and die Wiener Philharmoniker', in *Österreichische Musikzeitschrift* 29 (1974), pp. 183-88.

Schneider, Musikantiquariat. *Kataloge.* Tutzing, 1971- .

Schnürl, Karl. 'Drei niederösterreichische Bruckner-Orgeln. Tulln - Langenlois - Krems', in *Bruckner-Studien* (Vienna, 1975), pp. 163-69.

Schönherr, Max. 'Wer war Friedrich Eckstein?', in *BJ 1982/83* (Linz, 1984), pp. 163-72.

Schöny, Heinz. *Bruckner-Ikonographie.* Vienna, 1968.

——————————. 'Anton Bruckner zum 100. Todestag. Seine Ahnenliste als Geschichte seiner Vorfahren', in *Mitteilungsblatt der IBG* 48 (June 1997), pp. 10-24.

Schönzeler, Hans Hubert. *Bruckner.* London, 1970.

——————————. *Zu Bruckners IX. Symphonie. Die Krakauer Skizzen. Eine Bestandsaufnahme.* Vienna, 1987.

Scholes, Percy A., ed. *Dr. Burney's Musical Tours in Europe, II: An Eighteenth-Century Musical Tour in Central Europe and the Netherlands.* London, 1959.

Schorske, Carl E. *Fin-de-siècle Vienna.* London, 1979.

Schubert, Ingrid. 'Bruckner, Wagner und die Neudeutschen in Graz', in *BSL 1984* (Linz, 1986), pp. 35-58.

Schwanzara, Ernst. *Vorlesungen über Harmonielehre und Kontrapunkt an der Universität Wien.* Vienna, 1950.

Scragg, G.R. *The Pelican History of the Church IV.* London, 1962.

Sehnal, Jiri. 'Ein Brief A. Bruckners an den mährischen Orgelbauer Franz Ritter von Pistrich', in *BJ 1980* (Linz, 1980), pp. 129-32.

Simpson, Robert. *The Essence of Bruckner*. London, 1967, 2/1992.

Slapnicka, Harry. 'Bischof Rudigier und die Kunst', in *BSL 1985* (Linz, 1988), pp. 23-31.

------------------. 'Oberösterreich zwischen Wiener Kongreß und den Anfängen der politischen Parteien (1815-1970)', in *ABDS* 10 (Vienna, 1994), pp. 9-32.

Sonntag, Mariana E. 'A new perspective on Anton Bruckner's composition of the Ninth Symphony', in *BJ 1989/90* (Linz, 1992), pp. 77-114.

Spiel, Hilde. *Vienna's Golden Autumn*. London, 1987.

Stargardt, J.A. *Versteigerungskataloge*. Marburg and Berlin, 1978 - .

Steinmann, Hugo. '"Und Sie, sind Sie auch ein Prinz?" Die Erinnerungen des Schweizer Bruckner-Schülers William Ritter', in *Mitteilungsblatt der IBG* 33 (1989), pp. 9-15.

Stephan, Rudolf. 'Bruckner - Wagner', in *BSL 1984* (Linz, 1986), pp. 59-65.

------------------. 'Bruckner und Liszt. Hat der Komponist Franz Liszt Bruckner beeinflußt?', in *BSL 1986* (Linz, 1989), pp. 169-80.

Stradal, August. 'Erinnerungen aus Bruckners letzter Zeit', in *Zeitschrift für Musik* 99 (1932), pp. 853-60, 971-78 and 1071-75.

Strasser, Otto. 'Anton Bruckner und die Wiener Philharmoniker', in *Von Pasqualatihaus. Musikwissenschaftliche Perspektiven aus Wien* 3 (1994), pp. 5-21.

Taub, Susanna. *Zeitgenössische Bruckner-Rezeption in den Linzer Printmedien (1855-1869)*. Dissertation. Salzburg, 1987.

Thiel, Helga, Gerda Lechleitner and Walter Deutsch. 'Anton Bruckner - sein soziokulturelles Umfeld, seine musikalische Umwelt', in *BSL 1987* (Linz, 1989), pp. 111-19.

Timms, E. *Karl Kraus, Apocalyptic Satirist: Culture and Catastrophe in Habsburg Vienna*. New Haven and London, 1986.

Tittel, Ernst. 'Wiener Musiktheorie von Fux bis Schönberg', in Martin Vogel, ed., *Beiträge zur Musiktheorie des 19. Jahrhunderts* (Regensburg, 1966), pp. 163-201.

Tröller, Josef. *Anton Bruckner. III. Symphonie d-Moll. Meisterwerke der Musik* 13. Munich, 1976.

Tschulik, Norbert. *Anton Bruckner im Spiegel seiner Zeit*. Vienna, 1955.

------------------. 'Anton Bruckner in der Wiener Zeitung', in *BJ 1981* (Linz, 1982), pp. 171-79.

------------------. 'Der Bruckner-Schüler Josef Vockner', in *BJ 1989/90* (Linz, 1992), pp. 289-302.

Vielmetti, Nikolaus. 'Das Judentum in zeitgenössischen Musikleben', in *BSL 1986* (Linz, 1989), pp. 49-57.

Voss, Egon. 'Wagner und Bruckner. Ihre persönlichen Beziehungen anhand der überlieferten Zeugnisse (mit einer Dokumentation der wichtigsten Quellen)' in *Anton Bruckner. Studien zu Werk und Wirkung. Festschrift Walter Wiora* (Tutzing, 1988), pp. 219-33.

Vyslouzil, Jiri. 'Otto Kitzler in Brünn', in *BSL 1988* (Linz, 1992), pp. 65-70.

Wagner, Manfred. *Geschichte der österreichischen Musikkritik in Beispielen.* Tutzing, 1979.

--------------------. 'Bruckner in Wien' (*ABDS* 2). Graz, 1980.

--------------------. *Der Wandel des Konzepts. Zu den verschiedenen Fassungen von Bruckners Dritter, Vierter und Achten Sinfonie* Vienna, 1980.

--------------------. *Bruckner.* Mainz, 1983.

--------------------. 'Zur Rezeptionsgeschichte von Anton Bruckners Achter Symphonie', in *BJ 1991/92/93* (Linz, 1995), pp. 109-15.

--------------------. *Anton Bruckner. Sein Werk - Sein Leben.* Vienna, 1995.

Waldstein, Wilhelm. 'Bruckner als Lehrer', in *Bruckner-Studien* (Vienna, 1964), pp. 113-20.

Walterskirchen, Gerhard. 'Bruckner in Salzburg - Bruckner-Erstaufführungen in Salzburg', in *Mitteilungsblatt der IBG* 16 (December 1979), pp. 14-20.

Watson, Derek. *Bruckner.* London, 1973; 2nd ed. Oxford, 1996.

Weinmann, Alexander. 'Anton Bruckner und seine Verleger', in *Bruckner-Studien* (Vienna, 1964), pp. 121-38.

Wessely, Othmar. 'Anton Bruckner und Linz', in *Jahrbuch der Stadt Linz 1954* (Linz, 1955).

--------------------. 'Musik und Theater in Linz zu Bruckners Zeit', in *Anton Bruckner und Linz. Ausstellungskatalog.* Linz, 1964.

--------------------. 'Von Mozart bis Bruckner. Wandlungen des Linzer Musiklebens von 1770 - 1870', in *Österreichische Musikzeitschrift* 25 (1970), pp. 151-58.

--------------------, ed. *Bruckner-Studien.* Vienna, 1975.

--------------------. 'Bruckners Mendelssohn-Kenntnis', in *ibid.*, pp. 81-112.

--------------------. 'Johannes Brahms und Anton Bruckner als Interpreten', in *BSL 1983* (Linz, 1985), pp. 73-79.

--------------------. 'Anton Bruckner als Briefschreiber', in *ibid.*, pp. 89-93.

--------------------. 'Bruckner, Wagner und die Neudeutschen in Linz', in *BSL 1984* (Linz, 1986).

--------------------. 'Anton Bruckners Präparandenzeit', in *BSL 1988* (Linz, 1992), pp. 21-25.

--------------------. 'Bruckner-Berichterstattung in der Neuen Zeitschrift für Musik', in *BSL 1991* (Linz, 1994), pp. 127-47.

--------------------. 'Der junge Bruckner und sein Orgelspiel', in *ABDS* 10 (Vienna, 1994), pp. 59-96.

----------------------. 'Zu Bruckners Windhaager Jahren', in *BSL 1992* (Linz, 1995), pp. 49-56.

Winterberger, Hans. 'Die Hauptorgel der Ignatiuskirche ("Alter Dom") in Linz', in *Historisches Jahrbuch der Stadt Linz, 1971*. Linz, 1972.

Wolff, Werner. *Anton Bruckner - Rustic Genius*. New York, 1942, 2/1973.

Zamazal, Franz. 'Kultur- und musikgeschichtliche Situation in Enns', in *ABDS 3* (Graz, 1980), pp. 17-55.

----------------------. 'Leopold von Zenetti. Leben und Werk', in *ibid.*, pp. 57-108.

----------------------. 'Ein Beitrag zur Familiengeschichte. Ausgehend von einer Episode aus dem Leben des Vaters Bruckners', in *BJ 1982/83* (Linz, 1984), pp. 117-28.

----------------------. 'Der Bischof und sein Organist - Die Beziehungen zu Anton Bruckner', in Rudolf Zinnhobler, ed., *Bischof Franz Joseph Rudigier und seine Zeit* (Linz, 1987), pp. 157-65.

----------------------. 'Ein verschollenes Werk Bruckners: Die Rose', in *Mitteilungsblatt der IBG 35* (December 1990), p. 11.

----------------------. 'Bruckner als Volksschullehrer', in *BSL 1988* (Linz, 1992), pp. 27-34.

----------------------. 'Bruckners Namenstag-Kantate für Propst Michael Arneth (1852)', in *BJ 1989/90* (Linz, 1992), pp. 205-17.

----------------------. 'Johann Baptist Schiedermayr. Ein Vorgänger Bruckners als Linzer Dom- und Stadtpfarrorganist', in *BSL 1990* (Linz, 1993), pp. 119-60.

----------------------. 'Unveröffentlicher Bruckner-Brief an Julius Gartner', in *Mitteilungsblatt der IBG 41* (December 1993), pp. 27-34.

----------------------. 'Familie Bruckner - Drei Generationen Lehrer. Schulverhältnisse - Ausbildung - Lebenslauf', in *ABDS 10* (Vienna, 1994), pp. 97-251.

----------------------. 'Zeitgenössische Notizen über Anton Bruckner. Ludwig Edlbacher und Georg Huemer', in *BJ 1991/92/93* (Linz, 1995), pp. 197-204.

----------------------. 'Neues zu Bruckners Aufenthalt in Windhaag', in *BSL 1992* (Linz, 1995), pp. 57-72.

----------------------. 'Über Bruckner, sein Umfeld und einschlägige Publikationen', in *Mitteilungsblatt der IBG 50* (June 1998), pp. 17-20.

----------------------. 'Oberösterreich als Schubert-Quelle: Was kannte Bruckner von Schubert', in *BSL 1997* (Linz, 1999), pp. 117-76.

----------------------. 'Das Linz Landestheater zur Zeit Bruckners', in *Mitteilungsblatt der IBG 52* (June 1999), pp. 7-13.

----------------------. 'Bruckner besucht Mozarts "Don Juan" in der Wiener Hofoper', in *ibid.*, pp. 14-19.

----------------------. 'Hofrat Dr. Ignaz Zibermayrs Erinnerungen an St. Florian: Schulverhältnisse, Anton und Ignaz Bruckner', in *Mitteilungsblatt der IBG 53* (November 1999), pp. 5-8.

736

Zappe, Hermann. 'Anton Bruckner, die Familie Zappe und die Musik', in *BJ 1982/83* (Linz, 1984), pp. 129-61.

Zinnhobler, Rudolf, ed. *Bischof Franz Joseph Rudigier und seine Zeit.* Linz, 1987.

——————————. 'Das Bistum Linz zwischen Spätjosephinismus und Liberalismus', in *ABDS* 10 (Vienna, 1994), pp. 33-58.

Zwol, Cornelis van. 'Holland: ein Brucknerland seit 1885', in *BJ 1980* (Linz, 1980), pp. 135-41.

——————————. 'Bruckner-Rezeption in den Niederlanden und im anglo-amerikanischen Raum', in *BSL 1991* (Linz, 1994), pp. 149-60.

——————————. 'Ein Bibliothekar aus Den Haag und ein dirigiender Komponist in Amsterdam - die ersten Stützen Bruckners in den Niederlanden', in *BSL 1994* (Linz, 1997), pp. 95-106.

INDEX

This Index is restricted to Bruckner's compositions, relevant institutions and, with a few obvious exceptions, persons who were born during Bruckner's lifetime. Consequently, prominent Bruckner musicologists such as Robert Haas, Leopold Nowak and Alfred Orel, whose names appear frequently in footnotes, do not appear here.

STUDIES IN THE HISTORY AND INTERPRETATION OF MUSIC

24. Klemens Diez, **Constanze, Formerly Widow of Mozart: Her Unwritten Memoir**, Joseph T. Malloy (trans.)

25. Harold E. Fiske, **Music and Mind: Philosophical Essays on the Cognition and Meaning of Music**

26. Anne Trenkamp and John G. Suess (eds.), **Studies in the Schoenbergian Movement in Vienna and the United States: Essays in Honor of Marcel Dick**

27. Harvey J. Stokes, **A Selected Annotated Bibliography on Italian Serial Composers**

28. Julia Muller, **Words and Music in Henry Purcell's First Semi-Opera, Dioclesian: An Approach to Early Music Through Early Theatre**

29. Ronald W. Holz, **Erik Leidzen: Band Arranger and Composer**

30. Enrique Moreno, **Expanded Tunings in Comtemporary Music: Theoretical Innovations and Practical Applications**

31. Charles H. Parsons (compiler), **A Benjamin Britten Discography**

32. Denis Wilde, **The Development of Melody in the Tone Poems of Richard Strauss: Motif, Figure, and Theme**

33. William Smialek, **Ignacy Feliks Dobrzynski and Musical Life in Nineteenth-Century Poland**

34. Judith A. Eckelmeyer, **The Cultural Context of Mozart's Magic Flute: Social, Aesthetic, Philosophical** (2 Volume Set)

35. Joseph Coroniti, **Poetry as Text in Twentieth Century Vocal Music: From Stravinsky to Reich**

36. William E. Grim, **The Faust Legend in Music and Literature, Volume II**

37. Harvey J. Stokes, **Compositional Language in the Oratorio** *The Second Act*: **The Composer as Analyst**

38. Richard M. Berrong, **The Politics of Opera in Turn-of-the-Century Italy: As Seen Through the Letters of Alfredo Catalani**

39. Hugo von Hofmannsthal, **The Woman Without a Shadow /** *Die Frau Ohne Schatten*, Jean Hollander (trans.)

40. Bertil H. van Boer, Jr. (ed.), **Gustav III and the Swedish Stage: Opera, Theatre, and Other Foibles: Essays in Honor of Hans Åstrand**

41. Harold E. Fiske, **Music Cognition and Aesthetic Attitudes**

42. Elsa Respighi, **Fifty Years of a Life in Music, 1905-1955 / Cinquant'anni di vita nella musica**, Giovanni Fontecchio and Roger Johnson (trans.)

43. Virginia Raad, **The Piano Sonority of Claude Debussy**

44. Ury Eppstein, **The Beginnings of Western Music in Meiji Era Japan**

45. Amédée Daryl Williams, **Lillian Fuchs, First Lady of the Viola**

46. Jane Hawes, **An Examination of Verdi's** *Otello* **and Its Faithfulness to Shakespeare**

47. Robert Springer, **Authentic Blues–Its History and Its Themes**, André J.M. Prévos (trans.)

48. Paul F. Rice (ed.), **An Edited Collection of the Theatre Music of John Abraham Fisher: The Druids and Witches Scenes from** *Macbeth*